She just about undid him with a single touch.

"Lucy… stop."

She didn't move her hand. "I can't."

He couldn't have moved away if he'd tried. She was pure temptation. And he wanted her.

When he dipped his head, his intention clear, a tiny moan escaped her. It was the sweetest kiss he'd ever experienced, almost as though it possessed a kind of purity that had never been matched and never would.

Brant suddenly felt as if he'd been sucker-punched. Because he'd known, deep down, that kissing Lucy would be incredible. Everything about her had been tempting him for months. Every look, every word, every touch had been drawing them toward this moment. His pulse galloped, knees grew weak, until he pulled back and looked into those honest eyes.

What was he doing? Lucy was the hometown girl who wanted romance, marriage, the white picket fence. Brant didn't do any of those things.

Her eyes shimmered with a kind of longing that heated his blood even further. But he fought the urge to kiss her again, because he knew where it would lead. He'd want to make love to her forever… and that was the one thing he couldn't

LUCY & THE LIEUTENANT

BY
HELEN LACEY

First Published in Great Britain 2016
By Mills & Boon, an imprint of HarperCollins*Publishers*
1 London Bridge Street, London, SE1 9GF

© 2016 Helen Lacey

ISBN: 978-0-263-91996-7

23-0616

Our policy is to use papers that are natural, renewable and recyclable products and made from wood grown in sustainable forests. The logging and manufacturing processes conform to the legal environmental regulations of the country of origin.

Printed and bound in Spain
by CPI, Barcelona

Helen Lacey grew up reading *Black Beauty* and *Little House on the Prairie*. These childhood classics inspired her to write her first book when she was seven, a story about a girl and her horse. She loves writing for Mills & Boon Cherish, where she can create strong heroes with a soft heart and heroines with gumption who get their happily-ever-after. For more about Helen, visit her website, www.helenlacey.com.

For Robert... to the moon and back.

Chapter One

Brant Parker grabbed the T-shirt stuffed in the back pocket of his jeans and wiped his brow.

It was cold out, but he'd been working for four hours straight without a break and it was quite warm inside the closed-up rooms of the Loose Moose Tavern. He'd spent the best part of three weeks stripping out the old timber framing and flooring that had gone through a fire eight months earlier.

Most people said he was crazy for buying the place, like it had some kind of hoodoo attached to it. But he didn't believe in hoodoo or bad luck, and he wasn't swayed by anyone telling him what he should or shouldn't do. The Loose Moose had been a part of Cedar River for over thirty years and he believed the old place deserved another chance.

Maybe he did, too.

Brant dropped the piece of timber in his hands,

stretched his back and groaned. It had been a long day and he wanted nothing more than to soak under a hot shower and to relax in front of some mindless TV show for an hour or two. But first he had to go to the veterans home to visit his uncle, as he did every Tuesday and Friday.

Uncle Joe was his father's oldest brother and a Vietnam veteran who'd lost a leg in the war. He also had a heart condition and suffered from the early stages of Parkinson's disease. He lived in full-time care at the home adjacent to the small community hospital. Brant cared deeply for his uncle. The older man knew him. Got him. Understood the demons he carried.

He headed upstairs to the small apartment and took a shower, then dressed in jeans and a long-sleeved shirt. It was snowing lightly, a regular occurrence in South Dakota in winter, but quite unusual for mid-November. He shouldered into his lined jacket, pulled on woolen socks and heavy boots, and grabbed his truck keys. The home was a ten-minute drive in good weather from the main street in town and since snow was now falling in earnest, he knew the roads would be slippery. Brant took his time and arrived about fifteen minutes later. It was late afternoon and the parking lot was empty, so he scored a spot easily and got out of the truck.

The wind howled through his ears and he pulled the jacket collar around his neck. It promised to be a long and chilly winter ahead. But he didn't mind. It sure beat the relentless, unforgiving heat of a desert summer like the last one he'd endured in Afghanistan. The light blanket of snow made him feel as though he was home. And he was. For good this time. No more tours. No more military. He was a civilian and could lead a normal life. He could get up each morning and face a new day. And he could forget everything else.

Brant headed for the front doors and shook off his jacket before he crossed the threshold. When he entered the building, heat blasted through him immediately. The foyer was empty and the reception desk had a sign and a bell instructing to ring for attendance. He ignored both and began walking down the wide corridor.

"Hi, Brant."

The sound of his name stopped Brant in his tracks and he turned. A woman emerged from a door to his left and he recognized her immediately. *Lucy Monero.* He cringed inwardly. He wasn't in the mood for the pretty brunette with the lovely curves and dancing green eyes, and tried to stay as indifferent as possible. "Good afternoon, Dr. Monero."

"Please," she said just a little too breathlessly. "Call me Lucy."

He wouldn't. Keeping it formal meant keeping her at a distance. Just as he liked it.

Instead he made a kind of half-grunting sound and shrugged loosely. "Have you seen my uncle this afternoon?"

"Just left him about ten minutes ago," she said, smiling. "He said he's feeling good today. The nurses left food on the tray, so perhaps see if you can get him to eat something."

"Sure."

She didn't move. Didn't pass. She simply stood there and looked at him. Examined him, he thought. In a way that stirred his blood. It had been too long since anything or anyone had stirred him. But Lucy Monero managed it with barely a glance.

And he was pretty sure she knew it.

"So, how's the shoulder?" she asked, tossing her hair in a way that always made him flinch.

A trace of her apple-scented shampoo clung to the air and he swallowed hard. "Fine."

He'd dislocated his shoulder eight weeks earlier when he'd fallen off his motorbike. She'd been one of the doctors on duty at the hospital that night. But he'd made a point of ensuring she didn't attend him. He hadn't wanted her poking and prodding at him, or standing so close he'd be forced to inhale the scent of her perfume.

"Glad to hear it. I was talking to your mother the other day and she said you plan to reopen the tavern in the next few months?"

His mother had made her opinion about Lucy Monero clear on numerous occasions. She was Lucy's number-one fan and didn't mind telling him so. But he wasn't interested in a date, a relationship or settling down. Not with anyone. Including the pretty doctor in front of him. Her dark brows and green eyes were a striking combination and no doubt a legacy from her Italian heritage. She wore scrubs with a white coat over them, and he figured she'd just come from the emergency room at the hospital where she worked. But he knew she was also filling in at the veterans home a couple of times a week while one of the other doctors was on leave. Uncle Joe thought the world of her, too. And even his older brother, Grady, had extolled her virtues after she'd attended to his youngest daughter when the child had been taken to the ER a couple of months ago with a high fever.

Brant did his best to ignore her eyes, her hair and the curves he knew were hidden beneath the regulation blue scrubs. "That's the plan."

She smiled a little, as though she was amused by his

terse response, as though she had some great secret only she was privy to. It irritated him no end.

"I'm pleased your shoulder is okay."

He wished she'd stop talking. "Sure, whatever."

Her eyes sparkled. "Well, see you soon, Brant."

She said his name on a sigh. Or at least, that's how it sounded. There was a husky softness to her voice that was impossible to ignore. And it *always* made him tense. It made him wonder how her voice would sound if she was whispering, if she was bent close and speaking words only he could hear.

Brant quickly pulled himself out of the haze his mind was in and nodded vaguely, walking away, well aware that she was watching him.

And knowing there wasn't a damned thing he could do about.

Lucy let out a long sigh once Brant Parker disappeared around the corner of the ward. His tight-shouldered gait was one she would recognize anywhere—at the hospital, along the street, in her dreams.

He'd been in them for years. Since she'd been a starry-eyed, twelve-year-old mooning over the then-fifteen-year-old Brant. She'd lived next door to the Parker ranch. The ranch he'd left when he was eighteen to join the military. She'd left Cedar River for college just a couple of years later and put the boy she'd pined over as a teen out of her thoughts. Until she'd returned to her hometown to take a position at the small county hospital. She'd seen him again and the old attraction had resurfaced. He had been back from another tour of the Middle East and they'd bumped into each other at the O'Sullivan pub. Of course he hadn't recognized her. The last time they'd crossed paths she had been a chubby, self-conscious teenager with glasses. He'd seemed surprised to see her, but had said little. That had been more than two years earlier. Now he was back for good. Just as she was. He had left the military after twelve years of service and bought the old Loose Moose Tavern.

He could have done anything after high school—maybe law or economics—as he was supersmart and was always at the top of his class. One of those gifted people who never had to try hard to make good grades. He spoke a couple of languages and had been some kind of covert translator in the military. Lucy didn't know much about it, but what she did she'd learned from his mother, Colleen. The other woman regularly visited Joe Parker and also volunteered at the hospital where Lucy specialized in emergency medicine.

She'd known the Parkers since she was a child. Back then her parents had owned the small ranch next door. When she was fourteen her dad had died unexpectedly from a stroke, and then within a year her mother had sold the place and moved into town. A few years later her mother was killed in an accident. By then Lucy was ready for college, which would be followed by medical school, and had left town. The house her mother had bought in town was now hers and it was conveniently located just a few streets from the hospital. She was back in Cedar River to give back to the town she loved.

And maybe find her own happiness along the way.

Because Lucy wanted to get married and have a family. And soon. She was twenty-seven years old and had never had a serious romantic relationship. She'd never been in love. The truth be told, she'd never really been kissed.

And she was the only twenty-seven-year-old virgin she knew.

In high school she had been a geek to the core and had mostly been ignored by the boys in her grade. She hadn't even managed to get a date for prom. And by the time she was in college, her dreams about dating quickly disappeared. Three weeks into college and her roommate was assaulted so badly Lucy spent two days with the other girl at the hospital. It was enough to make her wary about getting involved with anyone on campus. She made a few friends who were much like herself—focused kids who studied hard and avoided parties and dating. By the time she started medical school the pattern of her life had been set. She was quiet and studious and determined to become a good doctor. Nothing else mattered. Though she'd gotten more comfortable over time in social situations, she was known as a girl who didn't date and, after a while, the invitations stopped.

One year quickly slipped into another and by the time she'd finished her residency she'd stopped fretting about being the oldest virgin on the planet. Not that she was hanging on to it as though it was a prize…she'd just never met anyone she liked enough to share that kind of intimacy with. Of course her closest friends, Ash, Brooke and Kayla, thought it amusing and teased her often about her refusal to settle for just *anyone*. She wanted special. She wanted a love that would last a lifetime.

She wanted…

Brant Parker.

Which was plain old, outright, what-are-you-thinking-girl stupid, and she knew it deep within her bones. Brant never looked at her in that way. Most of the time he acted as though he barely even *saw* her. When they were kids he'd tolerated her because they were neighbors, and in high school he had been three years ahead and hadn't wasted his time acknowledging her in the corridors. By the time she was in college he was long gone from Cedar River.

Her cell beeped and quickly cut through her thoughts. It was Kayla reminding her that she'd agreed to meet her and Ash and Brooke at the O'Sullivan pub for a drink and catch-up that evening. It had become something of a Friday-night ritual since she'd returned to town. Kayla had been a friend since junior high and worked as curator of the small Cedar River historical museum and art gallery, and Ash was a cop with the local police department. Brooke, who was Brant's cousin, was pure cowgirl and owned a small horse ranch just out of town.

All four women were good friends and she thoroughly enjoyed their company…most of the time. But she wasn't really in the mood for drinks and conversation tonight. She'd had a long morning in the emergency room and had been at the veterans home for the past few hours. She was tired and wanted nothing more than to go home, strip off and soak in the tub for a leisurely hour or so. But since her friend wouldn't take no for an answer, she agreed to meet them at the pub at six, which gave her an hour to get home, feed the cat, shower and change, and then head back into town.

Lucy ended the call and walked toward the nurses' station. She handed in her charts to the one nurse on duty and signed out. She had another two weeks at the home before her contract was up and then she'd return full-time to the hospital. But she'd enjoyed her time working with the veterans. And with Joe Parker in particular. He was a natural storyteller and entertained everyone with his charm and easy-going manner.

Pity his nephew didn't inherit some of those manners or charm.

Lucy wrinkled her nose and headed down the hall to

the small locker room. Brant made her mad the way he ignored her. It wasn't like he was some great catch or anything. Sure, he had a body to die for. And the sexiest deep blue eyes. And dark hair that she'd often imagined running her fingers through. But he was a moody, closed-off loner who didn't seem to have time for anyone. Except his closest family members. She'd seen him in town one morning with his young nieces and the girls clearly adored him. It had made her think about how he'd probably make a great dad one day. And the idea of that quickly had her womb doing backflips.

Idiot...

She shrugged off her foolish thoughts, hung up her white coat and grabbed her bag.

The cold air outside hit her like a laser blast when she walked through the hospital doors. She quickly made it to her Honda and jumped inside. Snow was falling lightly and she watched the flakes hit the windshield. She loved snow and everything that went with it. Skiing, snowballs, log fires and the holidays… It was her favorite time of year. And one day she hoped she'd have a family of her own to share it with.

If only she could get the silly and impossible dreams of Brant Parker out of her head.

She popped the key into the ignition, started the car and drove off. The roads were slick, so she took her time getting home. When she pulled up in the driveway it was past five o'clock and she spotted her ginger cat, Boots, sitting idle in the front window. The image made her smile, and she was welcomed by the demanding feline once she'd dusted off her shoes and entered the house.

The place was small and very much in need of a complete renovation. She'd painted the walls in the living area and main bedroom when she'd returned to town for good, but since then she'd been so busy at the hospital, anything else had been put on hold. The kitchen required a complete overhaul as the cupboards were decades old and styled in old-fashioned laminate paneling and bright orange trim. It was retro in the truest sense and not to her taste. But she couldn't really afford to get someone in to do the work until the following summer and wasn't skilled enough to tackle anything more than painting herself. So, it would have to wait.

She dropped her bag, fed the cat and quickly checked her email before she headed to the shower. Within half an hour she was dressed in her favorite long denim skirt, emerald green shirt and mid-heeled boots. She pulled her hair from its ponytail, applied a little makeup and grabbed a small handbag for her wallet and cell phone. She texted Kayla as she was leaving, grabbed her coat and headed outside. She dusted the thin layer of snow off the windshield before she got into her car. The vehicle took a few turns of the key to start, but she was soon on her way.

The O'Sullivan pub was in the center of town and possessed a kind of richly authentic Irish flavor. It was actually a hotel, with fifteen luxurious rooms, two restaurants, a bar, an outdoor garden for private functions and several conference rooms available for rent. The O'Sullivan family was rich and well-known. Although the old man, John O'Sullivan, had retired and his eldest son, Liam, now ran the place, he still walked around with his chest puffed out like he ruled the town and everyone in it. No one crossed the O'Sullivans. No one would dare. The hotel was one of the main draws in the town and that had a lot of pull with the mayor's office. Tourists came to see the old mines, the occasional rodeos, the horse and cattle ranches, and many used the town as a stopover before they crossed the state line. Since the O'Sullivan's hotel was the poshest place to stay, few people objected to paying for their amenities.

She did wonder if that's why Brant had bought the Loose Moose—as a way of sticking it to the O'Sullivans. There was certainly no love lost between the two families. Brant's older brother, Grady, had been married to Liz O'Sullivan, and Lucy knew her parents had never thought a rancher was good enough for their beloved daughter. When Liz died a few years ago things had gotten worse and, according to Colleen Parker, the feud between the two families was now quite intense.

It was early, so she found a spot outside the hotel and parked. She got out, grabbed her coat from the backseat and tossed it over her arm. A few people milled around the front of the hotel, and she recognized a couple of nurses from the hospital and waved as she made her way through the wide doors.

Kayla, Brooke and Ash were already seated at a booth in the bar when she arrived, with a pitcher of sangria between them. The O'Sullivan pub certainly wasn't the average run-of-the-mill kind of drinking establishment. If you wanted beer and a game of pool you went to one of the other cowboy bars in town like Rusty's or the Black Bull. She slid into the booth and raised a brow at the quarter-empty pitcher on the table. "You started without me?"

Brooke tossed her straight blond hair a little and grinned. "You're late. So, of course."

Blue-eyed Ash, whose bobbed hair was the color of copper, smiled and nodded. "I'm off duty."

"And being a museum curator is thirsty work," Kayla said and laughed. "Although I'll be stopping at one drink. But we got you a glass."

Lucy chuckled and stared at her friend, who was easily the most beautiful woman she'd ever known. Kayla's long blond hair and dark brown eyes stopped most men in their tracks.

She lifted the half-filled glass and took a small sip. "Thanks. Are we staying for dinner?"

"Not me," Brooke said. "I have a foal due within days and with this weather coming in…" She sighed and grinned. "You know how it is."

Yes, they all knew Brooke lived and breathed for her horses.

"Nor me. I only have a sitter until seven thirty," Ash replied and inclined a thumb toward Kayla. "And this one has a date."

Lucy's gaze widened. "Really? With whom?"

Kayla laughed again. "Assignments. Marking papers for the online class I'm teaching through the community college."

"Gosh, we're a boring group," Lucy said and smiled. "Just as well I have a cat to get home to."

"You could always ask Hot Stuff over there to take you to dinner," Kayla suggested and laughed again.

Lucy's eyes popped wide. *Hot Stuff?* There was no mistaking who she meant. Her friend had been calling Brant that name for years, ever since Lucy had admitted she was crushing on him when she was a teenager.

"He's here?"

"Yep," Kayla replied. "Over by the bar, talking to Liam O'Sullivan."

Lucy looked toward Ash for confirmation. "She's right. He was here when we arrived. Looks like he's not too happy about it, either. I don't think he's cracked a smile in that time."

Nothing unusual about that, Lucy thought. She itched to turn around and see for herself, but didn't want to appear obvious. But she was curious as to why he was with Liam O'Sullivan, considering the family history.

"You know, he's not a complete killjoy," Brooke said about her cousin and gave a little grin. "And if you like, I could ask him for you?"

Lucy almost spat out her sangria. "Don't you dare," she warned. "You know how I feel about—"

"Yes," Brooke assured her and chuckled. "We've known how you feel about him for well over a decade."

God, how foolish that sounded. And, if she were being completely honest with herself, a little pathetic. She certainly didn't want friends thinking she was still *pining* for Brant Parker after so many years. "Well, I *won't* be asking him to take me to dinner," Lucy assured them.

"Pity," Kayla said and chuckled. "Because he hasn't taken his eyes off you since you've been here."

Lucy's cheeks heated. So, he watched her. It didn't mean *anything*. She might be unkissed, untouched and naive, but she was savvy enough to know when a man *wasn't* interested. Even though there were times…well, *occasionally* she had thought that she'd seen interest in his blue eyes. But mostly she thought it simply *wishful thinking* and then got on with knowing he'd never look at her in that way.

She turned her head a little and spotted him. Handsome as ever, he was talking to Liam and she experienced the usual flutter in her belly. His dark hair, strong jaw and blue eyes never failed to affect her on a kind of primal level.

"You're imagining things," she said dismissively and poured another quarter of a glass of sangria to keep her hands busy.

"I know what I saw," Kayla said, still smiling. "I wonder what he's doing talking with Liam."

"I'm sure you'll find out," Lucy said with a grin.

Kayla sighed heavily. "For the last time, I am *not* interested in Liam O'Sullivan."

Ash and Brooke both laughed. "Sure you aren't," Ash said.

"We're just working together on the gallery extension plans, that's all," Kayla insisted.

Lucy was pretty sure there was more to it, but didn't press the issue. She was more interested in knowing why Brant was consorting with his brother's mortal enemy. But since neither things were any of her business, she concentrated on the cocktails and enjoying her friend's company.

Except, Brooke didn't drop the topic. "At least he hasn't wrecked his bike again."

"Not for a couple of months," Lucy said and frowned. "He was lucky he wasn't seriously injured," she added with quiet emphasis.

His last visit to the ER was his third in seven months and had landed him with a dislocated shoulder and cuts and scrapes. The first was another flip from his motorbike. The second was when he'd climbed Kegg's Mountain and taken a tumble that also could have killed him. Why he'd risk his life so carelessly after surviving three tours of the Middle East, Lucy had no idea.

"I guess he's just adventurous," Brooke said, and Lucy saw a shadow of concern in her friend's expression. This was Brant's cousin. Family. Brooke knew him. And clearly she was worried.

"Maybe," Lucy replied and smiled fractionally, eager to change the subject.

Ash bailed at seven fifteen to get home to her eleven-year-old son, Jaye. Lucy hung out with Kayla and Brooke for another ten minutes before they all grabbed their bags and headed out. Brant had left half an hour earlier, without looking at her, without even acknowledging her presence. Kayla managed a vague wave to Liam O'Sullivan before they walked through the doors and into the cold night air.

Lucy grabbed her coat and flipped it over her shoulders. "It's still snowing. Weird for this time of year. Remind me again why I didn't accept the offer to join the hospital in San Francisco?"

"Because you don't like California," Kayla said, shivering. "And you said you'd miss us and this town too much."

"True," Lucy said and grinned. "I'll talk to you both over the weekend."

They hugged goodbye and headed in opposite directions. People were still coming into the hotel and the street out front was getting busy, so she took some time to maneuver her car from its space and drive off.

The main street of Cedar River was typical of countless others in small towns: a mix of old and new buildings, cedar and stucco, some tenanted, some not. There were two sets of traffic lights and one main intersection. Take a left and the road headed toward Rapid City. Go right and there was Nebraska. Over three and a half thousand people called Cedar River home. It sat peacefully in the shadow of the Black Hills and was as picturesque as a scene from a postcard. She loved the town and never imagined living anywhere else. Even while she was away at college, medical school and working at the hospital in Sioux Falls for three years, her heart had always called her home.

Up until recently the town had been two towns— Cedar Creek and Riverbend—separated by a narrow river and a bridge. But after years of negotiating, the townships had formed one larger town called Cedar River. Lucy had supported the merger… It meant more funding for the hospital and the promise of a unified, economically sound community.

Lucy was just about to flick on the radio for the chance to hear the weather report when her car spluttered and slowed, quickly easing to little more than a roll. She steered left and pulled to the curb as the engine coughed and died.

Great…

A few cars passed, all clearly intent on getting home before the snow worsened. Lucy grabbed her bag and pulled out her cell. She could call her automobile club for assistance, but that meant she'd be dragging mechanic Joss Culhane out to give her a tow home. And Joss was a single dad with two little girls to look after and had better things to do than come to her rescue because she'd forgotten about the battery light that had been flashing intermittently all week.

Better she didn't. She was just about to call Kayla to come and get her when she spotted something attached to one of the old buildings flapping in the breeze. A shingle. Recognition coursed through her.

The Loose Moose. Brant's place.

A light shone through one of the front windows. He was home. She knew he lived in the apartment above the tavern. Of course she'd never been up there. But Colleen Parker had told her how he was renovating the tavern while residing in the upstairs rooms.

Lucy got out of the car and wrapped herself in her red woolen coat. Surely, Brant would help her, given the circumstances?

She grabbed her bag and locked the car before she headed toward the old tavern. The old adobe front was boarded up, apart from the two windows, and the heavy double doors were still blackened in spots from the damage caused by the fire eight months before.

Lucy knocked once and waited. She could hear music coming from inside and discreetly peered through one of the windows. There were trestle tables scattered with power tools and neat stacks of timber on the floor near the long bar, and the wall between the remaining booth seats and the back room that had once housed pool tables had been pulled down. She knocked again, louder this time, and then again. The music stopped. By the time the door swung back she was shivering with cold, her knuckles were pink and her patience a little frayed.

Until she saw him. Then her mouth turned dry and her knees knocked for an altogether different reason.

He wore jeans and a navy sweater that molded to his shoulders and chest like a second skin. His dark hair was ruffled, as though he'd just run a hand through it, and the very idea made her palms tingle. His blue eyes shimmered and his jaw was set tightly. He looked surprised to see her on his doorstep. And not one bit welcoming.

But, dear heaven, he is gorgeous.

She forced some words out. "Um, hi."

"Dr. Monero," he said, frowning. "It's a little late for a house call, don't you think?"

She swallowed hard, suddenly nervous. There was no welcome in his words. She jutted her chin. "Oh, call me Lucy," she insisted and then waved a backward hand. "My car has stopped just outside. I think it's the battery. And I didn't want to call for a tow because my mechanic has two little kids and I thought it was too much to ask for him to come out in this weather and I was wondering if… I thought you might…"

"You thought I might what?"

Lucy wanted to turn and run. But she stayed where she was and took a deep breath. "I thought you might be able to help. Or give me a lift home."

His brows shot up. "You did?"

She shrugged. "Well, I know it's only a few blocks away, but the paths are slippery and the snow doesn't seem to be easing anytime soon."

His gaze flicked upward for a second toward the falling snow and then to her car. "Give me your keys," he instructed and held out his hand.

Lucy dropped the keys into his palm and watched as he strode past her and to her car. He was in the car and had the hood up in seconds. Lucy tucked her coat collar around her neck and joined him by the vehicle. He closed the driver's door and moved around the front, bending over the engine block. Lucy watched, captivated and suddenly breathless over the sheer masculine image he evoked. There was something elementally attractive about him...something heady and fascinating. Being around him felt as decadent as being behind the counter in a candy store. He had a narcotic power that physically affected her from the roots of her hair to the soles of her feet. And she'd never responded to a man in that way before.

Not even close.

Sure, she'd crushed on several of the O'Sullivan or Culhane brothers back in high school. But Brant Parker had never been far from her thoughts. Returning to Cedar River had only amplified the feeling over the years. Being around him made her realize how real that attraction still was. She liked him. She wanted him. It was that simple. It was that complicated.

"Battery's dead," he said, closing the hood.

Lucy smiled. "Well, at least that means I remembered to put gas in the tank."

He didn't respond. He simply looked at her. Deeply. Intently. As if, in that moment, there was nothing else. No one else. Just the two of them, standing in the evening snow, with the streetlight casting shadows across the sidewalk.

"I'll take you home," he said and walked back toward the Loose Moose.

Lucy followed and stood by the doors. "I'll wait here if you like."

Brant turned and frowned. "I have to get my jacket and keys, and my truck is parked out back. So you might as well come inside."

He didn't sound like he wanted her in his home. In fact, he sounded like it was the last thing he wanted. But, undeterred, she followed him across the threshold and waited as he shut the door.

"You've been busy," she said as she walked through the room and dropped her bag on the bar. "The renovations are coming along."

"That was the idea when I bought the place."

Lucy turned and stared at him. He really was a disagreeable ass. She wondered for the thousandth time why she wasted her energy being attracted to him when he made no effort to even be nice to her.

Not one to back down, she propped her hands on her hips. "You know, I was wondering something… Is it simply me you dislike or people in general?"

His jaw tightened. Hallelujah. Connection. Something to convince her he wasn't a cold fish incapable of response. His gaze was unwavering, blistering and so intense she could barely take a breath.

"I don't dislike you, Dr. Monero."

She shook her head. "My case in point. I've asked you half a dozen times to call me Lucy. The very fact you don't speaks louder than words. I know you *can* be nice because I've seen you with your mom and brother and nieces. At least when we were kids you were mostly civil…but now all I get from you is—"

"You talk too much."

Lucy was silenced immediately. She looked at him and a heavy heat swirled between them. She wasn't imagining it. It was there…real and palpable. And mutual. As inexperienced as she was, Lucy recognized the awareness that suddenly throbbed between them.

Attraction. Chemistry. Sex.

All of the above. All very mutual.

And she had no real clue what to do about it.

Chapter Two

Lucy Monero was a walking, talking temptation. And Brant wanted her. It took all of his willpower to *not* take her in his arms and kiss her like crazy.

But he stayed where he was, watching her, noticing how her hair shone from the light beaming from above. Her dazzling green eyes were vivid and suggestive, but also filled with a kind of uncertainty that quickly captivated him. Lucy had a way of stopping him in his tracks with only a look. So he didn't dare touch her. Didn't dare kiss her. Didn't dare talk to her, even though there were times when he thought he'd like nothing else than to listen to her voice or to hear her breathless laughter.

When they were kids she'd hung around the ranch, often watching him and his brother break and train the horses from the sidelines, her head always tucked into a book. She'd been quiet and reserved back then, not trying to grow up before her time by wearing makeup or trendy clothes. When her dad died, her mom had sold the small ranch and they'd moved into town, so he hadn't seen her as much. His own dad had died around that time, too, and with twenty-year-old Grady taking over the reins at their family ranch and Brant deciding on a military career midway through senior year, there wasn't any time to spend thinking about the shy, studious girl who never seemed to be able to meet his gaze.

Not so now, he thought. She'd grown up and gained a kind of mesmerizing poise along the way. Oh, she'd always been pretty—but now she was beautiful and tempting and had firmly set her sights on what she wanted.

Which appeared to be him.

Brant wasn't egotistical. But he recognized the look in her eyes every time they met. And he wasn't about to get drawn into *anything* with Lucy Monero. She was pure hometown. A nice girl who wanted romance, a wedding and a white picket fence. He'd heard enough about it and her virtues from his mom and Brooke. Well, it wasn't for him. He didn't do romance. And he wasn't about to get involved with a woman who had marriage on her mind.

"You're staring at me."

Her words got his thoughts on track and Brant felt heat quickly creep up his back and neck. His jaw clenched and he straightened his shoulders. "So, I'll just get my jacket and take you home."

"Is everything okay?" she asked quietly.

"What?"

She tilted her head a little and regarded him with her usual intensity. "You seem…tense."

It irritated him to no end that she could see through him like that. "I'm fine," he lied.

Her brows came up. "I'm pretty sure you're not."

"Is there a point you're trying to make?"

She shrugged one shoulder. "You know, most times we meet, you barely acknowledge me. At first I thought it was because you were just settling back in to civilian life and that small talk was really not your thing. But then I've seen you with your family and you seem relaxed and friendly enough around them. And you were with Liam O'Sullivan earlier and didn't end up punching him in the face, so that interaction must have turned out okay. So maybe it's just me."

Brant ignored the way his heart thundered behind his ribs. *It is you.* He wasn't about to get drawn into her little world. Not now. Not ever. He had too much going on. Too much baggage banging around in his head. Too many memories that could unglue him if he let someone in.

"Like I said, you talk too much."

She laughed, the sound wispy and sort of throaty and so damned sexy it sucked the air from his lungs. He was tempted to take the three steps he needed to be beside her. Maybe kissing her would get her out of his system. Maybe it was exactly the thing he needed to keep her out of his thoughts. But he stayed where he was, both irritated and fascinated by the relentless effect she had on him without even trying. And he knew the only way around it was to stay out of her way. To avoid her. To ignore her. To keep himself separate, as he had for the past eight months, and not get drawn into the land of the living where he would be forced to take part. Instead he'd stay on the sidelines, pretending everything was fine. Pretending *he* was fine. So his mom and brother didn't work out that he was now a shadow of the man he'd once been.

"So, I'm right. It *is* just me?" she asked, stepping a little closer. "Why? Are you worried that I might work out that underneath all your brooding indifference there's actually a decent sort of man?"

"Not at all," he replied quietly. "*Dr. Monero*, the truth is I don't think about you from one moment to the next."

It was a mean thing to say. He knew. She knew it. And he hated the way the words tasted in his mouth. He wasn't cruel. He wasn't good at it. He felt clumsy even saying the words. But he had to try to keep her at a distance.

"I see." Her eyes shadowed over for a second. She looked…hurt. Wounded. And the notion cut through him like a knife. He didn't want to hurt her. He didn't want to have any feelings when it came to Lucy Monero. "Okay. Fine. You've made yourself perfectly clear. Now, I think I'll find my own way home."

She was past him and by the door in seconds. As she rattled the doorknob, Brant took a few strides and reached her, placing a hand on either side of the jamb. She turned and gasped, looking up, so close he could feel her breath on his chin.

"Lucy…"

The sound of her name on his lips reverberated through him, sending his heart hammering and his blood surging through his veins. She was trapped, but didn't move, didn't do anything but hold his gaze steady. And this, he thought as he stared down into her face, was exactly why he needed to keep his distance. There was heat between them…heat generated by a sizzling attraction that had the power to knock him off his feet.

"Don't…please…" she said shakily, her bottom lip trembling fractionally.

Brant stepped back and dropped his arms instantly. "I'm not going to hurt you."

She nodded. "I know that. I didn't mean I thought you would. It's just that…being around you…it's confusing."

She was right about that!

"It's like you ignore me as though I don't exist," she

went on to say. "But sometimes you look at me as if…
as if…"

"As if what?" he shot back.

"As if you do…like me."

"Of course I do," he admitted raggedly, taking a
breath, hoping she couldn't see how messed up he was.
"But I'm not in the market for anything serious. Not
with you."

There…it was out in the open. Now she could move
on and stop looking at him as though he could give her
all she wanted. Because he couldn't. He didn't have it
in him. Not now. He'd been through too much. Seen too
much. He wasn't good company. He wasn't boyfriend or
husband material. He was better off alone.

"Why not?" she asked.

Nothing…

Brant sighed heavily. "I'd prefer not to get into it."

"Oh, no," she said and crossed her arms, pushing her
chest up, which instantly grabbed his attention.

God, her curves were mesmerizing. He looked to the
floor for a moment to regather his good sense and hoped
she'd stop talking. But no such luck.

"You don't get to make a bold statement like that and
then think you're off the hook. What's wrong with me?"
Her brows rose again. "I'm honest, intelligent, loyal and
respectable, and have good manners. I even have all my
own teeth."

Brant laughed loudly. God, it felt good to laugh. There
was something so earnest about Lucy it was impossible
to remain unaffected by her. During the past few weeks
he'd often heard her soft laughter through the corridors
of the veterans home and wondered how it would feel to
be on the receiving end of such a sweet, sincere sound.
And he wanted to hear it again.

"Well, I guess if I was buying a pony, all bases would be covered."

Her chuckle started out soft and then morphed into a full-on, loud guffaw. By the time she was done there were tears on her cheeks. She wiped them away and thrust out her chin.

"Wow…you do have a sense of humor." Her eyes shimmered. "Your cousin was right, you're not always a complete killjoy."

"No," he said easily. "Not always."

"So, this being a jerk thing…that's something you save especially for me?"

Brant's mouth twitched. "I have to get my keys," he said, ignoring the question. "Wait here."

Her eyes sparkled. "Aren't you going to invite me upstairs?"

To his apartment? His bedroom? "Not a chance," he said and strode off without looking back.

Lucy wrapped her arms around herself and wandered through the tavern. Every sense she possessed was on red alert. By the door he'd been so close…close enough that she could have taken a tiny step and been pressed against him. The heat from his skin had scorched hers. The warmth of his breath had made her lips tingle with anticipation. It was desire unlike any she'd known before. And she wanted it. She wanted him. She wanted his kiss, his touch. She wanted every part of him to cover every part of her.

And she shook all over, thinking about her false bravado. She'd never spoken to man in such a blatantly flirtatious tone before. But being around Brant was unlike anything she'd ever experienced. As *inexperienced* as she was, flirting and verbally sparring with him seemed to have a will and a power all of its own.

"Ready?"

He was back, standing by the steps that led upstairs. Lucy swallowed hard and nodded. "Sure. Thanks."

He shrugged loosely. "My truck's out back."

"No motorbike?"

He raised a brow and began to walk toward the rear of the building. "Not in this weather."

He was right, but the idea of being behind him on his motorbike, holding on to him, being so close she'd be able to feel his heartbeat, made her pulse race.

"So you're only reckless with yourself. That's good to know."

Brant stopped midstride and turned. "What?"

Lucy held out three fingers. "That's how many times you've been in hospital in the past seven months. Twice off your bike because you were speeding and once when you thought it was a good idea to climb Kegg's Mountain—alone—and without the proper gear, I might add."

"You're still talking too much," he muttered and then kept walking.

Lucy followed him down the long hallway, past the kitchen and restrooms, and then through the rear door. He waited for her to walk outside and locked the door. It was still snowing lightly and she took quick steps toward the beat-up, blue Ford pickup parked outside. He opened the passenger door, ushered her inside, strode around the front of the vehicle and slid into the driver's seat.

"What's your address?" he asked.

Lucy gave him directions and dropped her bag into her lap.

She expected him to immediately start the truck and drive off. But he didn't. He put the key in the ignition but placed both hands on the steering wheel. And then he spoke.

"I wasn't speeding. My bike blew a tire the first time and the second time I swerved to avoid hitting a dog that was on the road."

It was meant to put her in her place. To shut her up. To end the conversation.

But Lucy wasn't one to be silenced. "And the mountain?"

"I was unprepared. Not a mistake I would make again." He started the engine and thrust the gear into Reverse. "Satisfied?"

Lucy's skin tingled. The idea of being satisfied by Brant Parker had her insides doing flip-flops. Of course, he wasn't being suggestive, but Lucy couldn't help thinking how good a lover he would be. Not that she would have anything to make a comparison with. But she had a vivid imagination and she had certainly fantasized about being between the sheets with the man beside her.

She smiled sweetly. "I guess I didn't hear the whole story because I didn't attend to you the night you were brought into the ER."

He shifted gears again and turned into the street. "I thought my mother would have kept you updated. You and she seem to have become quite the twosome."

"I like your mom," Lucy replied. "She's a good friend."

"Yeah, my mom is a good person." He turned left. "She also likes to play matchmaker."

Lucy's mouth twitched. She knew that. Colleen had been gently pushing her in Brant's direction for months. "Does that make you nervous?" she asked, turning her gaze. "I mean, now she's got Grady settled and engaged to Marissa, do you think you're next?"

She watched his profile. Impassive. Unmoving. Like a

rock. But he was trying too hard. The pulse in his cheek was beating madly. He wasn't so unmoved. He was simply reining his feelings in…as usual.

"She's wasting her time."

Lucy tried not to be offended and managed a brittle laugh. "Considering how happy your brother is now, you can't blame your mom for wanting the same for you."

"I'm not my brother."

No, he wasn't. She knew Grady Parker. Oh, he still had the Parker pride and was a teeny bit arrogant, but he was a good-natured, hardworking family man with three little girls to raise and had recently found love again with Marissa Ellis. The wedding was only a couple of weeks away and Lucy knew Brant was standing as his brother's best man. She'd been invited, more to please Colleen Parker than anything else, she was sure. And since Brooke and Ash were both going and she liked Marissa and Grady, she was delighted to be part of their special day.

"Have you got a speech prepared?" Lucy asked, shifting the subject. "For the wedding, I mean. I hear you're the best man. That should be a fun gig…even for you."

He pulled the truck up outside her house, set the vehicle into Park and switched off the ignition. Then he turned in his seat and looked at her, his jaw set rigid. Boy, he was tense. And the intensity of it crackled the air between them. Lucy met his gaze and held it. Felt the heat of his stare as though he was touching her, stroking her, caressing her. She shuddered and she knew he was aware of the effect he had over her. A tiny smile tugged at the corner of his mouth, as though he knew he shouldn't react but couldn't resist.

If he moved, if he so much as lowered his defenses in any way, Lucy would have planted herself against him and begged for his kiss. She wanted it. Longed for it. But he continued to look at her, into her, making her achingly aware of the intimacy of the small space they shared.

"Even for me?" he intoned, his deep voice as intense as a caress. "I do know how to have a good time, despite what you think."

Lucy's bravado spiked. "Really?"

He inhaled heavily. "What is it you want, Dr. Monero?"

The million-dollar question. Bravado was fine when it wasn't challenged. But under scrutiny, Lucy quickly became unsettled. "I'm not... I don't..."

"You want something. Is it me?" he asked bluntly. "Is that what you want?"

Color smacked her cheeks. "I just want—"

"Why?" he asked, cutting her off. "Why me? You could have anyone you—"

"Chemistry," she said quickly, dying inside. "Attraction."

"Sex?"

Lucy stilled. She didn't want to think her reaction to him was merely physical. But since she did find him more attractive than she'd ever found any other man, perhaps she was blinded by those feelings? Maybe her daydreams about getting to know him, being around him and spending time with him were exactly that. Dreams. And foolish remnants of an old teenaged infatuation. She'd spent college and medical school wrapped in a bubble—wary of involvement with anyone because of what had happened to her roommate. But once she was back in Cedar River—more confident and older and able to meet his gaze head-on—Lucy had believed she would somehow be able to capture his attention.

But that hadn't happened. He'd ignored her. Despite her smiles and friendly attention.

And the more he ignored her, the more she wanted

him. His indifference became fuel for her teenaged fantasies and starved libido. So maybe it was just sex and she was simply too inexperienced to recognize it for what it was.

"What's wrong with that, anyway?" she shot back as heat climbed over her skin.

His gaze narrowed. "What's wrong with sex? Nothing... if that's all you're after." He reached out and touched her hair, trapped a few strands between his fingertips. It was the first time he'd touched her and it was electric. "But you don't strike me as the casual-sex kind of girl, Doc Monero. In fact, I'd bet my boots you are the white-picket-fence, happy-ever-after kind."

God, if he only knew, he'd probably run a mile.

"That's quite a judgment. And what are you? Only casual, no happy-ever-after?"

"Close enough," he said and returned his hands to the wheel.

"Back at the tavern you said you...liked me...so which is it?"

"Neither. Both. You're wasting your time with me. I'm not marriage material. So, good night."

Humiliation coursed through her veins and Lucy grabbed her bag and placed it in her lap. She got the message loud and clear. He was awful. Just awful. She swallowed the lump in her throat. "Are you going to walk me to my door?"

"This isn't a date," he said quietly.

He was such a jerk, and he was right about one thing: she was seriously wasting her time being attracted to him. Lucy set her teeth together and opened the door. "Thanks for the lift. I'll get my car towed in the morning. Good night."

"Good night...Lucy."

She got out, shut the door and stomped up the path and to the front door. While she was opening the door she realized he was still parked by the curb. So maybe he did have some chivalry in him. Ha—but not enough. As she got inside and peeked through the lace curtains to watch him finally drive away, Lucy decided she was going to forget all about him and spend her nights dreaming of someone else. Anyone else.

And the sooner she started the better.

Brant had been visiting his mother's home for lunch nearly every Saturday since he'd returned from his last tour. Colleen insisted they have a family catch-up and he didn't mind. He loved his mom, even though she drove him nuts with her attempts to interfere in his personal life. He knew there were only good intentions in her meddling, so he usually laughed it off and ignored her. But today—the morning after the whole Lucy-Monero-and-her-broken-down-car thing—Colleen was onto him the moment he stepped foot into her kitchen.

"I went into town early to get eggs and milk and saw Lucy's car outside the tavern," she said, her wide-eyed gaze all speculation and curiosity.

Brant walked around the timber countertop, grabbed a mug from the cupboard and poured coffee. "Her car broke down. I gave her a lift home."

And acted like a total horse's ass.

"She didn't spend the night?"

Color crept up his neck. His mother looked disappointed. Boy, sometimes he wished he had one of those parents who didn't want to talk about every single thing. "No, Mom, she didn't."

Colleen smiled. "You know, it wouldn't hurt you to encourage her a little. She's a nice girl. Smart. Pretty.

Sweet. And she has a kind spirit. I think she'd be a good match for you."

Brant sighed. "Are we really going to do this every Saturday?"

She grinned. "Every Saturday? I don't think I mentioned it last weekend."

"Oh, yeah, you did." Brant sugared his coffee and sat at the table. "I'm not in the market for a relationship right now," he said for the umpteenth time. "I need time to—"

"I know that's what you think," she said gently, cutting him off. "But I'm concerned about you."

"I know you're worried about me, Mom, but I'm okay," he assured her.

"You went through a lot over there," she said, her eyes glittering. "More than any of us will probably ever know. You're my son and I'm always going to be looking out for you, regardless of how old you are. When you have a child of your own you will understand what I mean."

"She's right, you know."

They both looked toward the doorway. His brother, Grady, stood on the threshold.

Brant frowned as his brother came into the room and sat. "You said you wouldn't encourage her," Brant reminded him.

Grady shrugged. "When she's right, she's right. I don't think it would matter how old my girls are, I'll always be on hand to make sure they're all right."

"See," Colleen said and smiled. "At least one of my sons had the good sense to listen to me."

Brant groaned. "Just because you meddled in his life and got him on the way to the altar, don't think you are going to do that with me. I have no intention of getting married anytime soon."

"You're thirty years old," his mom reminded him quietly. "And a civilian. You can have a normal life now, Brant."

No, he couldn't...

But he wasn't about to go down that road with his mother and brother. They didn't know much about what had happened before he'd left Afghanistan for good. He hardly dared think about it, let alone consider sharing it with his family. If they knew, they'd close ranks, smother him, give him sympathy and understanding when he deserved neither. In his mind, despite how hard he tried to get the thought out of his head, he was still a soldier. Still standing on the ridge. Still hearing the gunfire and the screams of the men in his unit who'd lost their lives that day.

"So where are the girls this morning?" he asked his brother, shifting the subject.

"With Marissa, getting their hair done." Grady grinned. "It's a practice run for their wedding-day hair."

Brant admired his brother. He'd raised his three young daughters alone since his wife, Liz, had died a couple of years earlier. Brant admired Marissa, too. His soon-to-be sister-in-law adored his nieces and had effortlessly stepped into her role as stepmother to the girls since she'd accepted his brother's proposal. Grady was a good man. The best he knew. And Brant was pleased his brother had found happiness again.

"O'Sullivan increased the offer," Brant said and drank some coffee.

Grady tapped his fist on the table. "Son of a bitch!"

"I didn't accept," he said when he saw his brother's swiftly gathering rage. "And I won't."

"Liam O'Sullivan believes he can have and do whatever he wants, just like his old man," Grady said and scowled. "The whole bunch of them think they're so damned entitled. No wonder Liz couldn't wait to get away from them. He only wants the Loose Moose because he doesn't want the competition. I heard he's been sniffing around Rusty's again, too. When Ted Graham finally does decide he wants to retire, O'Sullivan will be circling like a hyena."

"I told Ted I'd be interested in Rusty's if it comes on the market. He's not foolish enough to let the O'Sullivans get hold of the place. He hates them as much as you do."

Grady grunted. "You want two pubs? That's ambitious."

Brant shrugged. "Gotta make a living doing something."

"I thought you might want to come back to the ranch where you belong."

"I'm not much of a cowboy these days," he said, grinning.

"You're good with horses," Grady said generously. "Would be a shame to waste that skill entirely."

"You know I'll always give you a hand if you need it. But not full-time."

Grady nodded. "What about school?" his brother queried. "You said you were thinking of studying business at the community college."

"I still might."

"You could teach French at the night school, too," Grady suggested.

"I could," Brant replied, thinking about his options. "If I wasn't so busy with the Loose Moose."

"How are the renovations coming?"

"Slow," he said. "But I knew it would take a while. Doing the majority of it myself saves dollars but takes more time."

"If you need money to—"

"It's fine." Brant waved a hand. "I don't need your money."

"It's family money," Grady corrected. "The ranch is just as much yours as mine. And I would consider the tavern an investment. Dad and Uncle Joe and Granddad used to love the old place, remember?"

He did remember. It was one of the reasons why he'd been so keen to buy the tavern. "I'll let you know," he said, trying to fob his brother off as gently as he could.

Grady had a good heart but still acted as though he had to shoulder the brunt of all family issues. It was an "older brother thing," he was certain. When Grady had taken over the ranch he'd made it into one of the most successful in the county. Brant admired Grady's determination and commitment to the family, but he needed to do this alone. He needed to forge a life for himself that was of his own making.

"So, about this thing with Lucy Monero?" Grady asked.

"There's nothing going on between us," he assured his brother and looked toward their mother, who was cracking eggs into a bowl at the counter and pretending not to listen. "So, drop it. That means both of you."

"Can't," Colleen said and grinned. "Not when one of my kids is troubled."

Brant looked toward his brother for a little support, but Grady was nodding. Great. Suddenly, Saturday lunch had turned into some kind of intervention. Next, his mom would be suggesting he visit the shrink at the local veterans home.

"I was just talking to Dr. Allenby the other day about…"

Yep, right on schedule, he thought, and pushed his mother's words out of his head as she rattled on. He didn't need a shrink. He'd seen too many of them after Operation Oscar had gone down so badly. Three of his team had lost their lives. It had been two days of hell he wanted to forget. And he would, over time. If only his mom and brother would let up.

"I don't need a shrink."

His mother continued to whisk the eggs. "Then what about talking to someone else. Like me? Or your brother? Or even Lucy?" she suggested. "She's a doctor...and a good one."

Brant expelled an exasperated breath. "Mom, I'm fine. You gotta let this go, okay? I am happy," he lied. "I have you guys and the Loose Moose... For the moment, that's all I have room for. Working on restoring the tavern keeps my head clear, if that makes sense. And it's all the therapy I need."

That was the truth, at least. Sure, he was lonely, but better to be lonely than to bog someone else down with the train wreck his life had become. He probably just needed to get laid. It had been a while. He did the calculation in his head and inwardly grimaced. Man, he seriously needed to get out more. He still had friends in town, but going out with his old high school buddies, drinking beer, playing pool and talking smack didn't really cut it anymore. He wasn't twenty years old. He wasn't blinded by youth or ignorance. He'd seen the world and life at its darkest and would never be able to escape who he had become. Finding someone to share that with seemed impossible. The occasional one-night stand was all he allowed himself. And since Lucy Monero was not a one-night-stand kind of woman, he knew he had to keep avoiding her.

By the time he left his mother's it was nearly two. He headed to the hardware store to pick up a few things and spent the remainder of the afternoon working on the walls in the front part of the tavern. Turning in to bed around ten, he woke up at six on Sunday morning to get an early start, planning to spend the day sanding back the long cedar bar. But at one o'clock he got a call from Grady to say Uncle Joe had been taken to the hospital and was in the emergency room. It took him five minutes to change and head out and another fifteen to get to the hospital. He called Grady again once he was out of the truck and headed for the ER.

By the time he reached Reception he felt as though his chest might explode. The woman behind the counter said she'd inquire after his uncle and told him to wait.

Great. Exactly what he didn't want to do.

He knew Grady was on his way to the hospital, so he paced the room for a few minutes and then finally sat. The hospital sounds reverberated in his eardrums. Phones, beepers, gurneys, heels clicking over tiles. Each sound seemed louder than the last.

He sat for five minutes, swamped by a building helplessness that was suffocating.

When he could stand it no more he got up and headed back to the counter. "Is there any news about my uncle?"

The fifty-something woman scowled a little and flicked through some charts on the desk. "No, nothing yet."

"Then can you find someone who might know something?"

She scowled again and Brant's impatience rose. He wasn't usually a hothead. Most of the time he was calm and in complete control. Twelve years of military training had ingrained those traits into him. But he didn't feel calm now. He felt as though he could barely stand to be in his own skin.

"Brant?"

He knew that voice.

Turning his head, he saw Lucy and relief flooded through him. In some part of his mind he wondered how she had the power to do that, to soothe his turbulent emotions. Just knowing she was there somehow made things easier. Better. He swiveled on his heels and watched as she walked toward him, wearing scrubs and a white coat. Brant met her gaze and swallowed hard.

"You're here."

"I'm here," she said and smiled fractionally. "What do you know?"

"Not much," he said and shook his head. "What happened?"

Her eyes gave it away. It was serious. "He had a heart attack."

A heart attack? Fear coursed through his blood. "Is he…is he dead?"

The second it took for her to answer seemed like an hour. "No."

Brant fought back the emotion clogging his throat. "Is he going to make it?"

She nodded slowly. "I think so."

"Thank God," Brant breathed and, without thinking, reached out and hauled her into his arms.

Chapter Three

Lucy melted.

She'd never pegged Brant as a hugger. Nor did she want to think about what was going on in the minds of the two nurses at the reception desk. Cedar River was a small town. She was a doctor on staff and the most gorgeous man on the planet was holding her so tightly she didn't dare breathe.

There might be talk. Innuendo. But she didn't care. In that moment he needed her. Wanted her. It might be fleeting. It might be the only time she would ever get to feel what it was like to be in his arms. She heard his heart beating and felt the steady thud against her ear. His chest was broad, hard, the perfect place to rest her head, and all her plans to get him out of her mind quickly disappeared.

When he released her she was breathing deeply, conscious of the sudden intimacy between them. He pulled away and dropped his arms, watching her, his gaze so intense it weakened her knees. There was something in his eyes, a kind of wary vulnerability that tugged at her heartstrings.

"Sorry," he said quietly, clearly aware they were being observed by the two women at the desk. "That wasn't appropriate."

Maybe not, she thought, but it sure felt good. It wasn't the first time she been embraced in the waiting room. Relatives of patients had done it before when they had received news, good and bad. But this was different. This was Brant. Lucy forced some movement into her limbs and gathered her composure. She was a doctor and needed to act like one.

"It's fine, don't worry about it. I can take you to see your uncle now."

He nodded. "Thank you."

"We've done a few preliminary tests and it looks as though he has an arterial blockage. So he may need surgery," she explained as she used her key card to open the doors that led to the small emergency room. "We'll keep him here under observation tonight and then he'll be transported to the hospital in Rapid City tomorrow. They have excellent cardiology and surgical departments there and he'll be in really good hands."

He walked beside her through Triage, his expression impassive and unreadable. Lucy linked her hands together and headed for the cubicle at the far end of the room. She eased the curtain back. Joe Parker was resting and she leaned a little closer toward Brant to speak.

"He's asleep. I know his pallor looks a little gray, but that's not unusual after an episode like he's had. We'll let him rest for a while and do his OBS again in half an hour. You can sit with him if you like."

Brant nodded and sat. "Thank you."

Lucy lingered for a moment. "We'll do our very best for him. He's a special man and, despite his age, he's quite strong."

"Yeah, he is."

She knew how much the older man meant to Brant. She'd witnessed his affection for Joe Parker many times when he'd come to visit him at the veterans home. And Colleen had told her about the special bond they shared. They were both soldiers. They'd both fought for their country and had seen war and destruction and death. It was easy to understand why Brant cared so much for his uncle and had such a strong connection to him.

"I'll come back in a little while," she said and lightly touched Brant's shoulder. He tensed immediately and she quickly pulled her hand away.

She left the cubicle and pulled the curtains together. There were three other patients in the ER. A woman with a nasty burn on her arm, a toddler with a fever and a teenage boy with a fishing hook through his thumb. She checked on the baby and was pleased that his fever had gone down fractionally, and then instructed one of the triage nurses to get the teenager prepared so she could remove the hook. By the time she was done a little over half an hour had passed and she headed back to Joe Parker's cubicle.

Grady and Colleen were both there, bending the rules since regulation stated only two visitors were allowed at a time. But Colleen was well-known at the hospital and sometimes rules needed to be broken. Colleen was sitting in the chair and her sons flanked either side of the bed. Joe was awake and smiled broadly when she pulled back the curtain.

"Here she is," he said. "My guardian angel. She's been looking after me since I got here."

Lucy grinned. "Well, you're a model patient, so it's been easy."

"Never a more beautiful girl have I ever seen," Joe said and chuckled. "Makes me wish I was forty years younger."

Lucy smiled at his outrageous flirting and glanced toward Brant. He was watching her with blistering intensity and she quickly shifted her gaze. "How are you feeling?" she asked, grabbing the chart from the foot of the bed.

"Better for seein' you, Doc," he said and winked.

"Joe," Colleen chastised her much older brother-in-law gently. "Behave yourself."

Joe Parker smiled again, wrinkling his cheeks. "Ha! There's no fool like an old fool, right, Doc?"

He made a breathless sound and Lucy stepped toward the bed and grasped his wrist. He was overdoing it. She urged him to lay back and rest. She checked him over and scribbled notes in his chart. When she was done she asked Grady to walk with her outside the cubicle. The eldest Parker son had his uncle's medical power of attorney and she wanted to keep the family updated on his condition.

"It was a mild-range heart attack," she explained once she and Grady were out of earshot. "But I'm concerned enough to send him to Rapid City for a full set of testing. He may need surgery sooner rather than later, but the cardiologist there will make that call. For the moment he is stable and out of pain."

Grady nodded and she was struck by how alike the brothers were. Same color hair, same eyes, same tough jaw. Grady was a little taller than his brother, but Brant was broader through the shoulders. And Grady always looked happy…like he had some great secret to life. Whereas Brant…? Lucy only saw caution and resistance in his gaze. For the moment, though, her only concern was Joe Parker's welfare. She explained the procedure for transporting him to the larger hospital and when she was done asked if he had any questions.

"No," Grady replied. "I do know Brant will want to go with him. They're very close."

She nodded. "I can arrange something." She turned to walk away when Grady said her name. "What is it?"

He shrugged loosely. "About Brant. I know this might not be the right time to say anything…but do you think you could talk to the counselor at the veterans home about perhaps having a word with him…kind of on the down-low, if you know what I mean?"

Lucy's skin prickled. "Do you think he needs counseling?"

"I think when he was a solider he went through some bad stuff and doesn't want to talk about it," Grady said and sighed. "Not even to me or Mom."

Lucy thought that, too. She knew enough about PTSD to recognize the signs. His isolation, irritability and moodiness could definitely be attributed to something like that. Of course, she had no idea what he'd witnessed in service to his country. But if his brother was concerned, that was enough for Lucy to do what she could to help.

"I could have a quiet word with Dr. Allenby. He comes to the home once a week and he's trained to deal with veterans, particularly combat soldiers."

Grady nodded. "Yes, my mom has mentioned him. That's great. I'd really appreciate it if you could do that. But we might want to keep this between us, okay?"

Going behind Brant's back didn't sit well with her conscience. This was a conversation the Parker family needed to have together. But she could clearly see the concern in his brother's eyes and that was enough to get her agreement for the moment. "Don't think there'll be a problem with that. Your brother hardly talks to me."

"Self-preservation," Grady said and grinned.

"What?"

His grin widened. "You know how guys are. We always do things stupid-ass backward. Ask Marissa how much I screwed up in the beginning. Ignoring her was all I could do to keep from going crazy."

Lucy's mouth creased into a smile. "You know he'd hate the fact we're out here talking about him, don't you?"

"Yep," Grady replied. "Just as well we're on the same side."

Lucy's smiled deepened. "I'll see what I can do."

Grady returned to his uncle's bedside and Lucy headed to the cafeteria for a break. She ordered tea and a cranberry muffin and sat by the window, looking out toward the garden, an unread magazine open on the table in front of her. The place was empty except for the two people behind the counter and a couple of orderlies who were chatting over coffee in the far corner. She liked days like this. Quiet days. It gave her time to think. The hospital was small but catered to a wide area and some days she didn't have time for breaks.

"Can I talk to you?"

Lucy looked up from her tea. Brant stood beside the small table. "Oh…sure."

He pulled out the chair opposite. "Can I get you anything? More coffee?"

"Tea," she corrected and shook her head. "And I'm good. What can I do for you?"

It sounded so perfunctory…when inside she was churning. He looked so good in jeans and a black shirt and leather jacket. His brown hair was long, too, as it had been in high school, curling over his collar a little—a big change from the regulation military crew cut she was used to seeing when he came back to town in between tours. There was a small scar on his left temple and another under his chin, and she wondered how he'd gotten them. War wounds? Perhaps they were old football injuries or from school-yard antics? Or when he used to work horses with his brother? He'd always looked good in the saddle. She had spent hours pretending to have her nose in a book while she'd watched him ride from the sidelines. At twelve she'd had stars in her eyes. At twenty-seven she felt almost as foolish.

She took a breath and stared at him. "So...what is it?"

"My uncle is seventy-three years old, and I know he has health issues and might not have a lot of time left. I also know that he trusts you."

"And?" she prompted.

He shrugged one shoulder. "And I was thinking that once he gets to the hospital in Rapid City there will be a whole lot of people there who he doesn't trust poking and prodding and making judgment calls and decisions about him."

Lucy stilled. "And?" she prompted again.

"And he'd probably prefer it if you were around to see to things."

She eyed him shrewdly. "*He* would?"

His other shoulder moved. "Okay... *I* would."

"You want me to go to the hospital with him?"

"Well...yes."

"I'm not on staff there," she explained, increasingly conscious of his intense gaze. "I couldn't interfere with his treatment or be part of his appointments with specialists."

"I know that," Brant replied softly, his attention unwavering. "But you could be there to explain things… you know, to make sense of things."

Lucy drank some tea and then placed the paper cup on the table. "With you?"

He shrugged again. "Sure."

"Won't that go against your determination to avoid me and my wicked plans to ensnare you with my white picket fence?"

His eyes darkened. She was teasing him. And Brant Parker clearly didn't like to be teased.

"This is about my uncle," he replied, his jaw clenching. "Not us."

The silly romantic in her wanted to swoon at the way he said the word *us*. But she didn't.

"I do have the day off tomorrow," she said, thinking she was asking for a whole lot of complications by agreeing to his request. But she did genuinely care about Joe Parker.

"So…yes?" he asked.

Lucy nodded slowly. "Sure. I'll arrange for the ambulance to leave here around nine in the morning and we can follow in my car."

"I'll drive. We'll take my truck."

Lucy gave in to the laughter she felt. "Boy, you're predictable. Clearly my little Honda isn't macho enough."

"I need to get some building supplies from Rapid City," he shot back, unmoving. "I don't think the footrest for the bar that I'm having made will fit in your *little Honda*, Dr. Monero. Besides the fact that your car is unreliable."

"I had my car towed and the battery replaced yesterday, so it's as good as new." Her cheeks colored. "And I thought we agreed you were going to call me Lucy?"

A smile tugged at the corner of his mouth. "Did we? Okay, *Lucy*, I'll pick you up around nine."

His uncle looked much better the following day, but Brant was still pleased he was going to be assessed in Rapid City. He was also pleased that Lucy Monero had agreed to go with him. He knew it was a big favor to ask. But she'd agreed, even when she had every reason not to. He'd acted like a stupid jerk the night she'd broken down outside the tavern.

He waited in the foyer while his uncle was being prepped for the trip in the ambulance, and Lucy sidled up beside him around two minutes past nine. She looked effortlessly pretty in jeans, heeled boots, a bright red sweater that clung to her curves and a fluffy white jacket. Her hair was down, flowing over her shoulders in a way that immediately got his attention.

"You're late," he said, grinning fractionally.

"I've been here for ages," she replied and crossed her arms, swinging her tote so hard it hit him on the behind. "Oh, sorry," she said breathlessly and then smiled. "The ambulance is about to leave, so we should get going."

Brant rattled his keys. "Okay."

It was cold out, but at least the snow had stopped falling and the roads were being cleared.

"Once you've finished renovating the Loose Moose," she said when they reached his truck and he opened the creaky passenger door, "you might want to consider giving this old girl an overhaul."

Brant waited until she was inside and grabbed the door. "Are you dissing my ride?"

She laughed. "Absolutely."

He shut the door and walked around the front. "That's cruel," he said once he slid in behind the wheel and started the engine. "I've had this truck since I was sixteen."

"I know," she said, and fiddled with the Saint Christopher magnet stuck on the dash. "You bought it off Mitch Culhane for two hundred bucks."

Brant laughed, thinking about how Grady had gone ballistic when he'd come home with the old truck that was blowing black smoke from the exhaust. The truck hadn't really been worth a damn back then, but he'd fixed it up some over the years. "How do you know that?"

She shrugged. "I think Brooke told me. We're friends, remember?"

He nodded. "I know that. She's another fan of yours."

"Another?"

"My mom," he replied, smirking a little. "Patron Saint *Lucia.*"

Her eyes flashed. "How do you know my real name?" she asked as if it was something she didn't like.

"I think Brooke told me," he said then shrugged. "We're family…remember?"

"Funny guy," she quipped sweetly. "And I didn't think the Parkers and Culhanes were friends."

"Grady and I used to get into some scrapes with the Culhane brothers," he admitted wryly. "But since we shared a mutual dislike of the O'Sullivans we were friends more often than not."

"He still shouldn't have sold you this crappy old truck," she said. "You took Trudy Perkins to prom in it."

That's not all he'd done with Trudy on prom night, he thought, but he wasn't about to say that to the woman beside him. Trudy had been the wildest girl in their grade back then. And she'd had him wrapped around her little finger. He'd been a typical teenage boy and at the time Trudy had been his every fantasy.

But he'd changed. He didn't want that now. He wanted...well, he didn't have a damned clue what he wanted. All he knew was that there was nothing crass or easy about Lucy. She was kind and innocent. The kind of girl his mother approved of. Hell, the kind of girl his mother kept pushing him toward.

"I wonder what happened to Trudy," he said as he drove from the parking lot.

"She lives in Oregon. She married some rich banker and had three kids. I guess she could be divorced by now."

Brant glanced sideways. "How do you know this stuff?"

She shrugged. "I'm a doctor. People tell me things."

"Clearly."

"Except you wouldn't, right?" she said and leaned back in the seat. "You keep everything to yourself."

"Not everything."

"Everything," she said again. "Say, if I asked you what you were doing talking with Parker enemy number one, Liam O'Sullivan, the other night, you'd shrug those broad shoulders of yours and say it was *just business*."

"Well, it was."

She laughed softly and the sound hit him in the solar plexus. "When everyone knows he's trying to buy you out because he hates the idea of competition."

"Everyone knows that, do they?"

"Sure. He told Kayla and Kayla told me."

"Kayla?" he inquired. "That's your friend with the supermodel looks?"

"The one in the same. Every man notices Kayla. She's the original blonde bombshell."

Brant made a small grunting sound. "I've always preferred brunettes myself."

She glanced at him and then looked to the road ahead. "Could have fooled me."

Brant bit back a smile. "It's true."

"Trudy was blond," she said, frowning a little. "Remember?"

"She was brunette," he replied. "Trudy dyed her hair."

She snorted. "I'm pretty sure that wasn't the only fake part."

Brant wasn't one to kiss and tell, but the disapproval in Lucy's voice about the other woman's surgically enhanced attributes made him smile. "You could be right."

Lucy Monero had a habit of doing that. Whatever transpired between them, however much he desired her, wanted her, imagined kissing her, there was something else going on, too. Because he *liked* her. She was sweet and funny and good to be around. A balm for a weary soul. Something he could get used to, if he'd let himself. Not that he would.

"Incidentally," he said, speaking without his usual reserve. "Don't confuse my reluctance for disinterest."

"You really do talk in riddles sometimes," she said and then gave a soft laugh. "But I least I have you talking."

She did. In fact, he'd done a whole lot more talking with Lucy than he had with anyone outside his mother and brother and Uncle Joe for the past six months. "Communicating is important to you, isn't it?"

"People are important to me."

"I guess they have to be, considering your profession. Is that why you chose to become a doctor?"

She didn't answer and he glanced toward her and saw her gaze was downcast. She was thinking, remembering. Lost in some secret world of her own for a moment. She looked beautiful and just a little sad.

"No," she said finally. "It was because of my mom."

Brant could vaguely recall Katie Monero. She'd spoken with an Irish brogue and had taught dance lessons at the studio above the bakery in town. She'd married an Irish/Italian rancher who'd had no idea about cattle and horses, and who had died when Lucy was an adolescent. The crash that had taken her mother's life a few years later was a tragic accident. Katie had lost control of her car while a seventeen-year-old Lucy had dozed beside her. Katie had been flung from the car and Lucy had survived with barely a scratch.

"Because of the accident? It wasn't your fault, though."

"No," she said and sighed. "But my mom was alive for over ten minutes before the paramedics arrived. I didn't know what to do. I went numb. If I had put pressure on the main wound she might have had a chance. But I didn't know…and I vowed I'd never be in that position again. So I decided to go to medical school and become a doctor. I wanted to know that if I *was* ever in that position again that I would be able to do things differently."

"I understand," he said. "But you might need to let yourself off the hook a little."

"I can't," she replied. "I was there. I was the *only* person there that night. My mom needed me and I couldn't help her."

Brant's chest tightened. There was guilt and regret in her words. And he knew those things too well. "Sometimes you can't help," he said quietly. "Sometimes… sometimes in an impossibly bad situation, there's simply nothing you can do. You have to live through the moment and move on."

"It sounds like you know what that feels like."

"I do," he said soberly.

"But you don't like talking about it, do you?" she asked quietly. "The war, I mean."

Brant shrugged loosely. "No point rehashing the past."

"Sometimes talking helps."

He shrugged again. "For some people. Anyway, your mom…she'd be really proud of you."

Lucy sighed. "I hope so. I hope she'd think I was a good person."

"How could she not? You're incredible."

Heat crawled up his neck once he'd said the words. But there was no denying it. Lucy Monero was one hell of a woman.

"You better stop being nice to me," she said softly, "or I might start polishing my white picket fence again."

The heat in his neck suddenly choked him. "Look, I'm sorry about that, okay? I shouldn't have said it. I must have sounded like some kind of egotistical idiot…and I'm not. I think I've just forgotten what it's like to be normal. For years I've been driven by routine and rules, and now I'm living an ordinary life, talking about everyday stuff, and it takes practice. And time."

"I know that," she said and smiled. "I can't imagine even some of what you've been through."

His stomach clenched. "I had it easy compared to some. I got to come home. And in one piece."

"I'm glad about that."

He was, too. Most days. Until the guilt got him. The unforgiving, relentless guilt that reminded him that while he was home and healthy and physically unscathed, so many of his friends had not made it.

Survivor's remorse. He'd heard about it. Read about it. Hell, he'd even had an army shrink tell him about it. But he hadn't wanted to believe it. He longed to be grateful that he was still alive. But there were times when he couldn't be. And there were times when he felt as though a part of him had died up on that ridge that day.

"So am I."

He tried to think of something else to say, some way to convince her that her mother would be very proud of the woman she had become, but she spoke again.

"Your brother thinks you have PTSD."

Brant flinched. "I don't—"

"You might," she said, cutting him off. "It can show itself in various ways. Do you sleep through the night?"

"Mostly," he lied.

"There are other symptoms," she went on to say, calmly, relentlessly. "Bad dreams, fatigue, isolation. I know Dr. Allenby would be available to talk to you. I can give you a referral if you like. Or make you an appointment."

Great, she thought he was a head case. A nut job. Weak. And he was pissed that his brother had been interfering. "Grady had to know I wouldn't be happy he'd said that to you."

She shrugged lightly. "I might have told him I wouldn't tell you."

"But you did."

She sighed. "I thought it was more important I tell you the truth than him."

"Why?"

Brant felt her stare from his hair to the soles of his feet. But he didn't dare look at her, because her next words should have rocked him to the core. But they didn't.

"Because it's not your brother I like, is it?"

Chapter Four

Lucy never imagined she would be sitting in his truck and telling Brant Parker she liked him.

Admit it...you more than like him.

To his credit, he didn't overreact. In fact, as the seconds ticked by, he didn't do anything. He simply drove, hands on the wheel, eyes and concentration directly ahead. Nothing about him indicated he was affected by her words in any way.

But as the seconds turned into minutes, her gratitude quickly turned into irritation.

Am I so completely unlikable in return?

She sucked in a breath, felt her annoyance build and crossed her arms. "Well...thank you."

"What?" he said and snapped his head sideways for a moment.

"Thank you for making me feel about as desirable as a rock."

More silence. But this time it was filled with a thick, relentless tension that she felt through to her bones. Okay, so he wasn't unmoved. But he wasn't saying much, either!

"Don't be stupid."

Lucy's jaw tightened and she glared at him. "Now I'm a *stupid* rock?"

"You're deliberately twisting my words to get some kind of reaction," he said, still not looking at her, still staring at the road ahead. "It's not going to work."

Lucy laughed humorlessly. "You know, Brant, you can be a real horse's ass sometimes."

"Around you?" He sighed heavily. "Sure seems that way."

"Okay… I take it back. I *don't* like you. Not one bit."

"Good," he quipped. "Let's keep it that way."

Lucy clenched her hands around her tote. "Fine by me."

Silence stretched between them like elastic. Lucy was about to shift her gaze sideways to stare out the window when she heard him chuckle.

"Something funny?" she asked.

"Yeah," he replied. "You are. We are."

"But there is no *we*," she reminded him. "Remember? I'm a hometown girl with picket-fence dreams and you're not marriage material… Isn't that how it went?"

His jaw clenched but she caught a smile teetering on his lips.

"Are you going to constantly remind me of every stupid thing I say, Lucy?"

"Probably."

"Don't know how we're ever gonna become friends if you keep doing that."

Lucy's breath caught. "Friends? You and me?"

He shrugged loosely. "Why not? It would sure beat

all that wasted energy I've put in trying to ignore you for the past six months."

She almost laughed out loud. Now he wanted to be friends after months of snubbing her very existence? The nerve of him. "So, you admit it?"

"Totally."

His honest reply quickly diffused her rising temper. "And now all of a sudden you want to be friends?"

"I want my mother to stop matchmaking," he replied. "I figure that if we're friends and she knows it's strictly platonic, she'll get off my back."

Lucy clenched her jaw. "Boy, you sure know how to make a girl feel good about herself."

"It wasn't meant as an insult," he said quietly. "On the contrary, I think having you as a friend could be the best move I've made in a long time."

She tried to smile. Friends? Sure. Whatever. "Okay, we'll be friends. To please your mom, of course."

"You're making fun of me," he said, his gaze straight ahead. "That's becoming something of a habit of yours."

"You could probably do with being brought down a peg or two."

He laughed and the sound filled the cab. "You think I need bringing down?"

"Sometimes. But I guess since you look the way you do…" Her voice trailed off.

"What does that mean?" he asked.

Lucy shrugged, coloring hotly and digging herself in deeper with every word. "You know…because you're so…so…"

"So?"

"Hot," she said quickly. "Handsome. Gorgeous. And if you had mirrors in your house you'd know that already."

"I don't spend time gazing at my own reflection," he said wryly.

Lucy smiled, pleasantly surprised to discover that beneath the brooding, indifferent facade he actually had a good sense of humor. "Here I was thinking all you pretty boys were the same."

His mouth twisted and then he laughed again. "You're making fun again. See," he said easily, "this 'being friends' thing is working out already."

Lucy laughed. "Yeah…it's a breeze."

The conversation shifted to more neutral topics other than their fledgling friendship and by the time they pulled into the parking lot at the hospital Lucy was in a much better mood. And it didn't take a genius to figure out that he had somehow diffused her temper with his deep voice and quiet small talk. So, he was smart. She knew that. It was one of the things she found attractive about him. There was an understated intensity about Brant Parker that captured her attention every time he was within a twenty-foot radius.

And now he wanted to be friends. That's all. And she'd agreed.

I'm an idiot.

What she needed to do was to stay well away from Brant Parker and his deep blue eyes and sexy indifference. Otherwise she was going to get her heart well and truly crushed.

They walked into the hospital side by side and once they reached reception Lucy quickly asked for directions to Joe Parker's room. Brant's uncle was sitting up in bed, pale and tired, but in good spirits.

"You're certainly keeping good company these days," Joe said to Brant and winked toward Lucy. "'Bout time."

Brant managed to look a little uncomfortable. "Dr.

Monero is here in case you have any questions about the tests you'll be having."

Joe patted the edge of the bed, inviting Lucy to sit. "Is that what he said, Doc?" He winked again, then glanced at his nephew. "Using a sick old man to get a date... shame on you."

"Uncle Joe, I hardly—"

"I insisted," Lucy said, smiling, certain that Brant didn't appreciate his uncle's teasing. "So this isn't really a date. I wanted to make sure you were okay."

Joe's eyes crinkled in the corners. "That's nice to hear. But all this seems like a big waste of time. I don't want a whole bunch of people sticking me with needles and poking at me. I feel fine."

"You had a heart attack, Uncle Joe," Brant reminded him seriously.

Joe waved a hand. "It was nothing, just a—"

"Mr. Parker," Lucy said gently as she perched herself on the edge of his bed. "You trust me, right?"

The older man nodded. "Well, of course, Doc."

Lucy patted his hand. "You're here because I thought it was the best thing considering what happened yesterday. And I'll be close by if you have any questions. So, promise me you won't cause a fuss and will do everything the doctors say."

He shrugged and looked toward his nephew. "She certainly has a way about her, doesn't she? Is she this bossy with you?"

Brant's mouth twitched. "Absolutely."

Joe laughed and it made Lucy smile. She knew Brant was watching her and feeling his gaze made her skin hot. She wished she wasn't so affected by him. It would certainly make getting him out of her system a whole lot easier.

Two doctors and a nurse arrived, and she shuffled off the bed and introduced herself and Brant. It took a few minutes for them to explain the testing and observations they would be doing over the next few hours and once Lucy was assured Joe was in good hands, she and Brant left the room.

"Should we stay?" he asked as they headed down the corridor.

"No," Lucy replied. "The less distraction your uncle has, the better. We'll come back in an hour or so. In the meantime, you can buy me a cup of herbal tea at the cafeteria."

Brant grinned slightly. "Sure, *Saint Lucia*."

She frowned. "I thought we agreed you were going to call me plain old Lucy."

"You're not old," he said as they reached the elevator. "And you're not plain."

Lucy's eyes widened as they stepped into the elevator. "Is that a compliment?"

He shrugged. "An observation."

She waited until the door closed and pressed the button. "Smooth," she said and crossed her arms. "But you obviously don't remember when I used to be a chubby teenager with braces and glasses."

The elevator opened and he waited while she stepped out before following her.

"I remember," he said, walking beside her as they headed for the cafeteria.

"And here I was thinking I was invisible back then."

When they reached the cafeteria he ordered her some tea and a coffee for himself and quickly found them a table. He pulled a seat out for her, waited while she settled in, then placed his jacket on the back of another chair and took a seat. "Are you always this hard on yourself?" he asked quietly.

Lucy frowned. "What?"

"You're smart, successful..." His words trailed off for a moment and he rested his elbows on the table. "And beautiful. Why would you think anything less?"

"I don't," she said quickly, feeling heat rise up her neck. "I mean...not that I think I'm beautiful...because I'm obviously not. Well, not compared to someone like my friend Kayla. But I know I'm—"

"Being tall and blonde isn't a trademark stamp of beauty, you know," he said, meeting her gaze with a burning intensity that left her breathless. "There's also beauty in curves and green eyes and freckles."

I'm dreaming...that has to be it. There's no other way Brant Parker would be telling me he thinks I'm beautiful.

She swallowed hard and took a breath. "Wow, you really can be charming when you put your mind to it."

He chuckled. "I figure I have some making up to do."

"You mean because you behaved like an idiot the other night?"

"Yes."

She laughed softly. "You're forgiven, okay? I'm not the kind of person to hold a grudge anyhow."

"That's very generous of you. My mother was right."

Lucy's expression narrowed. "She was?"

He half shrugged. "She said you were kind. And sweet."

"Wow, how dull does that sound," Lucy sighed.

Brant's eyes darkened and he stared at her with a kind of hypnotic power. Awareness swirled through the space between them and she couldn't have broken the visual connection even if she'd tried.

"Tell me something," he said so quietly that Lucy had to lean forward to hear him. "Why don't you have a boyfriend?"

Brant had no idea why he was asking Lucy Monero about her love life. He didn't want to know. The less he knew about the bewitching brunette the better. But he couldn't help himself. She looked so alluring with her lovely hair framing her face and her sparkling green eyes meeting his gaze with barely a blink.

She sat back, looking surprised. "A boyfriend?"

Her reaction was dead-on. It was none of his concern what she did or with whom. "Forget I—"

"No one's asked me out."

Impossible. Brant didn't bother to hide his disbelief. "No one?"

She raised a shoulder. "Not for a while. And I guess I wasn't all that interested in dating when I was in medical school. Since I've been back home I've been too busy at the hospital. You know how it is…it's easy to get caught up in work and forget everything else."

He *did* know how that was. Brant had deliberately focused on renovating the Loose Moose for the past month or so to avoid any entanglements. But something in her expression made him think there was more to it. "So there was no college boyfriend you left behind with a broken heart when you went to med school?"

"No," she replied. "I was a geek in high school and stayed that way in college."

He smiled, remembering how she'd always seemed to have her head in a book when she was a teenager. "Don't geeks date?" he asked quietly.

"Generally other geeks." She gave him a half smile.

"You know…when we're not sitting around doing calculus for fun or asking for extra homework."

He grinned. "You really were a geek."

"One hundred percent," she said and smiled at two nurses who passed close by their table. "It's how I got through high school," she said once they were alone again. "I hung out with my equally geekish friends, studied hard, avoided gym class and tried not to get upset when I didn't have a date for prom."

Her admission made him think of Trudy Perkins and the ordeal she'd put him through about prom. There was the dress, the suit, the limo she'd wanted him to hire and her displeasure at being forced to arrive at the event in his battered old truck—she'd made him crazy with her expectations and complaints. A week later they were done. He'd enlisted in the army and she didn't want to be with someone who wasn't going to be around. And he'd been happy about it. The last thing he'd wanted was to leave a girl behind when he went off to war. Not that Trudy was the love of his life. Sure, he'd wanted her…but it was little more than that. And she hadn't seemed heartbroken when they'd broken up.

Only sometimes, when he'd returned home in between tours or on leave, he'd wondered what it would be like to have someone waiting…to have warm arms and soft words to greet him. But there never was. He'd made a point of steering clear of anything serious. Hometown girls were off-limits. And now it was a complication he didn't need.

"Prom is overrated," he said and sugared his coffee.

"Easy for you to say," she replied and sipped her tea. "You probably had every cheerleader hanging off your every word during senior year in the hope you'd take them to the prom." She grinned slightly. "But in the end Trudy won your heart."

Brant smiled. "My relationship with Trudy had less to do with heart—" he saw her expression grow curiously "—and more to do with another part of my anatomy...if you get what I mean."

He watched, fascinated as color rose up her neck. She embarrassed easily, but wasn't shy about showing it. "Us geeks generally missed that class," she said, grinning.

Lucy had a good sense of humor and Brant liked that about her. He was discovering that he liked most things about her. She had a husky kind of laugh, for one, and it seemed to reverberate through him. And her green eyes always looked as though they held some sort of secret. There was an energy surrounding her, a magnetic pull that Brant found difficult to deny.

Over the past few months he'd deliberately steered clear of her. Of course, that hadn't stopped his attraction for her from growing. But he'd kept it under control, dismissed it, put it out of his mind most days. However, being around her now, sharing her company and listening to her soft voice, made it impossible to ignore the fact that he liked her. A lot. And it was messing with his head and his intentions. He'd suggested they be friends when it was the last thing he wanted. But if he made a move for anything else, he knew he'd make a mess of it. She was a nice woman. Too nice to fool around with. He wasn't a saint, but he wasn't a complete ass, either. If he asked her out, if they dated and started a relationship, she'd want more of him than he could give. And he wasn't ready for that. The truth was, Brant wasn't sure he ever would be.

"Thanks for coming today," he said and drank some coffee.

Lucy smiled. "No problem. I like your uncle. I like you, too," she admitted. "Even though you can be an idiot."

Her bluntness amused him and Brant grinned. "So... friends?"

"Isn't that what we already agreed?"

"Just making sure we're on the same page."

"I don't think we're even in the same chapter," she said. "You're something of an enigma, Brant. You're a good guy when you want to be, but underneath all that, I don't think you really allow anyone to see the real you at all."

She was so close to the truth he fought the instinctive urge to get up and leave. But he stayed where he was and met her gaze. "Is that your professional opinion?"

She shrugged lightly. "That's my honest opinion."

Brant drained his cup and looked at her. "If you've finished your tea we should probably get back to see how my uncle is doing."

"You see, that's exactly my point. I've pushed a button by getting personal and now you want to bail." She pushed her chair back and grabbed her bag. "You should talk to your mom and your brother," she said frankly as she stood. "They're genuinely worried about you."

He knew that. But he wasn't ready for an intervention. He wanted to forget. "I don't—"

"You can tell me to mind my own business," she said, cutting him off. "But your mother trusts and confides in me, and I like her too much to dismiss her concerns. And your brother is concerned enough that he asked me to talk to you. If you don't want to discuss it with the people who care about you, at least make an appointment to speak with Dr. Allenby."

She walked off before Brant had a chance to respond.

By the time he was on his feet and out of the cafeteria she was halfway down the corridor and heading for the elevator. When he reached her he was as wound up as a spring. He grasped her hand and turned her around.

"Have we stepped into some dimension where you get to tell me what to do?" he asked.

She didn't move, didn't pull away. Her hand felt small in his, but strong, and when her fingers wrapped around his, Brant experienced a pull toward her that was so intense he could barely breathe. The sensation was powerful and all consuming. He met her gaze and felt the connection through to his bones.

"Brant…"

She said his name on a sigh and he instinctively moved closer. Her eyes shone and her mouth parted ever so slightly. It was pure invitation and in that moment all Brant wanted to do was to kiss her. Only the fact that they were standing in a hospital corridor and people were walking past stopped him.

"I'll sort things out with my family, okay?" he said more agreeably than he felt as he released her.

"And Dr. Allenby?" she asked, relentless.

"I don't need a shrink," he said and pressed the elevator button.

When the elevator door opened she walked inside and Brant stepped in behind her.

"You know he specifically works with veterans, right?" she reminded him. "You were in a war, Brant. And you went through things a civilian like me couldn't possibly understand. But one conversation with Dr. Allenby doesn't mean you're his patient."

Brant ignored her remark and once they rode the elevator up two floors they walked out. Lucy's shoulders were tight and he knew she was upset with him. But he wasn't about to open up about anything. Not the war. And not what he went through. It was over. Done. It was the past and Brant was determined to live in the present... it was the very least he owed the men who had lost their lives on the ridge that day.

His uncle was awake and seemed happy to see them. Lucy discreetly grabbed the chart at the foot of the bed and glanced over it for a moment.

"As you can see, I've been poked and prodded." Joe grinned and then winked at Lucy. "Although I would've much rather you do the prodding, Doc."

"Uncle Joe," Brant said, frowning "That's not really appropriate to—"

"Oh, settle down," his uncle said and laughed. "I'm not seriously trying to cut in on your action with this lovely woman."

Brant shifted uncomfortably as heat rose up his neck. Uncle Joe had a wicked sense of humor and most days Brant found him amusing and enjoyed listening to his stories. But he wasn't in the mood for Joe's levity at the moment.

"Good," he said, seeing Lucy's brows rise slightly.

The cardiologist returned before any more was said and they spoke at length about his uncle's tests scheduled for that afternoon. Considering his history, the cardiac specialist made it clear that he would be keeping Joe at the hospital for a couple of days for further testing and monitoring, and to determine if he required surgery. Lucy asked several questions and Brant listened intently, thinking how grateful he was she was there.

Once the doctor left, Joe spoke again. "Now, I need a nap, so take this lovely young woman to lunch and let me rest."

He nodded. "Sure. I have to pick up some materials

for the Loose Moose while I'm in town, so we'll head over to Home Depot and come back later."

Joe already had his eyes closed and a minute later they were back in the elevator.

"If you have an errand to run I can hang out in the cafeteria," she said as they headed toward the ground floor.

"You'd prefer to be alone?" he asked as they stepped out of the elevator.

"Well...no, but I—"

"Let's go, then," he said and kept walking.

When they reached his truck, Brant opened the passenger door and stood aside for her to climb inside. He waited while she strapped into the seat belt and then closed the door. Once he was in the driver's seat, he started the truck and drove from the parking lot.

"Do you mind if we make a stop before lunch?" he asked. "I have the kitchen going in in the next couple of weeks and want to make sure the contractor has everything that I asked for."

"I don't mind."

Brant took a left turn. "So, how did my uncle seem to you?"

"Good," she replied. "The testing this afternoon will confirm how much damage was done to his heart from his attack yesterday. If he needs surgery he'll probably go in during the next few days. And if he does, then we'll speak with the surgeon together so you'll know exactly what will be done."

Her words calmed him. "Thank you. I appreciate your help with this."

She shrugged lightly. "I like Joe. He's a good man."

"Yeah," Brant agreed. "He's the best."

"He loves you a lot."

"It's mutual."

"You're lucky," she said quietly. "I mean, to have such a caring family."

"I know." Brant glanced sideways and noticed her hands were bunched tightly in her lap. He thought about her words and then realized how alone she was. "You must miss your mom."

"I do," she replied. "Every day."

He looked straight ahead. "I think… I think that sometimes I take my family for granted."

"You probably do," she returned bluntly. "But when you've always had something, it's easy to forget its value."

Brant bit back a grin. "That's very philosophical of you."

"I'm a deep-thinking girl."

She was a lot of things. Beautiful. Smart. Funny. Annoying. And kind. Lucy Monero was just about the nicest person he'd ever met. And if he had any sense he'd stay well clear of her and her knowing green eyes.

Yeah…that's what he should do.

That's what he *would* do.

Starting tomorrow.

Chapter Five

Tuesday was a long and emotionally tiring day in the ER and by the time Lucy pulled up in the driveway it was past six o'clock. Boots was in his usual spot in the front window and meowed loudly once she opened the front door and walked inside. She dropped her bag and keys on the sideboard in the hallway and walked into the kitchen. She needed a cup of strong tea, a shower and about an hour or two to unwind in front of the television.

Lucy filled the kettle, fed the cat and headed for the bathroom.

I look tired, she thought as she stared at her reflection in the bathroom mirror. Not surprising. Some days were harder than others. And today had been as hard as any ever got for a doctor.

Fifteen minutes later she was showered and dressed in gray sweats that were shapeless but comfortable. She pulled her hair into a messy topknot, shoved her feet into sheepskin slippers and wandered back into the kitchen. She made tea and left the bag in while she perused the contents of the refrigerator, quickly figuring she should have stopped at the grocery store on the way home. She was just about to settle on a noodle cup when her cell rang. It was Brooke.

"Hey, there," her friend said cheerfully. "How's everything?"

"Fine," she lied, thinking she didn't want to get into a discussion about her day. "Same as usual. You?"

"Okay. Spent the day repairing fences. And I had a dress fitting."

Brooke was a bridesmaid at Grady and Marissa's upcoming wedding. The event was only a couple of weeks away and Lucy knew her friend had been helping with the preparations. "Sounds like fun."

"It was more fun than I'd imagined," Brooke said then chuckled. "You know I'm not much into frills and frocks. I don't suppose I could get you to give me a hand with my hair and makeup on the day of the wedding? And Colleen wanted me to ask you if you'd help out getting the girls ready."

She meant Grady's three young daughters who were all flower girls. "Of course," she said and laughed. "Anything you need."

"Great," Brooke said, sounding relieved. "This is my first gig as a bridesmaid and I don't want to screw it up."

"You won't," she assured her friend who she knew was more at home in jeans and a plaid shirt than satin and high heels. "You'll do great. And just remember that—" She stopped speaking when her cell beeped, indicating an incoming call. "Hang on a minute, I have a call coming in. It might be the hospital." She put her friend on hold and checked the incoming number, realizing it wasn't one she recognized. "Hello?"

"Have you eaten, Lucia?"

Lucy stilled as Brant's deep voice wound up her spine. "Ah…no. Not yet."

He was silent for moment. "Feel like sharing a pizza?"

Pizza? With Brant? Was he asking her out on a date? *Maybe I'm hallucinating?*

"Oh…I…okay. But if we're going out I need to change my clothes so I'll—"

"No need, I'm outside," he said then hung up.

Seconds later there was a knock on her door. Lucy pushed some life into her legs and headed down the hall-way. She opened the door and saw Brant on the other side of the security screen, dressed in jeans, a soft green sweater and his leather jacket, a pizza box in one hand and a six-pack of beer in the other. She fumbled with the cell phone and took Brooke off hold.

"I gotta go," she said quietly and opened the screen door.

"Everything all right?" Brooke asked.

"Fine," she said as he lingered on the threshold. "I'll call you tomorrow."

Once she ended the call, Brant's gaze flicked to the phone. "Am I interrupting something?"

"No," she replied. "I was just talking to Brooke. Um… what are you doing here?"

He held up the pizza box. "I told you. Dinner." His eyes glittered. "With a friend."

Lucy wasn't entirely convinced. "So this is not a date?"

She couldn't believe the words actually came out of her mouth.

He shook his head. "No, just a pizza and drinks. But

only if you like beer," he added. "I wasn't sure. I can duck out and get wine instead if you'd prefer?"

"I like beer," she said and stepped aside. His cheeks were pink, she noticed, as if he'd been standing out in the cold night air for a while. "You look cold," she said and ushered him inside and then closed the door.

"I'm okay."

"At least it's stopped snowing," she said and started walking down the hallway. "But the air has a real bite to it tonight. I think we're in for a long and cold winter."

"You're probably right," he said and followed her.

"I have a fireplace in the front living room that usually gets a workout every winter."

When they reached the kitchen he paused in the doorway. Lucy noticed his expression narrow as he raised a brow. "Well, it's all very circa 1975 in here."

She managed a grin. "I heard that retro is making a comeback."

"Not to this extent," he said about the gaudy color scheme and old-fashioned timber paneling. "It's very bright."

"It's awful," she admitted. "But I can't afford any renovations until next summer, so it has to stay like this until then. Wait until you see the bathroom," she said and laughed a little, feeling some of the tension leave her body. "It's baby pink, all over. My mom loved all things retro so she was very much at home here. Me...not so much. I've painted a few walls in the living room and bedrooms, but the rest will have to wait."

He grinned and placed the pizza box on the table. "I hope you like pepperoni."

Lucy smoothed her hands over her full hips briefly. "Do I look like a fussy eater to you?"

He laughed and the sound warmed her blood. God, he

had the sexy thing down pat. Even though she was sure he didn't know it. She'd accused him of being egotistical, but didn't really believe it.

"You look fine."

Fine? Lucy glanced down at her baggy sweats and woolen slippers. Good enough for friends, she suspected. Since he'd made it abundantly clear that's all they were.

"So, were all your other friends busy tonight?"

He stilled. "What's that supposed to mean?"

She shrugged. "Merely curious about why you're really here."

"I told you," he said, taking two beers and popping open the tabs. "Pizza with a friend. But if you need a more complicated reason…let's call it a thank-you for your kindness toward my uncle yesterday."

Lucy nodded slowly. "Did you see him today?"

"Yes, this morning. He's scheduled for bypass surgery on Friday."

"I know," she said and sighed. "I called the hospital this morning. I thought I would go and see him Friday morning before his surgery."

"I'm sure he'd like that," Brant said quietly. "I could meet you there. Or pick you up."

That meant more time in his company.

Being around Brant Parker was quickly becoming a regular occurrence.

Spending six hours with him the day before had worn down her defenses. Of course, she'd convinced herself the day had been all about his uncle. And it had been… on the surface. But after he'd finished his errands and they'd had lunch at a café a few blocks down from the hospital, Lucy knew there was a whole lot more going on. She still liked him. Too much. Despite his sometimes moody ways and indifference toward her over the past few months.

"Sure," she said vaguely. "I'll let you know. So, where do you want to eat? Here, surrounded by this lovely decor?" she asked, waving a hand toward the gaudy cupboards. "Or on the sofa in the living room?"

"The sofa," he replied.

Lucy grabbed the pizza box and read the writing on the top. "JoJo's? My favorite."

JoJo's Pizza Parlor was something of an institution in Cedar River. In high school she'd hung out there most Monday nights with her calculus club. Kayla had also been part of her group. The token swan among a group of ugly ducklings. The rest of the group had moved on or moved away, but she and her friend had never strayed too far. Once Kayla finished college in Washington State, she'd returned home, and Lucy followed a few years later.

"It's all in the secret sauce," he said and followed her down the hall.

Lucy smiled fractionally. "Do you remember how Joss Culhane got caught trying to swipe the recipe from old Mr. Radici one night after the place was closed up? He used to work there after school and told me how he wanted to get the recipe and duplicate it."

"I didn't realize you were so friendly with the Culhanes."

"I'm not," she said. "But Joss was hoping that since I was half-Italian I'd be able to help with the translation."

"And did you?"

"Not a chance," she replied. "My Italian is about as good as my Latin. He should have asked you," she said, placing the pizza box on the coffee table. "You speak a couple of languages, don't you?"

He shrugged lightly. "A little French."

She knew it was more than a little. Colleen had told her he was fluent. But he was being modest for some reason of his own. "Your mother told me that from your years in the military you also speak Arabic."

"I speak some," he said casually and came around the sofa. He placed her beer on the table and sat, grabbing up the remote. "There's a replay of a game I missed on Sunday. Interested?"

Football? She'd rather stick a pencil in her eye. But she shrugged agreeably. "Sure."

Pizza, beer and football.

They really were just friends.

If they were more than that, the conversation would be very different. She'd be in his arms, feeling his strength and comfort seep through her as she told him about her awful day. But she wouldn't...because they weren't.

Lucy positioned herself on the other side of the sofa and flipped the lid off the pizza box while he surfed channels with the remote. It seemed all too civilized. Like they'd done it countless times before. But inside she was reeling.

"You were a translator in the army, right?" she asked as she took a slice of pizza.

"Something like that."

Her brows rose. "Secret stuff, huh?"

He carefully looked at the TV. "I prefer not talking about it."

"I'm not trying to get into your head," she said. "Just making conversation."

He sighed softly and rested the remote on his knee. "Okay...then, yes. When I was in the military part of my job was to translate intelligence."

"I thought they used civilians for that kind of thing."

"They do," he replied. "But there are times when the

front line is no place for a civilian. Part of my training included learning the local language and a few of the dialects."

"Because you have an aptitude for languages?"

"I guess," he said and fiddled with the remote.

"You were one of those people who breezed through high school without really trying, right?" she asked.

A pulse throbbed in his cheek. "You could say that."

"You would have made a good geek," she said, lightening the mood a little. "Well, except for the blue eyes and broad shoulders."

He turned up the volume a little and took a slice of pizza. "But I sucked at math," he admitted. "I still do. So I would never have made your calculus team."

Lucy shook her head, as if mocking him. "Shame… you missed some really exciting get-togethers where we discussed differential and integral calculus. Of course, you would have also missed out on having a date for the prom."

He groaned. "Are we back to that again? I told you, prom is overrated."

"Ha," she scoffed and took a bite of pizza. "So you say, Mr. Popularity."

He laughed and the sound filled her insides with a kind of fuzzy warmth that was so ridiculous she got mad with herself. *Just friends.* Remember that, she said to herself. She glanced sideways and observed his handsome profile. It was strange being with him…and yet, absurdly easy.

"I think you're confusing me with someone else."

"Really?" she queried. "Let's see, weren't you the quarterback with the pretty cheerleader girlfriend?"

"Are you trying to make the point that I was a cliché?"

"Nope," she replied and took another bite of pizza.

"You were too smart for that. But you did have a cheerleader girlfriend."

"It was over the week after prom," he said quietly.

"Was she mad at you for joining the army?"

"Kind of," he replied. "How'd you know that?"

Lucy shrugged. "Girls like Trudy are easy to read."

"But not girls like you," he said and drank some beer. "Right?"

She settled deeper into the sofa. "I've never considered myself easy on any level."

"No," he said, meeting her gaze. "You certainly aren't."

Lucy stayed silent as the space between them seemed to suddenly get smaller. There was such a sense of companionship in that moment...as if he knew her and she knew him. She took a deep breath and tried to concentrate on eating. And failed. She'd had such a bad day. One of the worse kinds of days for a doctor. A day when she couldn't do a damned thing to stop something terrible from happening.

"Lucy?"

His voice stirred her senses. "Yes," she said, not looking at him but staring straight ahead at the television.

"Are you okay?"

She shrugged and swallowed hard. Because he seemed to know, somehow, that she was barely hanging on. "I'm fine."

"I don't think you are."

She took a deep breath. "Today was just...a trying kind of day."

The volume of the television went down almost immediately and she glanced sideways to see he'd propped his beer and pizza on the coffee table. "What happened?" he asked quietly.

"You didn't come over here to hear about my bad day."

"No," he said honestly. "But I can listen if you want to talk about it."

Not in any stratosphere had she ever imagined that Brant Parker would be the kind of guy to simply sit on the couch and *listen*. She didn't want to think about how tempted she was to take up his offer. She *did* need to talk. Talking always helped. But this was Brant…and he wasn't the talkative type.

"I can't really—"

"Would you rather I leave?" he asked.

"No," she replied quickly, feeling emotion fill her chest. "I could probably use the company."

"Okay," he said and turned up the volume a couple of notches. "I'll stay. And we can eat pizza and watch football. Or you can talk if you want to."

There was something so earnest and at the same time so comforting about his words that she had to swallow back a sob. They were becoming friends. And friends shared things. After a moment she drew in a long and weary breath and spoke.

"The thing is… I'm a doctor. I'm trained to harness my emotions and, most days, I can cope with the bad things that happen," she admitted, twisting her hands in her lap. "But today…today was one of those hard days… when I have to wonder if I'm making a difference at all." She shifted on the sofa to face him and saw that he was watching her closely.

"What happened?" he asked soberly.

Lucy swallowed hard. "A woman came in to the ER today, six months pregnant, and I knew within minutes of examining her that she would lose her baby. There was no heartbeat and there was nothing I could do or say to comfort her and her husband." She stopped, took a breath and relived the moment again. "It was the third baby they had lost in less than three years. So, I'd witnessed their heartbreak before. And her husband…he begged me to do something…to help his wife…to save his son. And I couldn't do anything."

Heat burned her eyes and the tears she hadn't dare allow that day suddenly came as though they had a will of their own. She didn't stop them. She couldn't have even if she'd tried.

"Lucy." He said her name softly. "Sometimes you can't do anything. Sometimes bad things just happen." He grabbed her hand and held it, enclosing her fingers in a way that warmed her through to her bones. "You know that. We both know that."

"I know it in here," she said and tapped her temple with her free hand. "I know that, logically, I gave her the best medical care possible and nothing would have prevented their baby from dying. But it hurt so much to see their profound sadness. Her husband was hurting so much…hurting for the woman he loved and for the child they both desperately wanted. And I felt their pain deep down. I kept thinking, *This could be anyone…this could be me.* And then I felt like such a fraud because I've been trained to *not* feel."

His gaze was unwavering. "You know, I think your innate ability to feel compassion and share that sadness is what makes you a great doctor. I saw the way you were with my uncle—and that kind of caring is genuine and heartfelt." He squeezed her hand. "You're not a fraud, Lucy…you're kind and compassionate and amazing."

And that was enough to send her over the edge.

She began to sob and suddenly she was in Brant's arms. And he held her, tighter than anyone had ever held her. Lucy pressed her face into his chest, heard his steady, strong heartbeat, and slowly felt her sadness seep away. He pulled her against him and sat back into the sofa so she was lying across his lap, her hands on his shoulders, her head against his chest, her face pressed against the soft green sweater. She closed her eyes, took a shuddering breath and relaxed—in a way she never had before.

Brant had no idea what had made him land on Lucy's doorstep with a pizza and a six-pack. Or why he'd suggested they watch football in front of the television. Or why he'd taken her into his arms. But for the past half hour he had stayed still, holding her gently. She hadn't stirred. She lay perfectly still, her one hand resting against his chest, her head tucked beneath his chin. He was pretty sure she wasn't asleep, but she wasn't moving, either. Just breathing softly.

I should get up and hightail it out of here.

But he didn't. She felt too good in his arms. Her lovely curves fit against him in a way that was both arousing and oddly comforting. She was soft and womanly, and even though his arm was numb he didn't move. He couldn't remember the last time he'd sat with a woman and talked the way he'd been talking with Lucy. Maybe never.

She finally lifted her head and met his gaze.

"Okay now?" he asked softly.

She nodded and the scent of her apple shampoo assailed his senses. "I'm fine," she said as she pulled away. Brant released her instantly and she sat up. "Sorry about that."

He frowned. "Sorry for what?"

"Falling apart." She shrugged and crossed her arms. "I'm not normally so fragile."

"You had a bad day," he reminded her. "It happens."

She shrugged again. "Yeah…but I'm a doctor and I should be able to keep it inside. But thanks for under-standing," she said and picked up the untouched beer bottle. "So, about this football game. Explain it to me."

"Explain football?"

"Sure," she said and drank some beer. "Why not? I mean, I'm not much into sports, but I'm willing to learn new things."

Brant smiled. "Actually, football should be right up your alley."

"How?"

"You like math, right?"

She nodded slowly. "Uh, sure. Geek to the core, re-member."

Brant flicked up the volume and briefly explained some of the player's positions. "You see that guy there? He's the quarterback."

"Yeah…and?"

"And he's tracked by the percentage of completions attempted and made, along with completion yards. Plus, the distance he throws the ball and from which side of the field he throws it."

She raised a brow. "Still not following."

"These numbers are then used to develop a mathe-matical model of the quarterback, for statistical com-parison with other quarterbacks. Just like the receiver who catches the pass is judged on the number of passes thrown to him and the number of catches. It's all about statistics," he added. "Math."

She grinned. "Gee, if I'd known how important math is to sport I would never have spent so much time trying to ditch gym class."

Brant laughed softly. "Wait until summer. Baseball is even more rooted in stats and averages."

"Good to know," she said and smiled as she took a drink. "Although, I'm not particularly athletic. I don't think I've ever swung a baseball bat."

"There's a practice net at Bakers Field, so if you want to learn, I could show you."

"I'll probably get stuck on first base."

The moment she said the words the mood between them shifted. He was certain she hadn't meant it to sound so provocative, but in her husky voice and with their close proximity, it was impossible to avoid thinking about it.

About her.

About getting to first base with Lucy Monero.

That was exactly what he wanted to do.

He wanted to kiss her sweet mouth more than he'd ever wanted to kiss anyone…ever.

"You know, I'm pretty sure I could get you off first base, Lucy."

He watched, fascinated, as color crept up her throat and landed on her cheeks. Despite her bravado, there was a kind of natural wholesomeness about her that was undeniable, magnetic and as sexy as hell. Her lower lip trembled and he fought the urge to see if her lips tasted as sweet as they looked.

He knew she was thinking it, too. Her green eyes shimmered with a sudden sultry haze that wound his stomach in knots and quickly hit him directly in the groin. He shifted in his seat, trying to get the thought from his mind.

"Wouldn't that…?" Her words trailed off and then she tried again. "Wouldn't that nullify the fact we're only friends?"

"Absolutely."

"And since you only want to be friends…"

"Yeah," he replied when her words faded. "That is what I said."

Her eyes widened. "Have you changed your mind?"

"About you? About us?" Brant dug deep because he had to. "No. Friends is best. Uncomplicated. Easy."

"Strange," she said as she placed the beer on the table and pushed back her hair. "This doesn't feel the least bit uncomplicated."

"You're right," he agreed. "I guess I'm new to this 'having a woman as a friend' thing."

She cocked her head. "What? You've never had a female friend before?"

He shook his head. "I don't think so. I mean…in the military? Yeah, for sure. But that was work. As a civilian? No."

"What about Brooke?"

"She's family so it doesn't count."

"Marissa?" she asked.

He shook his head. "She's my brother's fiancée and I'm just getting to know her."

"So, if you meet someone you like or were attracted to you'd what…sleep with her and then not see her again?"

Brant nodded slowly. "I guess."

She was frowning. "Sex means that little to you?"

Discomfiture straightened his back. He didn't want to talk about sex with Lucy Monero. He didn't want any part of his life to be under the microscope. "It's just a moment…a few hours…maybe a night. Little more."

She met his gaze. "Well, that explains why you're lonely."

Brant's back stiffened and he sat straighter. "I'm not—"

"Sure you are. Isn't that why you're here with me?"

Chapter Six

First base. Second base. Third base. Lucy was pretty sure Brant would have all the bases covered. The conversation was heading way out of her comfort zone. His, too, from the expression on his face. However she wasn't about to back down. He'd turned up on *her* doorstep, not the other way around.

"I am, too," she admitted. "Sometimes. I know I have my friends and my job, which I love…but the nights can get lonely. Or a rainy afternoon. Or a Sunday morning. You know, those times that people who are part of a couple probably take for granted."

He was watching her with such burning intensity it was impossible to look away. "I guess I don't think about it too much."

She didn't believe him. Despite his loving family and how close he was to his brother and uncle, Lucy knew he'd kept very much to himself since he'd returned to town. "Well, I do," she said and grinned a little. "I want to get married. I want to have a family… I mean, doesn't everyone need someone?" She stopped speaking for a moment and met his gaze. "Well, except for you, of course. You don't need anyone, right?"

The pulse in his cheek throbbed. "It's not about… needing someone. It's about knowing what I'm capable of at this point in time. And having a serious relationship isn't a priority."

"Define 'serious'?"

His mouth twitched. "The usual kind. Marriage-and-babies kind of serious."

"What if you fall in love with someone?" she asked, feeling herself flush again.

"I won't," he replied flatly. "I'm not looking for love, Lucia. Not with anyone."

Not with you.

His meaning was perfectly clear. And even though she was humiliated by the idea he thought she was imagining they had some kind relationship starting, Lucy put on her bravest face.

"Just as well we're only friends, then," she reminded him and focused her attention on the television.

"Just as well," he echoed and hiked up the volume.

He stayed for another half hour and when he left, the house felt ridiculously empty.

I'm such a fool.

Fantasizing about Brant was only going to lead to heartbreak. He'd made it clear he wasn't interested. So they'd spent a little time together and shared a pizza and a football game. And maybe she did collapse in his arms and hold on as if her life depended on it. And maybe he did hold her in return and give her the kind of comfort she'd only ever imagined existed. It wasn't real. *It wasn't anything.*

I'm not looking for love, Lucia. Not with anyone.

His words were quickly imprinted in her brain. Exactly where they needed to be. And what she needed to do was to stop daydreaming and forget about him.

Still, as she lay in bed later that night, staring at the ceiling, she couldn't help but remember his kindness. There was so much depth to him. More than he allowed people to see. He was strong and sincere and oozed integrity. But there was vulnerability, too. And pain…she was sure of it.

Something had happened to turn his heart to stone. She didn't doubt he'd experienced something terrible while he was deployed. Something he'd been keeping from everyone, even his brother and mother. And despite knowing it was madness to dig herself in any further, Lucy wanted to know what it was. She remembered how Grady had asked for her help. Clearly, Brant's family was genuinely concerned about him and Lucy had said she'd do what she could. Getting him to talk about what he'd been through in the military wasn't going to be easy. But the doctor in her felt a pull of responsibility to do what she could. And the woman in her wanted to understand his pain.

Her shift didn't start until eleven the following morning, so she slept in an hour longer than usual, then showered and dressed. Once she had a late breakfast she headed into town at nine-thirty to meet Kayla at the museum.

"You look tired," her friend said as they sat in Kayla's small office and began sipping on the take-out lattes Lucy had picked up from the Muffin Box on her way over.

"I didn't sleep much last night," she admitted, feeling the caffeine quickly kick in.

Kayla immediately looked concerned. "Bad dreams?"

She shrugged. "Just a long day," she said, deciding not to dwell on what had happened at the hospital the previous afternoon. "And then Brant dropped over with a pizza."

Kayla's eyes almost popped their sockets. "Really?"

"Yeah," she replied. "But don't read any more into it. We're just friends."

Kayla chuckled. "Sure you are."

"It's true," she said. "He's made it abundantly clear that he's not in the market for a relationship and I—"

"Won't meet anyone else if you keep hanging out with Brant Parker," Kayla reminded her.

"I know," she admitted. "But I like him. I have no idea why, of course. He's temperamental and indifferent and sometimes downright unfriendly. But…" She paused. "There are other times when he's such a great listener and he's really smart and funny and—"

"Oh, no," Kayla said, cutting her off. "I know that weepy look. You're actually falling for him. For real. This isn't high school, Lucy…you could really get your heart broken here."

"I know," she said as if they were two of the hardest words she'd ever said.

"Then stay away from him," Kayla suggested. "I mean it. He's quicksand for a girl like you."

"Like me?" she echoed. "You mean the oldest virgin on the planet?"

Kayla, Ash and Brooke were the only people who knew she'd never had an intimate relationship. Her friend smiled gently. "So, all that means is you haven't met the right man yet."

But I have.

"Why don't we talk about your complicated love life instead?" Lucy suggested. "What's going on with you and Liam?"

"Nothing," Kayla assured her. "My father would disown me, for one. And I don't like Liam O'Sullivan in the slightest. He's arrogant and opinionated and thinks way too much of himself. We're working on the museum extension plans together because he's on the committee and putting up most of the funding."

Lucy grinned. "Yeah, and I wonder why he's doing that?"

Kayla's cheeks colored hotly. "Because he knows how important the museum is to the town."

"Or because he wants to keep you in town," Lucy suggested. "Which probably wouldn't happen if the museum was forced to close down. You'd have to leave to get a job in a big city and Liam would be devastated," she teased.

Kayla waved a hand dismissively. "Enough about me. We're talking about you…and how you get your mind off Hot Stuff."

Lucy laughed. "Don't worry about me," she assured the other woman. "I'll be fine. After Friday I probably won't see him much at all and—"

"Friday?" Kayla asked.

"His uncle is having surgery," she explained. "I said I'd be there."

Kayla tut-tutted. "See…quicksand."

"I know what I'm doing."

I have no idea what I'm doing.

"I hope so. I'd hate to see you get hurt. And this thing with you and Brant has been going on for a long time and—"

"It's nothing," she assured Kayla. "Look, I know I was

all starry-eyed about him back in high school, and maybe I have talked way too much about him since I moved back to town. But I'm *not* pining after Brant Parker," she said firmly. "I promise."

Kayla's eyes widened. "So, if someone else comes along you'll give him a chance?"

She smiled at her friend. Kayla had been her wannabe matchmaker since they were kids. "Sure. As long as you do the same."

Kayla grinned. "No question about that. I'm a free agent."

"Yeah," Lucy agreed. "Except for being secretly in love with Liam O'Sullivan."

Kayla rolled her eyes dramatically. "Ha! Good try. I heard that his brother Kieran is coming to Grady and Marissa's wedding. He's a doctor like you...now that's worth thinking about. You guys used to work together in Sioux Falls, didn't you?"

"Yes. But no doctors," Lucy implored. "Too many long working hours."

Lucy stayed for another ten minutes, where they talked about Thanksgiving and the upcoming wedding. Lucy usually worked the holidays and this year was no exception. She would celebrate in a low-key way with her colleagues who'd either volunteered to work the holidays as she had or were unavoidably rostered. She really didn't mind working the holidays. It certainly beat sitting around her house alone.

For the first few years after her mother's death she'd tagged along with Kayla's family and they'd welcomed her wholeheartedly. But as she'd gotten older her need for inclusion waned and she was content to work and free up the time for her colleagues who had families.

But this year she felt more melancholic than usual.

When she got to work Lucy quickly forgot about her lonely life. A double vehicle accident on the highway meant half a dozen people were brought into the ER, two with serious injuries and another four with minor cuts and abrasions. She spent five hours on her feet and didn't take a break until it was close to five o'clock. She headed home a couple of hours later and pulled into her driveway at seven thirty just as rain began splattering the windshield.

Lucy grabbed her bag and made a quick dash for the house and was soaked to the skin by the time she got inside and shut the door. She shrugged out of her coat and flipped off her shoes, dropped her bag and keys in hall and headed for the bathroom. Fifteen minutes later she was clean, dry, and dressed in flannel pajamas and her favorite sheepskin slippers. She was just heading for the kitchen when she heard her cell pealing in her handbag. Lucy hot-footed it up the hall and rushed to grab her phone without registering the number.

"Hello?"

"You sound breathless," a deep voice said. "Everything okay?"

Heat rolled through her belly. "Brant, um, hi. Yes, I'm fine. You?"

"I'm okay. I'm calling to confirm Friday with you," he said evenly. "My uncle is really grateful that you'll be there."

Lucy's insides lurched. "Yes…well, I'm happy to do it if it reassures him. Only…"

He was silent for a moment when her words trailed. "Only?" he prompted finally.

She took a steadying breath. "I'd like you to do something for me in return."

The strained silence between them stretched like a

brittle elastic. "And what is that?" he asked after a moment, his voice raspier than usual.

Lucy knew she'd probably only get one chance to ask for what she wanted. So she went for it. "I'd like to make an appointment for you to speak with Dr. Allenby."

Brant fought the instinct he had to end the call and never dial her number again. But he didn't. He stayed on the line, grappling with his temper.

A shrink. Great.

And cleverly done, too. No demands, no subtle manipulation...just asking for what she wanted. He'd bet his boots she also had a great poker face. But since having her at the hospital was important to his uncle, he'd do what he had to do.

"Sure," he said easily, his heart pounding.

"Oh...great. I'll make an appointment for you."

"No problem," he said, ignoring the churning in his gut. "I'll pick you up Friday."

"Fine. See you then."

Brant disconnected the call and leaned back on the workbench. Damn, she wound him up! He shoved the phone into his shirt pocket and took a long breath. Lucy Monero was the most irritating, frustrating, demanding woman he'd ever known. He really needed to stop spending time with her before she got too far under his skin.

Too late.

He shook his tight shoulders, pushed himself off the bench and grabbed the circular saw. He had plenty of work to do before the plumbing contractors arrived on Monday. By his reckoning he had at least eight weeks' worth of work to do before he could open the tavern. In that time he had to think about hiring staff, including a chef and a barman. He wanted the place to be family friendly with good food and service at reasonable prices. Not as rustic as Rusty's nor as highbrow as O'Sullivan's, but somewhere in between. A place where he would be too busy to dwell on the war, the friends he'd lost or how he was irrevocably changed by all he'd experienced there.

And he longed to be so busy he wouldn't spend time thinking about Lucy Monero.

He turned around, plugged in the circular saw and picked a timber plank from the floor. All the booth seats needed replacing and he'd been steadily working his way through the task for the best part of three days. Brant measured out the timber he needed, grabbed the saw and began cutting through the plank. Within seconds the safety clip on the circular saw flipped back and the tool vibrated, jerked out of his grasp and bounced against the side of the work table. He quickly turned off the power switch, but not before the blade sliced through the skin on his left forearm.

Brant cursed loudly, dropped the saw and placed a hand over the wound. He was reaching for the small towel on the main bench when his cell rang. He grabbed the towel, quickly wrapped it around his arm, wiped most of the blood off his hand and pulled the phone from his pocket.

"Brant, it's me," said a breathless voice.

Lucy.

"Oh…hi."

"I just realized we didn't make a time for tomorrow."

He looked at the blood seeping through the towel. "I can't really talk at the moment. I'll call you back in a—"

"Why not? What are you doing?"

He was pretty sure she didn't realize how nosy she sounded. It made him grin despite the pain in his arm.

"Because I'm bleeding and I need to get a bandage on this—"

"You're bleeding?" The pitch of her voice went up a couple of notches. "What happened? What have you done this—?"

"An accident with a power tool," he said and then made a frustrated sound. "Look, I'll call you back when I—"

"Stay still and keep pressure on the injury," she said quickly. "I'll be there in five minutes."

Then she hung up.

It was actually six minutes before he heard a car pull up outside and about another thirty seconds before she tapped on the front door. Once she'd crossed the threshold he closed the door and looked at her. She carried a bright yellow umbrella, wore a brightly colored knitted beanie on her head and had a brown trench coat tightly belted around her waist. Letting his gaze travel down, he saw the pants she wore had tiny cats on them and she had slippers on her feet.

"Pajamas?"

She shrugged and rested the umbrella against the door-jamb. "I was in a hurry." She held up a black bag and looked at his arm. "I need to see what you've done," she said and glanced around. "And not here around all this dust. Upstairs. Let's go."

Right. Upstairs. He'd lived at the tavern for a couple of months and had not invited a single soul into the three-roomed apartment upstairs. Not even his mother and brother. It was sparsely furnished and other than the new bed, sofa and television he'd bought, about as warm and cosy as an ice-cube tray. Still, it served his purpose for the moment. He hesitated and then saw her frown and realized he wouldn't win an argument while she was in such a mood.

He nodded and walked toward the stairwell. "Don't expect too much."

"You're an idiot," she said as she followed. "I don't care where you live. Besides, you've seen my retro abode."

Retro and shabby maybe. But there was a warmth and peacefulness to her house that had made it very hard for him to leave her company the night before. It was even easier to recall how good she'd felt in his arms.

Once they reached the landing he stood aside to let her pass. She took a few steps into the living area and stopped. She clearly had an opinion about the place but unexpectedly kept it to herself. The room was spacious, clean and freshly painted, and was a combined living and kitchen and dining area. But he rarely used the kitchen other than to make coffee or to heat up something in the microwave. There was a small dining table and she immediately headed for it.

"Come here," she instructed once she placed her bag on the table and opened it. "Sit down."

He did as she asked and rested his arm on the table. She pulled a few things from the bag, including surgical gloves, and quickly put them on. He watched, fascinated as she gently removed the towel and examined the gash on his arm. Her touch was perfunctory and methodical. But having her so close made Brant achingly aware of every movement she made.

"So, how did this happen?" she asked as she stepped back, undid her belt and slipped off the trench coat.

Her buttoned-up pajamas were baggy and shapeless and did nothing to highlight her curves. But he was pretty sure she wasn't wearing a bra and the very idea spiked his libido instantly. And she smelled so good…like apples and peppermint. He cleared his throat and tried not think about how one layer of flannel stood between him and her beautiful skin. "I had a problem with a circular saw."

Her mouth twisted. "You certainly did. It's deep and needs a few stitches."

"Can you do that here?"

"Sure," she said. "But I don't have any local anesthetic so you'll have to be a tough guy for a few minutes."

Good. Pain would help him stop thinking about her skin and curves. She was so close that her leg was pressed against his. She'd ditched the beanie and, with her hair loose, her baggy pajamas and silly slippers, she was more beautiful, more desirable, than any woman had a right to be. And it aroused him. Big-time. He swallowed hard and concentrated on the pain in his arm instead. "No problem."

It took her less than ten minutes to stitch up the wound and wrap a bandage around his arm. "Try to keep it dry. And let me know if there's any irritation with the stitches. Seven days should do it before they need to come out."

"Okay, thanks."

"Is there anything else?"

She sounded mad. Annoyed. Angry.

And he was sure of it as he watched her clean up and thrust equipment back into her bag.

"Lucy?"

He gaze snapped toward him. "What?"

"You're mad at me?"

Her mouth tightened. "Yes, I am," she replied honestly. "It's like you have some kind of death wish. Motorbikes, mountain climbing, dangerous power tools… What's next, Brant? White-rapid canoeing? Skydiving?"

He laughed loudly and stood. "A defective power tool is hardly my fault."

"What about the other things?" she snapped.

"Haven't we been through this already? I told you about the bike accidents. And admitted I was an idiot to climb Kegg's Mountain without the correct gear." He grabbed her hand and stepped closer. "I don't have a death wish, Lucy. I promise you."

She looked up and met his stare head-on. God, he loved how she did that. Eye to eye. As though, for that brief moment in time, there was no one else in the world but the two of them. It felt like tonic. Like salve. As though her green-eyed gaze had the power to heal.

Of course she didn't...that was crazy thinking. But the more time he spent with her, the more difficult it was to keep denying how much he wanted her. Because wanting might turn into *needing*. And needing was out of the question. He couldn't afford to need anyone. And not someone as sweet and lovely as Lucy Monero.

"Are you sure? Your mom's worried you're... She's scared because she thinks you take too many risks. As if you don't care."

Brant's stomach tightened. His knew his mother frequently talked to Lucy, and it would be naive to think he didn't regularly turn up in their conversations. But he hated the idea that his mother was worrying about him unnecessarily. "What are you saying? That my mom thinks I'm reckless?"

"That's part of it."

His stomach continued to churn. "And what else... suicidal?"

She shrugged as though she didn't want to acknowledge the idea. "Maybe. It happens to soldiers all the—"

"I'm not," he said, cutting her off as he squeezed her

fingers. "I'm very happy to be alive and plan to stay that way for a long time."

"I hope so," she said, whisper-quiet.

Brant tugged her closer. "I promise I'm not depressed *or* suicidal."

She didn't look entirely convinced. "Depression can show itself with varying symptoms. Do you sleep well?"

"Mostly," he replied, hating that he was suddenly under the microscope but inexplicably unable to move away from her.

Her expression narrowed. "I don't believe you."

The truth burned his tongue. "Okay, so sometimes I don't sleep…sometimes I pace this room for hours or stare at the ceiling. That doesn't mean I'm depressed *or* suicidal."

"No," she replied. "Not on its own, but when you combine insomnia with other things, it can manifest itself into more."

"There are no other things."

"No?" she queried. "What about moodiness? Solitude?"

"If I was as disagreeable as you seem to think, I wouldn't be reopening the tavern."

"I didn't say you were disagreeable," she shot back quickly. "In fact, you're very charming and easy to talk to most of the time—like you were last night. I needed someone and you were there for me."

It didn't sound much like a compliment. Still, he didn't release her. And she didn't pull away. "But?"

"But you rarely, if ever, talk about yourself," she replied. "And that can be harmful to a person's well-being."

"So, I'm not much of a talker. That doesn't make me a head case."

She flinched. "Now you're angry. Being vulnerable

doesn't make you weak, Brant. Something bad happened to you over there, didn't it?"

His tone grew hard. "It was a war zone…bad things happened all around me and to a lot of people."

"I know that," she said, reaching up to touch his face. "But it's you I care about."

Her fingertips were warm, her touch electric.

His stomach dropped. Damn, she just about undid him.

Brant groaned. "Lucy…stop."

She didn't move her hand. "I can't," she said and then fingered the small scar on his chin. "How did you get this?" she asked, moving her fingertip to the scar at his temple. "And this?"

"I don't remember," he said vaguely and stared into her face.

Her cheeks were ablaze with color. Combined with her glorious hair and bright green eyes, it was a riveting combination. And he was immediately drawn into her gaze. Into the very space she possessed.

Brant moved his free hand to her nape and gently rubbed the skin at the back of her neck with his thumb. Her eyes widened immediately and a rush of soft breath escaped her. He couldn't have moved away even if he'd tried. She was pure temptation. Pure loveliness. And he wanted her. Brant wanted her so much it was making him crazy.

He said her name again, watched as her lips pouted a little in pure, sweet invitation.

Her hair tangled between his fingers and his grip tightened. She was looking at him, all eyes, all longing, and when he dipped his head, his intention clear, Brant heard a tiny moan escape her.

Her mouth was warm against his as their lips met.

She shuddered, half resistance, half compliance, as if in that moment she wasn't quite sure what she wanted. But it only lasted a second and then she relaxed against him. Brant instinctively pulled her closer. Her lips parted fractionally and he deepened the kiss, felt her shudder again before she opened her mouth to let him taste the softness within. It was the sweetest kiss he'd ever experienced, almost as though it possessed a kind of purity that had never been matched, or never would.

Brant suddenly felt as if he'd been sucker punched. Because he'd known, deep down, that kissing Lucy was always going to be incredible. Everything about her had been tempting him for months. Every look, every word, every touch, had been drawing them toward this moment. Toward each other. In that instant there was no denying it, no fighting it, no way he could have stopped himself from getting pulled deeper under her spell. And she felt it as much as he did, he was certain.

Her hands were now on his chest and then his shoulders, and he wrapped his arms around her, feeling her soft curves press fully against him. Her breasts, belly and hips pressed to him so perfectly her body was suddenly like a narcotic, drugging him mindless as the kiss continued and she tentatively accepted his tongue into her mouth in a slow, erotic dance that felt so good his knees weakened.

He pulled back when he needed to take a breath and stared down into her face. She was breathing heavily, as if she'd just run a marathon. And her green eyes were luminescent and shimmering with a kind of longing that heated his blood even further. He fought the urge to kiss her again. And again. Because he knew where it would lead. He wanted to make love to her so much he could barely think straight. He wanted to take her into his bed and peel off her silly pajamas and make love to every inch of her, over and over. He wanted to drug her mindless with kisses and to caress her skin until she begged for him to be inside her and then lose himself in her body for all eternity.

And knowing that she'd allow it was suddenly like a bucket of cold water over his libido.

He wasn't about to confuse her picket-fence dreams any more than he already had.

Brant released her abruptly and stepped back. "You should leave."

She moved unsteadily and gripped the table with one hand. "Brant... I..."

Her hurt expression cut through him, but he ignored it. "I mean it. Go home, Lucy," he said coldly. "I don't want you here."

Chapter Seven

It took Lucy about three seconds to grab her things and leave. She didn't bother getting back into the trench coat and instead had that and her bag clutched between her hands as she raced out of the room and down the stairs. She picked up her umbrella on the way and was out the door and back in her car so fast she was out of breath and had a pain in her chest. She took a few deep breaths to calm her nerves as she buckled up and started the ignition.

And cursed Brant Parker the whole drive home.

Jerk.

She wasn't going to waste one more minute thinking about him.

I don't care if he is a great kisser.

Ha! She didn't have anything to compare it to anyhow. Perhaps he was a lousy kisser.

Yes...he's a terrible kisser and I never want to see him again.

Only…his kiss was incredible and the very idea of never seeing him again made her ache inside. And it confirmed what she'd suspected for weeks…she *was* falling for him. And it scared her to death. Because it was plain he would never return her feelings. He'd closed off that part of himself that was about emotion. It was a coping mechanism, she was certain. He'd experienced some trauma, something that had made him shut down. She'd seen it before firsthand…in herself. Right after her mother was killed and then in college when her roommate was raped. For years afterward she'd walked around wrapped in a kind of protective armor, never getting close to anyone, never letting anyone in. It had taken six months of therapy to help her heal and *only* once had she'd been able to self-reflect and realize she needed help. Brant was nowhere near that point. She knew it. And it made her ache for him.

Her lips tingled when she remembered their kiss. All her adult life she'd imagined that first kiss…what it would mean and who she'd share it with. In her most secret dreams she'd held on to the hope that Brant would sweep her off her feet and kiss her senseless. And for that brief moment he had…wholly and completely. And despite knowing it would probably never happen again, she couldn't and wouldn't regret it. Being with him, feeling his heart beat wildly beneath her palm, knowing he'd been as caught up in the moment as she had been, had fulfilled her every fantasy.

Still, she hurt all over thinking of his parting words.

Her cell rang and she let the call go. It beeped a few seconds later, indicating she had a message. By the time Lucy pulled into her driveway it rang again. She ignored it, got out of the car and headed inside. It took fifteen minutes to lock up the house, brush her teeth and hair and climb into bed. She stared at the cell phone for a good couple of minutes before she finally pressed the message button.

Brant's deep voice was instantly recognizable.

Her heart seemed to skip a beat. And then another.

"Hey…it's me." There was a pause. "I just wanted to make sure you were okay. And I'm… I'm really sorry about tonight. If you still want to come to the hospital on Friday I'll pick you up around nine." Another pause. "Thanks for the stitches. So…good night."

The message ended and she quickly let the next one play.

"It's me again." Another pause, longer this time. "It's just that a guy like me…can hurt a woman like you without even trying. Good night, Lucia."

Tears welled in her eyes a she ended the message and propped the phone on the bedside table. It was impossible to hate him. Even though good sense told her she should.

When she awoke the following morning she was weary and mad with herself for allowing him to invade her thoughts so much. She had an eight-hour shift at the hospital ahead of her and didn't need thoughts of Brant Parker distracting her while she was on the job. She had plenty of work to keep her busy and, when she had a chance, she made Brant an appointment with Dr. Allenby. She sent him a text message with the details and left out anything remotely personal. He replied with a brief thank-you text and she didn't respond further.

Thankfully it was a quiet afternoon in the ER and when she took a lunch break around two o'clock she spotted Colleen Parker sitting in the cafeteria. Colleen volunteered at the hospital a few times a month and was on the fund-raising committee. Lucy purchased a pot of tea and a savory muffin and walked across the room.

"Hello, there," the older woman said and welcomed Lucy toward her table with a friendly wave. "How are you?"

Lucy nodded, knowing she must look haggard and sleep-deprived. "Great. You?"

Colleen smiled warmly. "Very well."

"How's your brother-in-law?"

Collen nodded. "I saw Joe yesterday and he seems to be doing well, considering. I haven't seen you around much this week. Everything okay?"

Lucy shrugged and then nodded. "I've been busy."

Yeah...busy making out with your son.

"Not too busy for a cup of tea and a chat, I hope," Colleen said, motioning to the chair opposite.

Lucy sat. "Of course not. How's the fund-raiser going?"

Colleen waved a hand over the stack of files on the table. "I've been doing the rounds. We desperately need new recliners for the maternity rooms. You know, the ones that allow the new moms to nurse easily and new dads to sleep." She grinned ruefully. "But each one is a couple of thousand dollars and trying to raise that kind of money around the holidays is almost impossible. I may have to put aside my pride and ask the O'Sullivans to make another sizable donation."

Lucy knew Colleen had little time for the wealthiest and most influential family in town, given that they had treated her eldest son so poorly while he was married to Liz O'Sullivan, and often still did two and a half years after her death. But since they shared three grandchildren, she also knew Colleen remained civil and supported Grady's decision to keep his daughters in their lives.

"Maybe the holiday season will increase their generosity," she suggested.

Colleen made a face. "Nice idea. At least I only have to deal with Liam now and not the old man."

Lucy made a mental note to have a word with Kayla. Her friend seemed to have some influence with the older O'Sullivan son, despite her protests. "I'm sure it will work out. I'd like to believe that people *are* more generous at this time of year, so perhaps some of that holiday spirit will rub off on the O'Sullivans."

"Yes," Colleen replied, smiling. "You're probably right. So, how's your car? Brant said you had some trouble with it last week."

It was a subtle change in conversation and Lucy bit back a smile. Her car troubles seemed like an age ago. "Fine. I got a new battery and that fixed the problem."

Colleen's expression narrowed. "And I believe you're coming to the hospital tomorrow?"

"Yes," she replied, coloring when she realized Brant and his mother had been discussing her.

"That's very kind of you. Grady and I will be there, too. Marissa is watching the girls at the ranch."

Lucy would be surrounded by Parkers. But it didn't make her uneasy. She liked them all very much. Although the idea of seeing Brant again was tying her belly into knots. "I'm sure your brother-in-law will be fine."

"I hope so," Colleen said and looked unusually pensive. "Joe is a lot older than my husband and they were more like father and son than brothers. When Alan died," she said of her late husband, "Joe became both a father and uncle to my boys. He means the world to them, and to Brant in particular. I know he'd be devastated if anything happened to his uncle. And after what he went through on his last tour in the military... I'm scared for what this might mean."

Lucy saw the older woman's chin quiver. Usually, Colleen Parker came across as strong and self-assured and able to handle anything. But believing her youngest son was troubled was clearly more than she could cope with. And Lucy instinctively offered comfort.

"He'll be fine," she said and patted Colleen's hand. "Brant's been talking to me, starting to open up," she said, exaggerating the truth a little since Brant hadn't really told her anything. But Colleen needed reassurance. "He's strong, like you, and I truly believe he'll be okay."

"I hope so. And I'm glad he's been talking to you," she said, looking a little relieved. "As a child he was always much quieter than his brother…more serious. But he feels things deeply and that makes him sensitive, which is why he's such a good listener and a good friend to the people he's close to. When he chose a military career I knew he would give it one hundred percent of himself. I only hope he hasn't gotten completely lost in the process."

Lucy smiled. Yes, Brant was a good listener. "Like I said, I'm sure he'll be fine."

She wasn't about to discuss his upcoming meeting with Dr. Allenby. If Brant chose to tell or to not tell his family, then it was his business. She was a doctor, and although he wasn't her patient, she still had a moral and ethical responsibility to respect his privacy.

Lucy finished her tea and muffin, steered the conversation toward the upcoming wedding for a few minutes, and then left to return to the ER.

The next few hours were busy as a young man with a suspected spinal injury was brought in after he'd fallen off a horse at one of the local dude ranches while on vacation. He was immediately transferred to Rapid City for tests. Once he was on his way, a girl of eight with chronic asthma and very concerned parents came into Triage. As her shift was finishing she stitched up another boy who'd torn his earlobe on a fence.

She left around six. Once she was home Lucy fed the cat, showered, changed into sweats and made a toasted cheese sandwich for dinner.

She sat in the living room, crossed her legs lotus-style and grabbed her cell. She'd made a decision while showering to drive herself to the hospital in Rapid City the following morning. She didn't want to spend time with Brant in the close confines of his truck. The less time they spent together, the better it would be for her peace of mind. She sent him a text message to say she'd take her own car and then flicked on the television.

There was no point in pining over what could never be.

I don't want you here.

She didn't need to hear that again anytime soon.

He didn't want her in his apartment. Or his arms. Or his life.

And the sooner she accepted it the better.

For everyone.

Brant pulled into the hospital garage in Rapid City just after nine-thirty on Friday morning. His brother and mother were about twenty minutes away. They could have travelled together, but he was in no mood for chitchat and had opted to drive in by himself. Without company.

Without Lucy.

He headed for the surgical ward and stopped at the nurses' station to ask what bed his uncle was in. When he entered the room he discovered Lucy sitting on a chair beside Joe's bed, smiling at something his uncle was saying. He lingered by the door, watching her. She looked so effortlessly pretty in a bright green sweater and jeans. Her hair was down, framing her face. Her cheeks were flushed and her mouth looked fuller, softer... Just the idea of her lips against his made his gut churn. Recollections of kissing her, of holding her, bombarded his thoughts. Nothing had ever felt better and there was no way to erase the feel of her against him or the taste of her kiss from his memory.

She looked up as if she'd felt him standing there and their gazes clashed. It was electric. Powerful. If he'd had any doubts he'd been somehow pulled into her vortex over the past week, they disappeared. She was under his skin and in his thoughts. And he knew he was right to have sent her away the other night. If she'd stayed, they would have ended up in bed together, he was sure of it. They would have made love and then he would have been in so deep, Brant knew he would have no hope of pulling away from her without breaking her heart. Or his own. He didn't want that to happen. The closer they got, the more she'd dig away at him, which was out of the question. He didn't want anyone digging. He didn't want to see query and then sympathy in her eyes.

Because he would. She'd get him talking—that was her way. Everything he'd been through in Afghanistan would be out of the shadows and under the microscope. He'd be back out on the ridge again. Only this time he'd have no cover, no one watching his back, no one taking a bullet meant for him.

"You plannin' on hanging around the doorway all morning?"

His uncle's voice jerked him back into the moment. "No," he said and stepped into the room. "Of course not."

"Looks like you haven't slept for a couple of days," Joe remarked and frowned. "Everything all right?"

Brant nodded and didn't dare look at Lucy. "Fine. What time are you heading into surgery?"

Joe shrugged. "Anytime."

"The surgeon will make a final decision within the next half hour," Lucy said, pointing to the chart at the foot of the bed. "If the OBS are good, then it will go ahead as planned."

Brant moved toward the other side of the bed. Damned if he couldn't pick up traces of her apple shampoo in the air. He ignored it and started a conversation with his uncle, blindingly conscious of every move she made.

Grady and his mother arrived a few minutes later and he was grateful for the reprieve. His brother began talking to Lucy and while his mother chatted to Joe, Brant hung back and tried to ignore the sudden pounding at his temples.

Forty-five minutes later his uncle was wheeled from the room and taken into surgery. Grady and his mother took off for the cafeteria and Brant remained in the waiting room with Lucy. The room was small with half a dozen chairs, a small table covered with dog-eared magazines, a tea and coffee machine, and a water cooler. Brant sat at one end, Lucy at the other.

"Are you okay?"

Her soft voice echoed around the room. He watched as her gaze flicked from his face to his tightly clenched hands. Feeling her scrutiny, he relaxed his hands. "Sure."

"I know you're worried," she said quietly. "But the bypass procedure your uncle is having is fairly standard. I'm certain he'll pull through it without any problems."

Of course her words were comforting. That's what she did. She was a doctor—she knew how to phrase comfort and offer a soothing hand. But no matter how much he was tempted, Brant wasn't about to get drawn even further into her web.

"I'm sure you're right," he said flatly.

"And he wants to get out of here as soon as possible," she went on to say. "That's often the best motivator for a swift recovery."

"Sure," he said again and sat back in his seat.

Her expression narrowed. "How are the renovations coming along?"

Brant looked up. She was persistent, that's for sure. "You don't have to do this."

"Do what?"

"Try and take my mind off things. I'd prefer not to talk."

A spark seemed to fly from her gaze, as if she had an opinion but held it inside. He knew he was being a jerk. And that she was probably hurt by his words but was too stubborn to show it. It made him bite back a smile. Lucy Monero was full of opinions and passion and a kind of captivating intensity.

"Okay…fine," she said and pulled her cell phone from her tote as she shifted her eyes from his. "No talking."

Brant eased back into the chair and stared directly ahead. Within five minutes there was enough tension in the room to fill a stadium. He grabbed a magazine off the table and pretended to flip through the pages, but he was suddenly so restless he had to fight the urge to get out of his seat and pace. He could feel her, edgy and ir-ritated just a few seats away. Her perfume lingered in the air and the way her fingers fiddled with the phone made him want to feel those hands on his skin. His at-traction to her was relentless. Powerful. And certainly well out of his control.

"All right," he said, still not looking at her. "Let's talk."

She sighed sharply. "You're such a jerk."

He stilled. "Yeah… I know. I'm sorry. I guess I'm just worried about my uncle and–"

"I know that," she said, cutting him off as she dropped the phone back into her bag.

Tension tightened his shoulders. "So, did you switch a shift so you could be here today?"

Her head turned. "I start night shift tonight for a week so I didn't need to."

"When do you sleep?"

"Tomorrow," she replied.

He had a thought. "You're working over the Thanksgiving holiday?"

She nodded. "I usually do." Her gaze sharpened. "The other two doctors have families. So I work."

Brant considered her words. She had no family and gave up the holiday so that her colleagues could spend time with their loved ones. Her thoughtfulness made him like her even more. "That's very generous of you."

She shrugged lightly, but he wasn't fooled. She seemed a little sad. Strange, he thought as he looked at her, how quickly he'd gotten to know her moods. Like she'd gotten to know his. They'd developed a fraught, tense friendship over the past week and even though good sense told him otherwise, Brant felt compelled to get to know her even better. Despite her intriguing mix of strength and resilience, there were times when she seemed hauntingly vulnerable. And naive. Almost…innocent. Brant couldn't quite define it…couldn't work out what it was about her that drew him like a magnet. It wasn't just a physical thing. He'd been attracted to women before. But Lucy Monero was different. When he was around her it *felt* different. When he was around her *he* was different.

No…that's not it.

He was himself. Without armor. Without pretense. Without anything to hide behind. And that's why he'd avoided her since he'd returned home. The moment he'd met her again Brant had experienced a kind of heady awareness, deep down, that shattered all his plans to steer clear of involvement with anyone. When his mother had started matchmaking it was all the excuse he'd needed to act like a compete ass. And he had, again and again. On most occasions over the past few months he would barely acknowledge her when they were in the same room. Like a jerk. And a fool. And a coward.

"Lucy?"

She looked at him. "What?"

"I'm sorry about the other night." Face to face, the words were harder to say. "I didn't mean to, nor did I want to, hurt your feelings."

She shrugged. "You didn't. It was just a kiss, Brant. Nothing."

For a moment he thought she meant it and part of him was glad. But then she blinked and he saw the shimmer in her eyes. And in that moment he was done for.

Lucy was determined not to let him see her cry. She blinked a couple of times and willed the tears back. This wasn't the time or place to get all weepy. So they'd kissed and then he'd behaved badly.

Welcome to the world of being a grown-up.

"I did say that guys like me can hurt women like you without even trying," he reminded her. "And I'm not saying that to let myself off the hook. I genuinely don't want to see you get hurt. And if we get involved…you will."

Humiliation coursed over her skin. Was her sexual inexperience so obvious? Of course he must have noticed. No doubt he'd kissed many women over the years…like Trudy with her overt sexuality and bedroom eyes. No sweet wonder he'd acted like he'd wanted to run in the opposite direction after their kiss…he'd probably figured out she was a greenhorn in the bedroom department.

"Don't forget your appointment on Monday," she reminded him, quickly shifting the subject.

"I haven't," he said quietly. "Not that I think it's necessary. But I'll do it because I gave you my word that I would."

"He's a good counselor," she said. "He talks to a lot of the veterans at the home, including your uncle. So try to go with an open mind, okay?"

"I said I'd go," he replied. "And so you know, I have talked with a shrink before."

"Me, too."

His expression narrowed. "You have? Why?"

A week ago she wouldn't have dreamed of having such a conversation. But things had changed. They'd changed. Even without the kiss, things had altered between them. "It was a few years ago. I found myself withdrawn and spending way too much time alone. I knew I hadn't moved on from the accident and my mom's death and what happened in college so I—"

"What happened in college?" he asked, cutting her off.

Lucy took a deep breath. "Three weeks after first semester started my roommate was assaulted."

"Assaulted?"

"Raped," she explained and felt a familiar heaviness weigh down on her shoulders. "I found her and got her to the hospital and stayed with her for two days. She didn't press charges. She didn't tell anyone. She never went back to class and left school a month later."

She watched Brant's hands clench. "And the individual responsible?"

"He went about his life as though nothing had happened. I used to see him on campus and he always had a smug kind of sinister look on his face. He knew *I* knew what he'd done."

Brant got up and sat in the seat beside her. His back was straight, his shoulders tight. After a few seconds he spoke again. "Did he ever come near you?"

She shook her head. "I made sure I was never alone around him."

He looked relieved…as if the idea of someone hurting her was unthinkable.

She didn't want to imagine what it meant. She couldn't. Wouldn't. She was already halfway in love with him… Imagining he cared about her even a little was a catastrophe waiting to happen.

"And your friend?"

She shrugged. "We lost contact when I went to med school. I was still mourning my mom's death and with my course load and everything else… I don't think I had enough of myself to give. I think about her sometimes and wonder if she has had a happy life. Or if she let that one terrible thing outline the rest of her life. I hope not. I hope she managed to pull through and find some happiness. I still feel guilty, though… I still feel as though I could have done more to help her."

He grabbed her hand. "I'm sure you did everything you could."

Lucy's insides fluttered. Being so close to him wreaked havoc with her determination to keep him at a figurative distance. It was impossible when he was touching her. She wanted to pull her hand away but couldn't. "I hope so. But it reminded me of my mom all over again," she admitted, feeling a familiar pain seep into her heart. "I experienced the same helplessness, the same guilt. And yet, in a way, it confirmed my decision to go to med school."

He linked their fingers and held tight. "And look where you are now."

She glanced around. "In this room, you mean?"

"I mean," he said quietly, "that you're helping people again…because that's what you do."

Lucy's gaze flicked to their joined hands now resting on his jeans-clad thigh. "Looks to me like you're the one doing the helping."

"Don't kid yourself," he said and smiled so intimately it sent a shudder running through her. "The only reason I feel as if everything will work out with my uncle today is because of you."

As an admission it spoke volumes. This man, who she instinctively knew had been through hell and back and didn't want anyone to know it, trusted her.

"You know, it's hard to admit when we need help. Going to see a therapist was one of the most difficult things I've ever done," she said, feeling him flinch a little. But he didn't move his hand. The doctor in her suddenly made her cautious to get any more involved with him on a personal level. But the woman in her… She wanted to hold him in her arms and never let him go. "But I went because I wanted to feel whole again."

He expelled a heavy breath. "Whole? I don't even know what that means anymore."

"It means sleeping through the night," she said gently, looking straight ahead. "It means not waking up in a cold sweat at two o'clock in the morning. It means talking about what happened…it means sharing your fear."

"I can't."

Lucy heard the pain in his words but pressed on. "Why not?"

Silence stretched between them. Finally he spoke.

"Because I can't go back there."

Her insides constricted tightly. "Back where? To Afghanistan?"

He shook his head. "To that day. To that moment. To that second."

Lucy turned in the chair and grasped his arm. His muscles bunched beneath her touch. "Why can't you?"

"Because," he said quietly. "It will break me."

A sound interrupted them and they both looked toward the door. Grady stood in the doorway, two foam cups in his hand. Brant released her immediately and Lucy's hand dropped. She knew how it must have looked, being so close, their hands linked and her fingers digging into his arm. It would have looked impossibly intimate. Brant got to his feet and moved away, dropping into a seat by the water cooler.

"I brought coffee," Grady said as he entered the room. "It's not so great, but it's better than what comes out of that machine," he said and pointed to the equipment on the small counter. "Mom is walking around one of the gardens." He passed the coffee around and sat on one of the chairs. "So, what's new with you guys?"

Brant laughed first, because the question sounded so absurd considering Grady had walked into the room and caught them holding hands like a pair of guilty teens.

Lucy shook off her embarrassment and got to her feet. "I think I'll join Colleen in the garden."

She left the room and knew she would be the hot topic of conversation between the two brothers. But she didn't care. They could talk about her all they wanted. It wouldn't change the fact that she was falling in love with a man who was clearly so weighed down by his past he didn't have any room in his life...or his heart... for anyone.

By the time Joe came out of surgery it was past three

o'clock. Once she was certain he was out of danger and had come through the anesthetic, Lucy said goodbye to the Parkers. She was in the foyer, just about to walk through the automatic doors, when she heard her name being called.

Brant was about fifteen steps behind her.

"What?" she asked sharply, suddenly breathless.

"I wanted to thank you for being here."

"No problem," she said and clutched her tote.

"It means a lot to my uncle."

Lucy's brows came up sharply. "Is that the best you can do? Really?"

He thrust his hands into his jacket pockets. "Okay… if you need to hear it…it means a lot to me."

"Anytime," she said and managed a tight smile. "Make sure your uncle follows the doctor's orders. And good luck with your appointment on Monday."

She turned and began walking.

"Are you going to be there?" he asked.

He wanted her there? Did she dare? Her heart begged her to say yes. But her head told her not to make it too easy for him. Lucy nodded and tossed her hair. "I'll be around."

And then she walked out.

Chapter Eight

I'll be around...

Brant had been hearing those words in his head for three days.

Even with a busy weekend, traveling back and forth to the hospital to visit Joe, and then immersing himself in the renovation for the tavern, he couldn't get Lucy from his thoughts. He'd said too much. Admitted too much. And he couldn't believe he'd asked her if she was going to be at the appointment with him. No wonder she thought he was a head case who needed a shrink.

He lingered outside Dr. Allenby's small office at the veterans home five minutes before his appointment. He knew the doctor reasonably well and respected his abilities as a counselor. But that didn't mean he wanted to bare his soul to the other man. There was no one else in the office other than the middle-aged receptionist who kept glancing his way every time he moved.

Just over an hour later he was forced to admit that it hadn't been as bad as he'd expected. Dr. Allenby didn't try to force him to talk about the war. Instead Brant spoke about his uncle and the tavern and what it was like being back in Cedar River after so many years away. Of course, he wasn't entirely fooled. It was about gaining trust. Therapists employed tactics just as soldiers did. But at least Brant didn't break out into a cold sweat or completely shut down to the idea of conversation.

And he knew why.

Lucy.

He'd made a promise and he didn't want to disappoint her. Over the past week he'd seen enough hurt in her eyes and it was almost unbearable. Thinking about what she'd been through made him want to wrap her in his arms and protect her from the world. Of course he couldn't. He wouldn't. She wasn't his to protect. Besides, it sounded old-fashioned and foolish. She was a smart, independent woman who could obviously look after herself. Still…the thought lingered because imagining her hurt or in trouble somehow switched on something in his brain and made him feel protective and stupidly macho at the same time.

When he walked out of Dr. Allenby's office he saw Lucy sitting by the door, her head down, flicking through a magazine. He stopped in his tracks when she looked up and met his gaze.

"Hi," she said and placed the magazine down on the small table in the middle of the waiting area.

"Hi, yourself."

She got to her feet. "How did it go?"

He briefly raised one shoulder. "Okay."

She was just about to respond when the receptionist spoke. "Mr. Parker, will you be making another appointment to see the doctor?"

Brant's instinct was to reply with a resounding no. But he looked at Lucy and saw her gazing at him questioningly. As though she expected him to say no but hoped that he'd say yes. And, foolishly, he didn't want to disappoint her.

"Sure," he said, ignoring the heat filling his chest at the idea of another session under scrutiny. "How about the same time next week?"

Once the appointment was confirmed Brant thanked the receptionist and walked toward the door. He held it open and allowed Lucy to pass, catching a trace of her perfume as she moved ahead of him.

"So, it was okay?" she asked as they walked down the corridor.

"It was okay."

"I'm glad."

Brant slowed his stride a fraction. "I didn't think I'd see you here today."

"I said I'd be around," she reminded him.

His skin tightened. "I thought you were on night shift this week?"

"I am," she replied. "I changed at work and came straight here. I'll sleep this afternoon. How's your uncle?"

"Good," he replied. "He'll be home by the end of the week. Unfortunately not in time for Thanksgiving, but we'll celebrate with him over the weekend once he's back here. My mom is all about the holidays, so no doubt she'll make sure he gets some of her turkey and pumpkin pie."

"Sounds delicious," she said, smiling as she walked.

Lucy's heels clicked over the tiled floor. She wore a blue dress, shorter than usual, and her bare legs were impossible to ignore. Her hair was loose, flowing over her shoulders, and she wore a short denim jacket that accentuated the flare of her hips. And she had boots on, the short cowgirl kind with fringe on the side. For a moment he was poleaxed. He stopped walking and stared at her.

When she realized he wasn't beside her she came to a halt and turned around. "What?"

His gaze slide over her. "You look...really pretty."

"Oh...thanks."

Brant wondered if she knew how sexy she looked in her short dress and boots. Probably not. Most of the time he was pretty sure she had no idea how beautiful she was. "I appreciate you coming here today. It was very thoughtful of you. Especially considering that I haven't done much to deserve it."

Her cheeks colored and she smiled tightly. "No problem. Ah...how's your arm?"

"Good. No problems. You're something of a whiz with a needle."

"Yeah," she said almost breathlessly. "Shame I can't cook."

"Nice to know you have some flaws, Lucia."

The air between them crackled and he knew she felt it as much as he did.

"Well, I have to go," she said and swung her tote around her hips.

Disappointment foolishly rushed through him. "Hey, I was thinking we could have a late breakfast at—"

"I can't," she said, cutting him off. "I have a date."

A date?

He frowned. "Like an appointment?"

He watched her expression harden instantly. "No. Like a *date*. I'm not completely undatable, you know, Brant... despite what you might think."

"I've never said you were—"

"Goodbye. Have a good day."

How was he supposed to have a good anything when

she was out on a date with someone else? He reached for her and grabbed her hand. "Lucy...wait."

Her fingers felt soft and warm enclosed within his. He met her gaze, saw her lip tremble a fraction and felt an inexplicable urge to pull her close.

"That's just it, Brant," she said, wriggling her hand free of his. "I'm tired of *waiting.*"

He watched her walk down the corridor, hips swaying, head held high, and fought the need to chase after her. He knew what she meant. It was a direct hit. She wanted more...and he didn't know what the hell he wanted. Suddenly tired of his own company, Brant left the building, got into his truck and drove to his brother's ranch.

The Parker Ranch was one of the largest in the area. His brother had been successfully running cattle for a decade and also worked as a county brand inspector. He'd always admired Grady's work ethic and integrity. His brother was one of the most decent human beings he'd ever known. He'd been through a lot, too, with losing his wife more than two and half years earlier, and raising his three young daughters. Since finding love with Marissa Ellis, Brant knew his brother was truly happy again.

Grady was in the stables with Rex, the ranch foreman. Who, as it recently turned out, was also Marissa's father. It was a long and complicated story, but Rex had returned to Cedar River after twenty-six years and discovered he had a daughter. Marissa's mom had since passed away and Marissa had lived in New York, returning a couple of times a year to see her aunt and her best friend, Liz— Grady's first wife. Yeah, complicated didn't half cover it. Rex had stayed in town, gotten a job on the ranch and hoped he'd get a chance to connect with his daughter once in a while. Of course when Grady and Marissa had fallen in love, it had added a whole other level of complexity to the mix. But everything seemed to be working out. Marissa and Rex were getting to know one another, Grady's daughters were delighted by the idea of having a new mom, and his brother was head over heels in love with a woman who clearly adored him and his children.

Yeah…some people really did get a happy-ever-after.

Brant ignored the twitch in his gut and met his brother by the stable doors.

"Good of you to drop by," Grady said and clapped him on the shoulder. "The girls were complaining they haven't seen you for a while. You bailed on Saturday lunch at Mom's."

Brant shrugged. "I had stuff to do."

And he hadn't wanted to answer the inevitable barrage of questions he'd get from his mother about a certain brunette.

"Brooke's inside watching Tina," Grady said. "Coffee's on. I'll be a few minutes here."

Brant nodded, left his brother to his work and headed for the house.

He never ceased to be amazed by the sense of peace he felt whenever he walked into the ranch house. It was wide and sprawling, with verandas all the way around and shuttered windows. There was a love seat on the front porch area that he was pretty sure had been there for an eternity. Out the back was a pool and patio that Grady had put in a few years earlier.

The front door was open and he headed down the hall. His cousin Brooke was in the kitchen, chatting to Grady's youngest daughter, Tina. Brooke Laughton lived about as solitary a life as he did. She owned a small ranch out of town and had once been the queen of the rodeo circuit. That was before her parents were killed, her brother ran off and her fiancé left her for another woman. He liked Brooke, though—she was candid and easy to get along with.

As soon as the toddler spotted him she dropped the sippy cup in her hands and raced across the room. Brant scooped her up and held her close. She was a precious, loving child, and he adored her and both her sisters.

"Wow," Brooke said and smiled. "That was quite a welcome."

"I can be charming when I want to be."

She laughed and looked at the child clinging to him. "You know, that's a good look on you."

Brant shook his head. "Don't you start, too. I get that enough from Mom."

Brooke shrugged. "Just saying."

He dismissed his cousin's words. Mostly. But as he poured himself a mug of coffee and sat at the table while Tina proceeded to stack a pile of stuffed toys around him, he let the idea linger for a moment. Having a child was the biggest commitment a person could make. And yet he'd watched his brother do it seemingly effortlessly for years and a part of him had envied that ability. But every time he tried to see that future for himself the image always appeared blurred...as if he wasn't ready. Sometimes he wondered if he ever would be.

And then, deep down, a feeling suddenly stirred, a restless thought that quickly turned into something else... a picture...an idea. And if he closed his eyes for a second he could see it clearly...a woman and a child, both with dark curly hair and deep green eyes.

"Brant?"

His cousin's voice jerked him back into the present and he quickly dismissed the image in his head.

"How are things at the ranch?" he asked casually.

Brooke managed a smile. "Okay, I guess. I have creditors snapping at my heels and the land rezoning issue is still a problem. But I'm still there."

Brant knew his cousin had some serious financial concerns. "If there's anything I can—"

"There's not," she said quickly and then grinned. "So…you and Lucy, huh?"

"What?"

She shrugged lightly. "I hear things."

"You mean from Mom. I wouldn't believe everything you—"

"From Kayla, actually," Brooke said matter-of-factly. "She said you were there last week having dinner. Besides, Lucy is my friend…"

"And?"

Brooke's forehead wrinkled a little. "And don't break her heart, okay?"

Discomfiture spiraled up his spine. "I have no intention of doing any such thing."

"I hope not." His cousin half grinned. "Although you may have missed your shot."

"What?"

"Your shot," she echoed. "With Lucy. I spoke to her last night and she said she had a coffee date with Kieran O'Sullivan today. He's back in town for the wedding this weekend…you know how he's a friend of Marissa's. Anyway, he called Lucy last night and asked her out. I mean, it makes sense, I suppose, since they're both doctors so they'll have a lot in common. And they worked together at that hospital in Sioux Falls a few years back."

Kieran O'Sullivan. Great.

Not only did he have to think about the fact she was on a date, she was on that date with one of the Parkers' enemies. Well…maybe that was a stretch. Kieran was okay, considering he came from that family. They'd gone to school and been on the football team together. But *a date.*

The very idea twisted at his insides. But he didn't dare show it. "She's an adult. She can see who she wants."

Brooke laughed. "Gosh, you're a rotten liar. You're about as crazy as a bear in a trap just thinking about it." His cousin put up a hand. "But I won't say anything more about it. You're gonna have to figure this one out for yourself."

"What's he figuring out?"

Grady's voice from the doorway made them both turn.

"Lucy," Brooke supplied, still grinning.

His brother walked into the room. "Ah, the pretty green-eyed doctor with the heart of gold. Is he falling in love with her or something?"

"Looks like it," Brooke said and chuckled.

Brant jumped to his feet. "Would you two stop talking about me as though I'm not in the room? I am *not* falling in love with Lucy Monero," he insisted. "We're just friends."

"You looked pretty cozy together the other day at the hospital," Grady said then looked at Brooke. "They were holding hands. It was very sweet."

Brant's blood boiled. "We were *not* holding hands."

"Sure you were," Grady said and grinned as he winked toward their cousin.

"Sometimes you can be a real pain in the—" His words were immediately cut off when he remembered there was a child in the room. "I have to go. I'll see you both Thursday."

He bailed quickly, angry and so wound up he barely made it to his truck without tripping over his own feet. Sometimes families were nothing but trouble. He drove down the driveway and hit the main road into town.

By the time he'd settled his temper he'd pulled up at the back of the Loose Moose. And he got to work. It was still early, barely noon, and by three o'clock he'd finished building the new booths at the front of the tavern and was ready to start painting.

Is he falling in love with her or something? His brother's words kept slamming around in his head as he worked.

No. Absolutely not.

He was not falling in love. He didn't know how to. Lust, for sure. He wanted her like crazy. But love... That was out of the question. It was about sex, that's all. He wanted to make love to her. And, sure, he liked her. How could he not? She was smart and funny and kind and he enjoyed her company. But that was all it was. *Lust* and a little *like* thrown into the mix.

Not love.

That would be plain stupid.

Lucy enjoyed her coffee date with Kieran O'Sullivan. She liked Kieran and they'd always worked well together at the hospital in Sioux Falls. He was handsome and charming and had just enough of the O'Sullivan arrogance and confidence to make him good company. Of course, he'd never so much as made a blip on her radar. And they'd often joked about how they'd be perfect for one another—except for the fact they weren't attracted to each other in the least.

She left the café after accepting a chaste kiss on the cheek from her date and headed home. Once she was inside she fed the cat, changed into her pajamas, pulled the curtains closed to block out the light and dived into bed. She managed a few hours' sleep and by the time she roused it was past four o'clock. She ate a sandwich, had a cup of tea and spent an hour on her laptop paying bills and budgeting for the next month. She started her shift at seven and was just about to leave half an hour before when her cell beeped to indicate she had a text message.

Lucy grabbed the phone and checked the screen.

How was your date?

She sucked in a breath. Right. Suddenly, Brant Parker was Mr. Curious? She waited a few minutes and replied.

It was good. I had a soy latte and pecan cookie.

A minute passed and the phone beeped again.

Are you seeing him again?

Lucy stared at the screen. He had some nerve, that's for sure.

Maybe. Do you have a problem with that?

She waited for a minute, well aware that her provocative question would niggle him. *Well, he deserves a little niggling.* When a few more minutes passed and she didn't get a response, Lucy grabbed her bag, put on her shoes and headed out. It was snowing again and she covered her head with her coat as she raced to her car. She was just about to shove the key in the ignition when her cell beeped. She fumbled through her bag and pulled out her phone.

I think I do.

Lucy grinned foolishly.

I am seriously falling for this guy.

But she wasn't about to start imagining a few texts meant anything. Lucy fought the urge to write something in return and instead tossed the phone back into her tote. Then she drove into town and headed for the hospital.

It was a quiet but long night in the ER and when she got home at six the following morning she fell into bed after a quick shower and slept until noon. It usually took a couple of days for her body clock to kick in when she started a block of night shifts and this rotation proved to be more difficult than usual.

On Tuesday as she was getting ready to leave for work when her cell pealed.

It was a message from Brant.

How's work?

For a moment she considered ignoring him, but temptation got the better of her. She mulled over her response for several minutes and then replied.

Not busy. Which is good. Great to see you're keeping away from the place, too.

She grabbed her jacket and keys, and finished locking the house up. And waited for a reply.

Motorcycles and icy roads don't mix. Told you I wasn't reckless.

Lucy petted the cat, got into her coat, switched off the lights and headed outside. When she was inside her car she sent another message.

I guess you're not such a bad boy after all.

Ten seconds later he replied.

Lucia, I'm good. I promise you.

Even to her naive eyes the innuendo couldn't be missed and her body turned hot all over. She had so little experience flirting—*if* that's what they were doing— and didn't know how to handle the feelings running riot throughout her system. Of course she knew she wanted him. That one kiss had ignited her libido and she wanted to feel it again…and more. She wanted passion and sweat and heat and all the things she imagined were shared between two people who were lovers.

Because she wanted Brant Parker as her lover…no doubt about it. Only, she wasn't sure if that's what he wanted, too. Oh, he'd certainly kissed her that night in his apartment as if he was interested. But he'd also sent her packing. His hot then cold approach was confusing. And annoying. And *unacceptable*, she decided with a surge of confidence and gumption.

So by the time Wednesday evening came around and she was dressing for work, Lucy was almost back to being furious at him for behaving like such an impossible jerk.

Until her phone rang. She recognized the number and said his name almost on a sigh. "Brant…hello."

He was silent for a moment, and then spoke. "Lucia… I was wondering something… Do you think anyone would notice if I skipped the best man speech on Saturday?"

Lucy smiled to herself as the sound of his deep voice wound through her blood. She knew he'd never let his brother down like that.

"Yes," she said, laughing softly. "And you're an idiot for thinking it."

He chuckled. "Ain't that the truth."

Lucy dug deep. Making it too easy for him wasn't on her agenda. "Did you want something?"

She heard his hesitation. "No... I mean... I just wanted to say...that I think... I actually think I'm missing something."

Lucy's nerve endings twitched. Talking was much more intimate than texting and she could feel her nerves fraying. She took a deep breath. "Missing something in the speech you mean?"

"Not exactly."

"Then what do you mean?"

She heard him draw in a hard breath. "I miss... I think I miss...you. I mean, I think I miss talking to you."

God, he was impossible. "You think?"

There was more silence. "It's not...easy for me to say."

No...nothing was easy when it came to Brant.

She sucked in a breath, galvanized her nerves and spoke. "You're talking to me now."

Silence stretched again. "I guess I just wanted to see how you were."

"I'm fine. But I'm getting ready for work so—"

"Okay," he said quickly. "I'll let you go. Goodbye, Lucy."

She inhaled heavily. "Goodbye, Brant." She held the phone close to her ear. "And Brant...if you want to talk you know where I am."

By the time she got to work and swiped in, she was as coiled as a spring. Brant had a way of invading her thoughts like no one else. But she couldn't let anyone see that or allow her personal issues to impact her job. So she sucked in a few steadying breaths and got on with her shift.

She was about to take her first break around eight o'clock when Kayla unexpectedly turned up. Lucy met her by the nurse's station and gave her a hug.

"What brings you here?" she asked.

"I had a late meeting and was driving past and thought I'd stop by on the chance you might want to grab a coffee and have a chat."

A few minutes later they were in the staff lunch room, sipping coffee and tea.

"Don't forget my mother insists you stop by on Friday and have some Thanksgiving leftovers. She's pretty miffed you're not coming over again...you know how much my folks adore you."

Lucy was touched by Kayla's kindness. "I have to work a double shift. But I'll do my best to stop by, I promise. So, how are things?" she asked.

Kayla shrugged. "Same as usual. How's it going with Hot Stuff?"

"Would you stop calling him that?"

"I've been calling him that since the ninth grade," her friend reminded her. "I probably won't stop now. Is it true you were holding hands at the hospital last week?"

Lucy almost spat out her tea. "What?"

Kayla laughed. "Grady said something to Brooke. She told me. The great circle of life," she said and grinned.

"Circle of gossip more like," Lucy said, frowning. "And it wasn't *that* kind of hand holding."

"How many kinds are there?" Kayla asked, still grinning.

"Plenty," she replied. "We're friends and sometimes friends hold hands during a—"

"This is me, remember?" Kayla reminded her. "Your *best* friend. What's going on?"

"Honestly," Lucy said and let out an exasperated sigh. "I have no idea. Some days I feel like I'm back in high school again, as though I'm idly wasting my days doodling hearts with Brant Parker's name inside. Metaphorically speaking," she added. "I'm not really doodling. But I am spending way too much time thinking about him when I should be concentrating on my work, my home and my friends."

Kayla's perfectly beautiful face regarded her inquiringly. "And is he thinking about you, too?"

Lucy shrugged. "It's impossible to tell. Oh, he's civil to me now and we have spent quite a lot of time together lately and there's been a bit of texting this week so I—"

"Texting?"

"Yes," Lucy replied. "Texting."

Her friend chuckled. "That's kind of romantic."

"It's kind of confusing," she corrected. "And I can't allow myself to imagine it means too much. Even if I hadn't kissed him I probably wouldn't let myself believe it was—"

"Whoa," Kayla said, cutting her off as she waved a hand. "Back up. You kissed him?"

Lucy's skin heated. "Well, technically he kissed me," she explained. "And then I kissed him back."

Her friend's eyes widened. "And when were you going to share this tidbit?"

"Do you tell me every time you kiss Liam O'Sullivan?" Lucy teased.

Kayla groaned. "I don't kiss Liam. But enough about that—tell me everything… Was it fabulous?"

"Yes," she admitted and smiled. "You see, this *is* high school."

Her friend shook her head. "It's life, Lucy. So what happens next?"

She shrugged. "I have no idea. I'm new to all this, as you know. He keeps insisting he's all wrong for me—that I want a picket fence and he's not that kind of man. There's a part of him that's broken...or at least that's what he believes."

Kayla's eyes softened. "And can it be fixed?"

"I'm not sure he wants it fixed," she replied, exhaling heavily. "It's as if he's stuck somewhere...in some place, some moment in time, that he believes has suddenly come to define him. I don't know what it is and he's not talking. But I feel it whenever we're together. In here," she said and put a hand to her heart. "I feel as though he thinks he has to hang on to this thing from his past or he'll be *redefined*...somehow changed." She sighed and drank some tea. "Anyway, I really shouldn't be talking about him like this."

"Why not? It's only talking."

Heat filled her chest. "Because it doesn't feel right."

"Conflicting loyalty, hey?"

She nodded. "Something like that."

Kayla sat back in her chair and regarded her intently. "Lucy, have you considered that the reason you want Brant is because he *is* broken? Unfixable? Which also makes him unattainable?"

"That doesn't make sense."

"Sure it does," her friend said gently. "And it really means only one thing."

"And what's that?" she asked.

Kayla met her gaze. "That you're falling in love with him and it's scaring you to bits."

Lucy met her friend's stare head-on and knew she couldn't lie. "Yes...that's it exactly. I'm falling in love with a man who doesn't want to fall in love with me in return. And I'm terrified."

Kayla reached across the table and patted her hand. "So what are you going to do about it?"

Lucy sat back in her seat and tried to ignore the ache in her heart. "Nothing," she replied. "He has to figure this out for himself."

Chapter Nine

Brant stared at the huge cooked bird on the kitchen counter and impossibly bright vegetables piled onto a tray, and watched as his mother managed to attack three separate tasks at once without skipping a beat. Her skill in the kitchen never ceased to amaze him. She baked and grilled and sautéed like a head chef at a top-end restaurant and he suddenly had an idea.

"You know, Mom," he said and snatched a green bean from the plate. "You could come and work for me once the tavern opens. I'm still looking for a chef."

Colleen looked up from her task and smiled. "And have you bossing me around all day? I don't think so. Besides, I'm too busy to work. With the quilting club and volunteering at the hospital, I wouldn't find the time."

"It was worth a shot," he said playfully. "If you know of anyone worth interviewing, let me know."

Colleen grinned. "I hear chefs are a temperamental

lot. What about Abby Perkins? Didn't she study cooking in New Orleans for a year or so?"

"She works for O'Sullivan, remember?" he reminded his mother. Although he liked the idea of having a chef the caliber of Abby at the Loose Moose, he didn't like his chances of trying to poach her away from the O'Sullivans' five-star restaurant at the hotel. Abby had married Trudy's brother a year or so out of high school.

Brant had a couple of chefs lined up for interviews the following week and hoped to find someone from that. "So, how's the fund-raising coming along?"

"Slow," she acknowledged. "Although I did get a sizable donation from Liam O'Sullivan this week. Sometimes I think he's not as disagreeable as he likes to make out."

"Sure he is."

Colleen laughed. "Well, his brother is back in town for the week, so maybe that has something to do with his generous mood. Kieran always has been the peacemaker in that family."

Brant's shoulders twitched at the mention of the other man's name. "Yeah…maybe."

His mother looked at him oddly. "Everything all right?"

"Fine," he said, taking another green bean. "What time are the troops arriving?"

"Six o'clock," she replied. "You're the one who's here early."

"I had some time."

Her expression narrowed. "Something on your mind?"

Brant shrugged. "Not a thing."

"You're a worse liar that your brother," she said and smiled gently. "Grady will at least try and make a joke when he doesn't want to talk. So, have you seen much of Lucy?"

No...

And it was making him crazy. His brain was still scrambled by the idea of her being on a date with Kieran O'Sullivan. Texting her daily wasn't doing him any favors. Neither was calling her and saying he missed talking to her. He really needed to cut all contact to give himself a chance of getting her out of his thoughts. But he liked knowing what she was doing each day. He liked her sense of humor and how she didn't cut him any slack. He liked that they could share a joke or flirt or both and how it felt like the most normal thing he'd done since forever.

"Ah...not much," he said finally. "She's working over the holidays."

Colleen nodded. "Yes, I know. She's such a committed doctor. Everyone adores her at the hospital. But," his mother said, stirring the cranberry sauce simmering on the cooktop, "it's a shame she'll miss out on a real Thanksgiving dinner."

There was a gleam in his mother's eyes and Brant swallowed the tension suddenly closing his throat. "I'm sure they put something on at the hospital."

"Well, yes," Colleen said and nodded. "But it's not like a real home-cooked dinner with all the trimmings, is it?"

Brant didn't have a chance to respond because there was laughter and happy squeals from the front door that echoed down the hall. Within a minute his brother's family was bursting into the kitchen, with Grady behind them, his hands laden with bags. Marissa placed a Crock-Pot on the counter and moved around to help Colleen as the kids raced back and forth between Brant and Colleen, giving hugs and showing off sparkly nail glitter. Marissa's father, Rex, arrived minutes later and the kids quickly transferred their attention. There was lots of cheering and laughter and a kind of energetic happiness in the room that was palpable, and everyone looked incredibly content.

Everyone but him, he realized.

Grady slapped him on the back. "All set for Saturday?" his brother asked.

"Since it's your wedding," Brant reminded him, "shouldn't I be asking you that question?"

"I'm solid."

Marissa laughed. "Don't let him fool you. He's been a bag of nerves all week."

Grady groaned, swept her up into his arms and dropped a kiss to her forehead. "That is so not true. Don't believe a word she says."

As Brant watched their interaction, something heavy lodged in his chest. Although he was thrilled that Grady had found happiness, a part of him was almost envious. He'd never experienced envy before and couldn't understand it now. He certainly hadn't felt that way when Grady was married to Liz and had started a family. But things seemed different now. Back then Brant had been absorbed with his military career and hadn't had any time to think about relationships or having a family of his own. And, logically, he still didn't. However, in that moment, Brant didn't feel very logical. He felt...alone.

Lonely.

Which was plain stupid considering he was surrounded by the people he cared about most in the world. Still, the thought lingered as his mother shooed him and his brother and the kids to the living room while she finished preparing dinner. Marissa stayed to help in the kitchen and Brooke arrived about ten minutes later. It seemed strange not having Uncle Joe around on Thanksgiving, but he wasn't being released from hospital until the following day and the older man had insisted they all have their usual holiday celebration and not worry about him. Of course they all planned to visit him when he returned to the veterans home, but Brant missed Joe's corny jokes and craggy smiles.

By seven his mother called him in to the kitchen to carve the turkey and tossed an apron toward him when he entered.

"And slice it thinly," she instructed. "Not great chunks like your brother did last year."

Marissa laughed. "Don't let the master of the grill hear you say that, Colleen."

They all laughed and Grady popped his head around the doorway. "Too late."

Brant ignored the twitch in his gut. He should have been laughing along with the rest of his family, but he couldn't switch off the uneasiness running through his system. By the time the bird was carved and the table set, he felt so cloistered and uncomfortable he wanted to grab his keys and bail. Only his mother seemed to notice and once they were alone in the kitchen she asked what was wrong.

"I'm not sure," he replied honestly. All he knew was that he wanted to be somewhere else. He *needed* to be somewhere else.

Her expression narrowed. "Are you sleeping okay?"

Brant ignored the question and placed his hands on the counter. "Mom," he said quietly, "do you mind if I have dinner to go?"

"To go?" she echoed then frowned instantly. "You're leaving? But it's Thanksgiving."

Brant sighed. "I know and I'm sorry. But I think I need... I *feel* like I need to be somewhere else."

"Somewhere else?" Colleen's eyes widened and then her mouth slowly curved with a little smile—and a flash of understanding. "So, this dinner to go…is it for one or two?"

He swallowed hard, dismissed the heat in his face and spoke. "Two."

There was snow falling outside and enough cold air blasting through the hospital doors every time someone entered to remind the staff that winter was on its way. Thankfully it was quiet in the ER and even though they were on skeleton staff, by eight o'clock Lucy was ready for a mug of hot chocolate and fifteen minutes of watching a rerun of some mindless show on the television in the staff room.

She was just about to head that way when she was paged. Answering the call, she was told someone was waiting for her in the foyer. Thinking it was most likely Kayla coming to spread some holiday cheer, Lucy clipped the pager to her coat pocket and walked out of the ER and down to the general administration area. The place was deserted except for one of the maintenance staff pushing a janitor's trolley. She said hello as she passed.

And then she came to a standstill.

Brant stood beside the information desk, dressed in jeans, boots, a navy plaid shirt and sheepskin jacket. He had a Stetson on his head and carried a wicker basket. He turned as though sensing her arrival and immediately met her gaze.

"What are you doing here?" she asked, moving closer.

He held up the basket. "I thought… Thanksgiving dinner. For two."

"You brought me dinner?" Her legs suddenly stopped

working. "But shouldn't you be at your mom's? I know she was planning a big family—"

"I'm here," he said quietly. "With you."

Lucy almost burst into tears. It was the most utterly romantic thing anyone had ever done for her. Maybe even the kindest thing. She fought the burning sensation behind her eyes and tried to smile. "Oh, I...thanks."

His mouth twisted and when she stepped closer she noticed how a tiny pulse beat in his cheek. He looked wound up. On edge. Way out of his comfort zone.

And it made Lucy fall in love with him even more.

"Can you take a break?"

She nodded. "Sure. I'll just let the other doctor on duty know I'll be out of the ER for a while."

Lucy snatched up the closest telephone, put in a call to the nurse's station in the ER and said she'd be back in half an hour. When she turned her attention to Brant he was directly behind her and she quickly felt the heat emanating from his body. The edge of his jacket brushed her elbow and she looked up, caught in his gaze and without a hope of denying how pleased she was to see him.

"Where should we go?" he asked and looked around.

Lucy scanned their surroundings. The foyer was empty but still reasonably well-lit; there were a couple of vending machines against one wall and a small bench seat in between them.

"That looks like as good a spot as any," she said and headed to the other side of the room and sat.

He followed and sat beside her, placing the basket between them.

"It's quiet here tonight," he remarked, opening the basket.

Lucy peered inside and nodded. "It will probably get busier later tonight. Right now most people are eating dinner and celebrating. It's the MVAs or bouts of food poisoning that mostly keep the ER busy around the holidays."

He met her gaze. "Well, hopefully there's nothing poisonous in here."

She chuckled. "What are we having?"

"Turkey sandwiches on cranberry bread, sweet potato casserole and iced pumpkin cookies for dessert."

"Sounds delicious," she said and licked her bottom lip.

He pulled a few things from the basket and handed her a small stack of sandwiches wrapped in a gingham cloth. Lucy unwrapped the food and laid it on top of the basket while he bought sodas from the vending machine.

He sat, twisted the caps off the soda bottles and handed her one. "Happy Thanksgiving, Lucia," he said and clinked the bottle necks.

Lucy felt a surge of emotion rise up and fill her heart. "Happy Thanksgiving, Brant. And…thank you. I was feeling a little more alone than usual today."

"Me, too," he admitted and drank some soda.

Lucy passed him a sandwich. "But weren't you with your family tonight?"

Brant smiled warmly. "You can be in a room full of people and still feel alone."

He was right about that. "I feel that way, too. Sometimes when I'm at a party or out to dinner with friends, I get this strange feeling of disconnect. I especially felt that way after my mom died. For a long time I couldn't stand to be in crowds or around too many people at one time."

"It's a coping mechanism," he said softly. "But I understand what you're saying. You must think about your mom a lot around the holidays."

"I do," she said and sighed deeply. "She loved the holidays so much. And Christmas especially. She would decorate the house with a real tree and hang ornaments everywhere. And she and my dad would kiss under the mistletoe. There were always lots of gifts under the tree… Nothing extravagant, of course, since we didn't have a lot of money, just small things. Like, my dad would make her a footstool or she would bake his favorite cookies or knit him a pair of gloves that never really fit right. There was never much money but always a lot of love. And I miss that. One day I hope I'll have that again…if I get married and have children, that is."

"I'm sure you will," he said softly. "You're a marryable kind of girl."

Her cheeks burned. "I hope I am. I mean, I hope there's someone who will want to marry me one day. Someone who will want to have children with me and grow old with me."

"Someone like Kieran O'Sullivan you mean?"

He sounded jealous and it made her grin. "I'd never marry a doctor. They work terrible hours. Besides, there's no blip."

"'Blip'?" he repeated.

"Blip," she said again and took a bite of her sandwich. "You know, on the radar."

His gaze narrowed and she could see he was trying to work out what she meant. "I believe a blip is a malfunction or a problem."

"Well, thank you, Mr. Walking Dictionary," she said, drinking some soda. "But falling in love *can* be a little problematic, don't you think?"

"I don't really know," he muttered and ate some food.

"I thought smart guys like you knew everything."

He glanced at her. "Who says I'm that smart?"

Lucy chuckled. "Oh, you're smart all right. Your mom

told me you've been asked to teach French at the high school in the evenings, for the adult classes."

He looked faintly embarrassed. "Yeah… I'm still thinking about it."

"Why are you so uncomfortable with the fact that most days you're probably the smartest person in the room?"

He shrugged again. "I could say the same thing to you."

"Oh, no. I had to study long and hard to get good grades. And I was hopeless at French and Latin." Her eyes widened. "Maybe you could teach me?"

"Teach you French?" He stretched out his legs. "Teach you how to French kiss, maybe."

Lucy almost spat out her sandwich as humiliation raced up her neck. "Was I so terrible that I need lessons?"

"Not at all," he replied softly. "You have a perfectly lovely mouth, Lucia."

She turned hot all over and tried to eat the rest of her sandwich. "This is really good."

"My mom is a good cook."

"She is. I should get her to give me some tips." Lucy's smile broadened. "And, just so we're straight on this, I'm not interested in Kieran O'Sullivan in the least. And it wasn't really a date, just two former colleagues catching up over coffee."

"Glad to hear it. The O'Sullivans think way too much of themselves."

She laughed. "He told me that his brother is going to keep trying to buy you out until you buckle under the pressure."

The pulse in his cheek throbbed. "Did he?"

She nodded. "And I told him he'd be waiting a long time."

He glanced at her. "Why did you tell him that?"

Lucy nodded. "Because I think anyone who has been a soldier on the front line for twelve years knows more about pressure and resilience than someone who sits behind a desk at a fancy hotel and barks out orders to employees all day."

He smiled and drank some soda. "I can handle Liam O'Sullivan…but thanks, it's very sweet of you to defend me."

"That's what friends do for one another."

He didn't disagree.

When he stayed silent Lucy spoke again. "Do you miss it? Being a soldier, I mean."

He nodded. "Sometimes I miss the code…the knowledge that someone always has your back. I miss the camaraderie and the friendship. Do I miss holding a weapon, using a weapon and dodging enemy fire? Not at all."

Lucy shivered. "I can't begin to imagine what you went through."

"At times it was hell on earth over there. A different world. But it was my job, so I did it the best I could while I was there."

"Why did you leave?' she asked quietly. "You were a career soldier, Brant. You're smart and could have worked in many different areas of the military… Why did you leave so suddenly and come back here and buy a burned-out tavern? It doesn't make a whole lot of sense," she said gently. "Unless something terrible happened that made you leave."

A shutter came down over his gaze. "I can't talk about it."

"You mean you *won't* talk about it," she corrected. "There's a difference, believe me, I know. I spent years refusing to talk about my mom's death and how I was plagued by guilt because I couldn't help her. But when

I did open up I stopped feeling guilty and experienced an incredible sense of freedom. It's like I'd been living in a house of glass, too afraid of what would break if I made a sound. But then I was out of this glass house and I could wave my arms around without breaking anything."

He twisted in the chair, placed the sandwich and soda into the basket and faced her. "Getting inside my head isn't helpful, Lucy. I'm only interested in living in this moment."

"This moment?" she asked. "Right now?"

"Right now," he replied.

"Is that why you're here with me…to be in the moment?"

"I'm here because…" His words trailed as he reached out and touched her chin. "Because the idea of *not* seeing you tonight was unthinkable."

Lucy's lip trembled. "And are you going to kiss me?"

"Yes," he said and took the sandwich from her hands and dropped it in the basket. "If that's okay?"

Her heart pounded behind her ribs. "It's more than okay."

His mouth touched hers gently, coaxing a response, and Lucy gave herself up to his kiss without hesitation. She waited for his advance and then invited him closer, loving how he now felt so familiar, so warm and strong, and how his mouth seemed to fit perfectly to hers. It was a chaste kiss compared to the one they'd shared in his apartment, and since they were in the hospital foyer and anyone could have walked by, Lucy was content to simply feel his mouth gently roam over hers. His hand stayed on her chin, steadying her, and she kissed him back softly, loving the connection, loving the moment. Loving him.

"Lucy…" He suddenly spoke her name in a kind of

agonized whisper. "When your shift is over, come back to my apartment."

"Brant, I—"

"I want to make love to you," he said, trailing his mouth down her jaw. "You're all I can think about."

His words were like music to her ears. He wanted her. She wanted him. It should have been as simple as that. But it wasn't.

"I want that, too...so much."

He clearly heard the reluctance in her voice because he pulled back. "But?"

"But not until you talk to me. Really talk."

"Talk?"

She swallowed hard. "About your past."

He released her and was on his feet in two seconds flat. "Blackmail? Really?"

"Not blackmail," she said in defense. "If I'm going to *be* with someone, I'd like to know who he is."

He frowned. "You know me already."

"I know what you allow people to see," she said. "I know there are things about you that you keep deep inside and are afraid to let anyone see. Including me."

"There's not."

Lucy didn't back down. "I may be naive, Brant, but I'm not gullible. I want to be with you. But I want to get to know you, too. What you think, what you feel." She put a hand to her heart. "In here. And that includes knowing what you went through when you were—"

"How has you and I sleeping together got anything to do with what happened when I was in the military?" he asked, cutting her off.

"It just does."

"No," he said irritably. "This is simply some kind of female manipulation."

"It's not," she implored. "I'm not like that. And there's nothing simple about this."

"How's this for simple?" he shot back. "You want to know about my past because you want to *fix* me. Well, I'm not some kind of renovation project for you, Lucy. I don't need *fixing*. Save that for your patients."

He turned around and walked away, his straight back and tight limbs making his anger abundantly clear.

Lucy watched as he disappeared through the doors and a blast of cold air rushed through the foyer. Her heart sank miserably and she packed up the basket beside her. So much for a romantic dinner for two.

Lucy grabbed the basket, let out a long, unhappy breath, and walked back to the ER.

The Parker-Ellis wedding was being held at Grady's ranch. However, Lucy had stopped by Marissa's place, which was next door to Grady's, to help Brooke and Colleen get the kids ready for the ceremony.

She braided their hair and the three little girls looked so adorable in their lavender-and-ivory dresses. Lucy was a little misty-eyed when she saw how beautiful Marissa was in her lace wedding gown. The other woman positively glowed. Even Brooke, who was as tough as the most ornery cowboy, had a tiny tear in her eye. One day Lucy hoped to be a bride herself. *One day.* When she was over her foolish infatuation with Brant Parker.

She left with Colleen and the kids and took a seat at the back of the ceremony next to her friend Ash. The huge tent had been beautifully decorated, and heaters were discreetly in place to keep the area warm and comfortable for the guests. The white-covered chairs with lavender tulle bows had been laid out in aisle format and, even from the back, she had a great view of the altar. And of Brant.

He stood beside his brother as best man, dressed in a gray suit, white shirt and bolo tie. He looked so handsome. But tense. His jaw was tight and his back straight. And she couldn't take her eyes off him. He turned when the music started and their gazes clashed. In the past two days she'd gone from loving him to hating him, back to loving him and then hating him again.

As she met his gaze head-on and realized he wasn't looking at the bride as she walked down the aisle, as everyone else was, but that he was looking at *her*, Lucy's skin burned from head to toe.

Once Marissa reached the altar, everyone turned to the front. The service was moving and heartfelt, and Lucy wiped tears from her cheeks once the celebrant pronounced them as husband and wife. Grady's daughters were jumping around excitedly as he kissed his bride and the guests erupted into applause they walked back down the aisle. Brant followed with Brooke on his arm and he flipped her a look that was so blisteringly intense as he passed that Ash jabbed her in the ribs.

"Wow," her friend whispered. "What on earth is going on between you two?"

"Nothing," she replied and watched as he escorted Brooke from the tent. It was a gloriously cool but clear day and the wedding party headed out for the photographs to be taken. "It's a long story."

"I like long stories," Ash said as they moved from the seating area toward the other side of the tent where a dozen large round tables were set up with crisp linen and white dinnerware. It was elegant and understated and exactly what a wedding should be, she thought as they wove their way through the tables to find their seats.

But Lucy didn't tell the story. She wasn't in the mood for any kind of post mortem about her aborted relationship with Brant. Because she was pretty sure it was over. Well, whatever they had was over. He'd made no contact for two days and she hadn't garnered the courage to call him, either.

By the time the wedding party returned it was time to be seated for dinner and then the speeches began. If she'd imagined Brant would be nervous giving his speech, she was mistaken. He was charming and funny, sharing anecdotes about his brother that made the audience laugh, and at the end there was a toast and applause.

Then later the bride and groom hit the dance floor and swayed to an old Garth Brooks love song that was so sentimental Lucy wanted to burst into tears. Seeing Grady and Marissa together was seeing real love, first-hand. They'd somehow managed to find one another despite the obstacles they had endured and made a lifetime commitment. She envied them. And felt a little sad for herself.

She looked around and noticed Brant dancing with Brooke. More couples were on the dance floor. Since Ash had been chatting with Kieran for the past hour Lucy was now conspicuously alone at her table. A band of tension tightened around her forehead and she grimaced. The last thing she wanted was a headache.

She needed aspirin so she got up, left the tent and headed around to the back of the house. Lucy let herself through the gate and walked in through the back door. She could still hear the music and laughter coming from the tent, but the house was deserted. She'd been to the ranch several times and knew her way around, so she made her way down the hall toward the main bathroom.

She was just about to open the top vanity cupboard when she heard Brant's voice behind her.

"Everything okay, Lucy?"

She swiveled on her heels. "Fine," she said breathlessly. "I was hoping to find some aspirin."

He frowned. "Kitchen. Pantry. Top shelf." He grabbed her hand. "Come on, I'll get it for you."

Heat coursed over her skin at his touch and she longed for the strength to pull away. But he held her firm and led her down the hall and toward the huge kitchen. When he released her she crossed her arms and waited while he opened the pantry and took out a small container of painkillers. He filled a glass with water and placed both items on the counter.

"Thanks," she said and took the medication.

"Headache?"

"Almost," she replied. "Just getting it before it gets me. So, how's your uncle?"

He shrugged lightly. "He seemed okay when I saw him this morning."

"I checked on him yesterday afternoon and he seems to be recovering quite well."

"I hope so." He rested his hip on the counter. "He was miffed that he missed this today. So, are you enjoying the wedding?"

"Sure," she said, placing the glass down. "You?"

His mouth twisted. "Sure." He met her gaze. "That's why we're both in here."

"I was looking for aspirin," she said and shrugged. "What's your excuse?"

"I was looking for you."

Her heart skipped a beat and she was suddenly absorbed by him. "Why?"

"You know why."

His deep voice resonated around the room and even though she was desperate to leave, she couldn't. "I *don't* know. You're confusing me, Brant. Nothing has changed since the other night."

She was right to say it. Right to remind him.

His gaze darkened as he looked her over. "You look so beautiful in that dress."

The long-sleeved deep red soft jersey dress molded to her breasts and waist and flared out over her hips. She'd had it in her closet for two years with rarely an occasion to wear it. Sometimes she wondered if it was going to gather dust along with her old prom dress. "Thanks. You look pretty good yourself. It still doesn't change anything."

Silence stretched between them and Lucy was so caught up, so hypnotized by his dark blue eyes, she couldn't move. Couldn't think. She could only feel. He looked lost and alone, and she remembered how he'd accused her of wanting to *fix* him. And she did. She longed to make him whole again. Because she knew he would make her whole in return.

"Okay," he said finally, as though it was one of the hardest words he'd ever spoken. "I'll tell you. I don't know why I want to tell you. I don't know what it is about you that makes me want to talk about things that I try not to think about. But for the past two days all I've been able to think about is you when I should be doing a hundred other things."

Lucy's breath caught in her throat. She waited. The silence was agonizing. The hollow, haunted look in his eyes made her ache inside and when he spoke again her heart just about broke into pieces.

"Three men in my unit died," he said quietly, his voice little more than a husky whisper. "And they died because of me."

Chapter Ten

Brant knew there was no taking back the words once they were out. He'd kept them inside for over a year, never daring to say them out loud. It should have felt good. Cathartic. Instead, every morsel of guilt and regret he'd felt since that day came rushing back and almost knocked him over.

Three men—whose names would be forever etched into his blood and bones and his very soul—had died to save him.

"Tell me what happened."

Lucy's voice, soft and concerned. A voice that haunted his dreams and consumed his waking hours. When good sense told him to stay away, he was inexplicably drawn even more toward her. When everyone else made him clam up, Lucy Monero did the opposite. Talking to her was, somehow, salvation.

"They were protecting me," he said flatly.

Her gaze narrowed. "I don't understand."

"I can't tell you anything in detail. This is classified information, or mostly, anyway. I can tell you that I was part of a small team who infiltrated deeply and secretly. We were on a mission and deep in enemy territory. Intelligence is often gathered via listening devices, some high-tech, other times just basic radio-frequency stuff. We'd been listening for several hours and I had information," he explained and tapped a finger to his temple. "In here. I was a translator and because of the situation we were in there was no time to document all the intelligence."

She nodded. "And?"

"Radio contact was made. A pickup point was decided. And then the mission turned bad and we were suddenly surrounded by insurgents. There seemed no way out. We were bunkered down behind a ridge of rock and held that position for eight hours, randomly exchanging gunfire. We all knew it was highly unlikely we'd all survive. Decisions had to be made. And then three other soldiers in my unit lost their lives making sure I got back safely. For the greater good, you see," he said cynically. "Funny—but nothing felt good about any of it."

She took a step closer and grabbed his hands. "I'm so sorry."

"Yeah…me, too. Do you get it now? Do you understand why—?"

"I understand guilt," she said, cutting him off gently. "And I understand why you feel as you do. But they were doing their job, right? Just as you were? Which doesn't make it your fault."

"I know that…logically," he said and gripped her hands. "But there's this thing about logic—it has a way of camouflaging truth and grief and guilt. So it doesn't matter how often I tell myself I'm not to blame. It doesn't matter that the intelligence eventually got into the right hands. It doesn't matter that the insurgents were defeated because of that intelligence. Because all that matters is that three lives were lost…three families are mourning… three men are dead…and I'm not."

She sucked in a sharp breath. "Are you saying you wish you had been?"

Brant shook his head. "Of course not. I'm grateful that I survived. I'm glad my family isn't grieving and I'm certainly glad I'm here, in this room, with you."

She shuddered and he pulled her closer. The awareness between them amplified and Brant fought the urge he had to kiss her. He wasn't going to coerce her in any way. They had heat and attraction between them, and he knew it was powerful for them both, but if they went any further it had to be her decision.

"Brant…" Her voice trailed off and then she inhaled sharply.

"Yes, Lucia?"

"I want to be with you… I do. I want it more than anything. I want you to kiss me and make love to me. But I also want everything else that goes with that."

He knew that. He knew what she was looking for. Commitment. Security. A life. Probably marriage down the track. He'd never been one for commitment and didn't see that changing anytime soon.

"Then you decide what you want to do, Lucy," he said and released her gently. "You know who I am. I've told you what happened and even though you might not understand why, it closed off something inside of me. And because of that I won't make you promises I can't keep. But I want you…and that's all I can offer right now."

Brant turned and left the room. He wasn't going to deceive her.

He cared about her too much for that.

By the time Lucy left the Parker ranch it was past ten o'clock. She drove into town with a heavy heart.

I want you...

His words toyed around with her good sense. She should run a mile. She should forget all about him. Instead she pulled up outside the Loose Moose and stared at the big door. She looked up and saw there was a light beaming in the upstairs window. He *was* home. He'd left the wedding around the same time she had, without speaking to her. If she went inside now they would make love...no doubt about it. If she drove on, Lucy sensed she'd never hear from him again.

And that was...unbearable.

Thirty seconds later she was tapping on the door.

When he opened the door he was still dressed in his suit, minus the jacket. He looked so handsome and his dark hair gleamed in the lamplight overhead.

"Hi."

His eyes glittered brilliantly. "Hello."

"Can I come in?"

He stepped aside and she quickly walked over the threshold. The door closed and she turned. He stood excruciatingly still and Lucy's dangling courage disappeared.

"You look really beautiful tonight," he said softly.

"I think you said that already."

He shrugged. "I don't think you really know how beautiful you are...inside and out."

Heat spotted her cheeks as she stripped off her coat

and placed it on a workbench. "I'm not beautiful…not really."

"You are to me," he said and half smiled. "You're also argumentative and a little stubborn and have a bad temper. But you do look really great in that dress." He took a few steps toward her. "I should have danced with you tonight. I wanted to."

Lucy swallowed hard and then grinned. "It was like prom all over again. No date. No dancing."

Brant stared at her, his gaze unwavering. He came closer and grabbed her hand, linking their fingers in a way that felt so intimate, Lucy's entire body grew hotter with each passing second.

"Come with me," he said and led her across the room.

She thought they were going upstairs, to his bedroom, to his bed, and her nerves had her legs shaking. But he walked past the stairwell and toward the back of the tavern. It had once been a pool room but was now filled with several tables and a stage, as well as two new gaming tables. There was a dance floor and jukebox in one corner. Brant didn't release her as he headed for the jukebox and flicked a few switches before it roared into life. He took a moment to choose a song and then turned her toward the dance floor.

Lucy dropped her bag onto one of the tables and went with him into the center of the floor as the music began. Kenny Chesney's voice suddenly filled the room and Lucy curved herself into Brant's embrace. They fit together, she thought as his right arm came around her waist and his other hand cupped her nape. And then they danced. Slowly, closely, as though they'd done it a hundred times before. His hand was warm against her neck and he rubbed her skin softly with his fingertips.

Lucy gripped his shoulders, felt the muscles harden

beneath her palms and moved closer. There was nothing but clothing between them and she could feel the heat of his body connect with hers.

And then he kissed her, deeply, passionately, as if he couldn't get enough of the taste of her mouth.

Lucy kissed him back and heard him groan as his fingers tangled in her hair. She held on to his shoulders and lost herself in his kiss.

When the song ended Lucy pulled back, breathless, knees trembling.

"Take me upstairs," she said softly.

"Are you sure?"

Lucy nodded. Whatever happened, she wanted this part of him. She wanted his touch and his possession and body next to hers. In that moment, nothing else mattered.

It took about a minute to walk upstairs and into his bedroom. The big bed was covered in a functional blue quilt and, other than two narrow side tables, a small chair and a wardrobe, the room was clearly just a place to sleep. He pulled the curtains together, flicked on the bedside lamp and turned off the overhead light. Then he unclipped his watch, placing it on one of the side tables.

Lucy was so nervous she was sure he could hear her knees knocking together. But she didn't move. She only watched him, mesmerized, well aware that he'd certainly done it all before, many times and with many other women. But she didn't want to think about that.

He tugged at his tie, dropped it on the chair and then began to slowly unbutton his shirt.

She absorbed him with her gaze and her palms itched with the urge to rush forward and run her hands over his chest. He was broad and muscular and so effortlessly masculine. Once the shirt disappeared, his hands rested on his belt and she gulped. Of course she'd seen plenty of naked men in her line of work. But this was different. This was Brant. She was going to touch him. Kiss him. Make love with him. And he would do the same with her. She was suddenly filled with a mixture of fear and wonderment.

"Everything all right, Lucy?" Brant asked as he kicked off his shoes.

She swallowed hard. "Yes…everything's fine."

He pulled the belt through the loops and dropped it on the floor. "*Lucia*…come here." She walked across the room and he grasped her hand. "You're shaking. Are you nervous?"

She nodded. "A little."

"Don't be," he said as gently swiveled her around. "We'll just take it slow."

His fingers found the tab of her zipper and he slowly eased it down. His mouth brushed across her shoulder and she moaned, overwhelmed by the sheer longing she felt for his touch. The gown slipped off her shoulders and fell to her feet. She stepped out of it and inhaled as she turned to face him.

"You're so…" He raked his gaze over her, taking in the red-lace bra and matching thong she'd bought on a whim months earlier and was suddenly very glad she'd teamed with the red dress.

Normally, Lucy was self-conscious of her curves. She never dressed overtly sexy and her underwear was usually the sensible nondescript kind. But the desire in his eyes was hot and real and made her skin burn.

She flipped off her heels and stood in front of him. "I can't believe we're here."

"Believe it," he said and tugged her closer. "I've thought of little else for weeks."

His words enflamed her and Lucy abandoned her

nerves and accepted his kiss. They were on the bed seconds later and she was breathless as his hands caressed her from knee to rib cage. His kissed her throat, her shoulders and the curve of her breasts. Her entire body was on fire and her hands clamored to touch him. She felt his heart beat madly in his chest, twirled her fingers on the trail of hair on his belly and heard him suck in a sharp, agonized breath. He was as weak for her touch as she was for his and the knowledge gave her courage. She didn't feel out of her depth. Touching him felt like the most natural thing in the world.

He dispensed with her bra quickly and touched her breasts with his hands and then his mouth. It was delicious, exquisite torture, and she threw her head back as his tongue toyed with one nipple and then the other. He pushed her thong down her hips and for the next half hour he gave but didn't take.

He kissed her, caressed and stroked her skin. He touched her with his hands, his fingertips and his mouth to the point that every inch of body was übersensitive to his touch. She clung to him. She whispered words she'd never imagined she would utter to another soul and experienced such narcotic pleasure than she was quickly a quivering mass of need.

He knew, somehow, that the sensitive skin behind her knee was an erogenous zone and his touch there made her head spin. He knew that trailing his tongue along the underside of her breast would drive her wild. And, finally, when he touched her intimately, she was so aroused she almost bucked off the bed begging for him to give her the release she suddenly craved. As inexperienced as she was, Lucy somehow knew what she wanted.

"Please," she begged and met his mouth hungrily.

"Not yet," he said with a raspy breath as he caressed

her gently. "We have all the time in the world. There's no need to hurry, Lucia."

There was every need. She wanted to feel him above her, around her, inside her.

But he knew what he was doing. There was a gentle rhythm in his magical touch as he continued to stroke her. And then she was gone, caught up in a vortex of pleasure so intense she thought she might pass out. She moaned and said his name, felt her entire body shudder as she came back down to earth. It was beautiful, frightening, overwhelming…and she knew there was more.

When her hands stopped shaking, she fumbled with the button and zipper on his trousers. She heard laughter rumble in his chest at her eagerness and he quickly took over the task. In a second he was naked and above her, chest to breast, his arousal undeniable.

He reached across the bed and grabbed something from the bedside table. When she realized he had a condom in his hand, she blushed wildly.

"Oh… I didn't think about that," she said suddenly self-conscious.

He chuckled. "Now, Doctor, I don't have to tell you how babies are made, do I?"

Lucy's heart did a backflip at the very idea of having his baby. It was one of the things she wanted most in the world.

"Ah…no. Just caught up in the moment, I guess."

He smiled and kissed her. A deep, drugging kiss that had possession stamped all over it. And she didn't mind one bit. She wanted to be his. She longed for it. Right then and all night long. And forever.

He moved over her and Lucy ran her hands eagerly down his back, urging him closer. She closed her eyes and waited. She knew there would be pain, knew her inexperienced body would resist at first. But she wanted him so much, needed him so much, any fear quickly disappeared. He hovered over her, kissing her neck, her jaw, her mouth, and Lucy welcomed him.

He stilled, rested his weights on his arms and stared down into her face. "Everything all right?"

She nodded. "Of course."

"You're tense," he said and kissed her again. "Relax."

She tried and when he finally was inside her she felt a sharp, stinging pain that made her wince.

He stilled again, more pronounced this time, and his gaze sharpened. "Lucy?" There was query and uncertainty in his voice. And he still didn't move. "What…are you…have you never—?"

"Brant." She said his name urgently, cutting off his words. She held on to his shoulders when she felt him withdraw. "No…don't…please…stay with me."

He knew.

And for a moment she thought she'd lost him.

His gaze bore into hers, absorbing her, asking the question and getting the answer he clearly hadn't expected.

"Lucy…" He said her name again, as if he was torn, unsure.

She gripped him hard and pulled him closer. "Don't leave me."

He gaze wavered and it seemed to take an eternity for him to relax. But he did, finally. He stayed, and that was all she cared about. She felt complete for the first time in her life. Lucy wrapped her arms around him and urged him toward her intimately. He moved against her, kissing her mouth with a mixture of passion and disbelief. And she drew strength from his mixed emotions. She kissed him back. She touched him. She told him what she wanted.

She matched him. They continued that way, moving together, creating a rhythm that was mind-blowing. And when release came again it got them both. Lucy held on as he shuddered above her, loving him with all her heart as she got lost in a world of pleasure so gloriously intense she could only say his name on a sigh.

When it was over, he moved and rolled onto his back. Lucy stayed where she was, breathless and still mindless from the tiny aftershocks of sensation pulsing over her skin. After a few minutes, Brant got up and disappeared into the bathroom. When he returned Lucy still lay on the bed, a sheet half draped over her hips.

He sat on the end of the bed and his skin dappled golden in the lamplight. Lucy reached out to touch him and he flinched. Then he looked at her. There was no mistaking it. He was angry.

"Brant, I—"

"That was your first time?" he asked quietly.

She nodded. "Yes, but—"

"Goddamn it, Lucy! You should have told me."

"It doesn't—"

"Whatever you're going to say," he said, cutting her off as he got to his feet and pulled on a pair of jeans that were on the chair. "Just save it. Because if you think it doesn't matter, you're wrong. It matters, Lucy. It matters so damn much."

He walked out of the room and she heard his feet thump on every stair. Once he was downstairs she stretched and sighed. Her body was still humming, still remembering every touch. She'd imagined making love with Brant countless times and being with him had exceeded anything she'd imagined. She had never expected to feel such a deep, fulfilling connection to another person. If she'd ever doubted that she was in love with him, those doubts were now well and truly gone.

Lucy sat up and swung her knees over the edge of the bed. He was angry and, in typical Brant fashion, when he was mad he closed down. And since Lucy preferred to face an issue head-on, she knew they had to talk.

She got up, grabbed the shirt he'd discarded and slipped her arms into the sleeves. It felt warm against her skin and the scent of his cologne clung to the fabric. She made a bathroom stop. She was still a little tender, but he'd been so gentle with her she knew it would pass quickly. Then she took a deep breath and headed downstairs.

Brant rarely drank hard liquor anymore. But he downed a second belt of bourbon and let the heat slide down his throat.

He was wound up. He couldn't sit still. He paced the rooms downstairs and tried to work out what he was feeling. Guilt. Confusion. Disbelief.

I should have known.

The words kept chanting in his head.

There had always been something innocent about Lucy Monero. She was an intriguing mix of confidence and coyness. Her kisses were sweet and making love to her had been like nothing he'd felt before. Her touch hadn't been tentative, but exploring, inquisitive…like she was experiencing something new and exciting. Of course, now he knew why.

A virgin.

He could barely believe it. Okay, so she *was* kind of wholesome. But she was also twenty-seven. And a successful doctor who'd gone to college and medical school and had lived a full life. Never in his wildest dreams would he have imagined she would be untouched.

"Brant?"

He looked up. She stood silhouetted in the doorway. She was wearing his shirt and with the light behind he could make out every curve and dip of her naked body beneath. His libido spiked instantly. Her hair was mussed and loose around her shoulders and he couldn't help but remember how he'd fisted a handful of her beautiful locks and kissed her throat and neck and breasts. He'd wanted her as he'd never wanted anyone before. Damn…he still wanted her. Everything about her was pure invitation… her skin, her lips, her curves. She was so lovely. So sweet. And sexy, too, even though he was pretty sure she didn't know it.

Brant shook off his thoughts and sat on the edge of one of the tables. He knew they needed to talk. But first he had to ensure she was all right. "Are you okay?"

"I'm fine." She stepped closer and the light behind turned the shirt translucent. "Are *you* okay?"

He shook his head. "We need to talk about this, Lucy."

She bit her bottom lip. "I know you're angry and—"

"I'm not angry," he said. "I'm a little confused. Frankly, I don't understand why you didn't tell me."

She shrugged. "Well, it's not the kind of thing that generally comes up in conversation."

"You're twenty-seven years old," he said flatly. "And up until half an hour ago, you were a virgin. I think that warrants some kind of conversation, don't you?"

She took a few more steps. "Okay… I probably should have said something."

"Probably?"

"All right," she said on a sharp breath. "I just didn't want to make a big deal out of it."

"It *is* a big deal, Lucy," he said quietly. "And if you've waited this long, you know that."

She sat on a chair by one of the pool tables. "I just wanted to be with you tonight."

Brant pushed himself off the table and dragged a chair beside her. "I wanted to be with you, too," he said as he sat. "But it was your first time, Lucy...and that should mean something."

"It did," she whispered. "At least, it did to me."

Guilt hit him squarely between the shoulder blades. "Look, of course it was...great. You're beautiful and sexy...and it's obvious I'm attracted to you."

She raised her hands. "But that's all it is, right?"

"I haven't deliberately misled you, Lucy," he said soberly. "I try not to mislead anyone."

"You're not serious?"

"What does that mean?"

"It means," she said quietly, "that for the past couple of weeks you've been courting me and haven't even realized it."

His back stiffened. "That's not true. I only—"

"Pizza and a football game?" she reminded him. "Comforting me when I had a bad day at work? An impromptu Thanksgiving dinner? Text messages? Phone calls saying how much you missed me? Really...what did you think you were doing?"

He stilled. Was she right? Was he so blind? He liked her...a lot. But the idea of it being more than that made his head ache.

"I guess... I guess I *wasn't* thinking," he admitted. He took one of her hands in his. "Did I hurt you? The first time can be—"

"You didn't hurt me," she said and pulled her hand away. "And you're working yourself up about it for some

reason of your own. I made a decision tonight, Brant…
and I made that decision because I *am* twenty-seven years
old and know exactly what I want." She got to her feet.
"Yes, I have not had a lover before tonight. And maybe
I didn't tell you that exactly, but I've told you plenty
about my life and the kind of person I am. I was a geek
in high school, *remember*?" she said with emphasis. "I
was a bookworm. I didn't have boyfriends. I didn't have
a date for the prom. And I told you I didn't date in college. What did you think that meant? That I was amusing myself with one-night stands instead?"

"Of course not," he said quickly. "I only—"

"I didn't deliberately set out to be a virgin at twenty-
seven. And even if I did, I'm sure that doesn't quite make
me a candidate for *Guinness World Records*."

"That's not what I meant to—"

"I was grieving my mom," she said hotly. "I was still
coming to terms with the accident. And the truth is, I was
so *messed up*, I didn't want to get involved with anyone.
And then when my roommate was attacked it shut something off inside me and all I wanted to do was become
a good doctor. That's all I concentrated on. That's all I
wanted. Not a date. Not a boyfriend. Not sex."

She was breathing so hard her chest rose up and down
and Brant was instantly aroused. She walked away, hands
on hips, clearly irritated. He stood and followed her
around the pool table.

"But you want that now?" he asked. "A boyfriend?
Sex?"

She stopped walking and turned, glaring at him.
"You'd make a rotten boyfriend."

He couldn't help grinning. Even when she was mad-
der than hell she was beautiful.

"You're right about that."

She looked at his chest and then her gaze rose to meet his eyes. "So, I should probably leave."

"If that's what you want."

She scowled and still looked beautiful. "You'd let me go so easily?"

"I never said it would be easy."

She seemed to sway closer. "None of this is easy, is it? Feeling. Wanting. Maybe…" she said as a hand came up and touched his chest. "Maybe it's not meant to be easy. Maybe the struggle is what makes it worthwhile."

"Maybe," he agreed and placed his hand over hers.

"So," she said softly. "What do we do now?"

Brant clasped his hands to her hips and lifted her onto the edge of the pool table. "Now," he said as he settled between her thighs and wound his arms around her, "I guess we do this."

She sighed, all resistance disappearing. "For how long?"

"For now. For as long as it lasts," he said and kissed her.

He knew that Lucy was thinking forever.

And that was something Brant didn't believe in.

Chapter Eleven

Lucy didn't want to think…or imagine…that six days into their *thing* she actually had a boyfriend. But Friday night, after they'd spent two hours in bed together and were now in her kitchen, eating enchiladas and drinking coffee, she figured she could call it a *relationship*. Of sorts.

When they were together Brant was attentive and charming and certainly seemed unable to get enough of her. They made love a lot. He arrived at her place every afternoon at five thirty and was always gone by midnight. They ate dinner, watched television, talked about mundane things and regularly had hot, uninhibited sex that turned her sensible brain to mush. But he never slept over and always called her the following morning to see how she was.

She was on day shift at the hospital and got to sleep in until eight every morning to combat the fatigue she felt, which meant a mad rush getting showered and dressed and to work on time. But she didn't care. She was wrapped in a lovely kind of bubble that had everything to do with the fact that she was crazy in love with Brant and adored every moment they spent together.

"I have the weekend off," she said and sipped her coffee.

Brant looked at her over the mug in his hands. "I know."

She half smiled. "Did you want to do something tomorrow? Or Sunday?"

"I have the kitchen going in at the tavern this weekend," he said quietly. "And the new chef is arriving tomorrow, so I'll be tied up both days. Plus, I want to try and see Uncle Joe. I'll let you know, okay?"

"Oh…sure."

He drank his coffee and then stood, collecting their plates. "There's a game on if you're interested?"

Football? She was learning to like the game and if it meant cuddling up on the couch with Brant, all the better. She nodded. "I was thinking, if you're coming over tomorrow why don't you stay the night and we could go into town Sunday morning for breakfast?"

He stilled and stared at her. "We'll see."

Code for "no chance." Right. Lucy wondered if he was worried about being seen with her. It was a small town and people talked. Although, since his truck had been parked outside her house every night for close to a week, she figured they had probably been outed already. Of course, Kayla had called every day, and Brooke and Ash, who were a little more discreet, had been texting her off and on for two days. Colleen had been noticeably absent and Lucy figured the woman was giving them space.

"If you don't want to spend the night, just say so."

His gaze sharpened. "That's not what I said."

She shrugged. "Actions speak louder than words."

She immediately saw the gleam in his eyes. "They certainly do."

Lucy smiled, caught her bottom lip between her teeth and felt a familiar surge of desire pulse through her body. "Prove it," she said and got up and raced into the living room, well aware he would be ten paces behind her.

By the time he caught up she was turned on and ready for him. He hauled her into his arms and kissed her hotly. She kissed him back and wrapped her arms around his waist. They made it to the sofa in three seconds flat and began stripping clothes off in their usual hurry. She straddled him and linked her arms around his neck.

"Contraception," he said raggedly.

Lucy dug into the pocket of her robe, extracted a foil packet and then rattled it between her fingertips. "Voilà!"

He smiled against her mouth and kissed her hotly. "Sweetheart, you never cease to amaze me."

Lucy's heart surged. It was the first endearment he'd ever called her and she liked it more than she'd imagined. They made love quickly, passionately, as if they couldn't get enough of one another. It was hot and erotic and mind-blowing. Afterward, Brant grabbed the blanket from the back of the sofa and wrapped it around her shoulders.

"It's cold in here. I've let the fire burn down too low," he said and hooked a thumb in the direction of the fireplace. "Remind me to stock up your firewood next week."

His consideration warmed her heart. He was caring and kind and she loved him. And had almost told him so a dozen times in the past week. But she always held back. He wasn't ready for any kind of declaration.

Lucy nuzzled his neck and pressed herself against his chest. "Thank you."

They watched the football game, fooled around a little on the sofa and by eleven-thirty he bailed. She gave him a lingering kiss in the doorway and watched through the front window as he drove away. As usual, once he'd gone, Lucy experienced a kind of aching loneliness. She knew it was foolish. Knew that whatever she was feeling, Brant was certainly not on the same page. He liked her. He wanted her. But that was all he was good for. She'd tried getting him to talk more about what had happened in Afghanistan, but he would shut her down every time she broached the subject. She knew he'd been to see Dr. Allenby again, but had no idea if he was making any progress or if he'd made another appointment. Despite how close they'd become, there was a restless kind of energy around him that was impossible to ignore. It had her on edge...and waiting for the inevitable fallout.

Strangely, he didn't text her Saturday morning and by ten o'clock she gave in and sent him a message. He replied about half an hour later, saying he was tied up and would speak to her later. It left her with a heavy, uneasy feeling in her heart.

Kayla and Brooke dropped in to see her at lunchtime, carrying a pizza and a six pack of pear cider.

"It's about time you came up for air," Kayla said with a grin as they all headed for the kitchen. "By the flushed expression, I take it everything is going well?"

Lucy shrugged. She wasn't sure she wanted to have a post mortem about her relationship with Brant. It felt... disloyal. That was stupid, of course, because Kayla and Brooke were her closest friends and she could always rely on their support and understanding. But she'd essentially always been a private person, and being with Brant on the most intimate level was not something she wanted to discuss or dissect.

"Yeah…fine," she said and grabbed plates from the cupboard. "How are you both?"

Brooke, certainly the most diplomatic of the pair, gave her arm a gentle squeeze when they all sat. "We're worried about you, that's all."

"I'm fine," she assured them. "I promise."

Kayla's perfectly beautiful face was marred with a frown. "We don't quite believe you. And we're here if you need to talk."

She knew that. But, strangely, the only person she wanted to confide in was Brant. She liked the way he listened. She liked the way he stroked her hair when she'd talked about her mom and the accident and how helpless she'd felt. She liked how there was no judgment, no condescending advice…only his deep voice assuring her the pain and hurt would eventually pass. The irony was, it was exactly what she wanted to say to him. They were both broken in their own way. Sure, she'd moved on and seen a therapist and didn't have bad dreams anymore, but a part of her would always grieve for the years she'd lost with her parents. And Brant understood that grief better than anyone ever had.

Sometimes when he'd dozed a little after they'd made love, she'd witnessed his restlessness. He had bad dreams, she was sure of it. She hadn't said anything to him about it, but knew he was certainly reliving the horror of what he'd seen in the war. And it broke her heart that she couldn't help him through his pain.

She looked at her friends and felt their sympathetic stares through to her bones.

"I'm fine, like I said. It's early days, that's all."

"Good," Kayla said and sighed heavily. "We just weren't sure if you knew about the woman he was with this morning."

Her back stiffened. "What woman?"

"I saw him at the coffee place next door to O'Sullivan's. They were talking. It looked serious."

He was with another woman. And it looked serious.

Lucy wondered if there had ever been a bigger fool than her. But she pasted on a smile and shrugged. "I'm sure there's a perfectly reasonable explanation."

Her friends didn't look too convinced. Heat burned the backs of her eyes and tears threatened to spill.

"I'm in love with Brant," she said honestly.

Brooke patted her arm again. "Yeah, we know that."

"I've never been in love before," she admitted, aware her friends knew it already.

Brooke offered a gentle smile. "Does he love you back?"

Lucy shook her head, suddenly hurting all over. "I don't think he believes he's capable of loving anyone."

And knowing he believed he was that hollow inside made her heart ache.

Saturday lunch at his mother's wasn't generally a chore, but Brant was in no mood to be put under the microscope by his parent or his brother. He planned to stop in for an hour before he got back to the tavern to tackle the painting. He'd had half the kitchen installed at the tavern that morning and the contractors were coming back the following day to finish the job. He'd also interviewed the new chef and discovered the thirtysomething single mom had excellent credentials and stellar references. She also had nowhere to live, since she was relocating from Montana with her young son, and Brant had assured her he would help her find suitable accommodation. His apartment above the tavern would do the job, and since he hadn't planned on making it his permanent residence, he needed to think about getting a real home of his own. A house, with a yard and a porch and a maybe a swing set out back.

As soon as he had the thought, Brant shook himself. He had no place in his life for yards and swing sets. That was the kind of life his brother had. Not him.

Only…he kept thinking about it. About yards and swing sets and Lucy Monero.

"Everything okay?"

His brother's voice jerked him into the present. Grady and Marissa had forgone a honeymoon and instead planned to head to Nevada with her father, Rex, after Christmas to meet her newly discovered extended family. Brant hadn't been home for the holidays in six years and suspected this one was going to be filled with the usual family gatherings and gift-giving.

"Fine," he said and met his brother's gaze for a moment. They were in the living room, watching a game on television. "How's married life?"

"Amazing." Grady grinned. "You should try it for yourself."

He wasn't about to admit that he'd thought about it many times over the past week. About as often as he'd thought about *ending* his relationship with Lucy. Damn… he didn't want to think of it in terms of being a *relationship*, but how could he not? She'd gifted him the most intimate part of herself and the responsibility of that gift was wreaking havoc with his integrity and moral compass. Lucy wasn't a casual kind of woman. Lucy Monero was the *marrying* kind. If he kept seeing her that's where they'd end up. He was sure of it. And he couldn't. He wouldn't. Having sex with her was addling his brain. He felt weak. Out of control.

He stared at the television and spoke. "I've done something really stupid."

Grady glanced sideways. "And what's that?"

"Lucy."

His brother chuckled softly. "Yeah, I heard. Mom's over the moon. But you know it might just turn out to be the smartest thing you've ever done."

He shook his head. "I can't give her what she wants."

"What's that?"

"Everything," he replied.

"And why do you think you can't give it to her?" Grady asked, more serious.

He exhaled heavily. "Because I'm not made that way. I don't know…maybe I was once. But…"

"The war changed you?" Grady said. "No surprise there. It would change anyone."

Brant nodded. "I've been talking to Dr. Allenby…you know, at the veterans home."

"How's it going?"

He shrugged. "He knows his stuff. He's easy to talk to and doesn't push too hard. But I've talked to army shrinks before and it hasn't made any difference. What's in here—" he put a finger to his temple "—is there forever. I can't escape it. I can't deny it. I'm just trying to camouflage it so I can lead a normal sort of life."

"And Lucy?" Grady prompted.

"She rips through that camouflage without even knowing it." He ran a frustrated hand through his hair. "Or maybe she does. I don't know. All I do know is that when I'm around her I feel… I feel so damned…"

"Vulnerable?" his brother said and sighed. "I hate to break this to you, but that's got nothing to do with you being changed somehow by what you experienced in the war."

Brant frowned. "Then what is it?"

"It's because you're in love with her," Grady said frankly.

Every part of him stilled and he quickly dismissed his brother's words. "I'm not. I just feel...responsible."

Grady's eyes widened. "For what? She's not pregnant is she?"

Brant scowled quickly, looking around to make sure his mother or sister-in-law weren't nearby and spoke quietly. "No. But she..." His words trailed off. He wasn't about to betray Lucy's confidence, as much as he felt like spilling his woes to his brother. "It's private and not up for discussion. But let's just say that she...surprised me."

His brother shook his head. "You can be cryptic if you have to, but the truth is you've always had blinders on when it came to Lucy Monero. She was the girl next door, remember? The girl who used to look at you with puppy-dog eyes and who you never noticed because you were too busy trying to score with Trudy What's-Her-Name. Now you've come to come to your senses and finally noticed her and it turns out she still has a thing for you." Grady's eyes gleamed. "Sounds like love to me."

Brant shook his head. "You can make fun all you like, but I have my reasons for feeling responsible for hurting her. You're right, she waited for me," he said, flinching inwardly, wondering what Grady would think if he knew the true meaning of the words. "She chose me and I have no idea why. All week I've been trying to work out ways to end it. But then she looks at me, or touches me, and I'm done for. I feel as though I'm in a corner and there's no way out. And the thing is," he admitted wearily, "part of me doesn't want a way out."

Grady smiled and slapped him on the shoulder. "Well, I guess there's only one thing you can do."

"What's that?"

"You should do the smart thing and marry her."

When Lucy didn't hear from Brant again on Saturday, or on Sunday morning, she began imagining a dozen different scenarios. Maybe his coffee date had turned into something else. Something more. But by midday she'd worked herself up and was so mad with him she knew if she stayed home she'd stew all day and ruin what was left of her weekend.

She drove to Kayla's in the afternoon and ended up staying for dinner. Kayla was all commiseration and support and by the time they'd consumed three cups of coffee and a packet of Oreos, Lucy had convinced herself that Brant was seeing someone else and his silence meant he was breaking things off between them. She left at eight o'clock and drove down the street, pulling over beneath a streetlight. She grabbed her cell and sent him a text.

I need to see you.

A couple of minutes later she got a reply.

I'm kinda busy right now. But I'll call you later.

Later? Right. Her rage turned to hurt and then her hurt morphed back into rage. Well, if he was seeing someone else she certainly wanted to know about it. She might be foolishly naive…but she wasn't going to be a naive fool!

I'll be there in five minutes.

She didn't wait for a response and drove back into town. Six minutes later she pulled up outside the tavern.

Lucy didn't bother with her coat, instead she grabbed her tote, got out of the car, marched up to the door and banged so hard her knuckles hurt. The big door swung back and he stood in the doorway, dressed in old jeans that rode low on his hips, a long-sleeved, pale gray Henley T-shirt and sneakers.

He was also covered in paint from head to toe.

"What are you doing?" she asked.

"Painting myself," he said, grabbing her arm and hauling her across the threshold. "More the point, what are you doing out this late and without a coat? Are you trying to catch pneumonia?"

She shivered as the cold from the air outside seeped through her thin clothing. "My coat is in the car."

"There's a fire going in the back room," he said. "Warm yourself up while I grab you a sweater."

Lucy walked to the rear of the tavern and stood by the big fireplace. She noticed a couple of ladders with a timber plank between them and a tin of paint on its side and a pool of paint on the floor. He returned a couple of minutes later with a blue zip-up sweater. She took it and placed her arms through the sleeves.

"Um, it looks like you had a little accident?" She pointed to the paint spill.

"Someone texted me," he replied pointedly. "I was on the ladder with a bucket of paint in one hand and brush in another. I went for my phone, it slipped out of my hand and almost landed in the paint. I figured a tin of spilled paint was the lesser of two evils."

Lucy bit back a grin. He still had some explaining to do. "Are you seeing someone else?"

"What?" he shot back as he grabbed a towel from the bench top and wiped at some of the paint on his face and neck.

Lucy stepped forward and took the towel from him. "Someone else," she said again as she removed a smear of paint from his jaw. "As in, the woman you had coffee with yesterday."

He sighed, clearly exasperated. "Faith O'Halloran has just moved to Cedar River from Montana with her young son," he explained. "She's the new chef. The coffee *date* was an interview."

Lucy fought the sudden embarrassment clinging to her skin. Damn Kayla and her overly suspicious mind. "Oh… I see."

He took the towel back. "So, is the interrogation over?"

She shrugged lightly. "Mostly. You've got paint in your hair." She grabbed the towel again and started on the paint smear on his throat. "And everywhere else, by the look of things. Why are you working so late anyhow?"

"I've got some of the interior fit-out next week," he said, standing perfectly still. "I told you I was working this weekend."

She avoided his gaze and kept wiping his throat. "You said you were busy."

"Yes, busy…working." He shook his head. "The kitchen went in this weekend, remember?" He took the towel and tossed it aside. "I'm going to clean up this mess, take a shower and then we're going to talk. Or—" He grabbed her around the waist, careful not to get paint on her clothes, and looked down into her upturned face. "You could take a shower with me and we could skip the talking for an hour or two."

Lucy liked the sound of that idea.

An hour later they were lying side by side on his bed, spent and breathing hard.

"Incidentally," Brant said as he entwined their fingers. "I'm trying not to take offense at the fact you thought I was seeing someone else. I'm many things, Lucia, but unfaithful is not one of them."

Lucy grimaced. "I'm sorry. Put it down to inexperience. I'm not very knowledgeable when it comes to this kind of…" She waggled the fingers on her other hand. "Thing."

"You're not alone," he said quietly. "I haven't exactly embraced commitment for the past decade."

She grinned. "Your virgin heart. My virgin body. That's quite a combination."

He laughed softly and his grip tightened. "Lucy… I'd like to know something."

"Sure. What?"

"I don't quite know how to put this without sounding incredibly egotistical…but why did you really wait so long to have a physical relationship with someone? Did it have anything to do with me? Or to some old infatuation you may have had from when we were kids?"

Lucy shrugged lightly. "Not consciously. I mean, sure… I did have a little crush on you in high school. But I was so quiet and ridiculously self-conscious in high school. And once I got to college, sex seemed like some kind of tradable commodity. The bed hopping wasn't something I wanted for myself. And then when my roommate was attacked…it just seemed like one complication I didn't need."

"But once you were working and out of college, surely there were men interested in you?"

"Not so much," she admitted. "I think that when a person puts a wall up for long enough, people stop trying to find a way over the top. And I had a wall that was ten feet high."

"What about Kieran O'Sullivan?" he asked.

"A friend," she replied. "No blip, remember?"

"So…there was no one else you were interested in being with? Ever?"

Heat crawled over her skin. How did she respond without sounding like an immature, love-struck fool? "I guess I didn't want to kiss a whole lot of frogs before I discovered princes didn't really exist."

Silence enveloped the dimly lit room for a moment. Lucy could hear him breathing and watched the steady rise and fall of his chest. After a moment he spoke again.

"Are you saying you hadn't…" His tone took on a kind of wary disbelief. "That you hadn't—"

"That I hadn't really kissed anyone before you?" she finished for him. "I guess I hadn't."

She heard his sharp intake of breath and felt the tension seep through his body. "Lucy…why me?"

Heat caught in her throat and she swallowed hard. "You know why."

He sighed heavily. "You could have any man you wanted…someone who can give you what you're looking for…marriage…family…"

When his words trailed off, Lucy's heart twisted. "And that's not you, is that what you're saying?"

He sighed again, wearily, as though he had a great burden pressing down on his chest. "A week ago you said I'd been courting you and didn't even know it…and you were right. That was unfair of me. I don't—"

"Am I being dumped?" she asked hotly, jackknifing up.

He straightened. "That's not what I meant."

"Then what?" she demanded. "Your hot-and-cold routine is tiring, Brant." Lucy shook her head and sighed. "How about we get some sleep and talk about this tomorrow?"

Brant stood, unselfconsciously naked and so gorgeous

she almost crawled across the bed and pressed herself against him. But his next words turned her inside out.

"You can't stay here."

She watched as he grabbed a pair of fresh jeans from the wardrobe and slipped them on.

Lucy scrambled her legs together. "Now you're kicking me out?"

He ran a hand through his hair. "I just think it would be best if you went home."

Lucy got to her feet and stood toe-to-toe with him. His gaze raked over her, hot and filled with an almost reluctant desire. Even when they were in the middle of a crisis, the attraction they had for one another was undeniable.

Lucy stood her ground. "No."

His gaze narrowed. "No?"

"I'm staying."

He inhaled sharply and grabbed her dress from the chair in the corner. "Get dressed."

"Forget it, soldier," she said, hands on hips. "Because if I go, I go for good."

"Then go," he said coldly and walked toward the door.

"What is it, Brant?" she demanded as she quickly got into her dress and smoothed the fabric over her hips. "What is it you're so afraid of?"

He stopped instantly and turned. "Afraid?" he echoed, his blue eyes glittering. "I'm not afraid of anything."

"I don't believe you," she snapped, going for his emotional jugular because if she didn't she knew she would lose him forever. "So, what is it? Are you scared that if I spend the night, if I sleep in your bed, that at some point I'm going to witness the *real* you? The you who paces the floorboards at night? The you who breaks out in a cold sweat at two o'clock in the morning? The you who has bad dreams and cries in his sleep?"

He paled instantly. "How…how do you know that?" he asked raggedly.

Her heart ached for him and she pressed a hand to his chest. "Because I *know* you. In here. I'm connected to you in a way I've never been connected to anyone in my life. Don't you get it, Brant? *I love you.*"

It was out.

There was nothing for either of them to hide behind.

Just her heart on the line.

Lucy stared at him, absorbing every feature, every conflicting emotion, evident in his expression. But he didn't speak. He didn't move. He simply looked at her. Into her. Through her. Time seemed to stretch like brittle elastic until, finally, he spoke.

"It's late. Get some sleep."

He turned and left the room and Lucy didn't take a breath until she couldn't hear his footsteps on the stairs. She sat on the bed and sucked in an agonizing breath. Did the man have ice water in his veins? Had she given herself and her love to someone who was impervious to deep feeling?

No…

She knew him. He was kind and compassionate and capable of much more than he realized.

Lucy lay on the bed and closed her eyes. She was so tired, weary from tension and knowing she had to go to work the following day. She inhaled, relaxed her aching shoulders and tried to rest, hopeful that at some point Brant would join her in the big bed.

But he didn't.

Lucy woke up around six and, after a quick bathroom stop, headed downstairs. Brant was awake and behind the main bar, sorting through paint swatches. He wore jeans and a dark sweater and looked so gorgeous her mouth turned dry.

"Hi," she said as cheerfully as she could muster. "Did you manage to get some sleep?"

He hooked a thumb in the direction of a narrow cot in one corner. "A little. You?"

She nodded. "I could make breakfast if you—"

"No...but thank you."

She inhaled sharply. "I guess I should go. I'll just get my things."

Lucy didn't wait for a reply and swiveled on her feet. When she came back downstairs a few minutes later he was near the front of the tavern, piling cut pieces of timber into stacks. "Will I see you later?"

He looked up and straightened. "I'll probably be tied up here all day."

Lucy nodded and walked toward the door. She grabbed the handle, lingered and then turned back to him. "You know, Brant, I've pretty much been in love with you since I was fifteen years old."

He stilled instantly, his blue-eyed gaze riveting her to the spot. The silence between them was suddenly deafening. But she kept going, too far in to back down.

"Do you remember the day you took Trudy to the prom?" she asked but didn't wait for him to respond. "I was at your ranch with my mom. Your dad and Grady were helping my mother sell our ranch and they were all in the kitchen talking and I was sitting by the counter, my head in a book, as always. I used to hang around your ranch and watch you and your brother break and train the horses. Or your mom would give me baking lessons. But that day you came into the room dressed in your suit with a corsage for Trudy and you looked so handsome and grown-up. I knew once school was over that you would be leaving for the military and for the hundredth time I wished I was older, prettier, more popular... And I wished that the corsage was for me and you were taking me to prom."

She sighed, remembering the ache in her young heart that day. "Then you left town and I finished high school and went to college and med school. Years passed and occasionally our paths would cross and you would usually ignore me, and I got used to that. When I returned to town permanently I knew I wanted to work at the hospital and settle down in Cedar River and hopefully find someone to share my life with." Her voice quivered as tears filled her eyes. "Then you came back and I tried to act like I was indifferent and over my silly infatuation. But I knew I'd been fooling myself. Because," she said, putting her hand to her chest as tears fell down her cheeks, "in here...in here I was still that insecure fifteen-year-old girl, dreaming about corsages and going to the prom with Brant Parker."

She pulled her tote close to her body and grabbed the door handle. "I know you believe you can't make a commitment, Brant...and I think I understand why. But, despite how much I love you and love being with you, I need to end this now... I need to stop kidding myself into thinking that what we have is enough for me. Because it's not."

She left the tavern and walked to her car. There was a light blanket of snow on her windshield and she flicked it off before she climbed into the car and drove home.

But the time she arrived at work an hour later, she was hurting all over.

Brant didn't call her that day. Or the next.

However, Lucy called him late Wednesday afternoon and left three messages on his cell.

Because at one o'clock on Wednesday, Joe Parker had another heart attack and was rushed into the ER by the paramedics, but tragically died forty minutes later.

Chapter Twelve

Brant ignored every message on his phone for several days. His uncle was dead and Lucy had left him. She had her reasons and it was probably the right thing. But by Friday he was so wound up he could barely stand being in his own skin.

He met Grady at the funeral home late in the afternoon and finalized the funeral arrangements for the following Monday. The service was to be held at the small cemetery on the edge of town and his uncle would be laid to rest next to their father and grandparents.

"Are you coming back to the ranch?" Grady asked once they'd left the funeral home. "The girls would love to see you."

Brant shook his head. "I've got things to do."

Grady grabbed his shoulder, looked concerned and didn't bother to disguise it. "I don't think you should be alone."

"I'm fine."

When they got to the parking lot, his brother scowled when he saw the motorbike. "Really? In this weather?"

"It was clear when I left the tavern."

Grady held out his palm and caught a few flakes of snow that were now falling. "It's not clear now. I'll drive you back and you can pick the bike up tomorrow."

They both knew he would never leave his motorbike unattended. "Stop fussing like an old woman."

Grady made an exasperated sound. "All right, just be careful riding home in this."

"I will," Brant promised.

His brother nodded and then spoke. "So, have you seen Lucy?"

"No," he replied.

Grady pulled his coat collar up around his neck. "She was there, you know, at the end, holding his hand, giving him comfort."

Brant ignored the tightness in his chest. Yeah, she was good at holding hands. Good at comfort. And good at ending things. "I gotta run. See you tomorrow."

He grabbed his helmet, straddled the bike and was about to say goodbye when his brother spoke again.

"I've always tried to avoid telling you how to live your life or give advice. But I'm going to give you some now. You need to face this, Brant."

His back tensed. "Face what?"

Grady waved a hand. "This thing with Lucy. You served three tours in the military and much of that time was spent on the front line. You're a soldier and one of the bravest men I know. So tell me, what is it about loving this woman that scares you so much?"

"I don't love her," he said coldly as he kicked the bike into life and drove off.

Twenty minutes later, after circling Lucy's block for the third time, he pulled up in her driveway and killed the engine. She wasn't home. He checked his watch. Five-fifteen. She was probably out with her friends at O'Sullivan's. Or she was working. Or on a date.

Brant climbed off the bike and headed for the small porch. He zipped up his leather jacket and sat in the love seat. And waited.

She arrived home twenty minutes later. Wrapped up in a scarlet woolen coat with fake fur trim, black boots, knitted gloves and a white beanie, she looked like she belonged on a Christmas card. Her cheeks were spotted with color and her lips looked lush and red. And imminently kissable.

She seemed neither surprised nor unsurprised to see him as she sat wordlessly beside him on the love seat. He didn't touch her. He didn't dare, despite how much he longed to.

"You didn't reply to my text messages," she said quietly.

"I haven't been doing much of anything this week."

She nodded fractionally. "I was worried about you."

He knew she would have been. "I'm sorry. I've been keeping to myself...trying to make sense of it all."

"And did you?" she asked softly.

He half shrugged. "Not so much. I miss him already."

"I know," she said, her gentle voice somehow soothing some of the pain he felt. "Are you still seeing Dr. Allenby?"

One thing he could always rely on—Lucy Monero never pulled punches or talked in riddles. She was honest and forthright and demanded the same in return.

"Yes," he replied. "I saw him Monday and I have another appointment next week."

"It's helping?"

"I think so...yes."

"I'm glad," she replied and, after a small silence, spoke again. "But what are you really doing here?"

"Grady told me that you were with my uncle when he died," he said, conscious of the heavy weight pressing down on his shoulders. "I just wanted to thank you for that and for your kindness toward him these past few weeks. It's meant a lot to us." He paused, took a breath, felt an uneasy ache in the middle of his chest. "And to me."

She nodded. "I wish I could have done more."

"If yours was the last face he saw before he passed away," Brant said quietly, "then I'm sure he would have died with peace in his heart. So, thank you."

"He was a nice man and I cared about him a great deal." She met his gaze, unwavering. "But anything I did...I did for you."

The sensation in his chest amplified and he swallowed hard. God, she undid him with just a few words. He got up and grabbed the helmet. "I know that. Goodbye, Lucy."

She was frowning. "Should you be biking in this weather?"

Brant looked at the snow still coming down. "I'll be careful."

He got to the steps and then turned. She was still sitting, still looking lost and lovely. His heart thundered in his chest. "You know, I did hear you the other night. Everything you said...you were right to say it. The thing is, I came back to Cedar River to try and forget what happened in Afghanistan. But most days, I still feel as though I'm back on that ridge, back dodging bullets and back hearing the screams of men who died so I could live.

And knowing the only reason it turned out that way is because I had an aptitude for learning another language. If I'd been good at math instead, things would have turned out very different. So, when it's two in the morning and I can't do anything other than stare at the ceiling instead of sleeping, or when my dreams are so bad I wake myself up screaming, I think about how a high school French class probably saved my life."

She stared at him. Through him. Into the very depths of his blood and bones and then further still, right into his soul. No one else had ever done that. No one ever would.

When she spoke again he could barely stand to hear the words. "Part of me wants to wish you and your guilt a long and happy life together. But I can't...because that would simply be my broken heart talking." She got to her feet. "I'll see you at the service on Monday."

Brant looked at her and every conflicting emotion he had banged around in his head. Part of him longed to take her in his arms, part of him ached for her touch. "Thanks again...for everything."

She nodded. "Sure. Goodbye."

Brant watched as she turned, walked into the house and closed the door. Lights flicked on and her silhouette passed by the window, and he was suddenly overwhelmed by an inexplicable urge to knock on her door to beg her to let him stay the night. But then she'd witness his truth—the insomnia, the pacing at two o'clock in the morning, the dampness on his face when he jackknifed out of bed in the middle of a nightmare. He'd tried medication and all it did was dull his senses. Alcohol left him hung over and weary for days. The only solution was to ride through it in private. No one needed to witness his anxiety. She already thought he needed a shrink. If she saw him at two in the morning, drenched in sweat, shaking from fear, she'd run a mile. Or worse, she'd stay. Out of pity and concern. And *that* was worse than not being with her.

It was better this way. For them both.

Brant got through the weekend by working at the tavern and on Monday ran on autopilot during his uncle's funeral. About eighty people turned up for the service, half of them Joe Parker's former army buddies. The minister gave a short reading, as did Grady and then Brant, and while most of the military crew went to Rusty's afterward to celebrate their fallen colleague with a round of beer and shared tales from the war, Brant returned to the ranch with his mother and brother and about twenty close friends, including Lucy.

By the afternoon there were just half a dozen people left, most bailing before the snow came down heavier. Brant sat on the wide veranda, an untouched coffee in his hand. Grady and Brooke were in the kitchen and Marissa was in the playroom with the kids. He spotted Lucy walking across the yard toward the stables. She had on her red coat and it was a stark contrast against the white backdrop of snow. He watched her as she walked, like a vision in red, like a beacon for his weary soul.

A surge of feeling suddenly rose up and hit him squarely in the solar plexus and he couldn't quite get enough air into his lungs. He didn't know what to make of it. Or what to think. Only Lucy could do that. No one had ever had such a profound effect on his peace of mind. His body. His heart.

They'd barely spoken all day. Strangely, it was as though they didn't need to. But during the service he'd felt her behind him and then her small hand had rested on his back. It was all he'd needed to get through the moment. And she'd known that, wordlessly. Because she knew him better than anyone.

He watched her as she walked around alone, moving in circles, almost as though she was so deep in thought she didn't care where she ended up.

"Do you remember what I said to you a few weeks back?"

His mother's voice made him turn his head for a moment. Sometimes his mom had the stealth of a jungle cat. "What?"

"That she would be a good match for you," Colleen reminded him, inclining her head toward Lucy. "I still believe it."

"Not today Mom, okay?"

"Did you know that your dad was terrified of enclosed spaces and had night terrors?"

Brant snapped his gaze around. "What do you mean?"

"He fell down a mine shaft when he was eight years old. He was trapped there for two days. He used to wake up screaming some nights. Knowing he had fears, flaws...it didn't make me love him any less."

Brant's stomach dropped. "Mom, don't."

"The fact that he could admit it," she said pointedly. "That's what made him strong. And a better man for it. And it made me love him even more."

Brant watched Lucy wander by the stables as his mother spoke. He resisted the urge to join her, to hold her steady as she trudged over the thin blanket of snow, to keep her safe.

I've pretty much been in love with you since I was fifteen years old...

Lucy's words echoed in his head and then lodged in his chest. No one had ever uttered those words to him before…and certainly not with such heartbreaking honesty. But Lucy was always honest.

Right from the start she'd told him the truth. Right from the start she'd had a way of making him think and feel when he'd believed himself too numb to feel anything. The way she'd opened up about her own past had switched something on inside him. She had demons… regrets…but she'd forged ahead, carving out a successful career and becoming a kind, compassionate and considerate person. The best person he'd ever known. And she'd shared a part of herself with him so earnestly…so honestly. It wasn't just sex. Being with Lucy was like nothing he'd experienced before. Making love to her, feeling her touch, watching her come apart in his arms, was both spiritual and physical. The perfect moment. The perfect feeling. She was perfect.

"I know you were incredibly close to your uncle," his mother said quietly. "But don't go down the same lonely road that he did. When Joe came back from the war without one of his legs he thought he was somehow defined by that…so he never allowed himself to have a serious relationship with anyone. He never fell in love. He never had a family of his own. And I don't want the same thing to happen to you."

"It won't, Mom," he assured her. "I'm not an amputee for one—"

"Some wounds are on the outside, some are on the inside," she said with emphasis.

"She's right."

Grady's voice snapped his head around. His brother came up behind them and stood to Brant's left. Flanked by his mother and brother, he felt like he was suddenly in the center of an intervention. And in that moment all he wanted to do was to head down the stairs and find solace with Lucy. Looking at her walking through the snow alone made his insides ache. And the only thing that would appease that ache would be to be by her side… by sitting on the couch holding hands or watching football over cold pizza and beer. By kissing her beautiful mouth. By making love with her and feeling the tenderness of her touch. She was the tonic he needed. She was *all* he needed.

Brant stilled and every muscle in his body tightened. *He really needed her.*

When he'd convinced himself he didn't need anything or anyone. Only solitude and time to dilute the pain and guilt that some days seemed etched into his very soul. And yet, Lucy knew that. She knew that and still wanted him. *Still loved him.* Because she was strong and courageous. She'd traveled her own road, recovering from the grief of losing her mother so tragically, and still found the strength and fortitude to allow someone into her heart. To allow *him* into her heart…even though he'd pushed her away again and again.

And he knew why.

Because he was scared. Terrified that he wouldn't measure up, that she'd think him weak, unworthy. That she would see him at his worst and still stay…out of loyalty. And pity. And that would be unbearable. He didn't want her sympathy. He didn't want her thinking she needed to fix him. He wanted to meet her head-on. Without fear.

Because…

Because he was in love with her. Wholly and completely.

Lucy Monero held every part of his heart and body and soul.

He watched her, a breathtaking vision in her red coat,

her head bent and her beautiful hair spilling out from beneath her hat. No one could ever come close. No one ever would.

Brant looked at his mother and then at Grady, and finally let out a long breath before speaking the words that were in his heart. "I'm in love with Lucy."

Grady laughed softly and his mother squeezed his arm. "Yes, we know," she said.

"The thing is," his brother said, still smiling, "what are you going to do about it?"

Brant looked toward the stables, watched her as she walked, his heart and mind filling with a kind of peace he'd never know before. "I'm going to ask her if she'll have me."

And he knew just how to do that.

Lucy was glad to be back at work. It was two days after Joe Parker's funeral and she was trying to get her life back into some kind of bearable rhythm. The hospital was busier than usual for a Wednesday, and since Christmas was only a couple of weeks away, there seemed to be an increase in the number of tourists coming into the ER with everything from stomach bugs to blisters. Lucy put on her best smile and spent the first few hours of her shift in Triage.

And she tried to *not* think about her broken heart.

It wasn't easy. Everything reminded her of Brant. Every time she walked into the ER she remembered him the afternoon his uncle had been brought in so many weeks ago, and how she'd quickly found herself in his relieved embrace. She couldn't walk through the front foyer without remembering how he'd brought her dinner on Thanksgiving. And at home the memories were even more intense. Sitting on the couch drinking beer and eating pizza, watching a silly football game together, making love as though there were no other people on earth. *Everything* reminded her of Brant. And her dreams offered no respite. He filled them, consumed them, and each morning she woke lethargic and with a heavy heart.

Kayla stopped by with lattes at lunchtime on Wednesday and Brooke called her after lunch to ensure she was okay. Ash came in around two o'clock to question a young man who'd been in a minor vehicular accident and had whiplash. She stayed to chat for a few minutes and Lucy tried to appear to be her usual happy self. She knew what her friends were doing and loved them for it…but mostly, she just wanted to be left alone.

There was nothing anyone could say or do to ease the ache in her heart and she didn't want to burden her friends with her unhappy mood. She'd get over it in her own time. Once she stopped thinking about Brant. And dreaming about him. Only then would she stop loving him.

She'd considered calling him several times in the past couple of days, but every time she grabbed her cell phone she simply stared at the screen. They had nothing to say to one another and no words were necessary. She knew how he felt. He couldn't give her what she wanted and she couldn't settle for anything less.

I just need some time to get over him.

But as she thought the words she didn't really believe them.

By three o'clock the flow of patients into the ER had eased. Lucy was about to make a final walk around the ward before she prepared to go home when she was paged. She answered the call and was asked to go down to the main reception area as there was someone waiting to see her. Thinking it was one of her friends again,

Lucy grabbed her white coat and slipped it on before she headed out through Triage and toward the front of the building. When she stepped out of the elevator she took a left turn and stopped in her tracks, suddenly poleaxed.

There were several people walking through the foyer, but she only saw one.

Brant...

He stood by the small bench seat where they had shared dinner from a basket and drank sodas. But this time he was dressed immaculately in a tuxedo and shiny black shoes and he carried a small, clear box with a flower inside.

Lucy stared at him, mesmerized. He looked so good. So handsome. His blue eyes glittered and his dark hair shone beneath the bright overhead lights. He didn't move and Lucy somehow found the strength to take a few steps toward him. Suddenly she didn't see anyone else or hear anyone else in the room. Only him.

Finally, he held out the small box and spoke.

"I just want you to know," he said, his deep voice like silk, "that you will always have a date for the prom."

Lucy's breath caught and tears instantly heated her eyes.

It was the single most beautiful, romantic moment of her life.

She wanted to race into his arms. But she held back. That had a lot to talk about. A lot to think about.

"Is...is that for me?" she asked.

He nodded. "Everything is for you, Lucia."

Lucy experienced an acute sense of joy and stepped a little closer. He was in front of her, dressed in a suit and holding a corsage, with his heart on his sleeve and no walls between them. And in that moment she had never loved him more.

"Brant…" Her words trailed off as emotion clogged her throat.

"Lucy," he said softly and held out his hand. "Is there somewhere we can talk in private?"

She nodded, took his hand and walked away from reception and up the corridor. There were several empty offices and she tapped on one of the doors and entered. If anyone walked by she didn't notice. She saw only him. She didn't care if anyone wondered why the most gorgeous man on the planet was doing with a harried-looking doctor wearing scrubs and a white coat.

The room was a small and perfunctory—typical of any administration office, with a desk, filing cabinet and two chairs. She closed the door and turned to face him. He held out the box again. She took it with trembling hands and looked at the perfect orchid corsage. "It's beautiful."

He held her hand tightly and nodded. "Shall we sit down?"

Lucy sat in one of the chairs and waited while he pulled the other one close. As soon as he sat he grabbed her free hand and spoke. "I know I've repeatedly screwed things up from the start. I know I've behaved badly. I know I've pushed you away time and time again. And I know I have no right to ask this of you…but I'm asking without any agenda, without any notion that I deserve it…but would you give me another chance?"

Her heart contracted and she smiled, seeing the love in his expression. He'd reached out in the most amazing way and she felt confident enough to meet him halfway, so she nodded. "Of course."

He looked instantly relieved. "Thank you. For believing in me. For understanding me. For having the patience to wait for me while I came to my senses."

Lucy smiled. "Have you? Come to your senses, I mean?"

He nodded. "Absolutely. I can't bear the thought of my life without you in it."

Lucy had never heard anything more heartfelt in her life. "I love you, too."

He kissed her then, a soft, slow kiss that kindled her longing for him. When he pulled back, his blue eyes were so vibrant she could almost see her reflection.

He held her hand lovingly. "What time do you finish today?"

Lucy checked her watch. It was two minutes to three. "Just about now."

"So," he said, curling a hand around her nape. "How about we get out of here and you go home and put on your prettiest dress and I'll take you out somewhere and we'll do this properly."

"Do what properly?" she teased.

"You know very well," he said and lovingly tucked a lock of stray hair behind her ear. "I'm not going to ask you to marry me while we're sitting in a hospital office room."

Lucy's heart almost exploded in her chest. "Oh… you're going to ask me to marry you?"

He smiled. "I most certainly am. But not here."

"Well," she said and leaned closer. "How about we go home and I won't put on my prettiest dress. Instead," she whispered, going closer still, "you can get out of that ridiculously sexy tuxedo and we can kiss and make up for a while and then you can ask me. Because I miss you. I miss *us*."

Brant kissed her softly and took the corsage box from her hand. He extracted the flower and carefully pinned it to her white coat. "I miss us, too."

She looked at the flower then met his gaze. "Brant what happened...what made you—?"

"What made me see sense?" he asked, cutting her off gently. He grabbed her hands and held them close. "What made me realize that I couldn't live without you? A few things. The other day my brother asked me what I was afraid of and I couldn't answer him. And then after the funeral, my mom told me not to end up like my uncle... because I had somehow come to think that my past is what defines me...and not my present. But I think..." he said, his words trailing for a moment as he softly touched her cheek. "I think that it was you. I *know* it was you. I was watching you walk alone in the snow the other day at the ranch, wearing your red coat... You looked so beautiful it took my breath away. But you looked alone, too. And that was unbearable for me. In that moment I knew... I just knew."

Lucy's eyes burned and she managed a quivering smile. "You knew what?"

He took a long breath. "I knew that I was in love with you."

They were the sweetest words she had ever heard. She reached up and cupped his smooth jaw. "I will always love you, Brant. And I'll always be there for you... through fire and rain...through bad dreams and sleepless nights."

His eyes glittered. "I wish I could tell you that I was through the worst of it, Lucy. But I can't."

She kept her hand against him. "You were in a war. And you experienced something life altering. You have to get through this at your own pace, Brant...but you also have to forgive yourself enough to let that happen. And that will take time. And patience. And probably therapy.

But there are no judges, no one here to devalue your feelings. There's just you…and me."

He groaned softly and captured her mouth in a kiss. "I love you, Lucia," he said against her lips. "I love your strength and your goodness. I love how you make the most of every moment. And I'm humbled that you want to love me back. There's no one in the world like you," he said and smiled, love in his eyes. "And I will love you and protect you and honor you always."

Lucy's throat burned with emotion. He was such a passionate, strong yet gentle man. And knowing she had his love filled her heart with overwhelming happiness. She knew they had some hurdles ahead, but Lucy was confident they would get through it together.

"So, about this tuxedo," she said and toyed with the bow tie. "Although it looks great on you, I still like the idea about going home and getting out of these clothes. And you did promise me a proposal, remember?"

He laughed softly and pulled her onto his lap. "I certainly did. Speaking of homes, in a few weeks I'm going to be homeless. The new chef is taking over the apartment above the tavern," he explained. "So unless you want to see me out on the street, I might have to bunk at your place for a while."

Lucy smiled and pressed kissed to his jaw. "Oh, I think we could come to some arrangement." Her eyes sparkled. "But that means sleepovers, you know. Cold sweats and bad dreams and all."

"I know what it means," he said as his arms tightened around her. "And although I'm probably going to struggle at first with you seeing me like that, I know I need to let go of the fear that you'll think I'm…needy…and weak."

"You don't have a weak bone in your body, Brant Parker," she said, her heart aching for him. "But I understand. And we'll simply take it one day, and one night, at a time."

He nodded slowly. "Dr. Allenby was telling me about the group therapy sessions they hold at the veterans home, you know, for the veterans and their families." He squeezed her hand. "I was wondering if you'd come with me sometime."

"Of course," she said quickly. "Of course I'll come with you. From this moment I don't ever want to be apart from you."

"Me, either."

She pressed against him. "And I love the idea of us living together."

"Me, too." He held her close. "Let's get out of here, Lucy. Let's go home so I can get down on my knee and ask you to marry me."

Lucy smiled cheekily. "Do you have a ring?"

His eyes darkened. "Of course."

"Then I accept!"

He laughed and the lovely sound reverberated through her entire body. "I haven't technically asked you yet."

"That's true," she said quickly and jumped to her feet. "Then let's go. I don't want you changing your mind about this."

Brant stood and hauled her into his arms. "Just so you know, Lucia, I will never change my mind. You're stuck with me for the rest of your life."

And that, Lucy thought as she offered her lips for his kiss, was the best news she'd ever heard.

Epilogue

"You know, you can protest all you like, but I *am* going to carry you over this threshold."

Lucy stared up at him, all green eyes and red lips. "But it's bad luck if we're not married."

Brant shook his head. "We're getting married in nine weeks. A date that *you* set, if you remember," he reminded her. "*I* would have happily eloped over Christmas."

"If we eloped, your mother would never forgive us," she said and crossed her arms. "Nor your brother or Kayla or Ash or Brooke."

She was right, of course. Eloping had never been an option. And she was right to suggest a six-month engagement. They needed time to get to know one another better, for Brant to continue with his sessions with Dr. Allenby, to arrange a wedding and to buy a house. Which is why they were now standing on the porch of their new home and she was being typically stubborn about his insistence he carry her over the threshold.

"Well, I have these," he said and dangled the keys from his fingertips. "So, I either carry you or we stay out here."

She glared at him. "You can been a real pain sometimes."

He shrugged. "I thought you found me charming?"

Her glare quickly turned into a smile. "Yeah… I do."

Brant laughed. "Well, climb the steps and come here."

She trudged up the five steps onto the porch. "This is really silly. What if someone sees us?"

"Some like who?"

She shrugged. "Our new neighbors perhaps."

He looked left and then right. "Old Mrs. Bailey plays bridge on Thursdays and is out, and the other side is Joss Culhane's house. Which you know. So, stop making excuses and get over here."

She chuckled and the sound hit him directly in the heart. Everything about her made him smile. Lucy was an amazing woman—kind, considerate, supportive and a tower of strength. Much more than he deserved, he was sure. But she loved him and he loved her in return, more than he'd ever imagined he could love anyone.

The past three months had been something of a whirlwind. With planning a wedding, opening the tavern, taking a part-time job teaching French at the high school and buying a home, there never seemed enough hours in the day. But Lucy was always at his side and unfailing in her support. She always made time to accompany him to the group meetings at the veterans home and had been with him in several of his sessions with Dr. Allenby. She'd been right about that, too. Time was a healer. Truth was a healer. He'd discovered both those things with her love and support. He'd even begun sleeping through the night.

The nightmares still came, but he was better prepared to handle them. And he'd forgiven himself, finally, for surviving the war when so many people around him hadn't.

"Where do you want me?" she asked, standing beside him.

Brant opened the security screen and then the front door. The house was big, low set and had been freshly renovated by the previous owners. Exactly what they wanted. Three bedrooms, two bathrooms, a huge kitchen and dining area, a large living room and a yard that needed a little work. But he didn't mind. Seeing Lucy's delighted expression the first time they'd viewed the house was enough to ensure he'd made an offer to the Realtor on the spot.

"I want you right here," he said and held out his arms. He scooped her up and jiggled her playfully. "Hmm... you're heavier than I thought."

She scowled and tapped him on the shoulder. "That's not very—"

"I'm kidding," he said and crossed the threshold. "You're as light as a feather."

She smiled and he carried her down the hall toward the kitchen. Since there was no furniture in the house, he propped her on the Canadian maple countertop and she smoothed her skirt down over her thighs. He kissed her cheek and then waved an arm to the middle of the dining area.

"We need to buy a new table," he said.

"My furniture arrives tomorrow," she reminded him. "Let's get it in the house and then see what we need."

He grinned. "My logical love."

She nodded and met his gaze. "While we're on that subject... I was thinking it would be logical to move the wedding up a bit. Say, to April."

Brant frowned slightly. "April? That's next month. Why would you want to do that when everything's booked for June?"

He looked at her and realized she seemed on edge. Even nervous. It occurred to him that she'd been a little distracted for days. Now he was really concerned. He said her name and she sighed heavily.

"I just want to make sure," she said softly.

"Make sure of what?" –

"That I still fit into my wedding dress."

Brant stilled instantly. Her dress? He met her gaze and saw her expression change. Now she was smiling, a kind of delighted, secret smile that reached him way down. And she deliberately lay a palm on her belly.

Her belly...

A strange sensation tightened his throat as his gaze flicked from her eyes to where her hand lay. And in an instant he knew. "Are you pregnant?"

She nodded. "Sure am."

Emotion rose and hit him square in the middle of the chest. Pregnant. A baby. A dad.

And Brant didn't know whether he wanted to laugh, cry or pass out.

Lucy couldn't help smiling at the look on his face. She'd kept the secret for two days, wanting to break the news in their new home...for a new beginning...a new chapter in their life together.

"Are you okay, Brant?" she asked, taking in his sudden pallor.

"I...think so. Are you sure?"

She nodded. "Positive."

He took two steps across the room and settled between her thighs, hugging her tightly. "How far along?"

"About six weeks."

She could see him doing the math calculation in his head. "The night of the opening?"

"Yes," she replied, remembering how the night of the Loose Moose reopening they'd celebrated a little too hard and forgotten contraception. They'd joked about it at the time. Now, Lucy couldn't be more delighted that they'd neglected to use protection that night. She was over the moon, happier than she'd ever been in her life. Having Brant's baby was a dream come true. "Are you in shock?"

"A little," he admitted. "You?"

"I've had two days to get used to the idea," she said and smiled. "But I wanted to tell you here…in this house. *Our house.*"

He kissed her, long and passionately and filled with love.

"I'm gonna be a dad? Really?"

"Really," she replied.

He kissed her softly. "I can't believe how lucky I am. I can't believe I have all this. That I have you. And now…" He looked down at her belly. "And now we're having a baby together…it's as though suddenly I have this perfect life."

Lucy grabbed his hand and laid it against her stomach. "We do," she assured him and saw his eyes glittering with emotion. Lucy touched his face. "And you're going to be great. *We're* going to be great. Everything *is* going to be perfect, Brant."

When their beautiful son, Joel, was born a little more than seven months later, everything was perfect, just as she'd known it would be.

* * * * *

MILLS & BOON®

Cherish™

EXPERIENCE THE ULTIMATE RUSH OF FALLING IN LOVE

Lynne Graham has sold 35 million books!

To settle a debt, she'll have to become his mistress…

Nikolai Drakos is determined to have his revenge against the man who destroyed his sister. So stealing his enemy's intended fiancé seems like the perfect solution! Until Nikolai discovers that woman is Ella Davies…

*Read on for a tantalising excerpt from
Lynne Graham's 100th book,*

BOUGHT FOR THE GREEK'S REVENGE

'Mistress,' Nikolai slotted in cool as ice.

Shock had welded Ella's tongue to the roof of her mouth because he was sexually propositioning her and nothing could have prepared her for that. She wasn't drop-dead gorgeous… *he* was! Male heads didn't swivel when Ella walked down the street because she had neither the length of leg nor the curves usually deemed necessary to attract such attention. Why on earth could he be making *her* such an offer?

'But we don't even know each other,' she framed dazedly. 'You're a stranger…'

'If you live with me I won't be a stranger for long,' Nikolai pointed out with monumental calm. And the very sound of that inhuman calm and cool forced her to flip round and settle distraught eyes on his lean darkly handsome face.

'You can't be serious about this!'

'I assure you that I am deadly serious. Move in and I'll forget your family's debts.'

'But it's a *crazy* idea!' she gasped.

'It's not crazy to me,' Nikolai asserted. 'When I want anything, I go after it hard and fast.'

Her lashes dipped. Did he want her like that? Enough to track her down, buy up her father's debts, and try and buy rights to her and her body along with those debts? The very idea of that made her dizzy and plunged her brain into even greater turmoil. 'It's immoral… it's blackmail.'

'It's definitely *not* blackmail. I'm giving you the benefit of a choice you didn't have before I came through that door,' Nikolai Drakos fielded with a glittering cool. 'That choice is yours to make.'

'Like hell it is!' Ella fired back. 'It's a complete cheat of a supposed offer!'

Nikolai sent her a gleaming sideways glance. 'No the real cheat was you kissing me the way you did last year and then saying no and acting as if I had grossly insulted you,' he murmured with lethal quietness.

'You *did* insult me!' Ella flung back, her cheeks hot as fire while she wondered if her refusal that night had started off his whole chain reaction. What else could possibly be driving him?

Nikolai straightened lazily as he opened the door. 'If you take offence that easily, maybe it's just as well that the answer is no.'

Visit **www.millsandboon.co.uk/lynnegraham**
to order yours!

MILLS & BOON®

MISSING
IN CONARD
COUNTY

RACHEL LEE

DELTA FORCE
DIE HARD

CAROL ERICSON

MILLS & BOON

First Published in Great Britain 2019
by Mills & Boon, an imprint of HarperCollins*Publishers*
1 London Bridge Street, London, SE1 9GF

Missing in Conard County © 2018 Susan Civil Brown
Delta Force Die Hard © 2018 Carol Ericson

ISBN: 978-0-263-27396-0

0119

MIX
Paper from
responsible sources
FSC˚ C007454

MISSING
IN CONARD
COUNTY

RACHEL LEE

Chapter One

Day 20

The forecast called for a severe winter storm to move into Conard County, Wyoming, in the next two days, so animal control officer Allan Carstairs was out hunting for strays. By nightfall, the temperatures would be dropping rapidly, and while the storm itself wasn't moving fast, the cold was stampeding down on them. Subzero temperatures weren't good for animals that were used to warm homes and not used to dealing with Arctic weather. Al had seen cats with badly frostbitten paws and ears, and he would never forget the dog that needed a leg amputated. Nor would he ever forget the animals he had found frozen to death.

So when the weather was about to turn dangerous, he roamed the area outside town looking for strays, as well as a family of felines that a trucker had reported dropped by the roadside. A lot of people let their cats roam free, and any cat that didn't sense the changing weather as a reason to get home would be looking at trouble, even death. Then there were the dogs. The leash law didn't always keep them from escaping and having so much fun racing the countryside that they often didn't seem to realize danger was closing in.

At that moment he already had three annoyed cats in

cages and a miniature schnauzer that appeared to be sad because he couldn't keep chasing a prairie dog.

Then he spied Misty. A beautiful golden retriever with a distinctive prance to her step, she seemed to be running in circles about a hundred yards inside the fence line of the Harris family ranch. He was surprised to see her so far out here. The Avilas had always been careful owners who tried not to let Misty slip her leash, but she was an accomplished escape artist. With the weather turning so bitter, perhaps one of the kids had let her out in the backyard without watching and she'd burrowed under the fence. Regardless, at the times she proved to be Houdini's reincarnation, Al usually picked her up within or near the city limits.

Al pulled his van onto the shoulder, grabbed a slipknot leash and climbed out. Misty had never been a problem to round up, so he expected her to come immediately when he called. Just after he slid off the seat and his feet hit the ground, he felt a light weight land on his shoulder and hang on. Regis, he thought, and smiled.

He closed the vehicle door so the animals would stay warm and gave thanks that the wind hadn't really started yet. Just the faintest of breezes to chill the air, and a tang that hinted at coming snow.

For the first time ever, Misty wasn't in a cooperative mood. As she raced around, she tossed some kind of toy in the air, and although she occasionally glanced at him when he called her, she kept right on playing, pausing only occasionally to paw at the ground before returning to her private game of catch.

"Hey, Misty," Al called. "Come on. Don't be a pain. Seriously."

Just then a sheriff's SUV pulled onto the opposite shoulder of the road. It bore a rack of lights and Conard County Sheriff painted in green on the tan background. K-9, Keep

Your Distance was also labeled on the side. By that, before she even climbed out, Al knew it was Kelly Noveno.

She had apparently taken in the situation before she pulled over to approach him, and grinned as she climbed out. "Having a problem, Al?"

He had to grin back. Kelly was a wildly attractive woman to his way of thinking, but what he most liked about her was her sunny nature and readiness to tease. He also liked her dog, a Belgian Malinois named Bugle for his slightly strange bark. Kelly left Bugle in her vehicle, however, and sauntered toward Al, her khaki uniform and jacket looking scarcely heavy enough to withstand the chilling air. "Misty giving you trouble?"

"She's in a mood, all right," Al agreed. Apparently, Kelly had had her own run-ins with the dog.

Kelly whistled, but Misty barely spared her a glance as she tossed her toy in the air and caught it.

"What in the world is she playing with?" Kelly asked.

"I've been wondering. Rawhide bone? Heck, she knows I wouldn't take that away from her."

Kelly chuckled. "She's teasing you." Then she turned to look at Al. "What in the dickens is that on your shoulder?"

Al didn't even have to glance. "That's Regis."

"That's a *squirrel*! You can't keep them for pets."

"I don't. Regis decides for himself. Sometimes he likes to ride shotgun. What can I tell you, Kelly? The squirrel has a mind of his own."

Al felt her staring but heck, what could he do about it? He'd rescued Regis as an abandoned baby, fed the animal until it was strong enough to take off into the woods and live the squirrel life. Except Regis kept coming back to visit.

"Now I've seen everything," Kelly muttered. "Someday I want to hear this story."

While Al wouldn't have minded spending the next day or two chatting with Kelly, there was still business to attend to. "Misty, get your butt over here now." This time there was an edge of impatience to his voice and Misty didn't miss it. She froze, looked at him, then came trotting over with her toy.

Al squatted down, ready to reward the dog with a good scratch and rub, but as Misty drew closer something inside him began to feel as chilly as the day.

"Kelly?"

"That's not rawhide," she said too quietly.

Al didn't answer. He waited until Misty snaked through the fence and came to a halt before him, dropping her toy and looking at him with a proud grin.

Al reached out, scratching her neck automatically as he looked down at the "present" she'd placed before him.

"Tell me that's not human," he said.

"I can't," Kelly answered, her voice unusually taut.

Their eyes met and Al knew they were both thinking of the same thing: the three high school girls who'd gone missing nearly a month ago.

"I'll get an evidence bag while you put the dog in your van," Kelly said. But he noted she walked to her SUV with a leaden step. All her natural vivacity had seeped away. She'd be calling for help, he thought, to try to learn where the dog found the bone. Before they were even certain.

"Yeah," Al said, speaking to the icy air. "Yeah." Then he stood, slipping the loose leash around Misty and leading her to the back of his truck.

"God," he told the dog, "I hope it's from a deer."

But he was very afraid it was not.

Chapter Two

Day 1

Kelly Noveno rolled over in her bed with a groan, wishing she could knock the ringing phone off the hook and go back to sleep. Being a sheriff's deputy, she knew she couldn't do that even though she'd worked graveyard.

The night shifts ended in the wee hours with her being too wound up to sleep immediately. Inevitably while she worked she drank far too much coffee, and by the time she reached her snug little house near the edge of Conard City, she was wider awake than an owl. She unwound with recorded TV or music, and often didn't fall asleep until late morning.

Thus, no one should bother her this early. She'd made that much clear to the dispatcher. She and her dog, Bugle, must be allowed to sleep.

Right then Bugle, who was lying beside her on her rumpled queen-size bed, lifted his head and made a sound somewhere between a groan and a yawn.

"Yeah, me, too, boy." Except that as she pushed herself upright, she caught sight of the digital clock. Three in the afternoon was hardly early. If she were on shift tonight, she'd be getting up soon anyway.

"Hell," she muttered and stood in her red flannel pajamas, shoving her feet into warm slippers. "It's getting cold, Bugle." Even inside. The heat must be straining to keep up.

The phone jangled again, telling her it wasn't going to let her run away. Pushing her bobbed, straight black hair back from her face, she reached for the receiver and lifted it to her ear.

"Noveno," she answered, trying to sound alert and not groggy.

"Kelly, sorry to wake you," came the gravelly voice of the sheriff, Gage Dalton. She guessed her attempt to sound alert hadn't worked very well. "You found a car in the ditch along the state highway last night, didn't you?"

"Yeah." She closed her eyes, remembering. "About eleven o'clock. A trace on the tag said it belonged to Randy Beauvoir. I called and got no answer. Figured someone had picked the occupants up because it was so cold. No sign of any trouble, appeared to be a simple loss of control. I tagged it for tow because the rear end was dangerously near the edge of the traffic lane."

All of which had been in the report that she had typed at five that morning. Holiday weekend, lots of activity and lots of people not home. New Year's.

"I know you're probably still tired, but we need you to come in. Three girls are missing, last known to be in that vehicle. Their parents called us half an hour ago."

"Oh, God," she breathed. "I'll be there right away."

SHE FILLED BUGLE'S bowls with kibble and fresh water, then while he filled his belly she hurried into a fresh uniform. Which girls? The thought ran around inside her head like a hamster on a wheel.

Beauvoir. She didn't know the family well, but she'd met Randy and May's daughter briefly last fall during one of those "don't drink and drive" demos they put on every two years, showing the graphic aftermath of an accident. The girl, woman really, had been pretty and engaging and full of questions because she said she wanted to become an EMT. Eighteen and full of promise.

"Oh, God," she said aloud once more.

Bugle looked at her, forgetting his food.

"Go ahead and eat," she told him. "Who knows when this day will end." Or how.

SHE GRABBED SOME dry cereal from the cupboard, poured milk on it and ate it too quickly. A couple of power bars wound up in her jacket pockets after she donned her utility belt and gun.

Time to go.

Anyone who'd grown up here should know better than to wander away from a vehicle on a cold night. It was easy to get lost out there on those open expanses, and people ought to be aware how fast the cold could become fatal. She couldn't believe three high school women wouldn't be aware. It was possible, but she was more inclined to believe someone had offered them a ride.

It would have been considered criminal by most folks around here to leave someone with a broken-down vehicle in such cold.

But if someone had offered a ride, who? And where had the girls gone?

Her stomach kept taking one plunge after another as she drove to the office. Bugle whimpered in his caged-in backseat as if he felt her anxiety.

"It's okay, boy," she said, trying to sound calm. Okay? Less and less likely.

THE SHERIFF'S OFFICE was a beehive of activity, with barely enough space to move around other personnel. Conversation was quiet, weighted with gravity. It looked like the entire department's staff was here, along with the city police department under the direction of Chief Madison.

Before she heard a word, she recognized that a search was about to get underway.

"Kelly?"

Sheriff Gage Dalton waved her back to his office. She wormed her way through the crowd with Bugle, greeting everyone with a nod. She knew them all but there was no time for conversation, not now. Bad things were afoot.

Once inside the sheriff's office, she closed the door at his gesture and took the seat facing his desk. Every time Gage moved, pain flickered across his scarred face. The result of a long-ago bomb when he'd been with the DEA. While he tried to give the pain no quarter, she didn't mind his manual suggestion that she close the door herself. Why would she?

Bugle promptly sat beside her, ears pricked, at attention. He sensed something.

"Okay," he said. "You know we don't usually respond to a missing person report this quickly, especially not when the missing are legally all adults. Any one of those young women has the right to skip town and disappear."

She nodded. "But not right before high school graduation. Five months before college and vocational schooling or whatever."

"Exactly. Plus, how likely is it for three of them to pull a disappearing act and take nothing with them? One might, but not all of them. So we're going to start looking immediately. You found the car last night around eleven. We're not quite eighteen hours into this. Maybe a little more. I figure the first thing to do is start looking along the state highway. You said the car was facing west in the ditch?"

"Mostly. It might have spun out, I can't be sure, but I

had the impression it was on its way back toward town. I also didn't see any tire skids, but that doesn't mean much as dark as it was. I didn't spend a whole lot of time looking, because there was no injury and no damage."

Gage nodded. "I've sent some people out to look at the highway for any kind of marks. So what have we got east along that road that might attract three young women on a holiday weekend night?"

Kelly was sure he knew the answer. "Rusty's Tavern. You want me to take Bugle out there?"

He nodded. "They'll be opening soon enough. Maybe one of the bartenders will remember them. Regardless, Bugle will know if they've been there."

He sure would, Kelly thought. "So what made their parents worry?"

"They knew the girls were going out last night. Each of their families thought they were staying at one of the other girl's homes. Apparently nothing definite had been arranged except a pajama party at one house or the other. By the time parents started worrying and calling each other, it was late and they all figured it wasn't that…simple."

It was so unlike the sheriff to hesitate over a word. She guessed he was as worried about the young women as anyone. As certain this wasn't going to end well.

"There's still hope," she said, rising as she realized he was done. "I'll head straight for the tavern. Do we have a target for my dog?"

"The parents are each bringing some clothing. Guess you'll have to wait until they get here."

"Or Bugle could smell the car interior. It's in the impound lot now, right?"

"He might get more scents than the girls."

She shook her head. "The parents aren't going to pick up a piece of their clothing without touching it. He's going to get multiple scents. One of the wondrous things about him is that he doesn't get them mixed up."

He put up a hand. "Whatever you think best." Glancing at the old wall clock to his right, he added, "Another half hour at least before anyone will be at Rusty's."

"I'll be there when they are." She paused. "We've got photos and personal data?"

"Not enough. Ask Sarah Ironheart. She may have been able to pull a digital copy of the yearbook. It won't be printed for another two months. Otherwise we're waiting for photos and all the rest from the parents."

She didn't want to meet the parents. Cowardly of her, she supposed, but right now all they could do, once they provided necessary information, was slow her down.

It wasn't that she didn't care. It was that she would care too much.

Sarah Ironheart sat at a desk near the front of the office, images scrolling across her monitor. A woman in her fifties, partly Native American, she had features that had worn the years well. Her long black hair, now streaked with gray, was caught in a ponytail on her neck, and the collar of her uniform shirt remained unbuttoned.

There was a chair beside the desk, and Kelly slid into it, waiting for Sarah to reach a pause point. "Damn it," Sarah said finally.

"What's wrong?"

"The yearbook editors haven't organized much of this file. I don't know how they'll get it finished in time to print it and put copies in students' hands by the end of the school year. Heck, some items aren't even in the total file yet, but in separate pieces."

Sarah leaned back in her chair. It was old and groaned as it tipped backward. "Coffee," she said as if it were the answer to everything.

"Want me to run across the street?"

Sarah cocked a dark eyebrow at her and smiled. "Trying to escape?"

Kelly half shrugged, feeling rueful. "I'd like to avoid the parents. Guess I can't."

"All of us should be that lucky. You still need a target. They're bringing them."

Kelly didn't even try to argue. Yeah, Bugle could pick up the girls' scents from the car, but they'd be much stronger on items of clothing. "Stay," she ordered Bugle. He waited, still as a piece of statuary, while Kelly stood. "How do you like your coffee?"

"Black. Thanks."

"No problem." The coffee bar was against the back wall, a huge urn that simmered all day long. The coffee was famously awful, but it carried a caffeine charge. What amused her, however, was that just in the time she'd worked here, she'd watched the addition of about seven types of antacids to the table behind the foam cups.

Velma, the dispatcher who had been with the department since the dinosaurs had roamed the earth, still smoked at her desk despite the no-smoking sign right over her head and made the coffee. No one ever complained. But now there was that row of antacids. Velma ignored it.

Kelly smothered a smile at the incongruities but poured Sarah her coffee. She'd like some herself, but she'd wait until she could get something that wouldn't hit her stomach like battery acid.

Sarah thanked her as she returned and handed over the coffee. Then she rubbed her neck once and returned to scanning the images on her screen. "It would help," she said quietly, "if all these photos were labeled by name. Or sorted by class."

"Still early days, huh?"

"For the yearbook, evidently."

Just then the front door opened and a blast of cold air could be felt all the way across the room. Kelly immediately recognized Allan Carstairs, the county's animal control officer. Although he was loosely attached to the sheriff's department, he seldom wore a uniform. Today a dark blue down parka with a hood covered him to below his narrow hips—funny that she could see those hips in her mind's eye—above jeans. Thermal long johns, she guessed. A staple for everyone during parts of the year. Like the insulated winter boots on his feet.

She watched him ease his way through the room, pausing to talk to some of the gathered deputies. At last he approached the spot where she sat with Bugle and Sarah.

"How's it going?"

"I guess we're going to see," she answered.

He nodded, his expression grim. Sharp angles defined his face, giving him a firm look that rarely vanished, even when he smiled. Gray eyes met hers, but right now the gray looked more like ice. It wasn't a warm color.

"Which three girls?" he asked.

Sarah spoke. "Jane Beauvoir, Mary Lou Ostend and Chantal Reston."

Kelly felt her heart squeeze. Jane had been the only one she'd met, but still. So young. So entitled to a future.

"Hell," said Al. "Chantal volunteered with me last summer."

"We need to get the rest of the K-9 units in here," Gage suddenly called from the hallway that led to his office in the back. "Where the hell is Cadel Marcus? Jack Hart? What kind of search can we run without the dogs?"

"A sloppy one," Kelly muttered. Bugle eyed her quizzically.

Impatience grew in Kelly. She wanted to get on with

it, find out if the girls had been seen at the roadhouse last night. If so, there might be a clue about who had picked them up. Or might have. At this point, however, it had clearly been no simple offer of a ride home.

The door opened again, this time for longer and letting in more icy air as the fathers of the three girls arrived. Randy Beauvoir entered first, followed by Kevin Ostend and Luis Reston. Kelly knew all three of them by sight, but only vaguely as she'd never had any business with them or their families.

She rose to her feet just as Gage reappeared and greeted the three men. They looked tense, worried, even a touch fearful. "Come back to the conference room," Gage said. "You've got the pictures? The clothing?"

The men nodded and Gage turned. "Kelly?"

"Coming."

Velma's scratchy voice suddenly penetrated the murmur of quiet voices. "Boss? Connie Parish says they need some help with crowd control. Word is getting around and folks are gathering near where the car was found to start their own searches."

Gage cussed. "Send ten men out there before they trample any evidence. Get ten volunteers. I got some business here first, then I'll go out there, too."

"I'll go," said Al Carstairs. He might be the animal control officer, but he had the physical stature to be intimidating, and the military bearing to go with it.

Velma looked around. "Nine more?"

Before she could see who went, Kelly and Bugle were being ushered into the conference room. In the relative quiet once the door closed behind them, the room filled with a different atmosphere. Fear. Worry. Even some anger. These fathers were like rifles that didn't know where to point.

"We're helping with the search," Randy Beauvoir said.

"I never thought you wouldn't. But I need Deputy Noveno here to give Bugle his target scents, and I want pictures of your daughters to go out with her, and with damn near everyone else. We're going to digitize the photos. They'll be on every cell phone in the county, okay? And TV, as well. But first things first."

A SHORT WHILE LATER, after a quick stop at Maude's diner to get a tall, hot latte, with her truck heater blasting, Kelly and Bugle headed east out of town with evidence bags holding part of the girls' clothing and photocopies of the full-size portraits. Even as she was driving she heard her cell phone ding, and figured it was probably the digital photos with background info.

It was beginning to hit her. She'd found the vehicle that had been carrying the girls only last night. Shouldn't some instinct have kicked in? Made her look inside the car, study the ground around for signs of a scuffle? Anything?

But the scene hadn't struck her that way. Once she knew the occupants were gone, that even their purses had vanished, there seemed to be nothing to worry about. No one injured, because if they had been they would have been on their way to the hospital and her radio should have been crackling with information.

It had been quiet, dark. People misjudged and went into ditches all the time, especially on cold nights where even a small patch of black ice could cause loss of control. She hadn't seen or felt any ice, but that didn't mean it hadn't been there when the car ran off the road.

But without any damage to the car or any obvious sign of foul play, there was really nothing she could do except get the vehicle towed when she couldn't get ahold of the owner.

Randy Beauvoir and his wife had been in Laramie for the weekend. They'd come home midday today, Randy had told her and the sheriff. They'd received Kelly's voice mail but hadn't immediately worried. No messages suggested the girl was in trouble. Probably at a friend's house for the night, as discussed. They'd get the car out of impound later.

But then Chantal's family had phoned, and the dominoes started tumbling. The girls weren't at one of their houses. Their families had no idea where they might be. Kelly's message about the car had suddenly struck them as a blinding warning flare.

The early winter night had begun conquering the landscape. Bright floodlights warned her of the approaching accident scene. She felt ill to the pit of her stomach. As she passed the cordoned-off area where the car had been found and crowds were beginning to gather, all she could hope was that somebody at Rusty's would give her a clue.

THE GRAVEL PARKING lot was clear of all but one vehicle, an aging pickup truck. Neon signs in the windows didn't yet shimmer with life and wouldn't until Rusty officially opened his doors.

She knew Rusty. She'd been called a number of times to help when some customers grew rowdy. Rusty did a better job than most of keeping it under control, but sometimes even he needed help. Roadhouses farther out had more problems, but here only ten miles out of town, the clientele seemed less likely to want to tussle, especially with the law. Most nights people came, drank and danced to local live music, and peace ruled, if not quiet.

This was the place that drew the patronage of local couples as much as local cowboys, and while she doubted anyone would think it wise for an unescorted woman to come here, three teens should have been safe. Older folks would have kept an eye on them, and Rusty would have served them soft drinks.

The door was unlocked. She pulled the tarnished brass handle and the ancient entry squeaked open. Inside the lighting was dim. The table candles in their squat hurricane lantern holders hadn't been lit.

Rusty was behind the long bar, polishing it with a rag. Directly across the large room from him, across the big dance floor, was a stage still holding band equipment.

"Hey, Rusty," she said as she and Bugle entered. "How's business?"

"Pretty good, but it always is on a holiday weekend. Tonight we'll be damn near empty. Can I help you, Kelly?"

He was a tall, lean man who always looked as if he needed to eat more of his own sandwiches. A gray moustache curled around the corners of his mouth.

"Have you heard about the three girls who've gone missing?"

Rusty's watery blue eyes widened. "No. Is that why you're here?"

She nodded and opened the brown envelope she'd brought with her, the one that held the eight-by-ten photos of each girl. She recited their names as she pulled them out. "Jane Beauvoir, Chantal Reston and Mary Lou Ostend. All high school seniors. We found their car in a ditch about five miles west of here just last night. No sign of them anywhere."

"Jeez," Rusty said, leaning toward the photos as if his old eyes needed some magnification. Reaching up with one hand, he turned on a bright light over the bar. Kelly blinked.

"Anyone else here yet?" she asked, even though it didn't feel like it.

He shook his head. "We don't open for another hour.

Not much to do before then." He picked up the photos one by one and studied them.

"They were here last night," Rusty said slowly. "Seems like they might have showed up a little after eight. Early. I hardly noticed because we were already full. Holiday," he said again as if in explanation.

"All three?"

"I do believe so."

"They hang out with anyone?"

He shook his head. "They sat at that table over there—" he pointed "—and drank enough diet soda to float a battle-ship." He lifted his gaze. "No alcohol, I swear."

She nodded. "Can I let Bugle sniff around while we talk?"

"Go for it, although how he's going to smell squat over the stale beer and fried chicken beats me."

She didn't argue or explain, but squatted down and pulled the three evidence bags from her pocket. One by one she let Bugle sniff them, then said, "Seek." He was off.

Straightening again, she pulled out her cell phone and hit the record button. "I'm taping this, okay? Just in case you mention something that winds up being important to us. All right by you?"

"Happy to do it," he answered. His gaze had wandered over to the table where he said the girls had been sitting. "Damn it, Kelly, they're so young and were just having fun. Haven't heard that much giggling since my own school days."

Then he paused and looked at her. "I didn't pay close attention, though. I wish I had. I'm sorry. We were busy. All they were doing was sitting and drinking cola. Oh, yeah, and they ordered a BLT to share. That was it. I didn't see anything wrong so I wasn't staring."

She nodded. "I understand. Anything at all catch your attention? Did one of them dance with anyone?"

He scratched his head and closed his eyes, pondering. "Dance? I think I saw two of them dance together. Line dancing. Nobody feels awkward if they don't have a partner, you know?"

"I know. So that was it?"

"Maybe not," he said after another minute. "They're pretty. I saw some guys wander by to talk with them, but they didn't stay." His eyes popped open and met hers intently. "My opinion, if you want it…"

"Everything you've got."

"Those girls weren't looking for trouble of any kind. Now, I've had people their age in here before, skating the line of being unwise. Trying to get someone to buy them a beer, wanting to dance with anything in pants. It happens. These girls were different. It was like they were having a private party and everything else was background."

Kelly tipped her head a little. "Unusual?"

"For that age. I was impressed. Must have good mamas."

Kelly wouldn't know about that. Turning, she saw Bugle sitting patiently upright beside the table Rusty had pointed out. Yup, they'd been there.

"Seek," she told him again. Then the trail became more winding. It wandered out onto the dance floor, approached the bar, headed down the hall to the ladies' room, then back to the table. "Find," she urged him, envisioning the evening the three girls had spent here.

He lowered his head and wound up at the front door. They'd left.

She looked again at Rusty. "So…nothing concerned you. You didn't feel like getting out your baseball bat?" She'd seen him swing that thing once. It put a quick end to most arguments.

"I wish I could tell you something. Nothing got me concerned enough to really pay attention. Nothing raised my hackles. But I'll keep thinking on it. Dang, those poor girls. If the car was in the ditch I don't suppose they ran away."

"They didn't get far if they wanted to." Reluctantly, she turned off the recorder and slipped the photos back into the envelope. Then she passed him her business card, needlessly since he certainly knew her and how to call the department. It just made her feel like she was actually doing something. "In case," she said.

"In case," he agreed. "Can I post some photos?"

"They should be on everyone's cell phone soon, but if you want some copies to put up, I'll let the office know."

He nodded slowly. "Maybe someone saw something I didn't. I'll tell everyone to check their phones tonight."

"And I'll get you some posters. It's early days yet, Rusty."

"Forty-eight hours, isn't that what they say?"

Her nod was short, wishing she could deny it.

"You never know," Rusty called after her as if to be reassuring. "They could be somewhere safe."

"Sure. Thanks for your help. Someone else might come round." Because they were all going to get dizzy running in circles trying to find these young ladies. Every step would be retraced a hundred times.

Damn!

Chapter Three

Day 1.5

Al Carstairs stood by the roadside as the crowd grew around the yellow police tape. Nobody was wanted inside that sacred circle yet except the crime scene techs.

The ground beside the road, apart from being winter-hard and covered with bits of sprayed gravel, wasn't going to yield much, he thought. Even the grass in the ditch, long since in winter hibernation, could present only broken stalks.

But nothing was going to be overlooked. If they could find any sign the girls had been picked up, or if they'd wandered off into the night, they had to locate it.

For his own part, he stepped back and began to walk along the pavement. Not even rubber skid marks to indicate the girls had tried to stop in a hurry, or swerved to avoid something.

Squatting, safely within the orange cones around which light traffic was being directed by cops wearing bright yellow vests, he scanned every inch of pavement.

He couldn't imagine why the driver hadn't tried to stop. Ice? Possible, but then the shoulder should have been torn up by the locked tires.

Something wasn't right. Then it struck him.

He stood and wondered whom he should talk to. Then he saw Kelly Noveno's SUV headed his way. Kelly. She was a smart one, and he trusted her judgment. He knew damn near everyone in the sheriff's office, but not in the same the way he knew Kelly. His animal control job often brought them together because of Bugle. Yeah, there were others he trusted as much or more, but none of them were out here right now.

How could a car go off the road without the driver trying to stop it? How could someone abscond with three high school girls? Rudolph the Reindeer's nose couldn't have blinked more brightly in his mind.

Kelly pulled over, inside the cones, then climbed out and approached him. "Nothing?" she asked, waving at the crime techs.

"Not from them yet. Kelly... I had a nuts idea. Tell me I'm crazy and I'll shut up."

She tilted her head. A tall woman, she didn't have to look up very high to meet his gaze. Dark snapping eyes. Full of vigor.

She nodded slowly. "Talk to me, Al. So far I'm coming up dry. Rusty thought they were the most well-behaved teens he'd ever had in his tavern, not even remotely looking for trouble. He said they seemed to be having a private party among the three of them."

Al nodded, but felt anxiety running along his nerve endings. So the girls hadn't been looking for trouble. That didn't mean they hadn't found it. It just meant it had been harder to find.

"What are you thinking?" Kelly pushed.

"No skid marks."

"Black ice."

He shook his head. "They still would have braked, and if they'd been braking to try to avoid going in the ditch or to avoid an obstacle, the shoulder would be torn up. Frozen as it is, it would have shown some tire marks. So they didn't brake."

He saw realization dawning on her face. "You're suggesting they weren't conscious? At least the driver?" Then she paused and swore. "Rusty said some guys passed their table briefly and chatted with them."

"Enough time," he answered.

She nodded, her expression growing even grimmer. She squatted to take a look at the pavement for herself, then straightened to study the shoulder once again. "Okay, I'm heading back to the tavern. Maybe Rusty knows who some of those guys were."

"I'm coming with you."

Animal control was part of the sheriff's department, but Al wasn't a standard deputy. It wasn't exactly pro forma for him to go along on an investigation, but everyone else was busy at the moment, and Kelly thought extra brains could always be useful.

"Let's go."

Despite the traffic hang-up around the scene, they got through quickly and were soon whizzing toward Rusty's. Bugle, in his backseat cage, knew Al so didn't seem disturbed by the addition of another person.

"It makes sense," Kelly said, although she didn't want to believe it.

"That someone could have drugged them? It's a wild hair, Kelly. It just popped into my head and wouldn't let go."

"I get it, but it still makes sense. Some guys stopped by their table to talk. And frankly, Al, considering these were young women out on a holiday weekend for some fun, they left Rusty's awfully early. I found the abandoned car just before eleven. When you were that age, did you call it a night that early?"

"No," he admitted. "Never."

"Exactly. No one was waiting for them, it was New Year's, all the parties would have been the night before. It's entirely possible that someone slipped something into their drinks and when they started to feel odd they decided to go home."

And that was crossing a lot of bridges with very little evidence, she thought. But it *did* make sense. She had to at least find out what guys were talking to them, if Rusty knew. Then she could interview them to see what more she could learn.

"Anyway," she said more to herself than him, "I didn't think of trying to track these guys down when Rusty mentioned them because he made it seem like it was all brief and in passing. I think I ought to kick my own butt. I should have gotten suspicious right then."

"Cut yourself some slack," Al said. "Three girls together at a table. A lot of men would stop by, get the brush-off and move on. Normal behavior. Nothing to stand out."

"Except the girls are missing." She clenched her teeth until her jaw ached, and when she turned into Rusty's parking lot she sprayed gravel.

She climbed out, leaving Bugle in the car with a cracked window and the heater on. Ten minutes. If this took longer, she'd come out and get her dog.

She slammed the SUV door emphatically, glanced at the watch on her wrist and marched toward the door, hardly aware that Al was on her heels.

Just then she was feeling awfully stupid. Stupid, and cold as the night nipped at her cheeks and the wind tossed her hair. She hoped the missing young women were safe and warm.

But she seriously doubted they were.

A COUPLE OF people had evidently showed up for work. A woman of about forty, wearing a leather fringed skirt, was making her way around the tables, lighting the hurricane lanterns. A younger man used a push broom on the dance floor, clearing off any remains of last night's revels.

"Already?" Rusty said, arching a brow as he pushed a spout into the top of a whiskey bottle.

"Some thoughts occurred," Kelly said. "Al?"

Rusty looked at him. "I know you. The animal control guy. What's up?"

Al unzipped his jacket halfway. Rusty didn't keep the place overwarm, but warm enough that winter gear could be suffocating. "Al Carstairs. I've got just a couple of questions, if you don't mind."

"You looking for these girls, too? I'm not surprised. Half the county will be out there tomorrow. Wish it wasn't so late right now. So, what can I do you for?"

"There's a chance the girls, or at least the driver, were unconscious when they went off the road."

Rusty straightened until he was stiff. He looked toward the table where the young women had been sitting just the night before. "Yeah?" he said hoarsely.

"Not sure," Kelly hastened to say. "Just an idea we're looking into."

Rusty nodded. He turned his attention again to Al. "What do you want to know?"

"You said some men stopped by their table. Do you remember who?"

Kelly had turned on her cell phone recorder and placed

it on the bar so Rusty would know she was recording. He looked at it briefly.

"I gotta think," he said. "Like I told Kelly, I wasn't paying close attention. There was nothing that made me think anything was going on except three kids drinking soda together and having a great time. Two brunettes, one bottle blonde."

"Chantal," Al interpolated. "The blonde. Turned eighteen two months ago. Hard worker. Never heard a complaint out of her about cleaning my kennels. She did love the animals, though. Talked about wanting to be a veterinarian."

Kelly drank in the facts, but wondered why Al felt it necessary to add them. To make Chantal seem more real to Rusty?

Maybe it had worked, because Rusty's frown turned really dark. "Yeah, she stood out. The other two were cute, too. Having a great time together."

"Jane wanted to be an EMT," Kelly volunteered.

Without another word, Rusty leaned his hands on the bar and looked down, eyes closed. He appeared to be straining to remember the night before. After a minute, he looked up and called, "Martha? Those teen girls who were here last night?"

The woman, carrying her electric match, came over to the bar. Her fading red hair was caught neatly into a netted bun, and the harsh sun and wind had given her a few wrinkles around her eyes and mouth. "Blonde and two brunettes? Youngest gals in here? Yeah. They was cute."

"Some guys talked to them. I can't remember who. Maybe one was Don Blevin?"

Martha shook her head. "I saw a couple of guys. Let me think. Dang, Rusty, we had so many folks in here last night."

"I know," he answered heavily.

Martha's eyes suddenly widened and she looked at Kelly's uniform. "Is these the girls what's missing? Oh my God…"

"That's why it's so important that you tell us everything you can remember," Kelly said. "Everything. How did they get their drinks? Who talked to them? Did anything seem…off?"

Understanding dawned on Martha's face. "You think they coulda been drugged?"

"We're just theorizing here," Al hastened to say. "Call it a wild idea. We don't know. We *can't* know."

Martha nodded, her expression as sober as a judge's. Then she turned her head a bit. "Jack, you got a minute?"

Shortly they were joined by the young man who'd been pushing the broom.

"Jack knows the younger set," Martha explained. "Who was them guys who stopped by the table of the three teen girls who was sitting over there last night. You know the guys?" She pointed at the table.

Jack's forehead creased and a lock of greasy hair fell over his forehead to make a small curl. "Sure. First it was Hal Olsen."

Kelly had pulled out her patrol book and wrote quickly despite recording all this. "Tell us about Hal?"

Jack shrugged. "He ain't nothin'. Maybe thirty. His wife left him two months ago and he's pretty much been living here. He likes to get hisself a dance with the pretty women. The girls didn't want any so he walked away."

"And after that?" Al asked.

"He got hisself a dance with Margot Eels. Pretty enough so I don't think he was feeling dissed."

"Who else?" Al asked.

Jack worked his mouth as if it would help his brain to think. "Art Mason. He's another regular. Drinks too much sometimes and Rusty has to cut him off, but I don't think he was sober when he talked to them gals." He flashed a faint smile. "Was kind of weaving. The gals laughed a bit after they sent him on his way. I think he landed in a chair near the dance floor. Then there was Keeb Dustin. Everybody knows the guy. Got hisself the service station east of town."

"Never causes trouble," Martha agreed. "He comes one night a week, either Friday or Saturday. He occasionally hits on someone, but not in a way that makes them complain."

"Anyone else?" Al asked.

"Don't know," Jack said. Martha shrugged.

"How'd the girls get their drinks?" Al asked.

"I brought 'em," Martha said promptly. "Fill up my tray with drinks at the station there, then pass them around to the tables. Keeps the bar from getting too crowded."

Kelly looked at Al for the first time. She saw awareness in his gray eyes, too. "Martha? You ever set your tray down with drinks on it?"

"Have to," she answered. "Gotta rearrange those bottles and glasses so I don't spill them all over anyone."

"But you're watching it every minute?"

"No," Martha answered. "People wanna talk. That's part of my job."

Kelly's stomach sank like a stone. So it was possible the girls had been slipped a drug. "How about," she said slowly, "you three make a list of everyone you can remember was in here last night. I'll pick it up tomorrow."

All three were agreeable, but Rusty looked positively dour. "I can't keep my eye on everything," he said to Kelly.

"Of course you can't, Rusty," she said reassuringly. "You folks have been a ton of help. And as for this suspicion, it's just that. Keep it quiet. We don't know that anything happened here at all. We just need every bit of information we can find."

Outside in the cold night, hearing Bugle call to her from the slightly open window of her truck, Kelly tried to keep her step steady as she walked toward him. Other cars were arriving now, but the flow wasn't heavy. Most of the interest would be down the highway around the crime scene. Folks had gathered to help, or out of curiosity. Who could say? But the crowd, the tape, the lights would draw attention. Wetting one's whistle could wait a short while.

When she laid her hand on the door of her vehicle, however, she froze. Then she tilted her head back and looked up at the amazingly clear star-filled sky.

She hoped that somewhere out in those desolate spaces there weren't three young women looking up at the stars with dead eyes.

Al was suddenly beside her, touching her arm. "Nobody would go to all that trouble just to kill them."

She lowered her gaze to his face. "Maybe that's even worse."

"Then we have to keep going, push as hard as we can."

"Yeah." Her answer was short, but she squared her shoulders and shook off the despair that wanted to overtake her. They had to find them as quickly as possible. Somewhere there had to be an essential clue.

She just wished she knew where to look beyond this tavern.

"Let's go," she said. "We have at least three guys to track down and get someone out to them for interviews."

The car felt too hot when she climbed in, but a glance at the dash thermometer told her it was sixty-eight. A good temperature for Bugle. He woofed a welcome.

As soon as Al was in the passenger seat with the door closed, she reached for her radio. Velma's scratchy voice answered.

"Hey, Velma," Kelly said. "Is Gage around?"

"Yeah, in the conference room working out a plan for tomorrow's search. You need him?"

"Please." She waited a couple of minutes, then heard the sheriff's gravelly voice.

"What's up, Kelly?"

"We were talking to employees at the tavern. I need someone to hunt up three guys and question them about the interactions they had with the three missing girls last night at Rusty's." Flipping open her notebook, she read the names to Gage.

"Slower," he said. Then, "Okay, got it. I know two of them. I'll send some deputies out to talk to them. Thanks, Kelly. Good work."

"Thank Al Carstairs. He's been a great help."

"I will. Are you coming in?"

"Absolutely. We need to talk in person." No way was she going to put the drug theory on the air. God knew how many police band radios would pick it up. The names of the men she wanted questioned didn't worry her. They'd come up at the tavern and she was sure they were about to be shared with the evening's early customers.

Gage's laugh was dry. "See you shortly."

Kelly looked down at the tall cup of latte she'd allowed to grow as cold as the interior of the truck. "I think I'm going to take a brief break. I need some coffee to get through this night."

"I'll join you," Al answered. "It'd make some good time to run over what we just learned."

Bugle seemed to quietly woof his agreement.

Yeah, they needed to do that, Kelly thought as she put the SUV in gear, swung a wide circle and drove back onto the state highway. Time to think it all over. You could get only so far just by picking up the puzzle pieces. Sooner or later you had to try to put them together.

She glanced sideways at Al, and out of nowhere came the unbidden wish that this would be a social coffee. Nope. They could be friends but they had to remain professional or risk making a mess. If he was even interested.

Besides, the only thing that mattered tonight was three missing girls, girls who might be terrified out of their minds. Girls who might be suffering.

Girls who might be dead.

THE CROWD AT the accident scene had thinned out. She paused long enough to let Al jump out to get his truck while she surveyed the faces that looked so odd in the arc lamps. It was getting later and colder, and evidently people thought nothing more would happen tonight. Overhead the county's two choppers were flying a search pattern with bright spotlights sweeping over barren fields.

Fifteen minutes later, she pulled into a parking spot in front of the City Diner, also known as Maude's, and through the diner windows scanned the interior. Al pulled in beside her and climbed out, coming over to her window. She opened her door halfway but didn't get out.

"No discussion here tonight," she remarked. The place was jammed full.

"I'll run in and get the coffee, then," Al said. "Nobody will badger *me* with questions. Think Gage would like some? And if so how does he like it?"

"Are we going to offend Velma?" she asked almost absently. Her thoughts were far away, reaching out into the frigid, empty night, trying not to imagine horrible things.

"Do we care? Gage."

"Yeah, he always wants his black, I think."

"You?"

"The biggest hot latte Maude makes."

"I'll see you at the office, then."

She listened to her door squeak as she closed it. The thing always squeaked when it was cold. She glanced over her shoulder at Bugle and figured he was probably starting to get desperate for some room to move. He tolerated the caging part of the job, but he was naturally very active.

Smothering a sigh, she threw her truck into gear and drove it the half block to the sheriff's offices. Across the street was the courthouse square, where Bugle could run a few laps and deposit his business. She let him out, then grabbed a plastic bag to clean up after him. He was good about that, always doing his business near her so she didn't have to run around needlessly.

When he was done she dumped the bag in the trash can, then turned to cross the street to the office. She saw Al just about there carrying a tray and a big brown bag with handles from the diner.

"That looks like more than coffee," she remarked as they met at the door. Since his hands were full, she reached out to open it.

"Maude's clearing some things out for the night. I hope everyone likes pie."

"Maude's pies? I think half this county would crawl across hot sand to get to one."

He gave a short laugh. Relief. They needed something to leaven the horror.

Inside, the office was much quieter than it had been earlier. Only four officers sat at desks. Probably a great many deputies had been sent home to rest up for a search tomorrow. Any others might be out protecting the crash site. Even Velma had vanished, a very rare thing.

Al lined up four pies on the table near the coffee. They were going to make plenty of people happy in the morning. Right now, he cut into an apple pie and served himself the wedge on a paper plate. "Hey, guys," Al said to the others, "help yourself to the pie. What would you like, Kelly?"

For the first time in hours she remembered that all she had eaten was a bowl of cereal.

"There's apple, blueberry, mincemeat and cherry."

The thought of any of them made her mouth water. "Apple would be great."

Gage had apparently heard their voices because he came out of the back, thanked them for the coffee and dug into the mincemeat pie.

He led them to the conference room, where maps covered the table. "Planning for tomorrow," he said as he eased into a high-backed chair. "Now, what's going on with these three guys—who are being interviewed right now, I believe—and what didn't you want to mention on the radio?"

"I'll let Al tell you," Kelly said. "He thought of it."

"A wild hair," Al said yet again.

"It didn't sound so wild after we went back to the tavern and talked to Martha. Go on." She spooned a small bit of apple pie into her mouth, to make it clear she wasn't talking, and wished only that she could savor it as all of Maude's pies deserved savoring. Right now, as knotted with worry as she was, it might as well have been ash.

"Well," Al said slowly, "I was looking at the highway and shoulder. Everyone thinks the girls skidded."

"And you don't?" Gage asked.

"Not likely. If they'd braked, even if they didn't leave tread marks on the pavement because of black ice, they'd have chewed up the shoulder, frozen or not. That car is too old to have anti-lock brakes, so there should have been some sign."

Gage swallowed a mouthful of mincemeat, followed by some coffee. "You're right, and at last report from the scene, they're not finding any clues as to why the car went off the road." He paused, his dark gaze intent. "That doesn't mean they won't."

"I know. I'm not a crime scene tech. Hell, I'm only half a deputy."

"I beg to differ, but go on."

"Well, it was like a light going on in my head. Why wouldn't they brake when going off the road? Maybe they were unconscious or seriously drunk on soft drinks."

Gage sat up a little straighter and put his paper plate and plastic fork down. Pain rippled across his face but it didn't remain. The frown did.

"You think they were drugged? Before they left the tavern?"

Al shook his head. "I don't know. I can't prove it."

"But," Kelly interjected, "Martha, who served their drinks, said she often puts her drinks tray down, either to rebalance it or because people want to chat. In other words, nobody watched those girls' drinks every second between bar and table."

"Nobody would think it necessary," Gage murmured. He'd forgotten his pie and his coffee and rubbed his chin. "The problem around here is that people know one another. It wouldn't occur to them to question the trustworthiness of a neighbor. Over time, they've sometimes had to, but by and large those are considered isolated incidents, nothing to worry about. Most people still don't lock their doors. We've grown, it's no longer a place where everyone knows everyone else, but the attitudes are still mired in an earlier time. We don't even imagine anyone would drug three young women. And yet, it's entirely possible we've got a sicko running around. As the old sheriff, Nate Tate, liked to say, 'This county's going to hell in a handbasket.' Not really, but change has been happening for a while."

He fell silent for a few beats. "Drugs. Damn it all to hell, I can see it and it would explain a lot."

"They left the bar early, too," Kelly said. "Kids that age don't end their partying around ten o'clock. I imagine they started to feel unwell."

"Probably so." He shook his head, then reached for his coffee. "Okay, then. Things just got even more complicated. If they were drugged, it had to be someone who didn't stand out at Rusty's place or we'd have heard about him by now."

He eyed Kelly. "In short, one of our neighbors."

Twenty minutes later, Gage sent them both on their way. "You need to rest up for tomorrow. It's going to be a long, cold day."

"I want to know what kinds of answers we get from those three guys," Kelly argued.

"Unless one of them confesses, it'll hold till morning. Besides, we've got a team going out there to try to speak to everyone who was at the bar last night. You might as well get your sleep. If anything breaks, I'll let you know."

Kelly had to be content with that. She really didn't know what else she could do out there.

"Tips should start coming in," she remarked. "I can man the phones."

"There are already four deputies out there doing exactly that. Take Bugle home."

Out of arguments, Kelly obeyed. Al walked out with her but only around the corner to where she was parked. He needed to collect his vehicle from down the street in front of the diner. Kelly watched her breath blow clouds, and couldn't help but notice it was growing colder. Of course it was. It was night.

And the young women…

She truncated the thought. Running it ceaselessly through her head wasn't going to improve anything. With the rising sun at least they could search, maybe stop to ask questions at homesteads that weren't too far out.

Right now…right now they just needed to wait for word to spread. Then would come the tips, mostly useless.

But at the moment… She just shook her head.

Al spoke as they neared her vehicle. "You going to be okay?"

Her head snapped around and she stopped walking. "Why wouldn't I be?"

He faced her directly. "I'm a combat vet, Kelly. I know about second-guessing, delayed reactions and sometimes shutdowns. This has got you upset and worried. You give a damn. You're not just going to go home and turn on the TV to some romantic comedy or suspense movie."

No, she wasn't. Everything inside her was knotted with frustration and worry. She probably wouldn't sleep worth a damn. "Sometimes you just have to endure. Get through it."

He nodded. "I know. I'm just saying…" He turned his head away. "Forget it. You need an ear, I'm available. This is probably going to eat you alive until we find those girls."

She figured it probably would. She just hoped they found the young women soon and found them unharmed.

Then she and Bugle headed home for what she anticipated was going to be a very long night.

Chapter Four

Day 2

Bugle found the first scent. At the scene of the accident, he nosed the ground and followed it to the highway's edge. There he stopped.

It wasn't a good sign, but everyone hoped Bugle was wrong or that some kind person had picked the girls up.

Or at least everyone *tried* to hope. If the girls had been given a ride by a friendly person, surely they would have called home by now. The silence had become terrifying for their families, and for everyone else.

Despite Bugle's following the scent to the road, no one even thought of calling off the search. They might have walked down the pavement, the cold might have weakened their scents. Regardless, there was no way they'd stop this search, whatever the dog might indicate.

Cadel Marcus, part-time deputy and dog trainer, joined Kelly at roadside with his K-9, Dasher. "I'm with you. Those girls didn't wander off over the fields. No scents on the far side of the road either."

"We still have to look. Someone could have left them farther along."

"Maybe." He nodded to Al, who joined them. "How's the dog-catching business?"

"I get most of them home. Say, if you want a shepherd mix to train, I have one whose owners are apparently fed up with his wanderlust."

Cadel nodded slowly. "Wonder what they're doing to make him run. Yeah, I'll take a look at him later. See what kind of potential he has."

Al's voice turned dry. "He's working on a teddy bear right now."

That drew a laugh from Cadel and even a very sober Kelly smiled.

The helicopters flew above again, having taken off as soon as the light was good enough to see the ground below. The searchers, civilian and police, were divided up into about ten groups and spaced out along both sides of the highway, on either side of the wreck scene. Between the rough ground and brush, they had to move slowly in order to avoid missing something important.

At this point few of the searchers hoped to find the girls. Now most of them were hoping for a clue. An item of clothing, a shoe, a purse, anything that might indicate the direction in which they had disappeared.

To Kelly's dismay, Bugle didn't seem particularly interested. She knew that he could pick up a scent from quite a long distance, either on the ground or in the air above his head. His boredom was as loud as a paid infomercial.

No girls around here.

Her gloved hand tightened on his leather leash, and she had to force herself to pay attention anyway. Scents were harder to detect in the cold, she reminded herself. Bugle might need to get closer.

But at that point, she didn't know if finding the girls out here after a long cold night would necessarily be a good thing.

Damned if they did, damned if they didn't. Never had that phrase seemed more apt.

THE GROUND SEARCH was called off for the night. Not a thing had been found. Kelly dragged herself back to her snug little house on the edge of town, a place that needed far more attention than she gave it. All her plans for fixing it up had kind of washed away in the reality of being a deputy covering so much territory for such a relatively small department. Oh, they had enough people to cover the routine, and even a group of investigators and a crime scene unit, but when something blew up, it was all hands on deck.

Something had blown up.

She fed Bugle some extra kibble and treated him to some chicken livers she boiled for him from a frozen stash she kept. He'd had a long, cold day, too, and gratefully scarfed it all down.

For herself she did nothing but make a pot of coffee because she needed something hot, fast. Then she collapsed in her easy chair, pinching the bridge of her nose to try to stave off a headache. The sense of hopelessness seemed beyond defeat right now. Occasionally she caught the sound of distant helicopter rotors as the two choppers kept up a search by spotlight in areas farther away from the wreck. The frigid dark made a continued search dangerous for people on foot, but the choppers kept up their valiant duty.

They had long since passed the limit of how far the girls could have walked, so now they were in the territory of a possible body dump. Or an out-and-out kidnapping, although no one seemed willing to say the word out loud.

In fact, no one seemed willing to consider the possibility that it might be too late for the three women. No one. A whole lot of determined people had spent a very long, very cold day hunting in the brush and gullies.

Just as the coffeepot blew a loud burst of steam to announce that it had finished, she heard a sharp rap on her door. Sighing, she rose and went to answer it, trying not to hope it was good news about the missing women. Good news, however, would have crackled over her radio or come by phone.

She opened the door, half expecting to see one of her neighbors with questions about the day's search. Instead she found Al Carstairs. His cheeks were still reddened from the cold, and he was carrying two big brown bags with handles and a tray of tall coffee cups. "Don't know about you, Kelly, but I'm starved and I don't feel like cooking. Care to join me for dinner?"

She couldn't possibly have refused the offer. Not only was it kind, but she really didn't want to be alone with her thoughts. Weary or not, she smiled. "Come in. I just made coffee, though." She reached to help with the cardboard tray.

"I bet it isn't a latte."

Despite all, she laughed. "It sure isn't."

Once inside he carried the bags to the kitchen counter. Small as this house was, the living area and kitchen were a single room, divided by a small bar. Bugle evidently had taken a liking to Al, because as soon as his arms were empty, the dog nudged his leg, then sat expectantly with his tail sweeping the wood floor and displacing a colorful rag rug.

Al obligingly squatted and gave the dog a good scratch around his ruff. Then he straightened and smiled at Kelly. "Bugle's a great dog. Anyway, dinner. I hope you like steak sandwiches. They're the most filling thing on Maude's menu and after today I think we both need calories."

"A steak sandwich sounds wonderful," she said, meaning it. "As many hours as we were out in the cold, I could probably eat a whole one."

The sandwiches were famous, and their size was always huge. Maude had always catered to hardworking ranchers, and people with more sedentary jobs made use of doggie bags. Kelly usually thought of a steak sandwich as two meals for the price of one.

Not tonight, though. She had a feeling she could polish one off in its entirety.

Al began pulling insulated containers out of the bags. He enumerated as he went. "Steak sandwich, steak sandwich, tossed salad, extra rolls for the extra hungry and another pie. I think Maude hopes that if she stokes us all on sugar we'll find those girls."

"Energy will help," she admitted. "I'm worn out. The cold absolutely drained me today."

He smiled her way. "Probably because we never took a break to warm up."

Bugle's nose reached the countertop, and he sniffed, making a hopeful little whine.

"You already had a huge dinner," Kelly said to him.

"He's apparently got good taste, though." Al's great smile seemed to leaven the entire room.

They decided to eat at the bar right out of the foam containers. "No dishes tonight," said Al. "We've got another long day coming up."

She agreed, and felt no need to apologize for failing to retrieve any of her limited quantity of plates, bowls and utensils.

She'd known Al for several years, but didn't really know him. It was odd, when she thought about it, but his work in animal control didn't often cross with hers as a deputy.

"You have a kennel out behind your house?" she asked

him after she had swallowed the first juicy mouthful of the steak sandwich.

"Oh, yeah. Insulated metal building with twenty cages. More like a barn. I seldom need that much room but occasionally it happens."

"But don't the owners want them back?"

"First I have to identify the owners, and that's not always easy. When dogs slip out, they sometimes lose their collars and all too often they're not microchipped. Then there are the dumped dogs."

"Dumped?" She turned her head to look at him. He held up a finger as he finished chewing and swallowing a mouthful of his sandwich.

"Dumped," he repeated. "God knows why, but some idiots think their dogs are equipped to become self-sustaining. Now, mind you, these are animals that haven't had to hunt for a meal in their lives and are used to human care. Most of them, anyway. Some folks hope a rancher will find the animal and take it in. I hate to tell you how often that turns bad."

She nodded. "Why?"

"I've been called out too often by a rancher who's found a dead dog. He could just bury it, of course, or leave it for the vultures, but most ranchers care about animals more than that. So they call me, hoping I track someone down to tell them what happened to their animal. I wish I could. I wouldn't be polite about it."

"Nor would I," she admitted, feeling sickened by the thought of what those animals must have endured. "What a cruel thing to do!"

"Especially when you consider they could have turned them in at any vet's office if they didn't want to hunt up a shelter. The lucky ones get found and fed while a rancher waits for me to show up. They don't need another dog. Mainly because dozens are getting abandoned."

Kelly urged herself to eat more, and felt her appetite returning. "What do you do with the survivors?"

"Kennel them. The vet, Mike Windwalker, does his best to help get them adopted, but it's not like we're short on dogs around here. Or cats for that matter. But cats are better at looking after themselves, especially if they had some time with an older cat who taught them to hunt. And most of our ranchers and farmers don't exactly mind another barn cat showing up. They're useful."

"But the dogs aren't?"

"Not without a lot of training. Cadel Marcus takes some to train them as K-9s or service animals, but there's a limit to what he can do, too."

"It sounds like a serious problem."

"It is." He polished off his sandwich and some of the salad, then encouraged her to eat more. "Another long day ahead."

She didn't want to think about it. Not until it arrived. Reminding herself that she'd been famished, she focused on savoring her dinner.

At any other time, she realized she would have been feeling content. A pleasant, handsome man dining with her, and excellent dinner, Bugle pretending to sleep near the foot of her stool but alert for any falling crumbs.

"That fireplace work?" he asked.

"I believe so. I haven't given it much of a workout because I'm gone too often."

"Wanna try it?"

She shrugged as she was about to put the last bit of sandwich in her mouth. "Sure. It worked fine the one time I used it."

Shortly after she'd taken the job here, having moved

from Laramie County. It had been a big change for her in terms of a smaller department serving fewer people overall, but that's what she wanted. Community policing. She'd certainly found it here, and after five years had no desire to move on.

There were dry logs stacked in a box near the fireplace, and he laid them on the grate with some twisted newspaper beneath them. They'd probably light good and fast as long as they'd been sitting there. Then he reached in to open the flue and an empty bird's nest fell out onto the stack of wood.

"I hope that's the only one," he remarked.

"So do I." She'd never had that chimney cleaned and if it was packed with stuff like that, it'd become an interesting evening.

Grabbing a poker, he shoved it up inside the chimney and didn't even loosen any creosote.

"Well, here goes," he said, pulling a butane lighter out of his pocket and holding it to the paper. "If the flame and smoke don't head straight up, I'll put it out."

"Okay." She couldn't even work up any worry about it. Instead she began to gather up the remains of their dinner and put them away in the fridge. Except for the pie. That would be fine on the counter and she had a strong feeling both of them would want a piece before the evening was over.

She looked over and saw the flames were standing straight up and that no smoke was escaping. "I guess it's okay."

"Right as rain." He remained squatting for a few more minutes while she finally settled into her recliner. There was a gooseneck chair on the other side of the battered side table. Oh, it was apparent that she entertained a whole lot. Yup.

Mainly one girlfriend at a time.

Al straightened, brushing his hands on his jeans. "I guess I should go. I've imposed…"

"You haven't imposed at all," she interrupted swiftly. "Get comfortable. There's still that pot of coffee and…" She trailed off.

"You don't want to be thinking about those girls tonight."

"Not if I can avoid it," she admitted.

"Me neither."

The lattes were long gone so he hunted up two mugs from her cupboards and brought a couple of cups of coffee to set on the end table. "You want anything in yours?"

"Black is fine," she answered. "Thanks."

A silence followed after he settled into the gooseneck chair. She knew why. They were both thinking about the same thing and neither of them wanted to talk about it. Even distractions hardly worked. Three young women were residing at the corners of her mind and wouldn't go away. The second night.

They could be looking only for bad things now.

THREE TEENS HUDDLED beneath a ragged blanket in a dank basement that even during the day had barely let in a crack of light. A pile of protein bars had been dumped in with them along with a bunch of plastic bottles of water.

Their winter outerwear was gone, as were their shoes and phones. In trembling voices, they'd talked about finding a way to escape, but knew in the dangerous weather outside they wouldn't get very far in their thin clothes and bare feet.

All they could do was huddle together beneath a smelly blanket and wait. They tried to buck each other up, but young though they were they knew no good could come from this.

Over the last twenty-four hours, hopelessness had begun to settle in. Tears had been frequent, terror had been constant, and at one point Mary Lou had even suggested they stop using the blanket and huddling and just freeze to death.

The other two girls had gotten upset with her. Chantal pointed out tearily that they had hope only if they stayed alive.

They grew quiet for long spells, feeling wearier and wearier. No protein bar could stave off the fatigue of constant fear.

They sat in the dark, as close as they could get, while their nerves crawled, their bodies ached and their minds ran rampant with horrible ideas.

They had no idea how they'd gotten here, nor any idea of who had put them here, but they knew there was no good reason for it. None.

EVEN COFFEE COULDN'T keep Kelly from dozing briefly in her easy chair. Sounds drew her out of an unpleasant nightmare and she saw Al putting another log on the fire.

When he turned around, he saw that her eyes were open, and he gave her a half smile. "Want me to leave so you can get to bed?"

She shook her head. She wasn't a coward by nature but this event had disturbed her more than many. "I'm still feeling guilty."

"For what? I saw your report. No damage to the car, no occupants, no reason to think anything except a passerby picked them up to get them out of the cold. It was too dark to look for tire skid marks. I mean..."

She nodded. "I know all that rationally, Al. It's the irrational part of me that's having trouble."

He pulled the gooseneck chair over until he was close enough to offer her his hand. She couldn't help but reach over and take it.

Bugle, finding this something entirely new in his experience, came over to investigate as if he weren't certain anyone should be touching Kelly.

"It's okay, Bugle. Relax."

The dog sniffed their joined hands, then settled on the floor between them.

Al grinned. "He's still feeling protective, I see."

"Always. My buddy." But her mind wasn't on Bugle, and she needed to distract herself or she'd get no rest this awful night, but she had to be bright and ready for the morning. A quiet sigh escaped her.

"Where are you from?" Al asked. "Someone said you used to be with the Laramie police, but I'm sure that wasn't your entire life."

She summoned a smile. "No. Hardly. I've moved around. My dad is Puerto Rican and I was born there. My mom worked as an executive for one of the companies that had a business there, but she died five years ago. Cancer."

"I'm sorry."

"So am I, but given what she went through in the end, her death was a relief." She shook her head a little. She didn't want to go down this road. "Anyway, they moved to Florida when my mom was transferred. My dad was a police officer and he took a local job."

"So you followed in his footsteps?"

"So it seems. I can't remember ever wanting to do anything else, but I essentially won the lottery when I was tapped to be a K-9 officer. I love dogs. Dad wanted me to stay in Florida, but I wanted to come up here. I visit him when I can. At least living in Florida, for him, means people don't look at him suspiciously."

His brow rose. "Why would they do that?"

"He's Latin, Al. With a bit of Indio in him. I get cross-eyed looks, as well. A lot of folks still think I'm a foreigner. Many people seem to have a hard time believing Puerto Ricans are US citizens."

He was frowning faintly. "I hope you don't run into a whole lot of that around here."

"No more than the indigenous people. Maybe less. I have a badge."

At that he laughed quietly. "That does help."

The smile felt awkward on her face, but it lifted her spirits a bit. She needed that. There wasn't a damn thing she could do right now. She was about to ask him his story when the landline rang.

Forgetting everything, nearly tripping over Bugle in her eagerness, she ran to get the phone. It was Gage Dalton. "I'm sure you're wondering about those guys we questioned."

"Absolutely. Al Carstairs is here. I'm sure he wants to know, too. Speaker?"

"Go ahead. Just don't give me a reverb."

She punched the speaker button, then sat on one of the bar stools. "You're on, Gage."

"Hi, Gage," Al said.

"Howdy. Okay, the long and short of it is that our three interviewees were put off by the way the girls dismissed them. Including our infamous drunk, Art Mason. Judging by what some of the other patrons said, he was in no condition to cross a room, let alone get down a highway. Jack, the janitor, said they wouldn't let Art leave until he'd drunk a pot of coffee. Way too late for the accident. As for Keeb Dustin, he appeared so appalled by the idea he'd be interested in girls so young that the deputy believed him. Anyway, he only stopped by the table because they were laughing and he liked hearing they were having a good time. Warned 'em to avoid anyone who showed them too much attention, then moved on to the bar, where most folks saw him nursing a few longnecks until after midnight."

"So they're clear," Al said.

"Well, hold on," Gage answered. "At this point I'm not clearing anyone, but yeah, neither seems likely. The place was busy. I'm not sure anyone would have noticed if one of these guys left for a while. Then there's Hal Olsen. Always on the lookout for a pretty woman. Apparently he scored that night because Lydie Dern says he went home with her about eleven or so. In the other direction, so they didn't see anything on the road."

"Dang," said Kelly, who only then realized just how much she'd been hoping they'd get a good clue.

"We'll keep an eye on them, of course," Gage continued. "I've got a couple of men working the tavern tonight, to see if anyone remembers anything unusual about last night, but so far no go. It seems many of them weren't there, and those who were had more important things on their minds."

Kelly chewed her lower lips for a few seconds. "Gage? Were the girls involved in anything that might have drawn attention? What have we got on their backgrounds now?"

"Been working on that. Three young ladies, all with high grades, members of the soccer team and the debate club. If it weren't for the fact that Jane Beauvoir was a member of the chess club, I'd have said the three of them were joined at the hip. Families all attend Good Shepherd Church, no one seems to think they had any enemies, either the teens or their parents…although that can always be a mistaken impression. Enemies don't always announce themselves."

"True. You're saying we don't really have anything."

Gage snorted, audible through the speaker. "I'm saying we haven't found it yet. Abducting three young women from the side of the road before eleven at night is a bold thing to do. It's also stupid, because no matter how smart they think they are, perps always leave something behind. You remember that rule."

Kelly nodded even though she couldn't be seen through the phone. "The perp takes something away but he always leaves something behind."

"We've just got to find it. Anyway, you two catch up on your sleep. Tomorrow's going to be another long day."

Kelly disconnected and sat staring at the phone as if it might have something else to offer. The ugly truth was that it wouldn't. It was like being inside a dark bag without a ray of light.

Maybe like those girls.

She passed a hand over her eyes as if she wanted to erase her thoughts, then looked over at Al. "It's still early," she said, surprised as her eyes grazed the wall clock. Not even nine yet.

As long as she'd lived up north, some part of her still lived where she'd been born, when night didn't fall so early even in the winter.

"Yeah," he answered. "Not a very helpful call."

"Maybe, maybe not. Weeding things out counts, too. But listen, don't you have animals to look after?"

"Not really. All the pets have been taken home. The rest have enough food to look after themselves tonight. Minks, by the way, don't make friendly pets."

But he was standing and pushing the chair back to its original position.

Crap, Kelly thought. He'd brought her dinner, she'd asked him to stay just a short while ago and now he was apparently taking her question as a dismissal. She slid off the stool, saying, "Al."

He glanced at her. "Yeah?"

"I was asking about the animals, not hinting for you to leave."

"You should get some sleep," he answered. "You heard Gage."

She hesitated, then said, "What makes minks bad pets, and would you like some of that pie you brought?"

He laughed then. "Minks are hard to tame, even if you start when they're still kits. It takes a lot of patience. And that's just the start."

She pulled the aluminum foil off the pie and retrieved two small plates from the cupboard. A knife would have to do for cutting slices. "What's the rest?"

"They prefer a semiaquatic environment, not easy to do at home around here. They can be really aggressive and you can't let them out because they'll kill other minks if any are around, and foxes would love to dine on them. They should be solitary except during mating, and these folks made the mistake of keeping two. They weren't exactly getting along."

"Wow. Worse than ferrets?"

"Depends. They're part of the same family of carnivores, *Mustelidae*. There you've got ferrets, skunks, weasels, even otters. But as long as you get a ferret young and give it plenty to entertain itself, it'll be little trouble. Plus they can be truly affectionate. These minks?" He just shook his head. "Someone will think they're adorable. Someone always does."

"So what will you do with them?" She passed him a slice of peach pie that smelled richly of cinnamon.

He thanked her and slid onto a bar stool.

"Coffee?"

"With this?" he asked. "Absolutely. Maude's pie can make my teeth curl."

That drew a laugh from her. "Lots of sugar. One of the reasons I don't eat them often." She cut herself a slice, then poured coffee for both of them from the waiting pot. It really hadn't been that long ago that she'd made it. This day had been endless.

Well, until now, anyway. She was enjoying Al's company. "The minks," she reminded him.

"Oh, I'm looking for a facility to take them. A zoo, a rescue organization. We'll see, but since they've been fed ground meat by humans since they were tiny, I'm not sure they could make it on their own even if they survived predators."

"Probably not," she agreed, sliding onto the other stool. "I don't know that I'd want to take them on."

"You'd need the facilities to survive it. They're nocturnal but awake a lot in the daytime. They're carnivores. They don't like each other unless they're mating."

"Sounds like some marriages."

For the first time she heard his full-throated belly laugh.

"Well," she said, "it *does*."

"That's what made me laugh. Anyway, I'll find someone to take the minks. As for other animals…we're quiet at the moment. I keep an eye out for strays when the weather's dangerous like this, but most of them go home immediately. No pets have been dumped recently, at least none that have been found and reported to me."

The pie was an amazing combination of tart and sweet. She felt her mouth pucker and revel all at once. Closing her eyes, she gave herself over to the wonderful flavor.

Al fell silent, too, and she could sense he was enjoying

the pie as much as she was. It should have felt sinful, with those girls out there in some kind of terrible trouble, but somehow it didn't.

She couldn't spend every minute worrying and thinking about it or she'd soon be no use to anyone. She'd learned a while ago that the toughest part of her job was trying not to get so involved her emotions began to rule her. Separation was essential. Even if she had to go to the ladies' room and cry about it for a while until she could restore her balance.

God knew, she'd seen some awful stuff that still lingered with her.

"Did you grow up here?" she asked, once again seeking a diversionary train of conversation. Although, she admitted, she wanted to know more about Al.

"Yeah, I did. Family's gone now, though. The two of them operated a music store that mostly catered to students who wanted to rent instruments or take additional lessons. I used to love listening to my dad play the oboe. It's such a beautiful, haunting sound, but put him and my mother together on a pair of saxophones and the place would rock."

She smiled. "That sounds wonderful. You musical?"

"Me? Nah. I was at the wrong age to want to do anything my parents did. Bad enough I had to work at the store and sell sheet music and reeds. I used to go nuts sometimes watching a high-school-aged clarinetist try out a bunch of reeds before settling on one he or she liked. No thought to the cost of those discarded reeds, and sometimes I was never certain they could really tell the difference."

Kelly laughed. "I'm sure some could."

"Oh, yeah, but not all of them. I got the feeling it was a thing to do if you played a woodwind. Anyway, my folks didn't mind it, so who was I to get annoyed?"

"What made you leave?"

"Did you know you can die of a broken heart? For real?"

She turned on her stool until she faced him directly. He seemed preoccupied with reaching for another piece of pie. "Al?"

"It's true," he said, his tone changing, growing a bit sorrowful. "Dad took a road trip to Denver to get some supplies. Unfortunately, he was mugged and killed for fifty dollars and a credit card."

Kelly's breath snagged and her chest tightened, aching for him.

"Anyway," he went on, "Mom died two days later. Broken heart syndrome, they called it. It had a fancier name, of course, since it was discovered by some Japanese doctors, but whatever. Her heart stopped beating right, and she thought the pain was grief and...too late. She was gone."

Kelly instinctively reached out to grip his forearm. "I am so sorry, Al. So, so sorry."

"It was a long time ago." At last he turned his head and gave her a faint smile. His eyes were dry. "Still hurts a bit, but it *was* a long time ago. After I recovered from the shock and two funerals, I put the shop up for sale and went looking for the Marine recruiter. I needed to get out of this town."

She squeezed his arm, then let go. "I can imagine."

He shrugged slightly. "I turned tail, but at the time I was glad I did. Boot camp gave me a whole lot of ways to focus on something else and expend a bunch of anger."

To her it sounded like one rational solution to an overwhelming loss. Somehow she couldn't imagine him trying to run his parents' store after that, and feeling angry every time someone tossed aside a half-dozen reeds before finding the perfect one. He might have let them know what he thought.

That drew a quiet sound of amusement from her.

"What?" he asked, digging into a second piece of the pie.

"I was just imagining you dealing with the students who tossed aside reeds after all you went through."

That brought the smile back to his face. "It sure wouldn't have been pretty. For a while there I was one angry young man."

"Understandably. I was pretty angry after my mom died, but it wasn't as if there was anything she could have done. She had a particularly aggressive form of cancer. Oh, well." Thoughts kept getting dark, probably because of all that had happened in the last twenty-four hours.

Her mind kept wanting to wander out into the icy darkness outside, but she couldn't let it. What was she going to do? Race out into the night and run wildly around?

No, she had to wait for morning, for the briefing, for all the details that had been undoubtedly gathered today by various teams. Wait and hope for a major clue.

God, she hated this! She squeezed her eyes closed and battled all the feelings about what those young women might be experiencing, trying to put them away into a box until there was something she could actually act on.

"You care."

Al's voice reached into her dark thoughts and she opened her eyes. "Don't you?" she asked almost truculently.

"Very much. Thing is, being in the military I eventually learned to put things away until I had to deal with them. Once you've made your plans, done your end of it, there's nothing more except to wait for the fallout. If you can't sleep, if you're gnawing holes in your own stomach, it doesn't change a damn thing."

She knew he was right but didn't know how to get to

that pinnacle of detachment. It wasn't as if she'd ever had to deal with anything like this in her policing career. "I deal with accidents, robberies, even a rare murder...not abductions, Al. It's different."

"Of course it's different. Worse, maybe, because at this point we can't even be sure those girls were abducted. Maybe they *did* hitch a ride, get dropped off at some-place closer to home and just never made it because of the weather."

She sat up a little straighter. "That's possible." Then she started crashing again. "There's still the fact that they went off the road without even braking."

"Maybe we'll find out otherwise. Those crime scene techs could pull a needle out of a haystack. Let's wait for the morning briefing. We could well learn something hopeful."

He was right, of course. That didn't change the ugly, dark roiling inside her. Finally she gave up on her pie and covered the pan with the slightly crumpled aluminum foil. "You take this with you when you go," she said. "It's more temptation than I can stand and I need it like poison."

His gaze grew inscrutable. "Okay," he said after a few beats. "Are you going to be okay, Kelly? Seriously? You want me to sleep on your floor? Or you want to come to my place?"

His words made her acutely aware that she wasn't be-having professionally. This was a case, like any other she had worked. It was always tougher when the victims were young, but you had to wade through it. Do the job. Not let it overwhelm you. She was in danger of drowning, not a usual state of affairs for her. She prided herself on being a good cop, not a mess of tangled emotions.

"This is really getting to me," she admitted. "More than things usually do. But I've got to deal, Al. I can't use you as a crutch, no matter how kind your offer is. Call it my learning curve. Especially if I want to stay in law enforcement."

He nodded slowly. "It's learnable. This is just a rough case. Rougher than usual."

She fixed her gaze on him again, turning outward from her inner turmoil. "I can't imagine what you've had to deal with. You were in combat, right?"

"Unfortunately. You make contact once or twice, and you learn how useful a shell can be. You just can't afford to brood about it. The next mess will always come. All you can do is maintain optimal readiness. Consider this your first contact."

"But I've done other things…" She paused. "There was this crash of a light plane. I was among the first responders and…" Again she paused, squeezing her eyes shut. "You've seen it. It was more than a year before I could deal with raw chicken or spaghetti."

"I know."

She opened her eyes. "I've moved past it. Mostly. But you're right. This is so different it might as well be first contact for me. So I just have to push through."

"Take something to help you sleep. Got any melatonin?"

"That stuff is a natural hormone, right?"

"The same thing the body makes. I use it once in a while when memory starts bugging me. Best part of it is I can wake up and one coffee makes me alert again. No hangover."

"I'll keep that in mind." Right then her insides and emotions felt as if they'd been thrown in a blender. But she had to get through it. Tomorrow was another day, and she wanted to be able to help. To be useful in whatever way she was needed. "Thanks, Al. You've been great."

He glanced at the digital clock on her microwave. "I

should go. We both need some sleep and I *do* have a few animals I need to check on."

She wanted to keep him longer but knew that clinging wasn't going to fix a damn thing. She needed to find her objectivity and put this case into the realm of other cases, a problem to be solved. There *was* always a possibility this would turn out well. Heck, they might get a call in the middle of the night telling them the girls had turned up at some outlying farmhouse.

As Al was leaving, he paused at the door, pie in hand, then surprised her by wrapping one arm around her and hugging her tightly for a brief few seconds. "You're strong," he said. "You'll make it."

She wished she were as confident.

As she latched the door behind him, it struck her that she was being terribly self-indulgent, giving in to useless feelings and allowing them to run her.

She needed to be thinking, using her brain or sleeping. Either one would be more useful and less selfish.

When at last she curled up in bed, Bugle stretched alongside her, closer than usual, as if he felt her distress. With her hand digging into his ruff, she closed her eyes and finally, finally fell asleep.

Chapter Five

Day 3

Once again the sheriff's office was crammed with deputies and city police, and plenty of other people waited outside, wondering where the search would head today.

Because they were going to search. Even as the first, very faint light of dawn began to appear in the east, the helicopters could be heard taking to the air again, to hunt with their spotlights until daylight aided them, cabin crews alert for any movement, or any color outside the norm.

Today they had more information about the missing, however.

"All right," Gage said, rapping on one of the desks for silence. "Micah here is going to fill you in."

Micah Parish, of clear Cherokee ancestry, had been with the office since the days when Gage had first arrived in town. At first he had been greeted with old prejudices, but over the years he had knit himself into the fabric of the community.

"All right," he said, lifting a whiteboard and placing it on an easel. The photographs of the three missing young women stared back at them. "You know these are the young ladies we need to find. We learned something from the parents about what they might be wearing, so keep alert for colors of bright pink, royal blue and, unfortunately, light green. That won't stick out very well. But look for colors that don't belong out there at this time of year."

Murmurs and nods went around the room.

"You'll need to inform the civilians who are searching with us. Given our search area today, we'll have one deputy leading each group of searchers. We can divvy it up before you depart.

"As for other things, the enemies these young women might have…need I tell you that nobody has an enemy?"

A quiet laugh rolled around the room. Dark humor. The kind that kept cops, firefighters and soldiers sane.

Micah nodded in response. "We're going to be talking to some of their friends today, other kids at school. We may learn that there are a few people who actually don't like them, or that they've had a run-in with someone. Kelly?"

She raised her hand so he could find her in the crowd. "Sir?"

"I want you and Connie to do the interviews at school today. The principal is agreeable and will give you a private room. Kelly, I know Bugle is suited to other tasks but his presence may keep the atmosphere more relaxing for the students, okay?"

"Okay, Micah." She could see his point, and much as her body wanted to be outdoors moving, and much as she was sure that Bugle would prefer that, she knew he was probably right. Bugle always drew interested attention.

As the final bell rang for the day and students started piling out of the high school for buses and their own cars, Connie and Kelly sat back at the table they'd been using in a private room facing laptops and notebooks.

Kelly sighed.

Connie stretched and nearly groaned. "I'm getting too old for this."

Kelly laughed. "You're not that old. Don't make me feel bad."

"You know how I met my husband, Ethan?"

Kelly shook her head. "Before my time."

"Well, he's Micah Parish's son."

That snagged Kelly's interest. She twisted on the folding chair that could have done with a pillow and looked at Connie. "Yeah?"

"Yeah."

"I wondered because of the name but nobody ever told me."

"Well, that was an interesting story. Micah didn't know about him because his mother hadn't told him, so one day Ethan shows up at Micah's ranch with the news. But that wasn't the point of me bringing it up. I brought it up because years ago, when my daughter was about seven, I thought she was kidnapped."

"Oh my God," Kelly breathed.

"Ethan tracked her, believe it or not. We'd had days of this awful tension because a stranger had approached her on her way home from school. Deputies were crawling every street, parents were warned not to let their children walk home alone... The drill. You know it. Then my daughter disappeared during the night out her bedroom window. The thing was, Ethan's background in the military gave him the skills to track her. We found her up at the old mining camp...and the man who had taken her was her father, my ex. He'd just gotten out of prison."

"You must have gone through hell." Kelly couldn't begin to imagine it.

"I did. But it didn't last long and it turned out all right." Connie's mouth compressed, then she said, "It's not looking good, Kelly. Almost forty-eight hours now. The window's closing."

"I know. But it's not immutable." She needed to believe that. She *had* to believe that. Out in the fading afternoon light, dozens, if not hundreds, of people were hunting the countryside, knocking on every door, looking for any sign at all of the three girls. At some point they couldn't keep the search going at this level. Even with all the volunteers, there would come a time when they'd have to give up looking and start hoping for some other kind of clue.

How could three girls just vanish into the night like this?

Because someone had taken them.

She looked at Connie. "We need to start thinking about whether there's anyone around here who might be capable of this abduction."

"We're already thinking about that," Connie reminded her. "We just spent all day asking a bunch of high school students if they'd seen anything odd, if these girls had mentioned being afraid of someone or something, if anyone disliked them enough to want to hurt them. We're already doing it, Kelly."

"It doesn't feel like enough."

"Especially when we haven't learned anything that feels useful. Yet." Connie sighed and closed her laptop. "I need to get home, make dinner for the kids and Ethan, assuming he comes in from the search. I'm going to spend an awful lot of time thinking about what we heard today. You?"

"I'm not going to be able to think about anything else. Maybe somewhere in this shower of love is a needle."

Connie laughed wearily. "Exactly. It was creepy, if you ask me. Kids this age always have some gripes about one another. This sounded like a wake."

No one speaks ill of the dead.

"Yeah, it did. And that bothers me, Connie."

"Why?" Connie's gaze grew sharp.

"Because you'd expect people this young to be convinced these girls were going to show up. Instead they seem to have given up. Why?"

"Maybe because it's so damn cold out there they know no one could survive for long."

"Maybe." But Kelly had trouble believing it. "And maybe I'm overreacting. They're probably all scared about this and just as confused as anyone."

Connie nodded and stood, pulling her uniform parka on. "I'll pass all this non-news along to the sheriff on my way home. The students all have our cards. If they think of something, or suddenly want to open up about anything, they know how to reach us." She smiled wanly. "They'll probably call *you*. Bugle was a hit."

Indeed he had been. He'd even preened a bit, if a dog could preen. Kelly suspected he'd have been happy to stay even longer to enjoy all the pets and praise that had come his way.

But the fun part was over.

"Work," she said.

He needed to hear no more. He stretched and got ready to move. His tail even wagged a bit. He truly enjoyed working.

Which was more than she could say that particular day.

On the way home, she stopped at the diner to pick up dinner. On impulse, she bought enough for two and hoped that Al might be inclined to stop by when the search ended. She told herself it was a silly hope, but she needed something to look forward to, even if she was imagining it.

All this time, Al had never shown any interest in her. Well, occasionally she thought she caught a spark of heat in his gaze, but if so he masked it quickly. Probably she was imagining that, too.

She shook her head at herself as she carried home enough food for an army. No involvement, she reminded herself. She'd seen it happen, when two people in the same department got close, then broke up. The subsequent situation was often uncomfortable for everyone, and sometimes it could grow ugly.

Nope, none of that.

She fed Bugle, who'd lacked only food during the day because she had a special water bottle for him that opened to provide a tray for him to lap out of. No, he'd never go thirsty as long as she could refill that bottle.

He didn't seem especially hungry, however. He left nearly half his kibble in his bowl, causing her to wonder if she should heat some more chicken livers for him. But no, she didn't want him to expect that every day. It didn't take long for him to create a habit.

A hot shower helped ease some of the tension from her, especially her shoulders and neck, then she dressed in flannel pajamas and a bathrobe, wrapping her hair in a towel. As she emerged into the main part of the little house, she eyed the fireplace. The logs had long since burned out, but she wondered if she should make another fire just for herself.

She certainly needed something cheery after today. On the other hand, burning the wood for her own entertainment seemed wasteful and not especially good for the environment. Last night had been a true splurge but it had been so enjoyable.

The towel damp-dried her short bob quickly, so she went to hang it over a rack and run a bush through her hair. How many kids had they interviewed that day? She'd lost count at some point, although she could check it on her computer or her notepad, where each of them had been dutifully noted by name and age.

It still seemed odd that no one had anything negative to say. She hadn't been in high school for a while, but she easily remembered the cliques and the gossip and the way some of the students had avoided others like the plague.

These three girls were unusual in their pursuits. Not cheerleaders, the perennially popular, but nerds. Chess club? Debate club? Soccer, and not even first string? Either they'd become basically invisible or no one today had wanted to mention the petty kinds of comments students like them often drew.

She bet it was the latter. She'd seen their photos. Nerds or not, they were all pretty enough to attract attention at a hormonally driven age.

Sighing, she fluffed her damp hair a little with her fingers and decided she needed to eat before she took a complete plunge. This entire situation was so upsetting, and she'd never dealt well with the feeling of helplessness. Right now she felt helpless. Closing her eyes, she could all too easily imagine those girls out there somewhere, terrified out of their minds.

Someone had taken them. She believed that now after Al's recognition that the car hadn't braked before going off the road. And for all three of them to have been taken? Drugs.

She felt her heart lift a bit, leaving the worst of her despair behind when there was a rap on the door. She opened it and Al stood there. He spoke before she could even greet him. "I was thinking about picking up dinner for us if I'm not becoming a nuisance. You interested?"

"Already done. Come on in. There's plenty. How'd the search go?"

He was cold enough that when she stood near him she

could feel his body sucking the heat from the air. He tossed off his gloves and parka and knelt before her fireplace. "You mind?"

"I was thinking about doing it."

"Then let me. I need it. You know, like a candle in the dark."

She felt her heart and stomach both plummet. "Nothing?"

"Not a damn thing. A glove? A shoe? A scarf? Nope. Not even that much. You?"

"If anyone ever had a mean thing to say about those girls, we didn't hear it today. Tomorrow we'll talk to some teachers, too, but I'm not sure it's going to make any difference."

The dry logs he piled into the fireplace started quickly. He tossed the match onto the flames and remained squatting, holding his hands out toward the fire, lost in thought.

After a few minutes, she asked, "Hungry?"

"Famished," he admitted. A couple of seconds later he stood and came to the bar to help her unload the bags. "You went all out."

"I was seeking comfort," she admitted. And hoping he might stop by, but she didn't want to tell him that.

"You don't have to explain that to me," he agreed.

Tonight she brought out dishes. They had a lilac pattern on them, leftovers from her mother's collection that she'd never bothered to add to. A few dinner plates, salad plates and bowls remained. Enough for two people, at a pinch maybe three.

She'd skipped the steak sandwiches and instead had asked Maude for containers of tomato soup and thick grilled cheese sandwiches. More comfort food.

"Ah, man," Al said, "I love Maude's grilled cheese. It's

like eating Texas toast covered in melted Havarti. She seasons them, too. I hope you like dill."

"Love it. That's one of the reasons I decided to try them."

"It's a hit and I haven't taken my first bite."

The soup was rich and surprisingly good, Kelly thought. She wasn't the biggest fan of tomato soup but Maude's might change her mind.

Sitting at the bar with Al, feeling the heat from the fireplace warming her back, it was almost possible to believe everything was normal.

It was not.

She ate quickly, trying not to think about whether the missing students were eating anything tonight, whether they were warm enough, whether they were being terrorized. Later, she told herself, forcibly squashing the thoughts. They could talk about all this mess after they finished eating.

One of her previous partners had scolded her for losing her appetite. "You owe it to the victim to keep yourself in the best functioning shape possible."

But sometimes it was hard. Sometimes her whole body and mind wanted to rebel at the idea that anything, *anything*, could be normal in a situation like this.

Al kept the conversation general and light. She gave him credit for that because her attempts to respond in the same vein weren't exactly stellar.

She looked at Al. "After Connie and I talk to the teachers tomorrow, I want to go back to Rusty's tavern."

He raised a brow. "Yeah?"

"Everything seems to have started there, doesn't it? And they said they'd make a list of everyone who was there that night."

Al nodded slowly. "I'll go with you, if you don't mind."

Why would she mind? If police work had taught her nothing else, it had taught her that two brains were often better than one.

Settled in her plan, she resumed eating.

CLOSER THAN KELLY would have believed, and yet farther than it seemed possible, two girls awoke in a darkened basement, chilled to the bone despite the ragged blanket that had been tossed over them.

A single movement, and Chantal cried out. "Wire," she said. "Oh, God, wire." Her wrists and ankles were bound and every movement of the thin, bare wire cut at skin. "Mary Lou? Jane?"

"Me, too," answered Jane, her voice thick as if she'd been crying. "He drugged us again. Chantal, I don't think I can go without water, but it must have been in the water bottles."

"Yeah." Probably. Chantal's mind recoiled, then seemed to stiffen. "Mary Lou? Mary Lou?"

"I don't think she's here," Jane answered, her voice breaking. "She was right beside me earlier. Now she's not answering."

Helplessly, ignoring the cutting pain in her wrists, Chantal edged closer to Jane. "She's gone?"

Jane seemingly didn't even want to answer. After a few seconds she said in a cracked whisper, "Maybe she got knocked out more than we did."

"Shh," whispered Chantal. "Hold your breath and listen."

But there was no other sound in the dank space, not so much as soft breaths. A tomb couldn't have been any more silent.

Mary Lou was gone. But to where and for what?

"Oh my God," Jane whispered. "Oh my God. What did we do, Chantal?"

"That's not going to help," Chantal whispered fiercely. "We've got to get our heads working again. There's got to be something we can do *now*." She *had* to believe that. Never once in her life had she simply given up, even when a situation looked hard. Like trying out for the soccer team. She didn't have any real athletic ability, but she'd wanted to do it anyway because it was the kind of activity that was good for college applications. So she'd practiced until she'd become good enough to make the second string. Because she refused to be defeated by her own mind.

She believed in her ability to conquer the difficult, and she was trying to believe she could conquer this, as well.

But the wire around her wrists and ankles gave lie to that. Hopelessness, as cold and dank as the dark room, settled over her.

REVE HAD HAD ENOUGH. Maybe taking the three girls had seemed like a good idea at the time, but the one he'd just dealt with... No fun at all.

Well, he'd have no more to do with her. He still had two more and if he was careful, they'd probably work better. But he was going to keep them tied up in the dark longer, and keep them a whole lot hungrier. By the time he got done, they'd think he was their savior. Yeah.

In the meantime, he needed to ditch this one. Driving down back roads in the dark with his headlights off wasn't a whole lot of fun, but he was wary they might resume the helicopter search. They seemed to have called it off at dusk, though. Giving up, he supposed.

He didn't go far out of town, maybe ten miles. He knew of some wide-open ranchland that hadn't been used in years, and it would provide the perfect place to dump whatshername. Trash. That's all she was now.

He didn't bother to wrap her in anything. The last thing he wanted was for her body to be protected from the elements or scavengers. Nope, she'd come into this world as naked as a jaybird, and she was going out the same way.

The hard ground aided him, leaving behind almost no sign of his passing. When he got far enough from the road, he stopped.

Damn, she'd grown heavy. Or maybe he was just hurting.

Didn't matter. She was knocked out and would stay that way just long enough. With a grunt, he rolled her naked body into a ditch. Cold as this night was, she'd be dead almost before she woke up.

Then he dragged a couple of tumbleweeds over her, checking to make sure the ditch wouldn't let them blow away too easily.

In a week or so, she'd be nothing but bones. As for her clothes…he had a woodstove to burn them. No sign she'd ever been anywhere near his place.

As for the other two…that abandoned, run-down house was perfect, with a solid basement but everything else going to hell. Nobody ever went there. Not even kids looking for a thrill. In a few years there'd be nothing left of the house except the hollowed-out basement.

Turning slowly, he drove away, making sure he didn't leave any deep tracks behind him. He stuck to old tractor ruts, hard as rock in the dry winter. He wouldn't stir up anything noticeable, and once it snowed there'd be absolutely nothing to see.

The winter had aided him, he thought. Traditionally the area didn't get a whole lot of snow and what it did was dry and blew around. The last couple of years had been unusual with heavier snows, but not this year. Here they had reached January with nothing but a few light flurries that hadn't stuck. That wouldn't last, but it had lasted long enough for this job.

Damn, he ached from that kick. He'd have liked to treat her to a bit of a beating, but he was trying not to leave evidence, and even if all they ever found were her bones, assuming the wolves or coyotes didn't drag them away, they'd be able to tell she'd been hurt before dying.

Nope, teen girl freezes to death in January on the high plains of Wyoming. Wouldn't be the first. No clothes meant only that the carrion eaters had pulled them apart and dragged them away. It kind of amused him to think of the hours that would be wasted seeking scraps of cloth.

He realized he was thirsty and decided to go to Rusty's for a beer or two. He went several times a week and no one would notice him, except maybe for Spence and Jeff, if they were there and wanted to play pool. He had a life.

And the life provided cover.

CHANTAL AWOKE SUDDENLY. The jarring movement reminded her of the wire cutting painfully into her wrists and ankles. She drew a long breath, steadying herself, letting the pain wash over her and then away. Beside her, Jane still slept, a quiet snore escaping her. This basement was causing her allergies to act up, uncomfortable for Jane when she couldn't even blow her nose.

But those quiet snores hadn't wakened her. She listened intently but heard only the lonely sound of the wind. If their captor had come and left more food and water, she didn't know. Not that she wanted any of it now.

A headache pounded behind her eyes, either from hunger or from the drug they'd been given...when? She didn't even know how long ago they'd been knocked out and Mary Lou had disappeared.

All of a sudden she understood why people would find a way to scratch hash marks for days into the walls of their prisons. Except in here she could not be sure what was night and what was day. There was absolutely no way to keep track of time. That could prove maddening, she realized. As maddening as the endless night that swallowed them.

She stared into the unyielding dark and tried to think of something they might be able to do. Some way to put an end to this. She knew well enough that without shoes and jackets they wouldn't make it very far in the Wyoming winter weather. But some other way, because right now escape looked impossible.

Then, out of nowhere, a deep sorrow welled up in her and as if she'd seen it with her own eyes, she felt the truth in her very bones.

Mary Lou was dead.

She had to stifle a cry, to bite her lip until she tasted blood. How could she know? How could it be?

But she knew. And she didn't want Jane to know.

MILES AWAY, Kelly jerked out of a sound sleep. Bugle, who'd been snoring beside her, lifted his head. The small nightlight glowed, her protection against jumping out of bed in the dark for an emergency call and barking her shins or tripping. In that light she could see Bugle's focus. He'd become alert, very alert.

She listened, hearing nothing but the night wind and the occasional crackle from the banked fire in the living room.

Then Bugle made a sound she almost never heard from him. It came from deep within him, a low groan, not a growl, and it sounded so incredibly forlorn that it seemed laced with sorrow. But over what? A bad dream?

Then he put his head on her belly and whimpered softly.

Knowledge crashed in on her. She knew what had wakened her so unexpectedly and what Bugle was trying to tell her. She knew why she felt her chest squeezing as if it wanted to silence her heart.

One of the girls was dead.

Chapter Six

Day 4

His phone rang well before dawn. Al was used to it. He had no set hours and folks knew they could call him if their animal escaped in this dangerous weather. He didn't mind at all. Saving animals was one way he could make up for a bunch of things he'd done that he never wanted to remember. Besides, he generally believed that animals were kinder than people. Certainly more forgiving.

He threw back the comforter, slapped his stockinged feet on the rough would floor and leaned forward to grab the receiver for the landline. "Animal Control. Carstairs."

"She's dead."

He recognized Kelly's voice instantly. "Who is? What happened?"

"I don't know. I just know one of the girls is dead. Bugle feels it, too. Damn it, Al, I'm going to smash something!"

He'd worked with animals too long not to respect their intuition. Plus, Bugle had a link to those girls after smelling their garments.

"Hell, I'll be right over."

"I'm not crazy!"

"I don't think you are. I'm on my way. Give me a few. I need to make sure everyone's got some water."

"Okay." Her voice cracked. "Okay."

He dressed as swiftly as he could, wishing he had more zippers and fewer buttons, then ran out to the kennels in the insulated barn. Two felines and one canine raised their heads curiously but didn't seem at all disturbed. The minxes were snarling at each other from cages five feet apart.

Yeah, they had water. Plenty of food in their automatic feeders. The dog yawned at him and went back to sleep. The cats merely stared enigmatically. The minks ignored him.

Sure that his charges would be all right for a while, he headed out to his truck. The light from the lamp he'd left on in his cabin silhouetted a squirrel in the window.

"Hey, Regis," he said. "What are you doing out at this hour?"

He'd never get an answer. All he knew was that squirrels tended to stay in their dreys at night with the rest of their squirrel families.

Crap, was the whole world suddenly going nuts?

A million questions demanded answers but he refused to ask them until he got to Kelly's place. All he needed to know for now was that she was clearly distraught and probably didn't want to call anyone from her department. He supposed he ought to feel complimented that she didn't think he'd dismiss her or label her nuts.

Still, the only evidence a feeling? Hers or the dog's? Yeah, he wouldn't want to explain that to most people, although he wasn't the sort to dismiss it.

He'd been in situations in Afghanistan where feelings of that kind had been all that saved his life and the lives of his squad. The sense that something was about to happen. That someone lurked and was ready to kill.

Easy to dismiss by telling yourself you'd picked up on

some small thing in the environment that you hadn't consciously noticed.

This was going to be different.

At three in the morning there was no hope of finding any ready-made coffee unless he drove to the far end of town to the truck stop. That would take too long. Dang, he needed some caffeine as quickly as possible, but he was sure he could make it at Kelly's house even if he'd have to wait fifteen or twenty minutes. She'd probably need some, too, before this night was over.

The drive seemed endless, which it didn't usually, but eventually he reached her little house on the edge of town and pulled into the driveway, two strips of concrete that were wheel-distance apart. An old-fashioned driveway, the kind that had come about in the days of wheeled carriages and wagons.

No getting stuck in mud. Or snow. Or... He shut the stupid line of thought down. The lights were on in Kelly's small cottage. Another time they might have looked welcoming.

The instant he reached her door, the icy night wind whipping through narrowed streets like a hungry animal, she flung it open. She'd been worried over the last few days, but now she looked sunken, circles around her eyes. Bugle didn't even rise from the floor to acknowledge him but lay there looking as depressed as a dog could look.

She couldn't even speak his name, simply stepped back to give him entrance.

"Coffee?" he asked, deciding to start on safe ground.

"I didn't... My hands were shaking..."

This was not at all the competent deputy he'd come to know over the last few years. Not that he knew her very well. They hadn't become fast friends, just acquaintances. But he knew her well enough to realize she was in a place she'd never gone before, at least not in her job. That was saying something because he had a good idea of some of the things she'd seen and dealt with. Law enforcement was the pointy end of the stick in a lot of ways, first responders like firefighters and EMTs. Nightmares that clung.

"Sit if you can," he said quietly. "Get a blanket. I'll start the coffee and build up the fire again. You look like an icicle."

Indeed she did. If he hadn't known better, he'd have thought she'd been standing out in the cold for the last hour.

She needed warmth, maybe food, something to help with the shock.

"I'm not crazy," she said, standing her ground.

"I don't think you are. But let's take care of your immediate physical needs…and frankly mine…before we talk."

At last she settled into her armchair. Bugle unfolded himself and came to place his head on her thigh. Since she'd ignored his other suggestion, Al grabbed the afghan off the back of the chair and tossed it over her, careful not to cover Bugle's head. Kelly's hand dug into the dog's neck as if she were hanging on for dear life.

Her coffeemaker was about the same as his, so stacking it and starting it came automatically, with one difference. He made this coffee strong. Then he nosed into her refrigerator and found a frozen raspberry Danish on a plastic tray. He popped that into the microwave for a quick thaw. Sugar was a good antidote to shock.

It didn't seem like something she'd ordinarily eat, however. But then, what did he know? She had friends who probably came over on weekends. Most people did. Even him, the isolationist misanthrope. Sort of.

At last he got a mug of coffee into her hands, watching them shake a bit, but not enough to spill it. "Want a piece of Danish?"

"Not yet," she murmured.

There was an embroidered stool stuck in one corner, maybe for use as an ottoman. He had no idea, but he had use for it now. He pulled it over until he sat right in front of her with his own coffee.

"Feel any better?"

She gave an almost invisible nod of her head.

"Ready to talk?"

She chewed her lower lip until he feared that she might make it bleed. "I can't explain."

"Then don't," he said gently. "Just give me the facts of what happened. You don't need to explain them to me."

Long seconds passed before she tried to speak again. "It's nuts."

"Don't dismiss it. Just tell me."

She squeezed her eyes closed. "I was sound asleep. I woke up suddenly and it was like…like this tidal wave of despair, maybe anguish…it just filled me. And then I noticed Bugle had come to full alert and he made this groan… Oh, God, I hope I never hear him make that sound again. It was heartrending. Then he put his head on me and he whimpered."

She drew a long, shaky breath. "That's when I knew. Thought I knew. Hell, I don't know. I was absolutely certain that one of those girls had just died."

"I guess Bugle was, too."

She opened her eyes and looked down at her dog. Her real partner. "Yeah," she whispered. "He felt something."

Al rose, then returned with two small plates, each holding a piece of Danish and a fork. "Use your fingers if you want." He set it on her lap and Bugle sniffed at it but left it alone. A well-trained animal.

"The thing is," Kelly said, her voice still thin and a bit cracked, "I can't go to work with this. I can't even tell

Gage. He might believe me, but what good would it do? We've still got to look for those missing women."

"I agree."

"I also don't need half the department whispering that I'm losing my marbles if someone overhears me. But damn," she said, her voice nearly a cry, "what can I do? I've got to do something. What if he's going to kill again? Or what if I imagined all this? The stress since the disappearance…"

He reached out and covered her hand with his. Even as she used her fingers to try to hold on to the plate he'd practically forced on her, he could feel her tremors. And the ice that seemed to be running through her veins.

"Eat. Drink your coffee. You're half the way into shock."

"From a feeling?" She looked utterly dubious.

"From a feeling. That's all it takes sometimes." He knew that intimately from his time at war. Shock could occur from an unexpected emotional blow. She'd had one, regardless of what it was based on.

She managed to swallow half the coffee. He went to get her another cup while she picked at the Danish.

"I don't know what to do." She was gathering her strength again. He could hear it in her voice.

"I'm not sure you *can* do anything," he answered, hoping he sounded reassuring.

"I hope it's not true. I hope I just imagined it because I've been so worried."

"We can hope," he agreed. He was glad to see her drink more coffee and eat a larger piece of Danish. He swallowed his own drink and felt his stomach burn in response. She wasn't the only one who was upset. Usually his stomach was cast iron.

"I must have imagined it," she said a little while later.

"Is Bugle into imagining things?" he asked.

Her head jerked a little as she looked at him. "He might have been responding to me. To my feeling."

"It's possible. I'm going to tell you a story, if you're up to it."

"Why wouldn't I be up to it?"

"Because it doesn't have a happy ending. You're not the first or only person to get feelings like this. They aren't always accurate, but when they are…"

She hesitated, nibbled another piece of Danish. "This was for church on Sunday," she said absently. Then, "Okay, tell me your story."

"Long time ago, a couple of kids I was in high school with went on a family camping trip. The oldest two were avid kayakers. They loved white water. Anyway, the daughter was helping her mother cook dinner when she suddenly looked at her mom and said, 'If I don't go home tonight, I'll never go home.'"

Kelly drew a sharp breath.

"Mom talked her into a better mood, my friend seemed to forget all about it…but the next day she and her brother went kayaking together, they overturned and both of them were lost. So what do you make of what she said to her mom?"

"I know I wouldn't want to live with it," Kelly said, her entire face drooping. "Oh, God, that's awful."

He nodded. "I couldn't agree more. But it's not the first time I've heard a story like that. So maybe I'm less skeptical than most. I've sure heard some stories about people who knew that someone in their family had died before they got the news. It happens. I can't explain it, but I don't dismiss it. However, in light of the fact that we have no concrete evidence, it won't hurt us to go on hoping your feeling was wrong."

"No, but right now that feels awfully hard."

"I'm sure." It felt hard to him, too. What if one of those missing girls had died? Why? What was the abductor trying to accomplish? To satisfy some ugly need to inflict pain and death? Why three girls, anyway? Seemed like that would make everything more complicated. One you could handle. Three all at once? Difficult.

"I'm sorry," she said unexpectedly.

"For what?" He couldn't imagine.

"For waking you in the middle of the night over something like this. I just couldn't stand to be alone, and I knew if I called one of my friends from the department they might wonder if I'd lost it."

"I don't mind. I'm glad you called, actually." He offered a smile. "And as you can see, I don't think you've lost it." He rose again, stretching muscles that somehow hadn't quite made the transition from bed to being upright, and went to get himself some more coffee. "I get called in the middle of the night often enough. People get worried when their pets go missing in weather like this. I don't mind."

He had settled again on the ottoman in front of her before she spoke again. "So you're a one-man animal rescue team?"

"Sometimes. Mostly the animals haven't gone that far and by the time I show up they're looking to be warm again. Easy enough to find. Although there was one black Lab who didn't give a damn how cold or wet it was. To him, playing keep-away was a big game. I'll never forget that huge grin he'd give me as he pranced out of reach."

She was smiling faintly, a good sign.

"That dog developed quite a reputation in his neighborhood. Jasper. Lots of folks recognized him and got a kick out of him."

"I can imagine."

"You never ran into him? I'm sure he was here during your time."

"Never had the pleasure."

He wondered how circumscribed her life was. Maybe nearly as bad as his own? Nose-to-the-grindstone serious? Of course, he was sure she wasn't the only person in the area who'd never gotten to know Jasper. For most people, if they'd seen that dog he'd have been nothing but a black streak passing by.

The fire was burning behind him, just a small one, but a cheerful sound. However, it was the only cheerful thing in this room. He could feel the cold, as if it had seeped in from the night outside, but it wasn't that kind of cold.

It was the inky coldness of death. There had been times when it had been his nearly constant companion. Now this.

God, he hoped she was mistaken, that the chill he felt had merely arisen from her description of her experience, but he feared it had not. If one of those girls had died, it hadn't been an accident. It had been murder. All that did was make him worry even more about the other two, and worry had already been doing a damn good job of peaking the longer they remained missing.

She'd utterly lost interest in the Danish and coffee he'd given her, so he took them to the kitchen.

"Rest if you can," he told her. "Morning will come soon enough."

He moved the stool back and took the chair near hers, watching her as she stared into the fire, kneading Bugle's neck, her expression both dark and fearful.

At last, however, her eyelids drooped and sleep found her. As soon as it did, Bugle burrowed in a little closer and closed his eyes.

Dog and man kept watch through the silent, terrifying hours of darkness.

A little while later, she stirred and spoke drowsily. "You were in the military, right?"

"Marines."

"How'd you get here, Al? Just because you grew up here?"

But he didn't think that was the story she wanted the answer to. She wanted something more intimate. Deeper. Not superficial answers. Clearly she needed something from him, but what? He couldn't imagine, so he hesitated, maybe too long because she withdrew her question.

"None of my business," she said without opening her eyes. "Sorry."

"No need. I was just wondering how to answer. The facts are simple. I was wounded. Considered unfit for duty. Medically retired. Nothing all that great there. Me and thousands of other troops."

"Yeah." She sighed, and her eyes fluttered open a bit to look at him. "Sad."

"It's the risk you take when you sign up," he said flatly. So true. Except who in the hell really knew what they were signing up for? That was the great secret until you were in the middle of it.

"Anyway, after a while I realized I wasn't dealing well with people. Too angry. Like a firecracker with a short fuse. Animals… Well, they're a whole different story. Being around them is soothing. Uncomplicated for the most part."

"Even minks?"

That drew a quiet laugh from him. "They're predictable, anyway. With time my fuse is getting longer. I guess I'm finally coming home."

He'd never phrased it that way before, but he could see from her expression that had struck her. She ought to be sleeping but here she was pondering his past and his overwhelmingly philosophical statements. Oorah. Good job, Al.

Chapter Seven

Day 6

Reluctantly, the world resumed its normal course. The search was beginning to taper off. People needed to get back to regular work. The sheriff couldn't afford to keep such a huge manhunt going, and after five days it had become obvious that wherever the girls were, they needed more detective work than traipsing across the countryside.

The families were beside themselves, of course. From the next room, Kelly could hear the sheriff explaining that all they were doing now was shifting focus.

"We'll still be looking but we're not going to find them out in the open," he explained. "We've covered every inch of more than a thousand square miles with our helicopters and quite a bit of the ground on foot. Everybody's been helping and everybody's on high alert for any sign of your daughters. Those girls have either left the county or are indoors somewhere."

"So what do we do now?" Kate Beauvoir demanded. "We can't give up!"

"I didn't say we're giving up," Gage said patiently. Kindly. "We're shifting focus to other methods that we believe will be more useful. The girls clearly didn't run away across open ground. They weren't left out there. So now we concentrate our efforts at a different level. Someone took them and we need to get some clues as to who."

Then the conference room door closed, and the conversation became private. Still haunted by her dream or premonition from two nights before, Kelly was grateful not to hear any more.

The office was too small to offer each deputy his or her own desk, so they shared them, using them as necessary when they were on shift or just coming off and needing to tidy up paperwork. Kelly's share of a desk sat near a window looking out at the courthouse square. The computer that filled a large part of it was an older model, serviceable but needing replacement. A small tray pulled out on one side to provide extra writing space as needed. Creating a sort of wall behind her were three overstuffed filing cabinets. Insofar as possible, records were being retired and placed on microfiche in the basement of the courthouse, but there was still enough paper to jam every drawer.

She had a list of names in front of her, names gleaned from Rusty and his staff, and a few other people who had come forward. The names of those who had been seen at the tavern the night the young women disappeared.

Going through them, she tried to design the most efficient route for herself. Today, she and Bugle were going to knock on doors and ask questions. It was always possible that someone had seen something that might have been suspicious.

Yeah, this was the next level of detective work. Shoe leather.

She heard a door open and instinctively looked up to see the families of the girls leaving. The women all had puffy, red eyes. The men weren't looking much better. Not a one of them seemed happy about the changes.

She couldn't really blame them, she thought as she

dragged her eyes down to the paper in front of her. Of course they wanted everyone out there looking. The problem with that was at this point the returns were seriously diminishing. It was a virtual certainty that none of those girls was lying out in the open. Nor had the choppers picked up any sign of disturbed ground.

That meant they were inside somewhere or they were in another county, and Gage had already flashed alerts to every agency within a thousand or more miles. Those girls' photos were going to be burned into the minds of every law enforcement officer in three or more states. Two FBI agents were on their way in from the nearest field office, not that they'd be much help.

Hadn't the mention of the FBI helped the parents a little? Kelly simply couldn't put herself in their shoes. She had no idea how they were assessing all of this, whether FBI agents seemed like they would help.

Even the FBI needed evidence.

Rapping her pen tip on the paper in front of her, Kelly studied it while she listened to the front door close behind the agonized parents. God, she wished she had something to offer them. That anyone here could offer them hope.

But right now hope was fading, and even the parents must realize that. Too long. Too damn long. Even a ransom note would have provided a thread to cling to. But not even that.

Which meant the abductor was up to absolutely no good. None. And that was a whole new level of terrifying.

Much as she tried not to imagine things, she still suffered from the same imagination as everyone else. She'd read enough stories about what had been done to young women who'd been kidnapped and held, sometimes for years on end. Right now those news stories seemed very close emotionally, very personal.

She pulled out her satellite phone and used the GPS to enter all the addresses she wanted to visit today. Sometimes this county seemed empty, but when you looked at going door-to-door, it grew huge.

When she'd entered the last address, she scanned the map and made the best judgments she could for which order to visit the outlying ranches. The likelihood that anyone had seen anything out there was slender, but on the other hand, those were people who, if they *had* noticed something unusual, would have paid attention. In town, too many people passed through because of the state highway. Roads out by the ranches were an entirely different story.

Satisfied she'd done the best she could, she folded the list and put it in her inside pocket. Then she buttoned up for the cold day and picked up her tablet. Bugle was already moving impatiently. He'd been wanting to get on the road for hours.

Even after all this time and five years here, not to mention Laramie, the first step out the door into the frigid air always felt as if it stole her breath. Once upon a time, as a pup, Bugle had been fascinated by the clouds of steam that came out of his nostrils, but he'd long since learned to ignore it.

As she buttoned him into his caged backseat and climbed into the car that held not one bit of the warmth she had filled it with on her way over, she wondered what Al was doing.

Patrolling? Rounding up escapees in answer to calls? Someday, when she had the time, she thought she might like to go on a ride with him and see what exactly filled his days. It probably wasn't much different from what she did on a lot of days: patrolling in case she was needed. Answering calls that came in if she was nearby. Often the job wasn't exciting. Boring, even. Then there were the other times.

Domestic disputes were the ones she hated most, and they were reaching the time of winter when they ramped up in both number and savagery. Cabin fever, she often thought, was lousy for relationships.

Not knowing what she'd find when she drove onto each ranch and knocked at the door put her on heightened alert. Most people would be friendly, some would even want her to come in for coffee and cookies because they were so glad to see a fresh face.

Her anxiety eased a bit and she smiled through the windshield at a day that was sacrificing all its clouds in favor of bright sun. At this latitude the sun didn't get that high, not like Miami or Puerto Rico, but once the snow covered the ground it would be every bit as blinding.

Right now it was just turning into a beautiful day. She felt a twinge of guilt for even noticing.

She was a little over five miles out of town, driving slowly over a dirt road that was bad now and would be even worse come spring. Thank God it was frozen, but it was like riding on a rubbery roller coaster. To the west the mountains rose like dark sentinels, promising a safety she had never managed to feel. They were close here, and seemed to loom over the county below. The mountains to the east were farther away, beautiful but not quite as dominating. Or threatening. Odd thought.

Just then Bugle started barking his strange half howl, and he persisted demandingly until she pulled to the side on a grassy turnout and put the SUV in Park. "What the heck, Bugle?"

As if he could answer. She could see nothing at all in any direction but dried grasses, scrub and tumbleweed.

Oh, and the nearby mountains that right now felt as if they were pressing on her shoulder, leaning in.

He hurried to the left side of the truck and pressed his nose to the window, still howling his fool head off.

She wasn't stupid enough to ignore it when her dog acted like a fool. Something had gripped his attention.

"Okay," she said. She reached for the gloves on the seat beside her and pulled them on, leaving the car to run to keep it warm.

One thing for sure, she was leashing that dog. If he wanted to chase a rabbit, *she* wasn't going to chase him. He waited impatiently while she opened the door and hooked the long leather lead to the ring on his collar. Then, without so much as a command, he jumped down and began to pull her back the way they had just come. To the point where he'd begun to lose his calm.

Well-trained K-9 or not, Kelly was well aware that he was still a dog. Before she let him pull her completely away from the vehicle, she grabbed a tennis ball, his favorite toy, and shoved it in her pocket. She might need it to get his attention, the way he was behaving.

But he'd raised his head, as if pulling something out of the air. She waited while he sniffed and then blew to clear his nose for a fresh sniff. Okay, maybe not a rabbit.

Then he lowered his head and began to pull her along the shoulder, weaving a bit as he went. The odor he pursued hadn't settled into a straight line, but neither had it behaved that oddly. An animal carrying something? But what? Or was he tracking a scent from something left beside the road?

If he hadn't been so determined, she might have called him back to her vehicle, but she'd learned to read Bugle well. He was onto something that to him was awfully important. Considering his training, what he believed to be important often turned out to be important to her.

She hadn't realized how long she had driven past the point where he started his frenzied barking. Nearly half a mile. With every step she grew more aware of the icy wind. She couldn't imagine what had gotten into the car, but something obviously had, and he was determined to get to it. With each few steps, he grew more focused. More intent. Her K-9 was on the hunt.

She pulled her snorkel hood closer around her face but didn't zip it into a narrow opening. As a cop she knew how important her range of vision was to her safety. Better to have a frozen nose than be blindsided.

Finally Bugle paused. He lifted his head again, turning it a little this way and that, then dived into the field beside the road. Not far. There wasn't even a turnout here, just some sagging barbed wire. But when he dipped three feet into the runoff ditch beside the road, he stopped and sat. Then he looked at her and pawed at the ground.

She recognized the signals. He'd found his target. But what the hell was his target? Sudden worry made her heart accelerate as if she were running the last lap in the Kentucky Derby. She began to breathe more rapidly, which made her chest ache and her sinuses feel as if they were about to crack from the dryness.

Damn weather. Carefully she approached the spot Bugle sat facing. He reached out one paw, touching nothing, but seeming to point.

She saw a dark heap, small, unimportant. Until she got closer.

A glove. A man's glove. Nothing important. Something like that could have blown out the bed of any pickup truck.

It would have meant nothing at all except for her dog's intense interest in it. Target.

One of the missing girls? But none of them should have a glove like this. So if…

She didn't allow herself to complete the thought. She didn't dare hope, not anymore. Not after the last days. But hopeful or not, she had to treat it as evidence.

"Bugle, guard."

Now that he'd found the object of his fascination, she had absolutely no doubt he'd stay put. Not that she'd have had any doubt anyway. Bugle did his job with all the panache and dutifulness of the cop he was. Maybe better.

She trekked back to her vehicle and pulled out a rubber glove and an evidence bag. The glove had been worn. There'd be DNA evidence inside it if the cold hadn't killed it. It might be important, or it might just be some kind of mistake. Heck, it could be a glove belonging to one of the girls' fathers. Bugle sure wouldn't miss that. Probably nothing, she told herself with each step as her nose grew colder. Probably nothing at all.

But she trusted Bugle's instincts and could not ignore them. She thought about driving back to pick up the dog and glove, then decided against it. She needed to scour the ground with her eyes to see if something else might be there. This was a very isolated part of the county, mostly grazing land, few houses, but someone could have come along this road and dropped something else. Or left a track, not that the ground was lately in any condition to take tracks.

She took the walk more slowly this time, forcing her attention to the shoulder right in front of her. It yielded nothing at all, and the rusting barbed wire appeared untouched. Somebody had some work to do, she thought. She didn't envy anyone who had to replace all that fencing.

Then she reached Bugle, who was still at attention but starting to shiver a bit. So much for a fur coat. As soon as she reached his side, she squatted, snapped on a rubber glove after removing her own insulated one and picked up the ratty old glove to insert in an evidence bag.

As soon as it was secure, she said to Bugle, "Search."

But he sniffed around a small area and seemed to find the exercise pointless. Okay, the glove was it.

Taking his leash in hand again, she joined him in a quick jog back to the vehicle. He seemed glad to jump inside the warmth. For that matter, she was glad, too.

Dang, it was so cold. She wondered how the coyotes managed it, because she knew they were out on their rounds despite the weather. She received the occasional call to check out an injured animal. Personally, she thought self-respecting coyotes ought to join bears in hibernation.

Her fingers barely wanted to hold the marker as she scribbled the important information on the evidence bag: her name, the date and time, the location where the item had been found. Then she sealed it, and no one would be able to open it without leaving evidence of tampering.

So careful. She hoped like hell it would do some kind of good for the missing women.

Just a clue. She'd been repeating the words like a mantra at the back of her mind for days now. Just a clue. She hardly dared to believe this might be it.

THE REST OF the day was devoted to knocking on doors, drinking quick cups of coffee or tea as she talked to the ranchers, their families and their hired hands, if they had any. A pointless waste of hours, she thought as she pulled up to the last house on her list.

The road had taken her the long way around, but the ranch house itself wasn't that far from the outskirts of town. There just wasn't a direct road to it.

She had to knock twice, and her stiffening hands didn't

appreciate it. She had grown so cold with all of this that her nerves burned when jarred. Just one more, then she could drive back in the heated comfort of her car and hunt up a hot drink and meal. Loads of coffee today hadn't done her much good. In fact, no good at all. She'd quit after a single sip because, while she didn't want to offend, she also didn't want to ask to use people's facilities. Her mouth felt as dry as cotton now.

Bugle had it easy, she thought wryly. Every time she let him leap out, he took care of business.

After her third knock, the door opened. A bleary-eyed man of about thirty-five stared back at her and shook his head a little.

"Sorry to bother you, sir, but you're Walt Revell, the current owner?"

"Uh, yeah." He looked at her again. "Is… What happened?"

"We've had three young women missing for nearly a week now and we're trying to find out if anyone might have seen something unusual that might help us out."

"Oh."

God, she thought, was this guy drunk or drugged? Or had he worked all night? Mussed hair, clothes that needed ironing… Well, according to records he lived alone. He probably wasn't good at looking after himself.

He shook his head. "Heard about that at the tavern. Damn shame. But I didn't see nothing."

She doubted he could see past the end of his nose. "Thanks for your time." She handed him her card. "If you notice anything that seems unusual or out of place, give us a call, please?"

"Uh, sure."

The door closed even before she finished turning away. Guy probably wanted to get back to sleep.

As she walked back to her vehicle, she saw that Bugle had his nose pressed to the glass. He was probably sick of being cooped up and wanted to be let out to play.

"In a bit," she said to him as she climbed back in and turned her truck around to head back out to the road. "Soon, Bugle."

He gave a low groan as if that answer didn't please him at all.

JANE AND CHANTAL hardly twitched a muscle. At some point, they had been drugged again, probably because it was impossible to go indefinitely without water. At least the wire bindings had been replaced with chain. Kinder to the flesh, maybe, but no less miserable or escapable.

They both realized that Mary Lou was gone for good. They just hoped she wasn't dead, although in the darkness and quiet they sometimes whispered about it. Neither of them any longer nurtured much hope that they would survive this. At their age, that was an especially difficult conclusion to reach.

They'd lived relatively sheltered lives in this out-of-the-way county where, yes, bad things happened, but not all the time. Living on a ranch, or living in town, they hadn't feared walking the streets in the evening or even felt it necessary to lock their doors. Companies that wired houses for security would go broke out here except for some of the businesses.

But that didn't mean they were totally insulated. The news got through, either in newspapers or on the evening television. They'd heard or read stories of what could happen to young women who were kidnapped by unscrupulous men. The questions floating around in their heads now were whether they were to be sex slaves or sacrifices. Both possibilities terrified them equally.

But they certainly didn't expect to be let go. That left them only a need to fight to survive. No other motive existed any longer.

They huddled as close together as they could, giving in and sitting up to eat the food bars placed nearby, forced to drink water because their bodies demanded it. Sometimes the water knocked them out. Those were the merciful times.

It had gotten to the point where Jane told Chantal that she hoped one of those bottles would contain a lethal dose of whatever was putting them to sleep.

Chantal wanted to argue with her, but her arguments were growing wearier and weaker. To fall into sleep and never awake again was beginning to appeal to her, too, though she refused to admit it to Jane.

So cold. Under the ratty blanket, pressed close to each other, they still grew miserably chilled. Unfortunately, not chilled enough to never wake up. They ached from confinement, from cold, from the hard floor. They hated the smelly blanket that did little enough of what a blanket was supposed to do.

They pressed icy bare feet together, rubbing them to stimulate circulation. They switched sides trying to warm one half and then the other.

Survival drove them, but they couldn't even explain why. Giving up would have been so much easier.

Nobody would ever find them, Chantal thought. Ever. But even as she grew more dazed with time, she squashed that thought every time it occurred.

"You know this county," she said to Jane, her voice little more than a cracked whisper from a sore throat.

"Yeah. If we're in Conard County." Jane didn't sound much better.

"It doesn't matter. People around here won't stop looking for us. They won't. You know that."

"Then why aren't they here already?"

Chantal had no answer for that. Instead she said, "They'll come. They must be looking over every inch."

"So? We're buried in a basement."

Chantal couldn't argue with that, so she fell silent. But then Jane said, "You're right. They'll even look in basements."

To that they clung as much as they could.

"Just eat another food bar," Chantal said. "If the bastard shows up when I'm awake, I don't want to be too weak to give him a hard time."

So they choked down the dry bars and risked a few sips of water.

Keeping up some strength seemed to be all they had left.

NOT TOO MANY miles away, Al Carstairs had resumed his usual duties in animal control. Mostly. Like everyone else, he was knocking on doors asking if anyone had noticed anything unusual. Like everyone else he was getting a lot of negative shakes of the head.

How could this guy have been so invisible? How was it nobody noticed something odd about a guy pulling three girls out of a car and putting them in his? God, they must have been drugged, and as such Raggedy Ann would have seemed more like a human body.

But nobody had noticed?

Well, it was New Year's night, and he guessed a lot of people were either at home nursing hangovers, or sitting in the bars, roadhouses and taverns that dotted this county, enjoying the hair of the dog that bit them. Rusty had said more than once that his tavern had been hopping.

The girls had left early, too. With the next morning being Sunday, most people who went out to enjoy themselves probably hadn't called it an early evening. So it was entirely possible that not one soul had driven by during the time when the car went off the road, and the abductor moved them to his vehicle.

What if someone had stopped? The guy could have said, "My sister and her friends had too much to drink. I need to get them home."

And if the person who had stopped wasn't from these parts, why would the individual mention it to anyone? Why even question it?

Kelly had apparently been the first person to come upon the car once the girls were gone. No one else had reported a car off the road. A dead silence seemed to have filled the county that night.

He cussed, which didn't please the stray black Lab he'd picked up. Molly, her name was, and while she had a loving home now, there was no question she hadn't always enjoyed one. She was the only dog he'd ever known that would cower at a cuss word, even one in passing conversation.

He'd have loved to find out who her first owners had been so he could give them a piece of his mind. But she'd been dumped at Mike Windwalker's clinic by a guy who said he'd found her beside the highway. And the guy didn't even live in these parts.

No help. Not that it mattered now. Molly had a good home; she just liked to run. Usually she'd run for a couple of hours and then show up at her family's door. This time she'd stayed out longer than usual and Al had been advised the family couldn't find her.

Well, she'd wandered farther than usual. Much.

Then there was a raccoon back there who'd gotten herself tangled in some barbed wire while attempting to heist the contents of a trash can. She needed to see the vet as well as get a dose of rabies vaccine. Mike would probably keep the animal for a while to make sure it wasn't already sick. Unfortunately, even though it was the wrong time of year, she appeared to be pregnant.

But while he was usually very focused on the animals he looked after, it was different now. Now all he could think about was the missing girls. Acid chewed at his stomach lining, his mouth tasted sour and a beer sounded too good to a guy who'd been dry for five years now.

Not that alcohol had ever taken over, but he'd become nervously aware a year or so after he left the service that it could easily become a favored crutch. That he *could* become addicted. So he'd quit on his own. Not another drop. It hadn't been that hard because he'd taken charge of it before it took charge of him.

But right now he seriously wanted a beer.

Those girls. Those poor girls. And Kelly. He knew she was out there continuing the pursuit but doubted she was having any better luck. He kept remembering that nightmare or premonition she'd had that one of them had died.

He couldn't dismiss it, much as he'd have liked to, and now all he wanted was to discharge these animals and find her, to see how she was holding up. Because this whole situation was not only horrifying, it was weird.

It was as if something supernatural had swept them away.

He dropped Molly at home with her family. The Clancy kids were thrilled to have her back. Molly had apparently tired herself out, because she collapsed at their feet and grinned.

Mike Windwalker took the raccoon, handling her with

long leather gloves to avoid a bite, and agreed she needed rabies vaccine.

"Pregnant, huh?" Mike said as he looked her over before popping the angry animal into a cage. "Somebody mess up her clock?"

"I haven't a foggy. I take them the way I find them."

Mike laughed. "Yeah, me, too."

As he drove away into the fading light of early winter night, Al wondered where he could find Kelly. Then he remembered his damn radio. Duh.

"Actually," she answered, "I was just about to hit the truck stop for one of Hasty's burgers. You interested?"

"Save me a seat."

Maude made a good burger, but Hasty fire-grilled them. A whole different level.

For the first time that day, things seemed to be looking up a bit. A burger and fries. He smiled wryly knowing his doc wouldn't like it, but since he was fit as a fiddle except for certain lingering effects of a wound, he refused to worry about it. If a single burger had ever killed anyone, he'd never heard about it.

But riding his shoulder like a shadow was concern for those three girls. He hated to imagine what their families must be going through. Not knowing was bad enough from his end.

Hasty's truck stop was full of grumbling beasts as usual. Inside the café, truckers were scattered around, most of them eating heartily and drinking lots of coffee. They were allowed now to drive only eleven hours a day, and most trucks had trackers on them. For reasons of speed and ease of driving, that meant most of these guys slept in their cabs by day and drove all night. Unless the weather was bad, in which case they reversed, wanting all the clarity of sight they could get.

Tonight was looking to be a long night before breakfast came.

Kelly was already there, at a table near a window. He liked that. He never felt quite comfortable without an open view. He knew it was a leftover from war, but knowing it didn't make it go away.

He slid into the booth facing her and smiled. "Want a pregnant momma raccoon who got herself tangled in some barbed wire? She was dumpster diving."

Kelly blinked, as if she needed to change her location in the world. "Really? Pregnant?"

"Seems way early in the season. I left her with Mike Windwalker. First on the list, treatment for rabies and antiseptic for scratches. Anyway, how'd your day go?"

"It went nowhere," she said frankly. "I must have stopped at twenty or so houses. Nobody saw anything that aroused their interest. At least not yet. I'm hoping that maybe someone has a memory jog and calls. There was one interesting thing, however."

The waitress came over and took their orders. Lots of coffee, two burgers for him, one for her, and a heap of fries. It was the cold. He always ate more. So, he guessed, did she. "So what was interesting?"

"Bugle. We were a little over five miles out on a ranch road when he started to go bonkers."

Al arched a brow. "Is that like him?"

"Absolutely not. He wanted my attention and he wasn't going to let me ignore him. He howled and barked until I thought I'd go deaf. So I pulled over and let him hunt whatever scent had caught his attention. About a half mile back down the road he found a glove. A ratty man's work glove, and he wouldn't budge. I gave it to the sheriff before I came here."

"That's strange," he said, thinking it over. He knew a

lot about dogs. The idea that Bugle might have caught the scent of one of the missing girls didn't escape him. He leaned back to let their dinners be served, then leaned in again, keeping his voice low. "They're going to test it?"

"Damn straight. I don't know if it'll tell us anything at all, but it's worth a try."

"Definitely." He lifted his burger, his mouth already watering. "You know how amazing dogs are, Kelly. You don't need me to tell you that if he caught a whiff of one of those girls he'd recognize it even after all this time."

"I know," she said quietly, almost sadly. "I don't know whether to be hopeful or not. I mean, it was in the middle of nowhere. It could have blown off the back end of a pickup truck, and there's no way to know where it would have been headed. So…"

"You're afraid it might be false hope."

"Yeah." She stared down at her burger, then picked it up with obvious reluctance. "I guess it's better than nothing. What if we can identify the DNA? Some guy with a record. That'd be a fantastic clue."

"But you're afraid it won't be."

She raised her gaze. "I somehow think I don't need to tell you about the tightrope between hope and despair."

"No," he admitted. "Come on, eat. Your eyes are so sunken right now they might fall out of the back of your head."

That at least brought a smile to her face.

"Bugle out in your truck?"

"Yeah." She motioned toward the window. "See him?"

He did. The SUV was obviously running to judge by the steam coming off the hood as a gentle swirl of snowflakes fell.

"I'm going to get him a couple of burgers, too," she remarked. "Please don't go sanctimonious on me about a proper diet for him."

At that she drew a laugh from him. "I'm sitting here eating two burgers myself. I'm going to get sanctimonious?"

Her smile widened. "He likes a few fries, too."

"Then let's save him some. I'm betting he's salivating out there, smelling everything that's cooking in here."

At that she finally laughed. "The aromas that pour out all the vents and ducts in this place call to human stomachs and noses for miles. Why should he be different?"

The rest of the meal passed amiably, and apparently the waitress knew the drill when it came to Bugle, because along with their separate checks came a couple of cardboard containers holding burgers and even a few fries.

"No ketchup," said the waitress. "I know he loves it, but you'll never convince me it's good for his stomach."

"I don't want to find out," Kelly agreed as she put a twenty on the table. Plus another five she tucked in the waitress's apron. "You didn't see that happen."

Al laughed and followed suit. They were halfway out the door when his radio began to squawk.

"Carstairs," he answered as they descended the steps into the parking lot. Bugle, in the wise way of all canines, was already standing at the window, his tail wagging like a flag in gale-force winds. He knew a treat was on the way.

Al listened, standing still, while Kelly opened the back door of her truck and put the burgers and fries in for Bugle. The cardboard went into the nearby trash can while the paper wrappers remained with the dog. He knew to lick them, not to eat them.

"I'll be right there," Al said. His voice had lost all cheer. He signed off and shoved the phone onto its belt holster.

"What's going on?" Kelly asked him, disturbed by his change in tone.

"A neighborhood problem dog just burrowed under a fence and menaced a four-year-old girl. Gotta go."

"Can I follow?"

"Sure, I might need you to help me legally confiscate the animal. Bugle could be a help, too."

"Where are we heading?"

"Downy Lane. Four-oh-nine."

Kelly radioed dispatch as she followed Al's van down the road. Velma, on duty again, cracked a laugh. "I heard the call. Bet Al needs you and Bugle more than himself."

"Now, Velma…"

Velma laughed again. "He's good with animals. This one is not a good animal. There's a difference. Only reason that dog ain't gone is pure neighborliness."

The listed address wasn't that far away from the truck stop, maybe eight blocks on the far side of the railroad tracks that rarely saw any traffic these days.

It was a shame, Kelly often thought, that railroads had been replaced by trucks. However, given the mountains around here, maybe the trains couldn't be loaded as heavily as the trucks without becoming unsafe. What did she know?

The house in question was old but well cared for, a late-nineteenth-century structure built in the old "shotgun" style. With a narrow lot, every room added on had been added to the rear. The term came from the saying that you could walk in the front door and hit everybody in the house with one blast of a shotgun.

She was glad times had changed in that respect.

She pulled up against the shoulder—no curbs in this part of town—and waited while Al approached the house. Bugle had wolfed down his treats and was now noisily licking his chops.

The front door opened and a man's silhouette appeared.

He was clearly upset and waving his arms. Instinctively, Kelly climbed out, leashed Bugle and approached, standing far enough back that she wouldn't seem like a threat.

"—don't know," the guy was saying, his voice raised. "Do I have to put bars and special locks on every door and window to make my daughter safe? She's *four*! I thought she was in bed. It's basically early, though, and I guess she got tired of watching TV or saw the snowflakes… I dunno. But she went out in her own backyard—a fenced backyard I might add—and suddenly I heard her shrieking and that beast from next door growling and damn, I never came so close to shooting an animal in my life!"

"Was the dog on your property?"

"You better believe it. Not two feet from her, crouched with his teeth bared. I've had it. That damn dog has threatened people before. Especially her. This isn't the first time I've called you, if you remember. It's time to listen."

Al nodded. "I'm sorry, Mr. Jakes. I think we're past issuing warnings now. Is the dog still out back?"

"I don't know. Fences won't hold him. He could be anywhere by now. But just tell me, Al, who the devil buys a dog to keep it outside all the time? I don't think that hellhound has been indoors once since they got him. Doesn't matter. What *does* matter is that my child ought to be able to play safely in her own backyard!"

To a point, Kelly thought as she listened. There were snakes, raccoons, foxes…but she let the thought go. She could understand Mr. Jakes's fury. Whether the dog would attack the child was irrelevant. What mattered was that no child should have to be threatened in his or her own backyard by a dog that should be properly confined.

"I agree," Al replied, keeping his voice calm. "Is your daughter safely inside now? No one else outside?"

"We're all inside, feeling like prisoners in our own

house. Something has to be done about that animal or its owners. At this point I don't care which."

"All right. You all wait inside while we hunt for Cujo. That's his name, right?"

"Like some kind of prediction. Yeah. You got help? Because you're going to need it."

"Deputy Noveno and her K-9 will be helping. If we need more help, I can get it. Just relax indoors while we take care of this."

Still grumbling, Jakes went back inside, slamming the door for emphasis. Kelly really couldn't blame him. Apparently this Cujo had been a problem before.

Al came around to the back of his van and Kelly moved in close with Bugle. "Okay," Al said, opening one of the doors. "Time for long leather gloves. I'm going to give you a muzzle to carry in case we need it." Then he turned and faced her, and he didn't look at all happy. "While I don't advocate it, shoot if you think it's necessary."

Kelly looked down at Bugle. "I think a certain set of teeth will work better."

"I hope so. But I don't want Bugle to get messed up either. I don't know what this dog is capable of. Not yet. I know we've had complaints that he's killed pet rabbits and a couple of cats, but there was no proof to pin it on Cujo. So the owners have been slapped with warnings and some fines for not keeping him properly leashed. Here we go again."

They started by walking through a latched gate into the backyard of the Jakeses' house. It was obvious where the dog had dug his way under a wooden privacy fence.

"I wish the neighbors would put in some wire fencing about two feet down," Al remarked. "Most dogs won't dig that deep."

"What breed are we talking about here?"

"Rottie. Usually good dogs, but there are some…"

"There are always some," she agreed as they walked around the side of the house. She didn't know if it was lack of training or poor treatment. Or, if like some people, some dogs just weren't nice pets. They probably had all kinds of personalities.

The backyard proved to be a nice size for such a narrow lot. A metal swing set stood to one side, and what appeared to be a covered sandbox filled a corner. Large and small plastic balls were scattered about, along with a ragged stuffed doll. Al bent for the doll. "I guess Cujo had him some fun after all." He passed the doll to Kelly, who looked it over. The head had unmistakable teeth marks on it.

Bugle sniffed it and gave one quiet woof. He knew. Kelly just hoped the miscreant dog hadn't torn it from the little girl's hands. That would have utterly terrified her.

Al scanned the backyard, then walked up to the house and grabbed a shovel. He jammed it into the hole under the fence in such a way as to make it difficult for the dog to crawl under.

"Next door, now."

Kelly scanned one more time, looking and watching Bugle, but Bugle didn't seem to be much interested in the backyard after one sniff at the torn doll and a pass by the hole under the fence. Instead, he seemed more interested in pulling her back the way they'd come.

He'd be the best one to have a good idea of where Cujo was hanging out.

"You want Bugle to lead the way?" she asked Al as they passed through the gate in the other direction.

He eyed her over his shoulder. "Like I haven't done this before."

She flushed, grateful the darkness hid it. "I only meant he'll be able to smell the other dog."

"It hasn't rained shampoo recently," Al said wryly. "We'll *all* be able to smell Cujo."

He had a point there. Dogs weren't exactly odorless, even when dry.

The house next door was nearly a carbon copy of the Jakes place. Lights gleamed from the window, so someone should be there. Once again, Kelly stood back near the sidewalk. She knew that her presence might cause trouble if whoever answered the door felt belligerent. Best to let Al handle it. He knew these people.

Belligerence was definitely waiting for him. Before Al could say a word, the man who answered was on a tear.

"Bet that damn sissy Jakes called you. Look, a dog's a dog, and they do things like dig under fences. They get out and run. I don't give a damn. That man has been after Cujo since he was a pup! He just wants me to get rid of him!"

Kelly felt Bugle growing tense beside her, ready to spring into action if need be. She made no effort to calm him down. The way that guy was gesticulating, things could get ugly at the drop of a hat.

"Mr. Hays…"

But Hays didn't wait for Al to speak another word. "My dog ain't doing a damn thing but being a dog. Like anyone else's dog. If that sissy next door didn't have a bunch of cats, he'd understand better. He needs some schooling and I might just give it to him."

"Mr. Hays, are you threatening…"

"I ain't threatening nobody. I just want him to leave my damn dog alone."

At that moment the ill-famed Cujo decided to come running around the corner of the house. He didn't go sit placidly beside his master. No, he bared his teeth and growled at Al. Worse, his hackles were raised. That dog was ready to fight.

Kelly tensed but didn't want to intervene unnecessarily. This was Al's job and he probably knew a whole lot more about how to handle this.

"Call your dog off, Hays," Al said. His voice held the sharp edge of command, a voice that said he was used to being obeyed.

"Why? He ain't hurtin' you and *you're* the one trespassing. I'd be within my rights to sic him on you."

Not exactly, Kelly thought, but bit her lip. *Stay out of it.*

"Mr. Hays," Al said, his voice suddenly as cold and hard as steel, "either control your dog and get him to settle or I'll deem him dangerous and put him out of everyone's misery. Are you hearing me?"

Al, still wearing the elbow-length leather gloves he'd put on, reached to his hip and for the first time Kelly noted he was carrying a collapsible baton on his belt. He pulled it off. That baton could put human or dog out of commission without killing either. With a pointed snap, Al extended it.

Bugle sidled forward, as if he wanted to take action, but the gentlest tug on his leash caused him to settle quietly beside Kelly.

Something must have gotten through to Hays, because he snapped, "Cujo! Here!"

The dog, still snarling, obeyed, standing beside his master, facing Al.

"Leash him," Al said in the same steely voice.

Cussing a blue streak, Hays obeyed. Kelly was grateful to see that Cujo's leash was a chain. She figured he could chew his way through leather in no time at all.

"Now," said Al, "we're going to talk. Unless you want me to take Cujo tonight."

Some kind of sullen mumble emerged from Hays.

"You have been repeatedly warned about failing to keep your dog under control. He is to be leashed any time he's outside your front door unless confined by a fence. Your fence out back isn't doing a damn bit of good to judge by the way he tunnels into the Jakeses' yard."

"He's just a dang dog…"

"A dang dog with a mouthful of teeth and a bite powerful enough to break bone. And the Jakes have a four-year-old daughter who has as much right to play safely in her backyard as Cujo has to be in his…as long as he stays in his own yard. Is that clear?"

"They oughta watch her…"

"And you ought to watch your dog. Quit arguing or I'll get really angry. I'm only halfway there."

For halfway to angry, Kelly thought Al seemed remarkably calm. Although his voice still sounded like honed steel.

"Now, listen carefully because I'm through repeating myself. Cujo crawled under the fence and menaced a little girl…"

"He don't menace nobody!"

"He was just menacing *me* and I'm not four. What's more I've got Deputy Noveno as a witness. Clear?"

Finally Hays stopped arguing and just nodded.

"If Cujo had so much as scratched that little girl, I'd be taking him to have him put down right now. This is not a joke. Are you hearing me?"

Hays nodded glumly.

"Unfortunately," Al continued, "a lot of people want rotties because they're tough and dangerous. But the most dangerous dog is one that's thoroughly trained. You hear me? Ask the K-9 officer there if you don't believe me. Regardless, I'll give you two choices. The first is give the dog up to me tonight. The second is, tomorrow morning take him to Cadel Marcus to be trained. If Cadel can train him, you'll have a dog that won't give you any heartburn but will still protect your family. But if you can't do that…"

Finally Hays spoke. "Heard that Marcus guy is good."

"The best. But Cujo needs to be trained, not running wild. And I don't just mean that he sits and stays. There's a lot more to a well-trained dog than that. So those are your choices. In the meantime, you get a citation for animal at large, and you owe the little Jakes girl a new doll."

Hays cussed again, but didn't argue.

Al pulled his summons book from his jacket pocket, tugged off one leather glove, which he tucked under his arm, and began writing. "Okay," he said as he ripped the summons off the pad and handed it to Hays. "You know the drill. Pay the fine by the date listed and you don't have to go to court. But I'll give you one more warning."

"Yeah?"

"Yeah. If Cadel tells me you haven't left Cujo for him to train by ten tomorrow morning, I'll take the dog. No more chances, Mr. Hays. Not one. The life of a four-year-old girl is still worth more than a rottweiler. Clear?"

A couple of minutes later, as they were about to get into their vehicles to leave, Al came to stand beside Kelly. "I hate to put a dog down," he muttered. "I hope that jackass pays attention this time."

Kelly understood. "I wouldn't want to either, but that little girl…"

"Exactly. Listen, if you don't have other plans, want to come to my place? I know it's a ways out."

She smiled, her heart lifting a bit. How did he do that to her? "My place if you'll be comfortable. I've got an early call."

"Your place it is. Want me to grab some coffee from Maude's on my way over?"

"That would be super."

Chapter Eight

Chantal and Jane had passed the point of caring much anymore. The cold was gripping them constantly, and their bodies demanded that they eat. They gobbled down food bars without a thought for what might be in them, and when a big package of sandwich cookies showed up, those disappeared in record time.

They'd even stopped worrying about what was in the water bottles. Survival had come down to instincts they could no longer ignore. With chains holding them, they huddled close and were even grateful when a second blanket appeared with the food while they were sleeping. Sleeping or knocked out. They didn't know.

They felt they were being watched sometimes, but were past caring about that, too. They struggled to get the second blanket wrapped around them with the first. It, too, stank, but it smelled like an unwashed body.

"He never met a washing machine he liked," Chantal said, a weak attempt at humor. She couldn't see Jane at all, but heard what sounded like the breath of a laugh.

They'd stopped asking why. They couldn't imagine why they were captive, and they'd given up hope that Mary Lou wasn't already dead.

Chantal, though she'd never said so to Jane, remembered that moment when she'd felt as if Mary Lou had said goodbye. If she was dead, at least she was out of this. Safe. Free of the cold and the terror.

The food warmed them temporarily, as did the extra blanket, and this time when she started to fall asleep, Chantal thought it was natural sleep.

At least she hoped it was.

Walt Revell, Reve to his friends, came back from a pool game and a few beers at Rusty's Tavern and pulled off the road. It was dark, the moon dropping behind the Western mountains, but there was still enough light to see by. Grabbing a backpack out of the rear of his truck, he began the trek to the collapsing cabin where he was keeping his girls.

Day by day he could see he was winning them over. They talked less, they ate without trying to avoid the food or water. They'd become his creatures, without will of their own.

Not much longer now. He just had to decide which one seemed most ready to behave herself. He wasn't going to ask much, after all. Some cooking, some cleaning, a little sack time... Not much at all in exchange for continuing to live.

Oh, yeah. No talking. He'd hit 'em into next week if they gave him any lip.

He counseled himself to patience. He'd been too quick with the first one, thinking terror alone would control her. It had been a waste, but he still had two left. He just had to wait until they forgot how to hope.

And from what he could see, hope was beginning to desert them.

When he was sure the drug in the water had done its work, he unlocked the metal door and descended the steps into the basement. He dropped more food and water beside them, a roll of paper towels to let them know that if they behaved they might get more comforts from him.

He hesitated over the cookies, then decided it was too soon to give them yet another reward. Let them eat the dry food bars and drink the water.

When he kicked them lightly with his foot, they barely stirred. Just a few more days. Not much longer.

Already the cops were near to giving up. The female deputy who'd shown up at his door hadn't been especially inquisitive. He could feel her dismissing him mentally. He was a nobody. She probably thought he was stupid.

Good thing she'd left her dog in the car, though. He was scared of what a dog might smell.

Terrified if he were to be honest. Maybe it was time to suffer through another shower and throw some of his clothes in the rickety machine.

Smells could give him away. He didn't want to risk that, not when he was so close to achieving all he wanted.

OVER TWO WEEKS had passed since the girls had gone missing. A feeling of despair was beginning to settle throughout the entire department. Kelly felt it when she went into the office nearly every day. The girls, they had begun to believe, had been taken far away from here. How else could there be no trace of them or their abductor?

Kelly supposed that at this point they'd give anything for a ransom note, but it was getting too late for that. Way too late. For all anyone knew, the girls were already being moved underground by some trafficking outfit, long since out of the county and maybe out of the country.

Kelly couldn't bear to think of it. Nobody wanted to say it out loud, but she was sure they all feared the same thing. The girls' families were at the end of their rope. The

FBI agents who had promised to show up were acting on the idea that the women were no longer in the county and thus they were operating out of Denver.

They might be right, but it scalded everyone in the Conard Country Sheriff's Department to feel that the FBI considered them to be too useless to even talk to.

Each day as each shift set out, every single deputy was determined to find something that would help locate the girls. Despairing or not, they certainly hadn't given up. They all feared that some pervert had them in his clutches and was treating them like slaves and whores.

When they could, the helicopters took to the air for an overflight, but had found nothing. Everything out there on the open expanses of wintry range looked as it always had.

And they still didn't have the DNA analysis back from the glove yet but were expecting it hourly. If it would answer any questions, no one knew.

Kelly started visiting Rusty's Tavern on the weekends. Al joined her. A beer, a chance to watch everyone without being obvious. Bugle resented being left at home, but Kelly didn't want to take her departmental SUV. It would be like walking in in full uniform, and her personal vehicle didn't have accommodations for leaving Bugle for long periods. All she wanted to do was watch, anyway.

As if, as Kelly had told Al at one point, the kidnapper was going to be wearing a sign around his neck.

Leaving no stone unturned had begun to take on a new meaning. Martha knew why they came. She didn't mention it, but she once said in passing, "I'm paying attention."

Kelly believed her. If one person did anything suspicious, they'd be facing Martha, who looked perfectly capable of breaking a beer bottle and using it as a weapon.

Rusty greeted them with a nod, as if to say he was keeping an eye out, as well.

After two weekends, Kelly and Al were both beginning to recognize the regulars. Some of them Kelly had questioned in the days immediately following the abductions, like that Revell guy. Watching him play pool, she wondered if he'd ever learned to color inside the lines.

A silly, useless thought, but a couple of other guys at the bar seemed to like to play with him and bet him a dollar at a time. Nobody was going broke or getting wealthy.

Al talked her into line dancing the second night they were there. All of a sudden her body felt awkward, as if parts wouldn't move right.

"Just relax," he said. "Nobody's watching, everybody's too busy watching their friends."

He was probably right, but she'd never felt comfortable dancing. He slipped his arm around her waist, showed her the simple steps and murmured in her ear, "Treat this as undercover work, a chance to watch people."

Well, that darn near worked like magic. Forgetting about what she was doing, she stumbled only once and Al steadied her. But he was right about watching people. Standing in line with other dancers, facing yet another line, sometimes wheeling around the floor, gave her an excellent chance to take in faces without being obvious about it.

Not that a face was going to tell her anything, but she could hope.

"This is a waste of our time," she said as they returned to their table, the bowl of nuts and two sweaty beer bottles.

"Maybe so. You're the cop. But we're reasonably certain our guy had to find our gals here. Whatever he did, he might try it again." He gestured with this bottle. "See that table over there in the far corner? Take a peek but don't zero in."

She took a quick look and felt her heart slam. Seriously?

Two teen girls were sitting over there? They hadn't heard what had happened?

"Indestructible," Al remarked. "At that age, they all believe it."

Won't happen to me. Kelly could almost hear herself saying that from her high school days.

"Anyway," he continued, "unless you have an objection, I figure we'll stay until they leave and maybe follow them at a reasonable distance."

"That's a great idea." She was embarrassed not to have thought of it herself. But then, she'd failed to be observant. That was part of her job. Al had picked up on those girls.

"I must be getting too tired," she remarked. "I should have noticed them."

"Maybe so, but I had a lot of years where I couldn't afford to overlook so much as a misplaced pebble."

That snapped her thoughts to him. "You never talk about it."

"Most of us don't. Nothing like war stories to ruin a mood, ruin friendships or convince folks we're totally crazy."

"I don't think there's any way I could believe you're crazy."

"You haven't seen some of my finer moments." He turned the beer bottle in his hands, and she noticed not for the first time that he seldom drank any of it. He held it like a prop.

"War takes a toll on everyone," he said presently. His voice was pitched so as not to travel. "Some guys come home and put on a veneer that fools everyone. They're okay. Or so everyone thinks, and that makes it easy on the people who care about them. Some can't do that. They need help dealing with what they saw and did. Me, I was somewhere in the middle for a while. Now I'm on the smooth veneer side."

"But is that good for you?"

He shrugged. "Whatever works. I consider myself lucky that I don't have to wallow."

"I doubt I'd think of it as wallowing."

He smiled faintly. "I didn't use that word seriously. I just mean I'm lucky that I don't have to dwell on it all the time. Animals are my medicine. I love the critters."

"Even rotties? By the way, did that dog ever get to Cadel?"

"Cujo is in boot camp right now. And I made sure Cadel knows the situation. Cujo isn't going to get an easy graduation because he doesn't have an easy owner."

That was one way of thinking about it, Kelly decided. The dog was probably going to be more responsible than his owner. That could create an interesting set of problems.

When she thought about Bugle, however, she had some idea of a dog's capabilities absent someone to tell it what to do. "Did I ever tell you about the time that I caught one suspect and Bugle chased down the other?"

"What?" The word came out on a laugh.

"Yup. Pulled a car over. I was getting the data on the registration when the driver climbed out, hands up. So Bugle and I both exited our vehicle. Then for some unknown and unexpected reason, the passenger jumped out and took to his heels. So there I was with the driver at gunpoint and my dog haring off into the woods after the passenger."

Al laughed. "I can just see it."

"Wasn't much to see except his hindquarters and tail. Well, I knew the driver was under the influence but with a backseat full of Bugle's cage, there was no place to put him. Certainly not in the front seat of my vehicle."

"God, no!"

"So I handcuffed the guy and made him run with me as we chased Bugle. Not a happy suspect, I can tell you."

"I imagine not."

"Got lots of body cam footage of him complaining he was tired and could we please take a break. Me, I was worried about getting to Bugle before the other guy could hurt him. For all I knew he had a gun or a knife. Anyway, by the time I'd followed Bugle's bark, and caught up, Bugle had the other guy on his knees with his hands over his head. Never laid a tooth on him."

Now Al was really laughing. "I wish I could have seen that!"

"It *was* quite some scene. And not exactly what I expected. Bugle undertook to make an arrest on his own initiative. Very cool."

"Was it a good arrest?"

"Absolutely. The guy he chased couldn't quite ditch all the cocaine in his pockets before I got there. And there was more in the car. I'm glad to say backup wasn't far behind because at that point we might have been stuck there for a little while, two suspects and no place to put them."

Al smiled. "I love stories like that about animals."

"So you're really crazy about them?"

"Let's just say I think the world would be a better place if we took a few lessons from dogs and cats. They pretty much live in the moment, their spats are never designed to harm one another in any serious way. Think of wolves."

"Wolves?"

"Yeah. They create family groups and take care of each other. Yes, there's a hierarchy, and the omega may have to eat last, but she *will* get enough to eat. And her job is to be the family clown, basically. The social grease that prevents things from growing tense. And as near as anyone can tell, they don't bear grudges."

"We could all do with a few less grudges."

"The girls over there are getting ready to leave," he remarked. Before she could move, he threw some money on the table, then sat back and watched.

Finally he said, "They're out the door. Nobody seems to be watching or paying attention."

"Okay." She rose and he followed suit. Together they eased through the crowd. Kelly bumped into a guy she didn't know. Right behind him was a man that she seemed to recall interviewing. Revell, that was it. This time he looked a little neater and a bit drunk.

"Deputy Kelly," the first guy said heartily. "Going so early?"

"Cut it out," said Revell, looking nervous as if he expected trouble. "Jeez, Spence, not every woman on the planet wants you to take a pass."

Al slipped his arm through hers, his face smiling but a tightness around his eyes. His entire posture seemed to turn into a warning or a threat as he eased her toward the door once again.

It struck her, as they eased their way out toward the door, that their cover was useless. Spence or whatever his name was had made her as law enforcement. So sitting in this damn tavern was probably a waste of time. Hell. Sure, they were trying to make it look like they were dating, but how many believed that?

"Hey," Spence called after them, "you ever find them girls yet?"

At that instant the bar grew immediately silent. Even the live music from the small stage trickled away.

Kelly felt herself stiffening, wanting to turn around and give the idiot a piece of her mind. Those missing girls were no joking matter. Not even for a drunken jerk. Still, she refused to yield to her baser impulse.

"Pretty damn bad," said Spence, "when the law can't find three girls. Bet they're right under your noses somewhere."

"Let it go," Al said quietly.

Oh, she didn't want to let it go. The anger that had been growing in her in response to weeks of worry wanted to erupt into vesuvian proportions, to flatten the guy's face just for the pleasure of wiping that smirk away.

But Al kept her moving toward the door. "We've got some girls to watch," he murmured.

"Dammit, Spence," she heard Revell say from behind. His tone still sounded a little nervous, but few people wanted to argue with the law. "You tryin' to get yourself in trouble? You're still on probation, remember?"

"So announce it to the world," Spence said angrily. "Just pointing out that cops shouldn't be out havin' a good time when them girls is missing. Get off my case, Reve."

Kelly focused on the door and the girls they were going to keep an eye on. They mattered, not some drunken blowhard who couldn't resist poking at a cop. Almost as if on cue, the band on the stage burst into a rowdy rendition of "Friends in Low Places," singing it about as well as anyone could except the original artist. Which meant poorly.

She drew a steadying breath of icy air as they left the stale beer and noise behind them. Without a word, Al hustled her into her car in the passenger seat. When he held out his hand, she gave him the keys. He hadn't been drinking and frankly, given her response to the idiot back inside, she wasn't at all sure how much she'd put away. Two bottles? She usually had her temper on a tighter tether.

Al wheeled the car around and started down the state highway, following the only visible taillights, the ones that must belong to the young women who'd just left the bar. At least no one else had tried to follow them. Not yet, anyway.

"That Spence guy was right."

"No, he wasn't. He thinks we were there having fun. Far from it, and you don't need me to remind you of that."

"No," she admitted. "But we still should have found *something* about those girls by now."

"This situation stinks," Al announced.

"No kidding."

"You're certainly tied up in knots. I'm getting there."

She twisted in her seat to better see him in the light from the dashboard. "It's not like I can forget those girls. I'm positive my imagination has been doing its worst."

"It has for all of us." He surprised her and reached out, covering one of her hands with his.

She watched the taillights ahead of them, then squeezed her eyes shut briefly. "You know, I've been a cop for nearly ten years now. I'm good at separating the job from the personal. Usually. This time I can't do it, Al! Those girls are haunting my every waking moment. Yeah, I'm still doing my job, but I'd like to be a whole lot busier. Instead I spend a lot of time driving back roads hoping for a glimpse of something useful. Anything. And I keep praying the girls are alive and all right."

For long minutes he didn't speak. The car ahead of them reached the edge of town, turned down a street, then pulled into a driveway. Clearly these young women were getting home safely tonight.

"Job accomplished," he remarked before turning onto another street and heading for her place. "What's getting you wound up," he continued, squeezing her hand, "is that it's been so long and the outcome is not at all promising. You didn't need me to say that, did you?"

No, she hadn't needed to hear it. She felt it in her bones.

Since the night she'd wakened from a dead sleep to sense that one of the girls had died, she hadn't been able to believe this would end in any way other than tragically.

"I guess I'm begging for closure," she said after a pause.

"We all are. I can't imagine the hell those parents are living. Our share of it is nothing by comparison."

At that she felt embarrassed. "I'm being selfish."

"I didn't say that. I'd be worried about you if you didn't care this much. We aren't robots, Kelly. We do what we do because we give a damn, you know? There'd be something wrong with you otherwise."

She remembered her dad speaking about a case that had tormented him for years. "Maybe you're right. My dad had some cases that haunted him."

"Let's just hope this one doesn't have to haunt us. There *is* still hope."

But not much, she thought grimly. "The glove didn't tell us much." Their one clue. Basically useless.

"Well, we know it touched one of the girls. Bugle was right about that. But whoever wore it…"

Whoever had worn it wasn't in the database anywhere. So no criminal history, at least not since law enforcement had started to keep such records. "Useless," she said aloud.

"Not if we find the guy. The DNA can tie him to the girls, right?"

"To one of them, at least. Yeah, that could be useful." But only if they found the perp.

She sighed, thinking this was very unlike her. Hope was usually the last thing she tossed overboard when the seas grew choppy. Yet here she was, arguing with every possible strand of hope Al tossed her way.

"I need an attitude adjustment," she said. "Some separation and a tighter focus on solving the crime."

He didn't argue. He turned into her driveway and switched off the engine. "Shall I stay or go?" he asked.

"Stay. Please. Talk me down."

He gave a mirthless laugh. "Maybe you can talk me down, too."

Once again she felt embarrassed. She'd been so busy thinking about how she felt that she hadn't given enough thought to how he must be feeling, as well. The idea that men didn't feel anything…well, her own dad had raised her to realize otherwise. No stoic stiff upper lip for Hector Noveno. He was a man who hadn't been afraid to shed a tear.

As soon as she opened the car door, she knew something was wrong. She could hear Bugle barking, something he rarely did, and he sounded…seriously disturbed.

She hit the ground running, then realized Al had the keys. Had she locked the front door? She didn't think so. She heard the pound of his feet right behind her.

"He doesn't usually do that, does he?"

"No. No." He was upset and communicating it in the only way he could.

She was sure she'd left the front porch light on, but it was off now. Burned-out bulb? Maybe. Criminy, she'd come out for the evening without most of her usual gear, not even a flashlight. Only her service pistol rode on her belt, hidden by her jacket and a bulky sweater. But the streetlight offered almost enough illumination to see the door and try the knob. If they needed the key they'd probably need the car headlights, as well.

But the knob turned under her hand and she threw the door open only to have Bugle launch himself at her and push her backward.

"Is someone inside?" she asked as she staggered back and regained her footing.

"He doesn't want you in there," Al agreed. "All I've got is my baton."

She lifted her jacket and tucked it back. "I'm armed." Unsnapping her holster, she drew her Glock. "A flashlight could be useful."

But that would take time. She had plenty of them inside, and a couple of good Maglites in her official vehicle, but how long would it take to get them?

"Bugle."

The dog immediately came to her side. "Find."

Well, that didn't get his attention. "Seek," she commanded.

She could have sworn he shook his head but marched forward. Something in the way he moved told her the threat was gone but that something else had seriously bothered him. As soon as they were inside her small foyer, which gave a view of everything on the ground floor except her bedroom, she flipped the overhead light on.

Then she saw what had upset her dog, and wondered how someone had managed to do that without Bugle latching onto him.

A stuffed toy rabbit lay on the floor, and wrapped around its neck was a ragged piece of pink cloth. She didn't want to think about where the cloth had come from. "Time to call for help." Her voice had flattened with tension.

Then she moved slowly back through the house while Al called for reinforcements. She saw the damage before long.

Bugle had been in the bedroom, the door closed. Yeah, she must have done that. He liked to sleep on the bed while she was out, and closing the door was an almost automatic response on her part to dampen winter drafts.

But someone had taken advantage of that, and now her bedroom door had been clawed until Bugle had managed to get free. Long after the miscreant was gone.

Then she set the safety on her gun and sat in her armchair with her hands dangling between her legs, staring at the toy rabbit.

A message? A taunt? A threat? But why?

INSTEAD OF COOKIES, Reve's next reward to the girls was slipper socks. He worked weekends at the hospital as a janitor and had access to plenty of them. He also had access to the drugs he was giving the girls, but nobody would notice such small amounts missing. He didn't need much; it wasn't like he was going to perform surgery.

Anyway, he'd been hearing their complaints about how cold their feet were and it finally dawned on him that neither of them would be very useful or attractive without feet.

He'd seen a gangrenous limb at work once, and he was absolutely positive that he wouldn't want it in his bed. Besides, it would stink.

It was a good thing he'd decided not to let Spence in on his plans because after tonight it was obvious the guy couldn't keep his yap shut. Taunting a cop? That was a good way to get arrested and maybe worse.

The wrong cop, too. People thought Reve was dumb. He kept his head down, didn't say much and often pretended not to hear even when he had. He made himself invisible.

But Spence had drawn attention his way, however indirectly. And that cop Noveno with the dog…she wasn't giving up on the girls. He saw her prowling even when she wasn't on duty, crisscrossing the county like she hoped to spy something.

It might be necessary to get rid of her, he thought as he popped the top on another beer and settled at his own creaky kitchen table. Nearly everyone else seemed convinced those girls were long gone, vanished into some shadowy trafficking organization.

Which, now that he thought about it, might have been a good way to make some money. But no, he wanted those girls for himself. The guys with money could get plenty of girls to enjoy, but Reve…he didn't have the money. He had to find and catch his own or do without.

The catching part had come to him only lately, but after some thought and planning, he'd thought he'd done pretty well. Only one girl lost, and that was because he'd grown too impatient.

He'd learned something and was putting it into practice right now. A few more days, a week maybe, and those girls would be putty, willing to do whatever he said to get out of that basement, to get warm, to eat real food. Yeah. It was working.

But Spence had better just keep his mouth shut. He didn't want that cop's laser gaze trained his way. He swore that Noveno woman had the evil eye or something.

Regardless, if she started hanging around too much, he wouldn't hesitate to eliminate her. See, he wasn't dumb. He knew words like *eliminate*, and that's exactly what would happen to Kelly Noveno if she started hanging around this end of the county too much.

For that matter, Spence, too. He'd better just stop giving the cops a hard time. No need for that crap. Reve had waited too long to fulfill his dream. He wasn't going to let anyone get in his way, including Spence.

Damn, what had possessed the man, anyway? It was almost as if he was taunting Reve rather than the cop. But Spence didn't know what was going on, so how could he?

Reve rubbed his head, trying to ease a growing headache. Maybe he ought to just stay home for a while, avoid the tavern. Maybe he ought to let the girls be for a couple of days. They had enough water. Didn't matter if they didn't eat for a few days.

Yeah, time to lie low.

Chapter Nine

Day 18

Having the crime scene team crawl all over her house wasn't the most enjoyable experience in the world even though Kelly understood it all. It had to be done. The furry bunny with the odd bow had long since been bagged, but someone had entered her house and perhaps left traces behind them.

She patiently answered questions, but there were no real answers. Al stuck around and explained, too. They were hanging out at the tavern on weekends like a dating couple—two whole weekends, thought Kelly. Some dating—and keeping an eye out for anyone acting strangely.

Which led to the overwhelmingly huge report that they'd watched over several girls, making sure they'd returned home safely. Gigantic effort. Maybe they'd get a medal for valor.

Ah, damn, she thought, letting her head fall back in the recliner. As a cop she was messing up. Her stakeout at the tavern wasn't helping a damn thing. She was too emotionally involved, so much so that a piece of evidence could possibly walk right under her nose without attracting her attention.

And what was with the stuffed rabbit? Somebody's bad idea of a joke?

Gage had dragged himself out of a warm bed to come over here and keep eyes on things. He'd headed up the CSU before he'd been elected sheriff when Nate Tate retired, and he probably knew damn near as much as anyone in this room.

"The rabbit," Gage said, pulling the stool over to sit on.

Kelly came to herself. "Want this chair, Gage? You've got to be miserable on a stool."

"I'm probably less miserable than you are right now. The rabbit."

"Yeah, the rabbit. I have no connection with rabbits, Bugle doesn't especially want to chase them, and…" Suddenly she looked at Al. "There was that guy we spoke to about his rottie. You mentioned the dog had killed some pet rabbits."

Al nodded and shrugged all at once. He was perched on a bar stool. "If Spencer Hays wanted to make a statement about that, my place would make more sense."

"I was with you when you talked to Hays."

"And you stayed well out of it. No, this is something else. Damned if I know what."

Gage bent, wincing as he did so, and picked up the rabbit now safely encased in a clear plastic evidence bag all marked up for the chain of evidence. He stared at it, turning it over a couple of times. "That ragged cloth bothers me. It's impossible to tell if it's supposed to be a bow, or a noose."

Kelly felt her heart skip. "A noose?"

Gage didn't answer her, but instead looked at Al. "How well you know this Spencer Hays? Had many dealings with him?"

"Not many, unless you count the number of times I've

had to warn him to keep his dog under control. The dog, by the way, is with Cadel Marcus right now. Time for some decent training before a little girl loses a hand or her face."

Gage nodded thoughtfully. "Well, we'll take a closer look at Mr. Hays. If he thinks you two have been going to the tavern together often, this could be his roundabout way of getting to you, Al. I can't see any other reason to leave it here."

"I've been spending quite a few evenings here," Al said. He didn't offer an explanation, for which Kelly was grateful. He *had* been spending a lot of evenings here when she wasn't working, but she didn't place much importance on it except they were growing a friendship. A very special friendship, she believed, closer than she'd enjoyed in a while. But still just a friendship. How could anyone hope to get at him through her?

After a moment, she decided to bring up the scene at the tavern. "Hays did have something to say to me tonight about not having found the girls yet. He was loud and noisy about it. But I can't imagine when he could have left the rabbit."

"He had time," Al said. "While we followed those girls home. How long do you suppose he needed to dump a stuffed toy here? Was your door locked?"

"No." So maybe he *did* have time. "It still doesn't make sense. It's hardly a threat. A taunt? But why?"

Gage spoke quietly. "Or just to say he knows how to get to you."

Aw, hell, thought Kelly. Aw, hell. "But why?"

The answer to that was a ringing silence.

IT WAS NEARLY one in the morning. Kelly needed to be on duty at seven. She ought to be sleeping but sleep appeared to be far away.

Al examined her bedroom door. "Gotta hand it to Bugle. You're going to need a new door."

"I'm not surprised."

He sat cross-legged on the floor and looked across the room at her. "You're a beautiful woman, Kelly Noveno."

She caught her breath, morose thoughts flying away to be replaced by astonished wonder. "What brought that on?"

He smiled. "I've been thinking it for ages."

She shook her head a little. "You've avoided me for ages. Come off it, Al."

"Sorry, lady. Been avoiding you because I'm a bad bet for a relationship. But that didn't mean I didn't notice. Anyway, sometimes I'd see you and it was like I lost my breath. But...beauty isn't a foundation, and my foundations are shaky anyway."

"You keep saying that. Or versions of that. Just what do you think is wrong with you?"

"If I can't trust myself, why should anyone else trust me?"

He shook his head and stood. "I don't want to leave you here alone tonight."

"I have Bugle," she reminded him.

He nodded slowly. "You're on duty in the morning?"

"Yeah. I hear there's a storm coming so I'll probably be doing welfare checks most of the day." Looking in on older residents who lived out of town, who might need a better place to stay for the duration or who might need some help stocking the larder, in which case she'd give one of the volunteer groups a call.

"Okay, then. I'll see you around."

A moment later he'd disappeared out the door. *See you around?* Had she offended him? All she'd done was ask what he thought was wrong with himself.

Well, if he was going to react that way...

Shaking her head, she climbed into bed wearing her thermal underwear, with Bugle's warmth snuggled up against her beneath the quilt.

A dog was more reliable than a man any day, she thought. She should have figured it out years ago.

But as she drifted into sleep, she had dreams of a rabbit wearing a noose, of a girl in a torn pink jacket, of Bugle with his teeth bared.

Bugle stirred nervously beside her but didn't wake her. His eyes never closed, though.

It took a hell of a lot of effort. Chantal was past worrying whether she cussed in the silence of her own mind or if she did it out loud so Jane could hear. It didn't seem to bother Jane, anyway.

They were chained so that their hands could reach their mouths, but not much beyond. Her wrists were sore, so sore that she was sure they must be scabbed over. Every movement hurt, but she steeled herself to ignore it. Their ankles were tethered to some kind of ring in the floor, giving them a few feet to move around in, but no more.

Her body felt as if it were crawling in filth. It had been so long since last she'd been able to get clean. Living worse than an animal.

The man hadn't been back in a couple of days, but she was sure he'd return. He wanted something from them and she was certain it was nothing good. They had to find a way to get out of here, except there was no way out except by the stairs that led to the metal door. A storm cellar, she thought. An ancient storm cellar, except over her head was the remains of a window. That seemed odd, so maybe it had been mostly a root cellar.

Whatever it was, it was boarded over with just the slightest cracks that sometimes let in some pale, watery light. Not enough to illuminate the room, but enough to sometimes tell her whether it was night or day.

The nights and days had all run together, though, and she no longer had any idea how long they'd been here.

She just knew she couldn't take it any longer. She was past caring if she died.

She stirred a bit and felt her elbows touch her ribs. For the first time in her life, she could feel her ribs sticking out. To think she'd once wanted to be that thin.

If she ever got out of here alive, she swore she was going to eat herself sick on every kind of junk food she could get her hands on. Her mind played tricks on her now, and sometimes she was sure she could smell a hamburger. Or a French fry. Or even broccoli.

Broccoli? Man, that was desperation. Worse yet, sometimes she craved Brussels sprouts, what her little brother called cannonballs. She'd never liked them, but now she'd have traded a whole lot for a big bowl of something green.

It was dark again, and she could faintly hear a wind whistling. It seemed to be coming from the remains of the window above her head.

"Jane?"

"Yeah." Jane sounded flat, as if she'd totally given up. Chantal was on the edge of it herself, but not quite ready. She had to make at least one attempt, and out of the fog of hunger and darkness an idea had come.

"Can you reach that window above us?"

"You're kidding, right? That's no window, that's jail bars."

"I know, but there are these small cracks in places. You saw them when we talked about them a few days ago." Or whenever it had been. Time had ceased to have meaning.

"So?"

"What if I rip off a piece of my sleeve with my teeth? Do you think you could shove it out a crack?"

"What good will that do?"

"It's bright. If the wind blows it like a flag..."

Jane was silent for a long time. "If it'll make you feel better, I'll try it, but it's a waste of time, Chantal. If it blows away, it says nothing. Anyway, who's going to care about a scrap of cloth? I don't think anyone's been looking for us for ages. They probably think we're in Mexico or getting whisked away by a gorgeous European prince."

Chantal fell quiet for a while, then said, "Being in a palace sounds better than this."

For the first time in forever, she heard Jane laugh. The noise was cracked, almost broken, but it sounded so good to Chantal.

"I like that," Jane whispered. "A big, rich, handsome prince who'll fall head over heels for both of us and treat us like priceless jewels."

"I think your mom was right when she said you read too many of those books."

Jane snorted. "Better than your cowboy stories. Didn't you ever want to get farther away from here? You don't really want some cowboy to lasso you, do you?"

"Depends. Not the cowboy who has us now."

Once again their mood darkened.

She felt Jane stir beside her. "I can just about reach the bottom crack," she said. "Give me that piece of cloth."

Of course, it wasn't that easy. The way Chantal's teeth felt right now, she wasn't sure they wouldn't all fall out of her head if she tried to tear at something.

"I want a hot shower," she murmured. "I want to be clean again, all over. I want to eat a double cheeseburger."

Jane was silent for what seemed the longest time. "Give

me a piece of that cloth," she whispered finally. "If nothing else, it'll be a good grave marker."

Chantal caught her breath. "You think he's leaving us here to die?"

"How should I know? All I know is Mary Lou's been gone forever. If that guy ever wanted anything from us, it was probably before we looked like filthy scarecrows."

Chantal squeezed her eyes shut, holding back tears that couldn't fall anymore. It was as if she had gone dry.

"Come on," Jane said, sounding broken. "The cloth. At least it'll tell them who the skeletons are."

NOW REVE DIDN'T dare do anything about the girls. Not since Spence had opened his yap. He'd have to wait a few days, see if that damn woman cop homed in on Spence in any way.

Talk about skating near the edge. And Spence didn't even know what was going on. It was as if some evil demon had put words in his mouth, causing him to draw attention to the very thing that Reve wanted to keep buried.

Crap.

And that stupid man had actually entered the deputy's house to leave part of an animal skin, he said. To give her a scare, he said.

They'd been lucky her dog hadn't been able to break out of the other room. Reve had spent the whole time sitting in his truck wondering if he should just find a way to shoot Spence when he was out running his trapline.

Another stupid thing. Spence lived in town but thought he was some kind of mountain man. Setting traps for foxes and selling their pelts. Damn fool was lucky he didn't catch himself a bear. Didn't matter. Fox trapping was legal. Wasn't nobody who liked the vermin.

But still. An animal skin?. For the cop when it was the

animal control guy he was mad at? So what if the two had started dating. Only a fool went after a man's woman.

Spence was a fool.

Sitting at his kitchen table again, Reve pondered what he was going to do about those girls. He didn't dare go near the place right now, not after the cop had been warned something was going on. What if she drove out here and saw him approaching that tumbledown shack. She might wonder. She might even think he had something to do with that damned toy.

Oh, he'd planned it all so carefully, but he hadn't counted on his friend being an idiot. Hadn't counted that foolish remarks might draw the wrong kind of attention.

Well, he'd better come up with a plan now. The girls had enough food and water for another five or six days. Then there was that storm moving in. If it was as bad as they were predicting, he might not even be able to reach them for a while.

They could die out there.

And right then that didn't sound like such a bad thing to Reve. He'd be shed of the problem and there'd always be another day down the road where he could try this again.

One thing for damn sure: he couldn't do anything from a prison.

Damn Spence all to hell.

THE MORNING BEGAN with an eerie light, a flat grayness that was still quite bright. No shadows fell anywhere, but the breeze, strangely gentled, still whispered of dangers to come.

Al stood outside, making a mental plan for the coming storm. They still had a couple of days, so it was too early to be worrying about wandering animals that might freeze, but he still had his regular tasks. At least they gave him an excuse to roam the county, hoping for a glimpse of something that might tell him what had happened to those girls.

Because he seriously doubted that if they were in this county that they were still alive. Hiding them from neighbors, even out on isolated ranches, would be hard to do for long. People visited, saw each other at church. Only someone who'd been a recluse forever would be overlooked for long.

Kelly had said she was going to be starting her welfare checks. Most of the deputies would be dropping by homes to find out if anyone needed heating oil or supplies, or to come to shelter in town.

So another blanket of searchers was going to be out all day, setting up things to help folks out, but still getting a good look at the entire county. Two days wasn't a long time to set up deliveries of heating oil if very many people were getting low. Impossible to know now, too, how long people might be shut in after the storm. Sometimes the wind blew the snow away like so much dry powder. Other times it built it into huge banks that covered houses until they were nearly invisible.

Only time would tell on that one.

And three girls, if they were out there and weren't being properly cared for, were probably already dead.

The thought darkened his mood considerably as he climbed into his utility vehicle, the one that had been modified to hold four cages comfortably in back. More than four and he'd have to bring them back to shelter.

Today he determined to head outside town, because any lost or abandoned animals were likely to be facing the most trouble out there.

As he bumped along the roads, however, he drifted

into thoughts about last night. Spencer had been an ass, for certain, but the man always had been. At least he'd finally seen the light about his dog, Cujo.

But then there was that stuffed rabbit. What in the hell did that mean? That it was a threat was obvious, to him at least. Dismiss it as a toy, but it remained someone had entered Kelly's house without her permission in order to leave it. Not a friendly gesture at all. He made a note to check with her later to ensure she was locking doors and windows. She shouldn't need a reminder but there'd been no evidence of a break-in at her house last night. Someone had opened the door and just walked in.

If he were Kelly, he wouldn't be feeling terribly safe after that. But she hadn't wanted him to stay. Of course, she had Bugle. He was probably more useful than ten armed guards, but still, Al hadn't liked being dismissed in favor of a dog.

But she had Bugle. And he'd had to come home and worry about her.

Then there was that stupid moment when he'd blurted how beautiful she was. Holy cow, what had possessed him? It was like something had taken over his mouth and issued the words before he could stop them.

Then that stuff about how he wasn't good for a relationship. It was true, of course. He hadn't lied about that, but he could see the questions dancing in her dark eyes, and if a guy was going to say things like that, he ought to be willing to answer the questions.

He guessed he spent too much time with dogs and cats. The idea amused him, but it was true. A flick of a tail, a long look, a twitch of ears, those animals could communicate entire encyclopedias to each other.

Him, not so much. He needed to use the whole dictionary of words to make his points. He was out of practice, though. He'd come home from the US Marines, mustered out with a disability, and discovered he had more problems than some shrapnel-torn back muscles. Nope, he had a brain problem, a brain full of rage that could be triggered unexpectedly. He'd gotten better with time, but that monster still lay in wait, and he treated it with wary respect.

What woman needed that? Hell, nobody needed that.

Then, like a great big wheel, his thoughts returned to that damned stuffed rabbit. No mistaking it was a message, but what kind? Why would anyone want to scare Kelly? Yeah, she'd found the car by the roadside, but that had proved to be useless. No information there to explain how three young women could vanish from the planet.

He smiled into the brightening day, with its strange light that assured him the sun was rising somewhere, as he recalled a conversation he'd overheard the other day at Maude's diner. Two men were absolutely convinced the girls had been abducted by aliens.

Vehemently convinced, even to the point of arguing when another fellow had discounted it after overhearing them.

"Where else could they be?" one of the men demanded. "Not in this county, that's for sure. You ever tried to keep anything secret around here?"

Interesting question. If those teens had been taken by someone who lived here, even if he'd transported them out of the state, he'd managed to keep it secret. And the guy at the diner was right. Keeping a secret around here was nigh on impossible.

"Ah, hell," he said to his empty truck. "Just keep your eyes peeled. He had to have left a track somewhere."

Sure. Like he'd left traces they couldn't find in the car.

The abduction had been well planned, no question. But to what end? He hoped like mad those girls were still nearby and could be found somehow. That at the very least one of them escaped to seek help.

But with each passing day that hope seemed dimmer.

So did the sky all of a sudden. Though he seldom cared to listen to the radio while he cruised around looking for animals that were out of place, he turned it on now.

Wicked storm on the way. It would hit full force by the day after tomorrow. No searching in the middle of that.

His radio squawked and he picked it up. "Animal control, Carstairs."

"Al," said a familiar voice belonging to an elderly lady outside town, "my Ruffles hasn't come home since yesterday. Not even to eat."

"I'm coming, Mrs. Jackson. Did she seem all right yesterday?"

"She was fine when I let her out yesterday afternoon. Just fine. And she knows how to hide from them coyotes. Heck, I think they're terrified of her."

"Maybe so," he agreed as he used one hand to execute a three-point turn. "I'll be there in fifteen minutes."

She thanked him, her voice wavering as it only could when a person was really upset.

He hoped to God he found Ruffles, an independent, stubborn, single-minded Maine coon that had plenty to say about how life should work.

Yeah, he wouldn't be surprised if that cat scared the coyotes. She was almost as big as some of them, big even for her breed. And while Maine coons were sweet tempered, this one had a temper.

She was also bred to withstand the kind of weather that was coming. Which was about the only good thing Al could say about it.

WHEN HE REACHED Mrs. Jackson's ramshackle ranch about ten miles beyond town, she was standing on the porch bundled up head to foot and calling Ruffles.

This was not good, he thought as he pulled his own jacket on and bundled himself. Ruffles had never run away this long before. A few hours, maybe, but overnight?

As soon as he reached the porch, he urged Mrs. Jackson back inside. She was in her eighties and like many older people she had grown thin and a bit stooped. No meat on her bones to keep her warm, winter-weather wear notwithstanding.

"It's too cold for you to stand out here. You wait inside. You know I always find Ruffles."

"Ruffles has never been gone this long before," she quavered.

He hated to imagine how long she had worried before she finally decided to call him. Several hours at least. "I'll find her," he promised. He just hoped he'd find Ruffles alive and well. "Say, are you set for the storm? Heating oil? Food?"

Mrs. Jackson lived alone, something he couldn't afford to forget.

"I got my heating oil last week," she answered. "I've got food."

"Well, I'll take a look at things in the house once I find the cat," he said. It wouldn't hurt to make sure her heater was operating correctly, and that her idea of food didn't amount to a single can of beans or soup.

She nodded, looking forlorn, and disappeared inside. She continued to peer out the front window, however, pulling the sheers back so she could see.

Okay, Al thought. *Where the devil would you be hiding, Ruffles?*

Something must have scared her good, Al reasoned.

More than usual if she'd taken to hiding and didn't want to come out.

He walked around the house, peering at every possible place that cat could have gotten herself stuck. Troubling him, however, was that he didn't hear a single *mew*. If the cat was in trouble, it should be calling for help. They usually did.

A gust of wind caught him, reminding him the weather was about to turn bad and the cat must be found, Maine coon or not.

Sighing, he started to survey the area around the house. A culvert, maybe? But coyotes could get in there. Ruffles didn't seem like the kind of cat that would allow herself to be cornered.

Then he spied a big old cottonwood, bare of leaves for the winter, but still high enough to attract a climber. Giving a mental shrug because he'd never known a cat to get stuck in a tree—they always seemed to find a way down, usually by jumping—he started to walk that way anyway. He'd made a promise.

As he walked, he scanned the ground almost out of habit. He could read the tracks of animals that had wandered through here before the winter had hardened the earth to cement.

Yeah, lots of coyotes, he saw. A wolf? Maybe, although they usually came in packs. Probably someone's stray dog. Cat tracks, mountain lions. They didn't usually come down out of the mountains this far, but one of them would be big enough to give Ruffles a bad time.

Then he saw a scrap of pink cloth. Just a torn scrap, but a different color from the one from last night's stuffed rabbit. Bending, he looked at it, then scanned the area around. Nothing for over a mile. Still…

First he took a photo with his cell phone, crouching

close. Then, touching the scrap only with his glove, he picked it up and tucked it in a seldom-used breast pocket on his jacket. Screw DNA, he guessed, but if he left it here it would blow away. Probably a useless exercise anyway.

Standing again, he continued his trek toward the tree. It was beautiful in the spring and summer, when it was all leafed out. Worthy of photographing. Right now it looked like a bunch of skeletal fingers, something he didn't want to think about.

If that cloth in his pocket had come from one of the missing teens… No way to know. Pink fabric was everywhere, and where could anyone be out here? Mrs. Jackson would know what was in her basement, and she wasn't likely to be involved in a kidnapping.

Still, he'd bring it to the sheriff's attention. Maybe they'd want to look around more out here. In case.

And all the cases were ugly.

"Ruffles." He called for the cat, hoping to see a huge Maine coon come running out of the sagebrush. No such luck. A big tumbleweed came at him, though, brushing by before the wind died again.

It was then he thought he heard a faint sound. "Ruffles?"

Another gust snatched it away and he froze, waiting to hear it again. He needed to locate it, and one sound wasn't enough out here. Sounds, he'd long ago learned since moving here, could be terribly deceptive in the wide-open spaces. Almost as bad as when they echoed among the rocks of mountains.

He resumed his march toward the cottonwood but kept scanning the ground. Where there was one pink piece of cloth, there might be another. There might even be a trail.

Like bread crumbs in Hansel and Gretel, he thought with sour amusement. Yeah, they should be so lucky. Those girls should be that lucky. Damn near three weeks now, and he was holding out very little hope.

He'd had to stop by the Episcopalian church two days ago, a tiny little building, to help the pastor with a barn owl that seemed to be caught in the belfry. While he was there he'd seen Jane's mother lighting a candle. Lighting a candle. It was enough to tear out a man's heart.

But hope endured, somehow. That woman hadn't given up but by now she must be wondering if God was even listening.

He reached the foot of the cottonwood and saw the ground had been ripped up. Coyotes. Then he heard another, faint *mew*.

Looking up, he saw Ruffles, her flecked brown coat blending well with the tree branches. Well, that explained a lot, he thought. Coyotes had treed the cat and she was afraid to come down. Must have been a pack of them or she'd have used her claws and teeth and sent them packing.

"Hey, Ruffles," he said in a soothing tone. "Rescue has arrived. Wanna come down?"

Because he sure didn't want to climb that tree. Winter slumber had probably made a lot of branches brittle, and there didn't look to be many really strong limbs positioned for a man to climb.

But the cat, like most cats, had a problem. She couldn't back down the tree. Cats just wouldn't do that. They had to see where they were going.

"Come on," he said. "You don't want to be the first cat I've ever seen who couldn't get out of a tree. I bet there's a can of food waiting for you right now. Aren't you cold?"

Talking to a cat. Okay, he was crazy, but at least it was harmless crazy. Anyway, hearing his voice, Ruffles appeared to be relaxing a bit. No coyotes were going to come if the man was here. He just hoped she realized that.

He was also glad this wasn't their first encounter. Ruffles knew him so she had no reason to fear him. He wasn't a stranger. Given the solitude in which Mrs. Jackson lived, there probably weren't a whole lot of people whom Ruffles knew and would trust.

"Come on, sweetie. Did those mean coyotes scare you? I wouldn't have thought they could tree you like this. You prefer life on the ground, don't you?"

Maine coons were definitely not tree cats, preferring to be on the solid earth, but Ruffles must have been terribly scared to perch herself up there.

Not knowing what else to do, he unzipped his jacket and spread his arms invitingly, ignoring the cold and hoping he looked like a safe landing place.

Ruffles looked in every direction, assessing threats, he assumed. Then her green eyes fixed on him again. Much to his relief, she started to ease her way down. Not easy, head-first, and she froze often, as if uncertain of her purchase.

Then, in one daring leap, she jumped down on him. He just managed to catch her, feeling her claws trying to dig in through his sweater, and hold her close. Those green eyes stared at him, then a purr told him most of what he needed to know.

Good. He grabbed a flap of his jacket and wrapped it over her. Then he spied some flecks of blood, almost invisible on her mottled coat. Hell, those coyotes had gotten a piece of her.

"I'll get you fixed up," he told her soothingly. "Bet you'd never guess I have a first aid kit for animals in my truck, would you? But I do. Some safe antiseptic. If you get to licking your coat, it won't sicken you. I think of everything, don't I?"

Ruffles's purr grew louder. Happy cat. All was well. For the cat and Mrs. Jackson at least.

RUFFLES HAD SOME scratches and had lost a few tufts of fur but no apparent bite marks, even though he and Mrs. Jackson went over every inch of her. Of course, that thick coat of hers had probably protected her from worse. Once he'd put the antiseptic on her, Al went down into the basement and checked out the heater. Everything appeared to be in working order, and the battery in the carbon monoxide detectors both in the basement and upstairs appeared to be reasonably fresh. He found some new ones in a drawer and changed them out anyway.

Her cupboard wasn't exactly overloaded with food, but she had considerably more than a can of beans. She'd be able to heat food on her propane stove.

Then, as she sat in her rocking chair with a now-happy Ruffles in her lap, he squatted before her.

"The storm is going to get very bad, Mrs. Jackson. No one can say for sure how many days you might be cut off from the world after it passes through. Would you rather I take you and Ruffles to the church shelter?"

She shook her head. "I'm fine. Besides, I was born in this house and if I'm going to die, I'd rather do it here. Been through bad storms before, Al. We'll do all right."

He nodded. "Just call if you need anything. I'll find a way to get here. Promise me?"

"I promise."

He had to be satisfied with that, he supposed. Then he hit the road again, wondering if he should take the scrap of cloth directly to the sheriff or wait until he finished his rounds.

Damned if he knew what use it would be, but maybe he ought to just turn it in. It felt almost as if it were burning a hole in his breast pocket.

So at the end of the driveway, he turned back toward town. The eerie light had changed and become purely leaden.

Winter was about to do her worst.

Chapter Ten

Day 20

"That piece of cloth has been gone for more than a day," Jane remarked wearily. "I told you it wouldn't do any good."

"I think we should try another one."

"You would. Don't you *ever* give up?"

Chantal struggled until she could reach her friend's hand. "What's the point in giving up?" she asked, her voice raspy. "At least we're trying everything we can. Better than just waiting to die."

Which was what they seemed to be doing. As far as they knew, the guy hadn't come back. The water supply was diminishing. The food bars had become a smaller pile. Jane mentioned rationing what they had, but neither of them had the brainpower left to figure out how.

They just resorted to sharing the food bars when they absolutely *had* to eat and taking only small sips from the water bottles.

"You haven't given up either," Chantal said. "If you had you'd finish the water or food."

Jane was silent for what seemed like a long time. "It's night out there," she said finally. Her voice sounded rusty. "Night. You hear the wind? Bad weather."

Indeed Chantal could hear the wind. Whatever cracks this place possessed often whistled from it.

"That's why the cloth blew away."

"Then let's try a piece of my sweater instead of my undershirt. It's thicker. It'll jam in better."

"And unravel."

"God, don't be so down. I can tie off the threads. I'm a knitter, remember? I made this darn sweater."

"At least it's bright green."

"Most visible color in the spectrum," Chantal mumbled, remembering her physics class. "Chartreuse. Okay. It might take me a while, but I'll unravel enough to stick in the crack."

"Better than doing nothing, I suppose."

Yeah, it was, thought Chantal. She was so weary she had to struggle to keep her eyes open, and she couldn't seem to stop shivering. Shivering was a good thing, right?

She twisted, crying out once as her wrists screamed, but she got hold of the bottom of her sweater near the seam. She'd made that seam, she could unmake it.

Then they were going to fly another little flag.

REVE THOUGHT OF the girls in the cellar a mile or so from his house, but with the storm coming and the roads covered with cops doing welfare checks, he decided it would be smart to leave them alone. They'd either make it or they wouldn't.

Since Spence had shot off his fool mouth, though, Reve had been questioning if he'd been wise to abduct those girls so close to home.

He'd had his eye on them for a while, of course. Bright shiny faces, youthful healthy bodies. He saw them in church when he felt like going and then he'd heard they were planning a New Year's get-together at the tavern.

It had seemed like a golden opportunity to stop dreaming and start enjoying his fantasies in real life. He was good at planning, too. He'd even managed to slip them just enough of the drug that they'd been able to get out to their car and start driving home.

It would have been hopeless if they'd passed out in the bar. Instead they had grown cautious because they weren't feeling well and finally had drifted off the road as easily as they fell asleep.

A great plan, one leaving no tracks that would lead to him. But the first one had proved to be a mistake, and now the other two had been in that basement for so long that the smell was sour when he opened the storm doors.

He wasn't sure he even wanted them anymore. Yeah, they could shower, but that wasn't going to put meat back on them. At his last check a few days ago, they'd looked almost like skeletons.

He didn't find them attractive anymore. What was he going to do? Drag their submissive, weakened butts out of the hole and fatten them up again? Hoping they'd be grateful to him? That they wouldn't act like the first one once they got a little energy back?

Much as he hated to admit it, despite everything he'd done right, he'd messed up. He should never have taken all three at once. He shouldn't have done it so close to home, not when a so-called friend like Spence was going to shoot off his mouth.

He tried to tell himself that Spence had merely diverted attention with his behavior. After all, no cop would expect the kidnapper to draw attention to himself.

But maybe that wasn't true. Maybe the guilty often liked to needle the cops. Hell, he'd read about how many guys had been caught simply because they couldn't avoid going back to the scene of the crime to watch. To enjoy their own handiwork.

He for sure wasn't that dumb. Hence finding a place far enough away, long enough abandoned, that it didn't look as if anything could possibly live in there except some rats and ground squirrels. It wasn't even on his property. No one could conceivably know that he'd shored up the root cellar to make a small prison.

He hadn't even had to buy any materials for the job. His long-gone family had left enough crap in his barn that he could probably build an ark for Noah. The thought amused him while the TV, with a snowy picture as usual, blathered on about how bad the storm was going to be.

At least he didn't have to go to work at the garage. His boss, Keeb Dustin, had told him to stay home. After the storm they'd probably work around the clock trying to jump-start dead batteries and repair bent fenders and snapped belts. The cold, this kind of cold, was cruel to cars.

And then there'd be the tows. A lot of people might well get stuck trying to get out of their own driveways, especially outside town. Or stuck in ditches because it was a strange fact that every single year people needed to learn to drive on snow all over again, and this would be the first snow this year.

So yeah, he'd be plenty busy for a few days after the storm. He might even pick up a few hours driving a plow if they got really buried.

Which left the girls. And leaving them was just about what he'd convinced himself to do. Too much trouble. Try another time. Learn from this and move on.

Hell, the cold from this storm would probably kill them in a few hours, and damned if he was going to drag them out of their hiding places and bring them here. Just his luck some cop, like that Kelly Noveno, would stop by to check

on him and one of those damn teens would start screaming her fool head off.

Leave them, he thought. Let nature take care of them.
There were plenty more where they came from.

AL TURNED IN the scrap of cloth he'd found while rescuing Ruffles and Gage slipped it into an evidence bag with
tweezers before looking it over. "Did you record where
you found this?"

Al pulled out his cell phone and showed him the information. "I got it all, including the GPS, but I don't know
what good it does us."

"Maybe nothing yet. Maybe nothing ever. But one of
those girls was wearing a pink parka when she disappeared
and this appears to be the right kind of nylon fabric. Then
look, did you see the teeth marks?"

Astonished, Al leaned forward for a closer look. "It was
chewed," he said.

"Yeah, it was. Which is an odd thing to do with one's
parka, I have to say. Looks like it was deliberately ripped
off."

Al's heart stuttered to full speed. "Maybe I should look
around some more near Mrs. Jackson's. I didn't see any
buildings anywhere near but…"

Gage nodded. "Wind," he said. "It's lightweight." Then
he motioned Al over to a wall map of the county, one that
was decorated with pushpins. "Here's Mrs. Jackson's place.
Nearest structure is probably…five miles? There might be
some old line shacks out there, but nothing that's occupied.
Wouldn't hurt to look around some, if you feel like it."

Then Al's radio clamored for his attention. A family
of felines had been dumped by the state highway, spotted
by a trucker who couldn't stop for them. "I've gotta go,"
he told Gage.

"Yeah. I'll think about this," he said, indicating the swatch of fabric. "Maybe something will come to me."

"It better come soon. That storm is supposed to hit tomorrow night or the next morning."

Gage merely nodded. Because, of course, he already knew.

KELLY WATCHED THE sky thicken with threat and was glad she was out doing the rest of the welfare checks. The predictions for the storm had grown so much worse that sometimes entire families were telling her they were moving into town to stay with relatives and friends, or at one of the church shelters.

Few wanted to be caught out here if something went wrong. One grizzled rancher wanted a few minutes of conversation and she was happy to provide it.

"Can't go into town," he said. "I got me some forty cows in the barn I gotta look after. Thank the good Lord I could get them all in."

"Can someone stay with you?"

He laughed. "I'm moving in with the cows. They'll keep me warm as toast and I'll have ice cream fresh from the tap."

She joined his laughter. "It *is* going to be bad."

"I reckon." He looked up at the sky. "You can laugh if you want, Deputy Kelly, but I'll tell you anyway. Spent my whole life out here. This ain't normal weather we been having, not for a few years now. And this storm? Nothing like it ever before. Them folks can laugh at climate change all they want, but I'm living close to it and I see it. It's not the same, not the way it was. So let 'em tell me it's just one storm and doesn't mean a hill of beans."

They probably would say exactly that, she thought as she drove away with a wave. Not everyone, but some. She'd been listening to the arguments for a long time now. She did, however, listen to her dad.

"Streets are flooding all the time down here, Kelly. Never used to see that. Houses that were safe except in the worst hurricanes are getting flooded at high tide, especially if we've had some rain. Streets undrivable. Things are changing. I'm glad you're up there."

Things are changing. Maybe that was the only thing people would agree on. But behind her Bugle let out a low moan, reminding her she hadn't given him a chance to take care of his business for a while now.

"Bad, bad Kelly," she said aloud. In the rearview, she could see Bugle cock his head inquisitively. "Next turnout," she promised him. It'd give her a chance to give the binoculars on the seat beside her a good workout. At every opportunity she'd scanned the surrounding country because she couldn't stop hoping she'd find some sign of the missing teens.

The rabbit in her house seemed like a minor thing compared with that. So somebody wanted to make her uneasy. Big deal. They probably also didn't want to mess with Bugle. She didn't need the Glock on her hip to feel safe.

But unless those girls were being held somewhere right around here, hope was nearly pointless. They were gone, one way or another, maybe not even in this county anymore. And if someone was holding them prisoner somewhere around here...well, something should give him away soon. A trip to a store, a pharmacy, extra food...if he had to care for three teens, he was going to need supplies. Supplies that wouldn't be on his usual shopping list.

Maybe.

But so far nobody had come to the sheriff remarking that they'd noticed something unusual. The most unusual thing had been that dolt Spence poking at her, and that hadn't been the first time she'd run into a jerk who liked to give a cop a hard time.

In fact, given the kidnapping, she was surprised that she and other cops hadn't suffered a whole lot more from impatient, angry people. They must seem like total failures.

And from Kelly's perspective, she felt like one. It seemed next to impossible that someone could have taken those girls and left no evidence behind. That was one of the almost unbreakable rules of crime scene investigation: take something, leave something behind.

But if he'd left anything behind, they didn't know what it was. They might stare straight at it and not know it. That glove was all they had. It linked to one of the girls, but not to the perp. No help until they had someone to charge.

Sometimes she found that the most frustrating part of police work, to be able to develop a mountain of evidence that you couldn't link to anyone specific until you put hands on the guy.

How many men in this county—assuming it was a man—might be enough of a pervert to take those girls? Did any of them have families they were hiding this from? Or did they all live alone? How many of *them* were there, solitary men?

Plenty, unfortunately. Women seemed more eager to leave this town and county than men by far. They wanted something more than the smell of cow poop and skunk in the morning.

She found a turnout and let Bugle out without a leash. He needed to run off some energy. Then she pulled out the binoculars and began to scan the countryside from east to west toward the mountains. A tumbledown line shack that looked like it should have collapsed long ago. No houses immediately in sight, but yeah, she thought she could see one farther out. A couple of miles? Possibly next on her checklist.

The mountains, for all they had prepared for winter, still looked dark and forbidding, probably because the sky was trying to work itself into an early version of night with lowering clouds.

The air felt oddly warm, though. Strange, but maybe it was an effect of the approaching cold, sucking heat toward it from somewhere else. Her weather knowledge was miserable, but as she stood there studying the barren countryside and a few cattle that really needed to be on their way into a barn, she wondered if she should have majored in meteorology.

Following in her father's footsteps had seemed like the thing to do for so many years, but how often had Hector tried to talk her out of it?

"You don't know, *muchacha*," he'd say to her. "The things we have to see. I'm not talking about risks. Sure there are risks but it's more dangerous to cut down trees or catch crabs. No, I'm talking about what we *see*. Things that get stamped in the brain and never go away. Why would you want to do that?"

Because that's what he had done and she admired the heck out of him. He'd been right about the things stamped in her brain, however. Absolutely right. At least she saw a lot fewer of them here in Wyoming than she had during her brief stint in Fort Lauderdale.

When Bugle apparently felt he'd run off enough energy, he came back to her with his tail wagging, ready to go on patrol again. It seemed he hadn't noticed anything untoward, and only then did she realize how much she'd been hoping that he'd find another piece of evidence, like that glove.

No such luck. She put him back in his cage in the backseat and wondered absently how soon it would get so cold that she'd need to put his quilted vest and booties on him. Not yet, anyway.

By comparison with the last few days, the air felt almost balmy.

Before she pulled back out onto the road, her cell phone tweeted at her. She almost laughed. She thought she'd been out of range for a while.

"Hey," said the now-familiar voice of Al Carstairs, "how are your rounds going?"

"Nearly done, for today at any rate. You?"

"Couple more houses. I'll be out on 581 for the next half hour or so. Listen, when you want lunch, look me up. I've got a story about a Maine coon for you, and I found a scrap of pink cloth that even Gage isn't sure means anything."

"Pretend you just heard me sigh. Okay, I'll see you on 581. Maybe an hour?"

"I'll be there. I'm running back to my cabin first, though. Some people call me on the landline and talk to my answering machine. Can you believe it? An answering machine in this day and age."

She laughed. "Hey, you heard of voice mail?"

"County won't pay for the additional service. Nope, I'm a tape man. Play and erase. See you shortly."

A Maine coon and a good story. Sounded like it might be a nice lunch break. Plus a piece of fabric. Her heart did one of those nervous little skips it had been doing ever since this case exploded.

She closed her eyes a few moments, sending a prayer for those girls winging heavenward, then pulled back onto the road.

She believed in a benevolent God. Absolutely. But she also figured the human race had him or her so overworked that single prayers might get lost in the tsunami.

"We make most of our own problems," her father had told her once. She wasn't sure if he was speaking as a cop or a dad, nor did it really matter. They'd just come out of Mass, and she'd donated her babysitting money to the poor.

"What do you mean?" she'd asked him.

"People don't starve because God wants it. They starve because other people are hard-hearted."

That philosophy had stuck. So maybe her prayer was useless. A bad guy was involved in all this. He had made this problem. Unfortunately, entirely too many people were in the perp's class, harming others for their own satisfaction.

But that didn't keep her from saying yet another prayer as she drove.

BACK AT HIS CABIN, Al got word of two missing cats, and he still had the ones dropped by the roadside to worry about. Kittens. If he hurried up, he could grab them and get to 581 with the missing cats who'd been out since last night.

Cats were a piece of work, he sometimes thought. He loved them as much as any animals, but cats could be especially difficult. Somehow, they'd managed to keep their own minds and wills intact. They could be cuddly companions one minute and troublesome isolationists the next.

As he jumped back into his truck, ready to rescue the local feline population, he felt a light weight land on his shoulder.

"Regis," he said, twisting his head to look at the gray squirrel. "You really don't want to come along to look for cats."

But Regis, like the cats, had his own mind. He chittered, then settled into the space between Al's collar and shoulder.

And that, thought Al, was what he got for rescuing an

infant squirrel last spring and nursing him to health before releasing him. Regis still had a bit of human in him.

FIFTEEN MINUTES LATER he'd rescued the family of cats, the kittens no more than a week old, and placed them on a towel together in a cage in the back of his truck. Mama immediately wrapped herself around them, protecting them. The two other missing cats showed up on their home porches, so he erased them from his mental list.

Once he approached 581 he saw Salty, a schnauzer from an outlying ranch that shouldn't be anywhere around here. So Salty was placed in a cage a distance from the cats and began to whine. Of course. He'd probably been having a great time chasing a ground squirrel, had indeed chased it so far he was too far from home.

At last he turned onto 581, looking forward to seeing Kelly. She was occupying a whole lot more time in his thoughts than was probably good for him, but he was past caring. There were enough bad things to think about.

Kelly was like a bright shining oasis in a world full of ugliness.

Then he spied Misty. A beautiful golden retriever with a distinctive prance to her step, she seemed to be running in circles about a hundred yards inside the fence line of the Harris family ranch. He was surprised to see her so far out here. The Avilas had always been careful owners who tried not to let Misty slip her leash, but she was an accomplished escape artist. With the weather turning so bitter, perhaps one of the kids had let her out in the backyard without watching and she'd burrowed under the fence. Regardless, at the times she proved to be Houdini's reincarnation, Al usually picked her up within or near the city limits.

Al pulled his van onto the shoulder, grabbed a slipknot leash and climbed out. Misty had never been a problem to round up, so he expected her to come immediately when he called. Just after he slid off the seat and his feet hit the ground, he felt Regis dig in his claws. He had to smile.

He closed the vehicle door so the animals would stay warm and gave thanks that the wind hadn't really started yet. Just the faintest of breezes had begun to chill the air, starting to vanquish the unusual warmth of the last few hours, and now held a tang that hinted at coming snow.

For the first time ever, Misty wasn't in a cooperative mood. As she raced around, she tossed some kind of toy in the air, and although she occasionally glanced at him when he called her, she kept right on playing, pausing only to paw at the ground before returning to her private game of catch.

"Hey, Misty," Al called. "Come on. Don't be a pain. Seriously."

Just then a sheriff's SUV pulled onto the opposite shoulder of the road. It bore a rack of lights, and Conard County Sheriff painted in green on the tan background. K-9, Keep Your Distance was also labeled on the side. By that, before she even climbed out, Al knew it was Kelly.

She had apparently taken in the situation before she pulled over to approach him, and grinned as she climbed out. "Having a problem, Al?"

He had to grin back. Kelly was a wildly attractive woman to his way of thinking, but what he most liked about her was her sunny nature and readiness to tease. He also liked her dog, but Kelly left Bugle in her vehicle and sauntered toward Al, her khaki uniform and jacket looking scarcely heavy enough to withstand the chilling air. "Misty giving you trouble?"

"She's in a mood, all right," Al agreed. Apparently, Kelly had had her own run-ins with the dog.

Kelly whistled, but Misty barely spared her a glance as she tossed her toy in the air and caught it.

"What in the world is she playing with?" Kelly asked.

"I've been wondering. Rawhide bone? Heck, she knows I wouldn't take that away from her."

Kelly chuckled. "She's teasing you." Then she turned to look at Al. "What in the dickens is that on your shoulder?"

Al didn't even have to glance. "That's Regis."

"That's a *squirrel*! You can't keep them for pets."

"I don't. Regis decides for himself. Sometimes he likes to ride shotgun. What can I tell you, Kelly? The squirrel has a mind of his own."

Al felt her staring but heck, what could he do about it? He'd rescued Regis as an abandoned baby, fed the animal until it was strong enough to take off into the woods and live the squirrel life. Except Regis kept coming back to visit.

"Now I've seen everything," Kelly muttered. "Someday I want to hear this story."

While Al wouldn't have minded spending the next day or two chatting with Kelly, there was still business to attend to. "Misty, get your butt over here now." This time there was an edge of impatience to his voice and Misty didn't miss it. She froze, looked at him, then came trotting over with her toy.

Al squatted down, ready to reward the dog with a good scratch and rub, but as Misty drew closer something inside him began to feel chillier than the day.

"Kelly?"

"That's not rawhide," she said too quietly.

Al didn't answer. He waited until Misty snaked through the fence and came to a halt before him, dropping her toy and looking at him with a proud grin.

Al reached out, scratching her neck automatically as he looked down at the "present" she'd placed before him.

"Tell me that's not human," he said.

"I can't," Kelly answered, her voice unusually taut.

Their eyes met and Al knew they were both thinking of the same thing: the three high school girls who'd gone missing weeks ago.

"I'll get an evidence bag while you put the dog in your van," Kelly said. But he noted she walked to her SUV with a leaden step. All her natural vivacity had seeped away. She'd be calling for help, he thought, to try to learn where the dog found the bone. Before they were even certain.

"Yeah," Al said, speaking to the icy air. "Yeah." Then he stood, slipping the loose leash around Misty and leading her to the back of his truck.

"God," he told the dog, "I hope it's from a deer."

But he was very afraid it was not.

Chapter Eleven

Days 20–21

An hour later, Cadel Marcus showed up with four of the K-9s he was training, and Jake wasn't far behind with his dog. Soon deputies began to congregate, filling the shoulders of the road, cutting it off to traffic.

The only thing they knew for sure was that a doctor at the hospital had said it was definitely a human thighbone, the growth plates hadn't fully hardened and he wouldn't be surprised if it belonged to one of the missing girls. The bone was now on its way to a forensics lab, but there was no time to waste.

Gage was blunt about it. "Figure we've got twenty-four hours max," he told everyone. "We've got to find the scene, find the body, find the evidence before this storm makes working impossible, or buries the remains again."

And none of that meant they'd find the perp.

Al had used the time to take the animals in his truck home or leave them in his kennels, and now he was ready to take one of Cadel's dogs to aid in the search.

"Same commands you've heard Kelly use with Bugle," Cadel told him. "Except these dogs are trained to hunt for cadaverine."

Cadaverine. The odor of death, something dogs could

sniff even if it was way more than six feet underground. "Bugle doesn't do that?"

"Around here, not much call. Three of these dogs are in training for other police departments. One body hunter is probably all we'd ordinarily need in this county. Today is different."

Different in so many ways, with a severe storm moving in that could hide evidence until much later in the spring. That would give scavengers more time to devour it and disperse it. Important traces, like cloth and hair, could vanish in a strong wind. Even teeth...

Al drew himself up short. He'd seen it in Afghanistan. He didn't need to think about all the stages of decay.

Kelly approached him, her face drawn. "I'd like to miss this day entirely."

"I think we all would," he agreed. "I'm sorry. I had funny stories to tell you."

"Where's that damn squirrel of yours?"

"Being smart. When I got back to my place, he headed for his drey. I don't know if he made himself a family yet, but I'm sure he's got other squirrels to hunker down with."

"I definitely want to hear that story."

"You will."

As if they were hunting for someone buried in a landslide or avalanche, they all carried long, thin metal poles to stick into the hardened ground. It wasn't easy, but they were thin enough to penetrate with reasonable effort. Even so, Al felt it all the way through his injured back.

But what they all really wanted was for the dogs to alert. To give them a narrower area to search.

They set out almost shoulder to shoulder, heading toward the area where Misty had been playing with the bone. Unfortunately, Misty had probably found it somewhere else and had carried it with her while she played.

Cadel had spread his dogs out with other deputies so they covered a much wider area. They offered more hope than rods and eyes right now. At least they still had visibility, but it seemed like the winter night was moving in even faster than usual. Al wished he had some night vision goggles. Detail was beginning to vanish as the light grew flatter by the minute.

Even if they found remains, all they could do was cover them until morning and hope it didn't grow too cold for the crime scene folks to gather everything in the morning light.

But mostly Al thought about the girl that bone had belonged to, about all three of the missing girls. How awful all the way around, from their disappearance to their parents' hoping and praying they'd be found alive to this.

He doubted anyone wanted to tell the parents about the bone. It might not belong to one of the girls. It could have come from somewhere else. Why terrify them any more than they were already terrified. Why steal the hope they had been depending on for weeks now.

Not without damn good reason.

But for him, as for many of the searchers, he suspected, hope was clinging by one last, thin thread after the bone. No reason to think only one of the girls had been killed. That would make no sense at all.

Not that any of this made any sense.

The wind was picking up as the last light faded from the day. They were done until first light in the morning. The dogs hadn't even signaled, and Al was quite sure they'd long since passed the spot where Misty had been playing. The question now was where she had found it.

They marked the place where they stopped looking with pin flags, then tramped dispiritedly back to the cars. For some reason, a hope of another kind had been born in the searchers: hope of closure. Even that was denied to them tonight.

Back at his car he saw Kelly loading up Bugle. He turned his charge back over to Cadel and headed her way.

"Say, Deputy," he said. The wind tried to snatch his words.

She looked at him, her expression sober, her hand on the driver's door latch.

"Come to my place tonight," he said. "It's a good night for not being alone."

To his amazement, she nodded. "I'd like that. Bugle, too?"

"I can't imagine you without that dog. Of course he comes."

She smiled lopsidedly. "Do you need me to bring anything?"

"Yourself and your dog. The pizza place is on the way if that agrees with you."

"I love pizza. Any kind, except anchovies. They're too salty for me."

"Done. See you there shortly. And oh, by the way? I have food for Bugle, too, so just bring something warm to hang out in. I have a feeling the temperatures tonight will make the North Pole seem balmy."

In fact they were already headed that way, he thought as he climbed into his truck. He really needed to check the weather so they'd know what they were facing tomorrow.

Of course, the weather was going to be only a small part of it.

KELLY PACKED HER usual flannel pajamas, slippers and robe, as well as a fresh set of silky thermal underwear for the morning, a clean uniform and Bugle's tug rope. From the way the air was feeling outside, she wasn't sure this storm was going to wait until the day after tomorrow.

So when they started in at dawn, they were going to have to give the search a massive effort. If only Misty could show them where she'd found the bone. Of course, any carrion eater could have dragged it away from the rest of the body. Whoever the poor victim was, he or she could be scattered over acres by now.

The pressure of time rode her like a goad. The coming storm could hamper them so much, could blow away evidence, could even bury things and freeze them so hard that the best dog might have trouble picking out a scent.

Maybe that had been part of their problem this afternoon. The body had been frozen, had lost a great many of its scents, those scents had been overlaid by whatever animals had torn at the flesh...

Cold as it was, a corpse should have been preserved, but not in the open where coyotes, bears, mountain lions and even wolves could get to it. Food was in short supply and high demand in the cold of winter. And bears, while they hibernated, often emerged from their dens in the course of the winter to hunt for food, as well. If there were easy pickings...

She didn't want to think about it. They couldn't do much until morning. At this point an air sweep probably wouldn't find a thing. Why should it? It hadn't directly after the girls had gone missing. No brightly colored clothing had given them away then, so why expect it now when the elements and the animals had had their way?

With her carryall packed, she hesitated, looking around her little house for anything she might have forgotten. The heat was on, the water was dripping so pipes wouldn't freeze, and she could think of nothing else she needed.

She and Bugle climbed into her official vehicle, which

she'd left running, and a blast of warm air from the heater thawed her cheeks, which had started to freeze on the way out the door. Colder and colder.

Cold weather was nothing new here, but this was going to be a killer cold if the forecast was correct, maybe hitting thirty or forty below. That wasn't a regular event. Sure it happened sometimes in the winter, but compared with places farther north, this part of Wyoming was usually much gentler.

Regardless of what was *usual*, the approaching storm was going to be a winter beast and would curtail them in their search for a body and evidence. Every minute tomorrow was going to count.

Al's cabin and kennels took up a couple of acres about five miles away from town along a paved county road. A big wooden sign, deeply carved and recently painted, announced that this was Conard County Animal Control, Chief Allan Carstairs. Two phone numbers, in smaller lettering, filled the bottom.

His driveway was in fairly good shape, given the time of year and that it was gravel, and soon she was pulling up to his front door and parking beside his van and his truck with the high cab on the bed to make room for cages.

Sitting out front was a cute wood cutout of a dog and a cat looking welcoming. She wondered if Al had created them.

The cabin itself, while looking like a leftover from the frontier days, was in great shape and the light pouring from windows was inviting. Smoke, caught in the gleam of her headlights, rose from a chimney. He must have built a fire.

It was almost as if all the bad things that had been riding her shoulders lifted and drifted away. There was nothing to be done tonight except enjoy time with a man she had come to like a whole lot more than she probably should.

Plus, tonight she wouldn't have to sit in her own house counting on Bugle's protection. Because whether she wanted to admit it or not, the stuffed rabbit had unnerved her. Someone had entered her house for no discernible reason and left behind a toy that might have been wearing a bow but might also have been wearing a noose.

She'd have to be made of steel not to be uneasy about that. Nor could she imagine any possible reason for it. Who the hell did *she* threaten?

Well, she had a night off from that, too. Maybe when the whole case got sorted out, she'd find out what that rabbit meant along with all the rest of it.

Then Al opened the front door, a powerful silhouette against the light behind, and waved her to come in.

For the first time in hours, she genuinely smiled. Sight for sore eyes, she thought. Bugle even gave a woof of approval.

Yeah, they'd made the right decision to accept his invitation.

REVE CAME BACK from checking on the girls. It would be his last check. He figured the coming cold would kill them, but since he wasn't entirely heartless, he'd left them some more water and food bars. Lucky the cold had put them to sleep or he wouldn't have left them anything.

Then he headed back to his place, headlights out as always, beneath a sky that had been blotted by clouds until he was practically driving into a black hole. Only once he was on the county road again did he turn his lights back on.

Nobody flying tonight. Nobody searching tonight. He felt free as a bird.

Until he got home and his landline rang. It was Spence.

"What do you want?" he asked irritably. Spence was an okay friend to have at the tavern, but Reve didn't much care for socializing in general. He'd go to church once in a while, smile at a few old ladies and grab some baked goods. The baked goods were free and were always delicious, and the old biddies pressed him to take loads because he was so thin.

Lean and mean more like, he always told himself. But he wouldn't turn down a whole pie, or an entire plate of brownies.

But friends? They had to be kept in their proper places, and Spence's proper place was at the tavern, at the pool table. Besides, he was mad at Spence for giving that deputy a hard time.

Cripes, a man on probation ought to know better.

"Hey," said Spence, "you see all the excitement of them looking for those gals this afternoon? Did you hear about the bone?"

Now Reve no longer felt like hanging up. Spence had piqued his attention. "What bone?"

"Story is some dog found it and was playing with it. Deputy Dawg took it to the hospital and they identified it as a human thighbone. You should have seen the show. They were out there for hours this afternoon with searchers and dogs. Didn't find anything."

Reve tried to decide if that was good or bad. "Sounds bad," he said finally, though he didn't mean it.

"Well, I had my fun."

"What fun?"

"You know the cars them gals was drivin'? Before Deputy Dawg came along I found it. Nothing inside. I was hoping for a wallet. Instead I found a damned stuffed rabbit. I brought it home to give to my dog for a toy, then decided to have some fun."

Reve's stomach had begun to knot. "What kind of fun?"

"I left it at the deputy's house. Only seemed right. They

can't find them missing gals, and after the look she gave me at the tavern when I said something about it, I thought I'd give her a little fright."

"You said you'd left part of an animal skin!"

"Fooled ya," Spence laughed.

Reve swore. "Let me guess. You left your fingerprints all over the toy and her house!"

"Man, I ain't no fool. Had too many brushes with the law. Nah, I wore gloves. Jeez, it's cold out there. Everybody's wearing gloves. Like I'd grab something like that with my bare hands, or use them to leave it at Noveno's house. Give me some credit, Reve."

Oh, Reve gave him credit, all right. Credit for being the biggest fool to ever walk on two legs. Taunting the deputy hadn't been enough. No, he had to go drop a big fat threat at her doorstep. "If you get picked up again, blame yourself."

Spence snorted. "No way on earth they can find out it was me. Wish I'd got to the car earlier, though. I wish I'd seen what happened to those girls."

You're lucky you didn't, Reve thought as he hung up his phone. Although at this point he was wondering if Spence wasn't a liability he needed to get rid of, the sooner the better.

But how?

He sat at his table, oil and whetting stone in front of him as he followed his monthly ritual of sharpening the kitchen knives. The process soothed him, and he enjoyed seeing how the blades had worn away with time, becoming narrower but no less sharp. When he finished each one, he would wipe the oil from it and test his arm to make sure it was sharp enough to cut the hair from him, like a razor. Better than a razor.

For now, he forgot about the girls. They were rapidly

passing into the rearview mirror of his life, little to interest him, soon to be gone. Their bones might be found in a century or two.

But the other one, the one he had taken out to the gully and covered with tumbleweed. A bone. So the animals had done their work, but that meant that the cops had renewed their search.

And Spence had just put his ham-fisted "joke" in the middle of it all. Damn, if those cops started taking a close look at that rabbit, they might find something from one of the girls on it. A hair. Whatever. And Spence in his absolute idiocy had thought it would be funny to try to scare the deputy with it, sure in his folly that no link would ever be made to anything.

The regular grating sound of the metal on the whetting stone created a comforting rhythm, but Reve wasn't comforted at all. Damn Spence, he might have created a serious problem for him. No, there was nothing that should link Reve to the girls, but the rabbit… How had he overlooked the rabbit when he pulled everything out of the car? What if it had *Reve's* hair on it? Just because he'd been wearing a watch cap didn't mean strands of his hair weren't elsewhere, ready to fall off him like mini grenades.

Crap, that thought really disturbed him. There he'd been trying to be so careful and only *now* did it occur to him that there might have been a stray hair or two on his jacket or jeans?

Not that it mattered unless they caught him. He'd never been arrested, nobody had his DNA that he knew of…

He twisted on the chair, putting the knife down, and reached into the fridge for another longneck. He was worrying too much. The girls would be gone, nobody would find them for a hundred years. Think how much harder he'd have made it on himself if he'd tried to bring them here and make them behave. Nah, that first girl had taught him a lesson. He just hadn't taken it far enough.

Next time, he'd know better how to accomplish this. And he'd start with one girl at a time.

AL'S LIVING ROOM was hardly any bigger than her own, and it, too, had a kitchen in one corner, except he didn't have a bar as a divider.

A fire burned warmly on a fieldstone hearth, adding cheery light and warmth. As he took her bag and leaned it nearby against a log wall, she turned slowly to look. Yes, it was a log cabin, but the whole feel of it, dark wood and all, made it seem so cozy, much more so than her house, which she had already thought was cozy.

Then she spied a small white Christmas tree in the corner near the front door and wide window. She couldn't help smiling.

"I know," he said, as if reading her mind. "It's still there. But some nights I just like to light it up and watch it change colors. It's fiber optic with one of those color wheels."

"Red and green?"

"Nah. More pastel. If you like, I'll show you later. But while the pizza is still warm…"

He'd gotten a pie with everything except anchovies. Maybe he'd made the store put extra veggies and pepperoni on it, because she couldn't remember seeing one loaded with so many green peppers, onions and mushrooms.

Two plates sat beside the box, and he served her a piece, inviting her to sit on his sofa. He actually had a sofa. But before he served himself, he opened a kitchen cupboard and pulled out a rawhide bone for Bugle. He looked at Kelly. "Is it okay for me to give this to him?"

She appreciated his understanding of the bond between

her and Bugle that had to be protected, but it didn't need to be protected every single second.

Bugle knew exactly what Al was holding, and sat at attention, his mouth framing his version of an eager smile.

"Bugle, okay." At once the dog trotted over to Al and quickly accepted the gift. Al grinned.

The dog decided this place was okay and the offering pleased him. Soon he was sprawled on a colorful area rug, gnawing intently and happily.

Al joined her on the sofa with his plate. "TV might be hard to come by. They never ran the cable all the way out here, but I have a dish. I use it mostly for internet, but I can get a few stations if you're in the mood. Otherwise I have a collection of movies that ought to embarrass me."

"Why?"

"Because every time I think about how much I've spent on DVDs, I think how much healthier my bank account could look."

She laughed, then took a bite of her pie. "This is great. What magic wand did you use?"

"A credit card that was willing to pay for extra toppings. I mean, I like the sauce and cheese well enough, but it's the toppings I'm really after."

"One piece will be an entire meal!"

He winked. "For you, maybe." Plate in hand, he rose from the couch and walked over to his little Christmas tree. It wasn't very large, just over three feet, but when he flipped a switch it became a gorgeous panoply of slowly changing lights. To her delight, she thought the nearly pastel colors were prettier than the usual Christmas colors.

"There," he said, returning to her side. "A little ambience. We could sure use some. Today was tough."

In so many ways. The bone, a virtual guarantee that at least one of the girls was dead. As for the other two…

Kelly sighed and closed her eyes. A moment later she started as she felt a weight on her thigh. Opening her eyes, she saw Al's hand.

"Don't stop eating. I shouldn't have mentioned it. Even on the battlefield we took breaks when we could. Otherwise you go nuts or become useless."

He probably had a point, she thought. It was hard to shed the feeling of wasted time, of guilt, but there was nothing they could do out there tonight. It was dangerously cold. How many people did they want to put in the hospital from frostbite or hypothermia when they didn't even have a definite place to look?

If only they could ask Misty where she'd found that bone, but the dog wasn't likely to learn to talk. Then she had a thought and sat bolt upright.

"What?" Al asked immediately.

"Misty," she said. "What if we took her back out there? She might want to find another bone to play with. If they were close enough, she might be able to guide us to others."

He nodded slowly, evidently thinking about it. "It might work. She was sure having fun with it, and a dog would remember where there were others."

"I never had a dog lose a rawhide bone. Hide it maybe, lose it never."

"I think we should try it. I'll give the Avilas a call in the morning and ask to borrow Misty. Better clear it with the sheriff, too, I guess."

Her appetite was coming back and just before she took a bite of pizza, she said, "I think Gage would try anything that had even a remote chance of helping."

"I'd walk barefoot on desert sand right now. I think he's probably feeling about the same."

"I know I am."

She managed to finish the slice, but her mind was wandering down the rabbit hole again. What if she'd found the car a little earlier? What if she'd looked a little closer for some evidence? Why hadn't she been more suspicious?

That was really killing her, that she'd treated a car in the ditch as a matter of no importance once she found that no one was in it and hurt. While that might have been true most of the time, it sure as hell hadn't been that night.

God!

But even so, she wasn't sure what she might have done differently. She'd been beating her head on that wall since the instant she learned that three young women had been in that car and that all of them were missing.

What *could* she have done differently? She didn't even know who was involved. She'd called the phone number on the registration and left a message when there was no answer. It wasn't as if she could have even done a thing to raise the alarm earlier.

Fingers snapped in front of her. Startled, she drew back a little and looked at Al. "What?"

"Come out of that hole you're digging. It's not going to help anything at all, Kelly. Beating yourself up is no help either. I should know."

She shook her head a little, but he wouldn't let her look away. He placed his finger beneath her chin and turned her head toward him. His gray eyes had grown distant and dark, like windows on hell.

"I was on a mission. Afghanistan. We were supposed to be training a local unit in mountain patrols. Unfortunately, we trusted the wrong people. I lost two men. Two. Our supposed allies turned on us, right when we were vulnerable because we were supposed to be working together. You wanna know how many weeks I spent beating myself up over that?"

She drew a long breath, unable to look away now. He

was sharing something deeply personal and painful, and deserved her full attention. Her heart felt as if it were squeezing in her chest. So much anguish, so carefully controlled.

"There should have been a clue, I thought. I should have seen some sign that they were plotting, that they weren't trustworthy, that they meant us harm. How in the hell could I have eaten with them, joked with them, traipsed shoulder to shoulder with them on that patrol and never, *never* picked up on any warning sign?"

"Al…" she breathed.

"Yeah," he said after a few beats. "I know that hole you're digging. I've plumbed it all the way to the bottom. Thing is, I never got an answer. I just kept hating myself until another officer who'd gone through the same thing finally asked me, 'Are you supposed to be psychic? Prescient? None of us is that. None.' I got his point. It was a while before I could let go, and I still get angry, but I've had to accept I didn't do anything *wrong*." His gaze lost a bit of its edge. "You didn't do anything wrong either. Get used to it. It'll never feel good, but the guilt is wasted. You did everything right."

She had a feeling it might be a while before she'd be able to believe that, but she could accept what he was saying about not digging herself into a deep hole. Beating herself up hadn't done a bit of good so far. Not one little bit.

He stirred, setting his plate aside on an end table, then scooted over until he could wrap his arm around her shoulders and draw her into a loose but comforting embrace. "I can't dictate the best way for you to handle this," he said quietly. "We're all different and I'm no shrink. But I honestly feel that you didn't do anything wrong. Not easy to live with, but not everything is easy. Especially stuff like this."

She placed her plate on the arm of the sofa and turned into him, enjoying the warmth and strength of his embrace, only in those moments realizing how *lonely* she'd been feeling in the past few weeks. His scents, of the outdoors, of man, filled her, touching her deeply in ways she hadn't felt in a long time.

Yeah, she was surrounded by comrades who'd joined the search, but she still felt alone, probably because she'd been the one to find the car. No one else had to deal with that.

But Al understood, and he was offering comfort. And while she tried to remain strong at all times, she could remember tears in her own father's eyes from time to time, and it didn't seem like weakness to accept the comfort Al was offering.

He tightened his arm around her shoulders just a bit, making her feel more secure, letting her know that she was welcome. Resting her head on his chest, she listened to his strong, steady heartbeat and watched the play of firelight and his silly little fiber-optic tree. It felt almost as if she'd stepped into some kind of dream.

Another world, one far away from her worries of the past few weeks. Could it be so bad to take a break for just one evening, especially when the temperature was dropping dramatically outside and no one could possibly continue the search?

The sight of Bugle happily gnawing on his rawhide added to the feeling of contentment that was trying to rise in her, offering her that break she probably needed. No reason to feel guilty. No reason to beat her head on the problem until morning. She said another prayer for the girls out there and hoped that they'd finally get a break in the morning. But until then…

Al murmured her name.

At once she lifted her head and looked at him.

"I'm no good at this," he said, brushing a strand of hair back from her face.

"At what?"

"I told you. Relationships. But…" Almost as if an invisible force tugged them together, their faces came close and their mouths met. At first it was a tentative kiss, a feeling-out, but not for long. Kelly reached up a hand to cradle the back of his head and draw him closer, to deepen the kiss that soon grew hard and demanding.

Oh, man, it had been too long, she thought. Entirely too long because of all her scruples about her job but all those scruples seemed to be vanishing before the force of her need for this man.

This one man, not just any man, she realized hazily as her body began to awaken to desire long suppressed. Man, she should have jumped his bones ages ago. The idea nearly drew a giggle from her.

Apparently he felt it because he pulled back a little, letting her catch her breath. "What's funny?"

She could feel her cheeks heat. She hoped he thought it was the heat from the fireplace, although it wasn't *that* warm. "It's silly," she said, sounding as if she had to force the words out.

"Oh. That's okay. I always thought you were the most wildly beautiful woman I'd ever seen."

Wildly beautiful? Her heart slammed and began a rapid tap dance of delight. "I was just thinking…" She drew a breath and blurted it. Truth for truth. "I was just thinking I should have jumped your bones a long time ago."

The smile that spread over his face would have lit the arctic night brighter than the aurora. "Oh, I do like the sound of that."

With a gentle hand, he cupped her cheek and drew her

in for another kiss. "Jump away," he murmured against her lips. "Anytime."

She was falling into him, all wariness and reluctance fading away, her world becoming Al Carstairs. Everything else vanished as her body felt a new tide rising, a tide of need and longing, a tsunami of desire long denied. It was washing through her and over her and driving out everything else.

The world drifted away, the universe became this one man and their embrace.

She felt as if everything inside her were quivering, steadily working her into a rhythmic need that made her clench her thighs and start to roll her hips. Oh, man, she needed, wanted...

A woof startled her. She and Al separated quickly.

Hazy-eyed, with her lips feeling swollen, she turned her head and saw Bugle eyeing them quizzically.

"Oh, boy," said Al. "Jealous?"

"I'm not sure." She shook her head a little, trying to come back to reality, much as she didn't want to. She was, however, acutely aware of what this dog could do if he thought she was in trouble.

"Maybe," she said slowly, "it's his training. He's not supposed to let anyone touch me except casually."

Al snorted. "This could get fun."

"This could be maddening," she replied, regaining some of her sense of humor. "Now I've got to figure out how to let him know you're okay."

He laughed. "Are you sure that's wise?"

She liked the twinkle in his eyes, and the way he was taking this with humor. At that moment she wasn't very happy with Bugle. Interference at exactly the wrong time. Her body was still humming with the forces Al had awakened in her, but she had to deal with Bugle first. He probably wouldn't bite Al without a command, but he could easily insert himself between them as a matter of protection.

"Hmm," she said.

"Yeah," he answered.

"Bugle, it's okay."

He tilted his head the other way, as if trying to figure out this new and perplexing situation.

Kelly leaned slowly into Al's side and took his hand in hers. Bugle whimpered quietly. "It's okay," she said firmly.

He didn't budge, but his gaze was skimming over the entire situation.

"I should have asked Cadel for a command to tell him someone's a good person," she remarked dryly. "I could lock him in another room."

"I saw what he did to the door in your house. Nope, we gotta win him over. I have an idea."

He slid off the couch until he was on the floor. He reached out his hand, letting Bugle sniff him. "Now you come down here, too."

Kelly dropped to the floor beside him.

"Now start petting him like you're playing a little rough. When he seems happy I'll get in on the action with you."

Made sense, Kelly thought, but she never in her life would have imagined that she'd have to get her K-9's permission to make love. "Let me pull out his tennis ball, too. You can toss that for him a few times when he seems to be mellowing. That's his signal for playtime."

Al smiled. "He's not exactly *un*mellow right now. Just unsure."

She had several tennis balls in her tote, but brought out only one. She made a big ceremony of giving it to Al. Bugle was instantly engaged.

"Okay, big boy," she said, using both her hands to

scratch around his neck, then playfully push him side to side. It took a minute or two, but soon he adopted the play posture, lowering his front legs until he rested on them. A happy woof escaped him.

She moved in for some more easy wrestling, and when Al joined her, Bugle didn't object. Soon he was bounding around the room and coming back to them both to nudge at them with his nose. Then Al threw the tennis ball.

And Bugle fell in love.

Kelly was laughing aloud at her dog's antics, and Al grinned from ear to ear. Bugle ran back with the ball and dropped it on Al. One more toss and he brought it back to give it to Kelly to throw. The bond was happening.

Eventually, Kelly fell back against the sofa, laughing, worn out from dog wrestling and ball tossing, as well as a long workday. She wasn't totally worn out by any means, but Bugle and Al had managed to ease her emotional turmoil.

Bugle could probably have kept at it for a long while, but he sensed the humans were done, so he returned to gnawing his rawhide as if it were all that existed on the planet.

Kelly looked over at Al and enjoyed the sight of him sprawled on his back on the floor. He seemed so relaxed now, the kind of relaxation she'd seen in him before only when he was helping animals. He'd reached his place of serenity.

His position also revealed his body in a way she'd never really noticed before. Oh, she'd always known he had a great build, but as he rested there, she could see how deep and powerful his chest was, how broad his shoulders and how incredibly flat his belly. Narrow hips, long legs with thigh muscles that showed even through his jeans...

He was a man in prime condition. Her heart fluttered, and the heat he'd ignited in her renewed. Every cell in her body quivered with anticipation. If only he would roll over, reach for her, touch her in places no one touched her. She lost her breath just thinking about it. His hands on her breasts, between her legs.

Oh, man, the bug had bit badly. She'd locked away her womanly impulses for so long, acutely aware that she was trying to make her way in a man's world. In Fort Lauderdale, in Laramie, there'd been plenty of guys ready to remind her that she was "just a woman." There hadn't been any of that here in Conard County, maybe because they'd long had female deputies, and two of them were closely related to one of their most prominent, Deputy Micah Parish. She was sure nobody wanted to ever get on Micah's bad side.

But Sarah Ironheart and Connie Parish were both related to him through marriage, one to his brother, one to his son. Nope, they were accepted, all right, and that acceptance seemed to have extended to her and the few other women on the force. Connie hadn't always been a deputy, she recalled, but after Ethan joined the department, so had she. Then Ethan had left to help Micah with his ranch and Connie had remained.

Micah, she sometimes felt, was easing his way out of the department, working fewer hours, spending more time at home with Faith and their family. But with Micah, it was hard to be sure of anything.

And why was she thinking of him and his family, anyway? He was a solid man, an excellent deputy, and as far as she could tell blessed with both a deep spirituality and strong compassion.

None of that had anything to do with right now except that she was trying to divert herself before she did something incredibly forward, like jump Al's bones.

Her cheeks grew hot as she remembered saying that out

loud, but she'd said it, and she'd meant it. And he'd called her wildly beautiful. Wow. That compliment reached all the way to her very core. Never once in her life had she ever felt that way about herself, nor had anyone ever told her that. But Al had, lifting her self-image in a new way.

Her thoughts were starting to drift to the frigid night outside, and the missing girls. One maybe dead, but what about the others? She couldn't know. No one could. All they could do was hope and restart the search in the morning.

In the meantime, Al was right, she shouldn't dig herself into that hole. Right now it could do no good except ruin this entire night.

Al seemed to be watching the patterns the firelight and his Christmas tree made on the ceiling. The logs dulled the glow quite a bit but didn't entirely erase the dancing color. It all looked so warm.

And he looked so inviting.

Hardly aware of what she was doing, she pushed away from the couch and crawled across the floor toward him. She felt Bugle's eyes on her, then heard him resume his gnawing.

Al spoke. "If you're about to do what I think you're about to do, should we let the dog take a walk, first? He's already proved he has a talent for timely interruption."

He wasn't looking at her, but she could see the corners of his firm mouth twitch. In spite of the tension and excitement that filled her, she had to laugh. She loved that he could make her laugh.

"Probably," she answered, hearing the huskiness in her own voice.

To her surprise, he reached out and tugged her gently until she fell on his chest, then arranged her so she lay squarely on top of him. "I want you," he said boldly. "But the damn dog…"

Then he kissed her so hard and so deeply she felt as if he took possession of her very soul. Soon the niggling needs that had been tempting her with excited anticipation had become a wildfire of hunger.

"The dog," he said, tearing his mouth from hers. "Damn, do you feel good."

Then he rolled her gently to the side and rose to his feet in one smooth movement. "Bugle, walk."

Kelly tried to clear her throat and brain. "Business," she said.

Bugle at once dropped his rawhide bone and headed for the door where Al awaited him. A moment later he darted out into the frigid night.

"I bet he doesn't take long," Al remarked. "I think we've lost another ten or fifteen degrees. Must be on their way to Texas."

A thought that another time might have made her laugh, but right now impatience was riding her like a goad. If one more thing kept her from discovering what sex with Al was like, she might groan in frustration. She was hardly able to think of anything else at all. Unfortunately, he'd been right about the dog.

A few minutes later, a bark alerted them. Al opened the door and Bugle trotted in, a few snowflakes dotting his coat like diamonds. Then something else followed him at top speed.

"Regis?" Al said, disbelieving. "What the—"

Kelly sat up instantly. A gray squirrel had darted across the floor, then turned around and set himself up in the tiny Christmas tree.

It was too much. Bugle looked befuzzled, Al looked

astonished and there was a gray squirrel sitting in an artificial tree amid the fiber-optic lighting.

Kelly started to laugh. Maybe it was hysterical laughter, but it felt damn good, and she wound up leaning against the couch and holding her sides. "Regis? What?"

"Exactly. What?" Al squatted and studied this new conundrum. "You didn't really want to go to bed with me tonight, did you?"

"I did."

"Well, we seem to have a whole bunch of busybodies here."

"Bugle will behave."

"I'm sure," Al retorted. "But Regis? I may have hand-raised him when he was orphaned last spring, but he's never been what I would call trained."

"So he doesn't have a family?"

"How would I know? He's been pretty much living as a free squirrel since I was able to release him last spring, but whether he hooked up with other squirrels, or had a family of his own, I have no idea. He just shows up from time to time, like he wants to visit."

"Or maybe tonight is just too damn cold and you opened a warm door."

"Entirely possible." He sighed, then settled cross-legged on the floor. "I'd feel like a monster throwing him out if he's too cold but we *do* have a dog in here."

There was that inescapable fact. Just because she'd never seen Bugle chase squirrels or rabbits or anything like that didn't mean he wouldn't suddenly take a notion. "So you raised Regis, huh?"

"Well, I wasn't going to leave him to starve to death."

She was loving this view of Al. Hand-raising a squirrel? Letting the animal ride with him sometimes? The squirrel trusting enough to come inside even though there was a dog in here?

She looked at Bugle, who was still eyeing the animal as if unsure how to react. "Bugle, okay. Relax." *Relax* was a word she'd been using with him for the last few years and she had no idea if he grasped the concept. She was sure that dog understood more English than anyone realized, but she couldn't always be certain *which* words made sense and how he might interpret them.

Bugle shifted from one side to another, watching the squirrel, which seemed to be regarding him with at least some suspicion. He lowered himself slowly, reluctantly.

"Solution," said Al, rising. He walked out into his small kitchen and returned with a custard bowl full of sunflower seeds. "This'll keep Regis happy. As for Bugle…we could take him and his rawhide into the bedroom with us if you're still interested."

Still interested? She felt like a pot simmering on low heat, just waiting for the right time to boil. "Oh, yeah," she answered.

He smiled and held out his hand. "Not exactly the most romantic way to start out."

"I'm not looking for romance." And she wasn't. If there was ever to be any romance between them, it could come later. Tonight she wanted passion, fire and forgetfulness.

Bugle picked up his bone and followed them into the bedroom. Behind her, Kelly could hear the squirrel cracking sunflower seeds.

It was indeed as if she had entered a whole new world with Al, and when he drew her into his arms, she went with a leaping, eager heart. Had she spent all this time avoiding her attraction to him? Because it felt as if it had been deeply rooted in her forever.

Impatience was winning, however. They'd spent enough

time dealing with dogs and then a squirrel. She wanted him and wanted him now before anything else happened.

He laughed quietly as she pulled at his shirt, and as their eyes met she saw both heat and delight in his gaze. He was as eager as she, and with every touch she seemed to lift out of herself until she felt she was floating in space.

Their clothes vanished, although she couldn't remember how and didn't especially care. At long last came the moment when they tumbled onto his bed in glorious nakedness, nothing left between them but bare skin.

The feeling of skin on skin was beyond compare, like nothing else in the world. She could feel the shackles of the everyday world letting go, could feel the freedom of being naked with a man and free to touch however she chose.

An amazing exuberance filled her, joining the growing heat that made her breasts ache and caused her to throb hungrily between her legs.

Running her hands over him, enjoying the way he moaned softly at her touches, she felt scars and signs of old injuries but ignored them for now. Nothing, absolutely nothing, was going to get in the way now. There would be later.

His small nipples were already hard, as hard as hers seemed to be, and she couldn't resist tonguing them and nipping gently, causing him to writhe and grab her shoulders. So much here to explore and discover. Sliding her hand down over his flat belly, she reached for his groin and found him stiff and ready, jerking at her lightest touch.

Excitement rushed through her, stronger than ever. She had wakened this in him. The sense of power and delight overwhelmed her.

She held him, stroking his silkiness softly, teasingly while she continued to torment the small buds of his nipples.

Then he apparently had enough.

He rolled her over and suddenly he was above her on his elbows, and the drowsy smile on his face promised more tortures to come. Tortures for her.

His tongue trailed over her neck, at first making it warm, then a chill followed, a delicious shiver. She'd never guessed her neck could respond that way. She grabbed his shoulders, feeling as if she would fall over a cliff edge if she didn't hang on for dear life.

Evidently he was as impatient as she, because soon he trailed his kisses to her breasts, sucking gently at first, then so hard she felt as if he were going to consume her. With each movement of his mouth, he sent another wave of desire racing through her, making her feel as if electric wires joined her breasts and her loins. Like being strung on a welder's arc, she burned for him.

His fingers found the sensitive nub between her legs, and at his first touch she learned that pain and pleasure could be the same. He rubbed her, his touches growing harder until her hips bucked helplessly, and moans escaped her. She had become a mindless bundle of need and want and he seemed to know it.

Then, at last, he slid over her and into her, filling her until everything inside her clenched with pleasure. Yes-sssssssss…

His thrusts were powerful, each one causing another happy moan to escape her. She felt as if he were pushing her, driving her ever higher into a world of magic, a place where stars exploded and filled the night with wonder.

Then came one last endless, almost painful moment when everything inside her seemed to pause in an infinite time of anticipation, where she almost feared she wouldn't tumble over the edge into satisfaction.

But with one last thrust, he brought her more pleasure and pain, the ecstasy of completion. Her world seemed to turn white like flame, and satisfaction rolled through her whole body like a powerful wave.

A cry escaped her, then him, and she felt him shudder as he followed her over the cliff into completion.

The world had slipped away, leaving her spent and happy, and secure in his arms. Nothing could be more perfect.

Chapter Twelve

The night passed too swiftly, yet not swiftly enough. Kelly slept better than she had any night since the teens disappeared, but even before the sun was up the anxiety began to fill her. The storm would arrive later today or early tomorrow. If they hoped to get any forensic evidence from where Misty had found that bone, this might be their only chance for a while.

The girls' lives might hinge on their speed.

Al appeared to feel pretty much the same. They'd managed to put the pizza in the fridge last night before it could spoil, and now he pulled it out. "Cold pie okay? I wanna start calling."

"Absolutely." Instead of feeding herself immediately, she took her bag into the bedroom and pulled out her fresh uniform. Bugle, who had spent the night at the foot of the bed, behaving himself, at once became alert. He loved to work.

Once she'd dressed and straightened herself up in his small bathroom, she emerged to smell coffee, to see a squirrel watching the world from his artificial tree and to hear Al on the phone. Now he was talking to Gage.

"It was Kelly's idea. She's thinking that Misty might remember where she found the bone, and I agree with her. Dogs don't lose their bones."

Gage must have agreed, because a minute later Al was on the phone with Misty's owners. It was early yet, but not as early as it might have been with the winter sun rising so late. The Avilas were agreeable to sharing their dog. They didn't know exactly why, and she gathered that Al had never mentioned the bone to them. They were, however, glad to do whatever they could to help with the search.

Good. They didn't need to be feeling uneasy around their dog because he'd been playing with a human bone. He was just a dog, making no moral connection to the idea of not disturbing a corpse.

They scarfed the pizza down with unseemly speed, and Al filled an insulated bottle with the fresh coffee before turning the pot off. Then he opened the door. "Out, Regis. You can't stay inside all day."

"Will he make a mess?" Kelly asked.

"He already has with those seed shells, but that's not what I'm worried about. He needs to be out doing squirrel things or I'll start to feel like I've deprived him of a real life by hand-raising him."

Kelly flashed a grin even as her stomach turned over nervously in anticipation of the day ahead. "You made sure he has a life. Right now he looks pretty happy."

But Regis was still a squirrel at heart, and with the door open he dashed out into the cold day. A wind had begun to batter the world, heralding the coming bad weather.

"I hope this storm doesn't show up earlier than expected," Kelly remarked as she pulled on her gloves and her watch cap.

"We'll do what we can. I'll catch up with you once I have Misty. The place where we found her?"

"Best place to start."

He caught her at the door before she could slip out and pressed a hard kiss on her mouth. "Later," he said. "Tonight."

Oh, she had no problem with that idea.

Bugle leaped up eagerly into his cage, and Kelly closed him in. He was going to need booties and his quilted vest today, she thought as the wind turned her cheeks almost instantly to ice.

It was a relief to climb into the cab of her truck and get out of the wind. She suspected the heater would take a while before it started blasting. Worse, she saw that snowflakes were falling again. Lightly. Almost like a promise more than a threat.

She had to face something, she realized as she drove back to the place on the country road where she'd found Al trying to corral Misty: finding the remains might not tell them a damn thing.

She'd been hoping—she supposed everyone was still hoping—that they'd find the remains and find a clue. A clue as to what had happened, a clue as to who had done it. Would they? With a sinking stomach, she seriously feared they wouldn't learn a single useful thing, and maybe not in time to save the other girls even if they did. How long would forensics take?

No answers. They were racing into the teeth of a winter storm to gather evidence that might not save a single life. That might not help them find the perp.

This was the part of police work she most hated, finding evidence that didn't lead to the perp. Evidence that would be useful only once they found the baddie. Great in court, but no lighted road to the door of a killer or rapist.

Nor any guarantee that they would find something to

lead them to the other girls, if the bone did indeed come from one of them. No guarantee they could save their lives.

No guarantees at all.

JANE AND CHANTAL huddled together beneath the stinking blankets. Upon awakening, Jane had remarked that there was more food and water. The thinnest stream of light that came through a crack in the boards over the window had become, for the girls, almost as bright as a midday sun. It was the only light they ever saw, and somehow they adapted.

They found, too, that they'd each had one hand released from the chains. They used the slightly increased mobility to double the blankets and give themselves a little more warmth in their cocoon as they downed the power bars with the aid of water. Neither of them cared anymore if the water was drugged. Sleep was now preferable to wakefulness.

"We're never going to get out of here," Jane said.

"We can't be sure." But in all honesty, Chantal figured she was going to die in this hole. All eating and drinking did was forestall the inevitable. But she didn't want to say that to Jane. Having both of them suicidally depressed would help nothing at all.

She pushed up as best she could to pick out the place where they'd stuffed strands of yarn from her bright green sweater. Only one strand appeared to be left in the crack. Not enough to be seen by anyone.

"Finish that bar," she said wearily to Jane. "We're going to unravel some more of my sweater, make a bigger flag to shove out there."

Jane merely sighed, as if an answer required more strength than she had. Minutes passed before she appeared to find energy to reply. "You tear down that sweater too much and you're going to freeze to death." She paused. "It doesn't matter, does it?"

"Of course it matters or I wouldn't be trying. We're going to make this as big as we can fit into that crack. This color ought to stand out like neon." The winter countryside now was so washed out with shades of winter brown and gray-green that any bright color ought to catch attention. She pulled at the yarn, trying to gather her exhausted thoughts into an idea of what to do with this to make it more noticeable. That crack, after all, wasn't very big. Long streamers had evidently been pulled out by the wind. So maybe a big ball to anchor them. She yanked more yarn out of the sweater.

Then Jane caused a new and different kind of chill to run through Chantal. "When he brought this last water and food, I saw his face. If we could get out, I could identify him."

Chantal stared blindly into the near darkness, her fingers growing still. If he hadn't concealed his face, he meant for them to die here. She'd begun to suspect it but facing the reality made her quail deep inside. She didn't want to die. She was only eighteen. There were so many things she had always wanted to do. A tear burned in her eye, but it was wasteful and she was almost perpetually dehydrated in the icy air, despite the water bottles. The tear never escaped and she sought to stabilize her reeling emotions. "Jane?"

"Yeah. I know. God help me, if I get a chance…"

"Who is he?"

"We saw him playing pool at the tavern with another guy. I could point him out. I could describe him. So could you. He was the shorter one."

Chantal flashed back to what had since become the last happy moments of her short life, and she did indeed remember. Ick. What a creep! Was she going to let him win?

Sudden strength infused her limbs and she started pulling at the yarn of her sweater once again. "We're going to get out of here, Jane. Our parents won't quit. They won't let anyone quit. We'll get out of here if I have to knit us booties for our feet with my teeth. But right now we need to poke out the biggest flag I can put together. Someone will see it because I swear they haven't stopped looking."

"Maybe not," Jane said tiredly. "Mary Lou…"

"We can't afford to think about her now. I'm afraid…"

"Me, too." Jane fell silent, then said, "Want me to try to braid some of those strands?"

"Good idea. The wind's probably getting strong enough to blow them around. Let's make them longer and fatter."

As she ruthlessly ripped yarn from her sweater into long lengths, she sawed it with her teeth to separate it so Jane could braid it.

"I never imagined," Jane muttered, "that braiding my horse's mane for the county fair would come in useful."

Under any other circumstances, Chantal would have laughed. But some creep had stolen her laughter. She wanted it back.

THE CREEP IN question had closed the shutters over the windows of his ramshackle house to better withstand the coming storm. He pulled his pickup into the lean-to that would provide some shelter. He'd already stocked up on supplies, and even had extra thanks to all the energy bars and water he'd bought for those girls. So if he got snowed in and for some reason lost the use of his water pump, he'd be fine.

And they'd be dead.

Crazy, he thought. He'd wanted to make them his slaves, to whip them into line and make them serve him in any way he decided. Now they were going to die because of

Spence's stupidity and a coming storm that would probably suck the last life out of them with its cold.

He ought to be furious. Instead he only felt two things: fear that he might have left evidence on that stuffed rabbit he'd overlooked, and a strangely warm feeling about those girls dying.

Odd, he'd been mad when he killed the first one. She'd infuriated him and gotten her just deserts. He hadn't felt then what he was feeling now: a kind of pleasurable delight not unlike sex.

Those two girls would die on his say-so because he refused to set them free. They were totally at his mercy, and he liked that. Although he could have let them out, he supposed. They'd die quickly enough in their thin clothes with nothing but slipper socks on their feet. He'd made sure that they had no warm winter gear for protection.

Once that storm started howling, he could throw them out into its fury and let it erase them until long after they were dead. By the time anyone found them, they'd probably be as chewed up as the one he'd already tossed aside. He kind of liked that image, too. On the other hand, forcing them to lie in that basement and just die because he *wouldn't* let them go appealed to him even more. *He* was the man in charge, in charge of something more important than shoveling manure and fixing old cars for the first time in his life.

A few nights ago he hadn't been able to resist visiting the body of the first girl. He wanted to see what the animals and elements had done to her. Bones had been tossed about, little flesh was left at all, and the only thing that caught his eye was a small gold necklace with a cross that he'd missed at the outset.

He considered taking it, then decided it didn't matter anymore if they identified the body.

They wouldn't be able to trace it to him. Let her family have that stupid keepsake…if they ever found the body.

He was sitting there, enjoying a longneck, patting himself on his back mentally, thinking just how smart he was.

Then there was a hammering at his door.

MISTY FOUND THE BONES, all right. At first she seemed to have no interest in helping, as if she couldn't understand what they expected of her. But then Kelly decided it was worth a try and retrieved the target bags. The bags containing pieces of clothing from the girls. Just maybe Misty would remember the scent and along with it the bones, although her hopes weren't really high.

"The cadaver dogs didn't find anything," she remarked to Al as she zipped the bags closed. "Why should Misty?"

"Maybe the cadaver dogs didn't get close enough." He shrugged one shoulder as Gage joined them. A line of searchers, already looking cold, edged the road again.

"I think," Gage said, "that it's time we got some luck on this. By the way, that rabbit left at your place? I sent it to the lab for forensics. Something not right about any of that."

"Tell me," Al said dryly.

"Okay, let's see what Misty can do for us. Maybe Bugle can follow the scent."

"I don't know," Kelly answered honestly. "Misty may remember she smelled it before when she found the bone. Bugle wouldn't be able to track it from here unless the victim passed this way."

"Good point." Gage shook his head. The last three weeks seemed to have aged him. "All right. Go for it, Al."

Misty suddenly became eager. Maybe she wanted to get back to her toys. Maybe she just wanted an excuse to run around the countryside. Only time would tell.

The rest of the searchers were told to keep back about twenty feet in case something turned up. They didn't want the scents to become muddied.

For a while it seemed as if Misty was prancing around the field as she had the day Al had found her with the bone. But Misty had her own methods of operation, and eventually the dancing gave way to a more directed movement. She *did* seem to know where she was going.

Kelly followed a little more closely with Bugle but was careful not to get in the way in case Misty made a discovery. Behind her, crime scene techs were ready to get to work, the sooner the better given the increasingly bitter cold.

Then Misty came upon the remains, over two miles in from a county road, in a gully now filled with tumbleweed. She jumped around, then wanted to dive in, but Al restrained her with a powerful arm.

Bugle walked a little closer and announced with a whimper that he recognized the odor. At once he sat at attention.

There was nothing left, Kelly thought as the team cautiously pulled away the tumbleweed. Nothing but some hair. Not even a scrap of cloth. Teeth and DNA would probably be necessary for ID, and the bones were pretty well scattered around.

Gage stood at the edge of the gully for long moments, then said, "My God, I recognize that cross." He looked up, closed his eyes and appeared to steel himself. "Mary Lou."

A HALF HOUR LATER, Kelly felt so helpless and hopeless she could barely stand it. Bugle kept pulling her west, toward another county road, as if he was after something. Finally, she decided to give him his head.

"Bugle scents something. I'm going to let him lead."

Gage nodded. "Go."

Al, who was still hanging on to a disappointed Misty, looked as if he wanted to go with her.

"Take Misty home," she said. "You'll be able to find me at the road out there. How far will I go without my truck?"

"Give me your keys. I'll bring it to you after I return Misty."

She watched him and the dog trot away, then looked at Bugle. "I hope you know what you're doing."

Because it was utterly unlikely that girl had gotten here under her own steam. If she had, there'd at least have been some patches of cloth left.

Bugle put his nose to the ground but after about five yards lifted it, indicating that whatever he was looking for was in the air.

It never ceased to amaze her that dogs could detect odors up to three hundred feet above their heads, and odors that might be weeks old, even in the air. The dang air was moving all the time, right?

But maybe he wasn't getting the scent out of the air. There was enough dry grass and brush around to have caught those odors and retain them even through the cold they'd been having. Or maybe some of the predators that had gotten to Mary Lou's body had left their own trail and he was following *them*.

Sometimes she really, truly wished Bugle could talk. She'd have loved to question him for hours about how he perceived the world.

But he was on a determined trek, and since she couldn't do anything back at the body, she might as well keep following. As the sky grew more leaden, and the wind stiffer, it occurred to her that once Al caught up to her with her truck, she could perhaps do one more swing of welfare checks along this road.

There'd been enough badness over the last few weeks. They didn't need people dying in this storm.

The hike was fairly long, well over a couple of miles before they reached the crossroad, but at least the quick pace of the walk was helping to keep her warm. She wondered if Bugle was glad of his quilted vest or if it annoyed him. But these temperatures must be as dangerous to him as to anyone else. In one of her pockets she'd tucked his booties in case it started to snow heavily. Right now he was okay, but if ice started to build up between his toes, he wouldn't be.

Not that there was any danger of that yet. Snowflakes were in the air, but so light it hardly seemed possible a killer storm was headed in over those mountains.

At last they reached the road, but Bugle wasn't done. He tugged her to the right and she followed, after closing the sagging ranch gate behind her. She just wished she knew what he was after. She guessed she'd find out when he discovered it.

So much of this county looked all the same—ranchlands and fences and wide-open vistas until you ran up against the mountains—that if she hadn't known which county road she was trotting along, she might have been anywhere.

But then something caught her eye. Something she remembered about the way the road looked. Too recently familiar. Hadn't she stopped here the other day? Somewhere just up ahead?

At that moment, Bugle came to a halt. Full stop. He sat, telling her he'd found it. She stared at him, then looked around, trying to figure it out until she remembered.

The glove.

The *glove*.

This was where they'd found that glove, and he'd tracked it from Mary Lou's remains. Her heart began to race and her stomach tried to flip over. A connection. No way to know what it meant, but it was a connection according to Bugle, and she absolutely couldn't afford to ignore it when he was doing his job.

She had yet to see him make a mistake when it came to his olfactory sense. This dog said that body was linked to this spot where the glove had been found.

Pulling off her own glove, she reached under her parka for her radio and called.

AL HEARD KELLY'S radio call shortly after he returned Misty to her owners and expressed his gratitude. He offered them absolutely no idea of the grisly task she'd been asked to perform; let them think she'd helped him round up another dog.

They wanted to talk about the storm, but he eased away from that, just warning them not to let Misty out off her lead.

"If she decides to go for a run, I may not have time to find her."

He looked at the kids, the usual aides to Houdini-dog, and they nodded solemnly with wide eyes.

He picked up Kelly's truck, leaving his own behind, and headed out to the county road where he'd promised to meet her. So Bugle had tracked the glove all the way from the remains. Although she didn't mention the body directly, only that he'd followed the trail from where she'd started her walk. Damn, dogs were amazing.

Not that this was going to tell them enough to find the other girls or the kidnapper. But it was still an essential link.

He listened to the chatter. Gage asked Kelly to flag the location and said he'd send some deputies out her way if she found anything else. Right now they were busy searching the current area for other signs.

"So far," Gage said irritably, "our dogs have found two raccoons and a fox. Yee-haw."

"Must have had a fight over the body," someone else remarked.

"Not on the air," Gage snapped. "How many police scanners do we have in this county? Keep it all under your hat. Face-to-face or shut up."

All that skirting around the word *body* and someone had blown it with one statement. Al might have been amused under other circumstances. There was nothing amusing about this.

When he caught up with Kelly, she was standing by the road and the pin flags she'd used to mark the spot Bugle had led her to. They might not survive the storm, probably wouldn't, but he was sure she'd marked the GPS coordinates and saved them. Routine for her.

He offered to let her drive as she piled Bugle into his cage and into the warmth of the SUV. She shook her head and climbed into the passenger seat.

"I am so *cold* I'm not sure my fingers could manage the steering wheel," she said as she fumbled at the seat belt clasp. "Dang, that dog dragged me quite a distance in this icy weather. Three miles? Maybe more? He seems fine, though."

"Well, he *does* have that quilted vest."

"It's not like I'm running around out here naked," she answered a bit tartly. "Damn, Al. The glove. The body. So they're linked but where do they get us?"

"That the glove fell off a truck and Bugle says it was near the body. That's good for something."

"You'd think. But *who*?"

Which, of course, was the big question.

He let the vehicle idle, blowing heat into the compartment, while neither of them said a word. He suspected they were both trying to figure out what this could mean. That the kidnapper lived somewhere along this road? Or that he'd just driven through here? Hardly a guided tour of his whereabouts.

"I was thinking of driving out along here for a final welfare check," Kelly said after a few minutes. "Might as well since I'm here. But could you drive? Slowly? I want to use my binoculars to scan the countryside. Just because I didn't notice anything a few days ago doesn't mean nothing is out there. I saw a tumbledown line shack that's probably empty, but there's another house up this way a few miles. Maybe the guy noticed something."

Without a word, Al put the SUV in gear. Unlike many vehicles, it proved to be capable of moving at five miles an hour. Kelly kept her binoculars pasted to her eyes. Big binoculars, the kind he used to carry. Those long lenses could see a long way.

"Just don't hit a rut," she muttered.

Yeah, it would jam those eyepieces into the bones around her eyes. An unpleasant experience.

Then all of a sudden she said sharply, "Stop!"

He obeyed, trying not to ram the binoculars into her eyes. The instant the vehicle stopped rolling, she hopped out and resumed scanning the countryside.

He put the vehicle in Park and locked the brake before climbing out to join her. "What did you see?"

"I thought I saw something like chartreuse. There's nothing that should be that color out here."

"Where?"

She lowered the binoculars and pointed. "Believe it or not, near the base of the line shack."

"Oh, that's not a line shack," he said as he began to

scan the area she indicated, adjusting the focus to make the building even larger to his eye. "Old ranch house. Man, somebody must have abandoned it two generations ago. It was tiny! Nobody could…"

His voice trailed off as his gaze fixated.

"Al?"

"I see it, too. It looks like some fabric poking out of a boarded-up window."

"Then let's go."

He lowered the binoculars, eyed the terrain and figured they might be lucky to have suspension after this drive. Lucky if their axles weren't broken. "It's going to be rough." It also might be a humongous waste of time, although at this point it was beginning to feel like wasting time was all they were going to do, anyway.

"All right, let's go. And put your gloves back on. You need those fingers."

He could sense Kelly's impatience in the way she leaned forward against her seat belt, but she didn't press him to a higher speed. She evidently was as aware as he that Bugle was in the back and didn't want him to be banged around inside his cage.

Steadily, with plenty of stomach-dropping dips and jaw-jolting rocks, they approached the shack.

And there was no question but what something green was fluttering from a boarded-up window. Detritus blown there by the wind? Maybe, but it looked more purposeful.

This time Kelly leaped out before the vehicle fully stopped and ran toward the fluttering green strands. She leaned her face toward it and called loudly, "Girls? Are you in there? Is anyone in there?"

The wind almost snatched her words away, but he heard the response of faint cries.

"We're coming in to get you out. Sheriff."

Well, that settled that, Al thought. He couldn't even begin to describe the feelings that twisted up his insides. Good. Bad. Relief.

God help them. He feared they'd find nothing good.

Going round to the other side of the shack, he found the cellar doors, heavy steel, chained and padlocked.

"Kelly," he said, "I'm going to use my gun. Call the sheriff to send an ambulance and more help while I open this up."

Then, standing to one side and hoping a ricochet merely bounced away into the weeds, he fired at the padlock.

He heard faint screams from inside, but he had to get this damn thing open. If he'd had his own truck, he'd have had bolt cutters. But he didn't, and his gun it was going to have to be.

"One more time," he shouted, hoping that was all it would take.

Kelly came round. "Help is on the way. We could wait but I'm not sure…"

He agreed. More than anything, those girls needed to be freed. They probably needed a lot of other things, like medical help, but primarily they needed to know they were safe now.

He leveled his gun again and took another shot at the lock. This time, probably with the help of the cold, it shattered and released the chain.

Kelly beat him down the steps. He listened to girls sob. And he waited for the sirens.

They had the teens. Now they just had to find their tormentor. He went to Kelly's SUV and hunted up the blankets he was sure she must carry for use at accident scenes. When he found them, he took them downstairs and fought back a wave of fury as he saw the girls' condition. Scarecrows. Filthy scarecrows.

It had been a while since he'd killed anyone, but he wanted to kill right now.

Then he heard Chantal's friend say, "I know who took us."

Chapter Thirteen

Day 22

Walton Revell tried to blame the kidnapping on his friend Spencer. There was the stuffed rabbit, after all. Jane defeated him, however, because she'd seen him.

And when he was arraigned before Judge Wyatt Carter and looked into the black gaze of Al Carstairs, he knew he was peering into hell. For the first time it occurred to him that he might be safer in prison than in walking away from the sheriff.

He was remanded into federal custody for the kidnapping, but there were also charges of murder and attempted murder, and a whole bunch of other things that added up to false imprisonment and torture. Maybe some other stuff, too, but the feds would put him away for life, whether the state decided to pursue the other charges. His public defender, who looked as if she'd be happy to kill him herself, didn't hold out much hope.

Not even a plea bargain.

Finally, Walton Revell began to wonder what had possessed him and why he'd ever thought this would be a good idea. All he'd done was end his own freedom, not make slaves out of the girls.

Now he'd be a slave to someone inside the pen. *Great thinking, idiot.*

At least he had the pleasure of seeing Spence have to explain why he'd put the rabbit in Kelly Noveno's house. "She was taking too long," Spence answered simply. "They weren't finding them girls. I admit I took it out of the car when I saw it along the road, but I got mad when she wouldn't answer my questions about the investigation and I decided to give her a scare. Speed her up."

He got a B&E for entering her house. The county attorney said there might be additional charges, like interfering with evidence, but no one seemed in much of a rush to hang Spence. No, Spence was all too eager to hang Reve, ready to talk about how they'd often discussed what it would be like to have some women as slaves.

He thought they were just kidding around.

Apparently, Reve hadn't been.

LEGS AND HANDS SHACKLED, Reve was led out toward a cell. The FBI would be coming to get him as soon as the blizzard passed. Yeah, the same FBI who hadn't shown much interest until they got word the arrest was made.

"Better late than never," Kelly remarked.

"Well, we didn't have a heckuva lot to go on when we first contacted them," Gage said. "I'm more interested in what they'll do now."

The storm had arrived. The outside world looked dangerous and bleak, but Al insisted Kelly and Bugle come to his place. He could tell she was dragging anchor, as if someone had let the air out of a balloon that had been overinflated.

He had some idea of how she'd been beating herself up, but now that could stop. The girls' families were with them at the hospital, and he told Kelly they'd go visit once the storm passed and it was possible to move around again.

She simply nodded. He was sure she was thinking of the lost Mary Lou, but there wasn't a thing that could be done about that.

At his place he barely unlocked the door before Regis darted in, but he didn't come alone. He had a bunch of smaller squirrels with him. His kids? Who knew. He brought out a bigger bowl of sunflower seeds and a small bowl of water and let them take up residence in his Christmas tree.

Bugle found his rawhide bone, ignored the squirrels and settled down to a happy chew. Kelly was the only one who couldn't seem to settle. She changed from her uniform into a set of flannel pajamas, a royal blue fuzzy robe and slippers and looked comfortable.

But nothing about her felt comfortable.

He made coffee, pulled out the leftover pizza and a Danish he'd bought a couple of days ago, and motioned her to eat something.

"I've got cereal and soup, too," he offered.

"This is fine." She took a mug of steaming coffee, then sat and ate two whole pieces of cold pizza. The weather and stress had made her hungry.

Heck, everything was making him hungry, too. Without apology to himself or the world, he pulled out a package of chocolate chip cookies and opened it, dumping them in a bowl. Then he sliced himself a huge piece of Danish and dug in.

Sitting beside her on the couch, he said, "I can think of no one else on this planet I would rather be snowbound with."

That snapped her into the present. A smile began to play over her lips. "Truly?"

"Truly." He just hoped he could trust himself now, but the last few weeks had made him believe in his ability to control himself around Kelly. No out-of-control rages, no desires to smash something other than that kidnapping creep. Being around her made him feel centered.

KELLY FELT HER heart skip a few beats, then begin to rise as it hadn't risen much since the disappearance of those girls. Their kidnapping had drained most of the joy from her life, except last night in Al's arms. She wanted to know that feeling again.

Just past him she could see out the windows. He hadn't drawn the heavy curtains yet, and the blizzard was now concealing the whole world. They were locked away together for at least the next day if not longer. Her gaze trailed back to him, and she saw something new in his expression, something she hadn't seen before: hope.

"I know what I told you about me and relationships," he continued. "It might still be true, but there's only one way to find out. I've enjoyed all the time I've spent with you over the last few weeks, and I didn't get triggered, at least not much. So it's possible…if you're willing to try. Kelly, will you date me? Formally. Like movies, and dinners, and maybe…some cohabitation while we try it on?"

As if her face had been frozen for three weeks, she felt a smile crack her cheeks, almost painful in its intensity. "Yes," she said simply.

"Yes to what?"

"To dating, to cohabiting…at least if you think your squirrels can live with my dog."

His face brightened as if the sun was rising on it. Outside a storm raged, but inside peace had settled.

"I think we can all get along. Besides, Regis has his own drey if he doesn't like it here."

She glanced toward the Christmas tree, where about four squirrels seemed to be sleeping. "I think *they* like it here. I know I do."

Then, throwing the stress of weeks, along with all doubts and fears, out into the storm, she wound her arms around him and looked deeply into his eyes. "You won't escape easily, Carstairs."

"I don't want to, Noveno."

Then they dissolved into laughter and fell on the floor, rolling together and hanging on tightly. The animals left them alone.

It was happy time for people.

* * * * *

DELTA FORCE
DIE HARD

CAROL ERICSON

Prologue

The boy, who'd introduced himself as Massoud, prodded his back with the old rifle as they made their way over the last of the rocks down the mountain.

The Afghan kid didn't seem to know much English beyond the words he'd used to threaten his life, or maybe his elders had ordered him to keep his mouth shut in front of strangers—especially American soldiers.

He didn't have any intention of harming the boy and hadn't taken the kid's earlier threat of bodily harm seriously. If that old Russian rifle could even shoot, Massoud barely looked big enough to hoist it and take aim. It worked well as a prop, though, giving his captor a false sense of courage.

He'd rather wind up wherever Massoud was leading him than lay waste to the kid in the mountains and be stuck making his way down by himself. He didn't lay waste to children anyway, despite what the US military believed about him.

Massoud had actually helped him navigate the terrain, which would've been difficult to do with his bum leg. Probably saved his life. Of course, he could've been saving it just to have someone else take it later.

He drew up and tripped to a stop, the boy's rifle jabbing him in the hip. He pointed to the huts with smoke rising from the center and a few goats tied up outside. He asked in Pashto, "Is this your village?"

The boy answered in English with the only words he seemed to know. "You die now, American soldier."

"Okay, okay." He held up his hands. "But you can call me Denver. I told you that. Denver."

The boy patted his own chest. "Massoud."

"I know, Massoud. Thank you for taking me down the mountain."

A flush seeped through the dirt on Massoud's grimy face as he pushed past him and greeted one of the goats with a scuff beneath its chin, his prisoner momentarily forgotten. "My home."

"Food?" Denver straightened his shoulders. He could eat one of those goats by himself—if Massoud's family didn't kill him first.

Nodding, Massoud pushed through the flap that functioned as a front door and waved him inside with the rifle.

Denver blew out a breath and shrugged his own weapon off his back. He leaned it against the side of the hut, leaving his sidearm strapped to his thigh. Massoud's family had to realize that if he hadn't used his weapons to kill their son, he didn't plan to use them against the other family members, either.

He ducked inside the dark, smoky room, and his eyes watered. A pot of something savory hung over a fire, bubbling with a thick concoction that made his stomach growl.

A small woman hunched over the fire, stirring the contents of the cauldron without looking up from her task.

Massoud rattled off something in Pashto, too fast

for Denver to catch all the words except *American*, but whatever he said had an instantaneous effect on the woman cooking.

She whirled around, the spoon in her hand dripping hot liquid onto the dirt floor. She swung the spoon at Massoud, the words tumbling from her lips and droplets flying from the utensil. When she stopped to take a breath, she scuttled into another room—probably the only other room in the structure.

Massoud pushed Denver in the direction of the flap at the front, and he stepped outside again, breathing deeply of the fresh air. The woman didn't seem too happy to see him, but at least nobody had shot him between the eyes...yet.

Massoud put two fingers in his mouth and whistled. Less than a minute later, a middle-aged man appeared at the door of another hut. He squinted at Massoud and his...guest and then jerked back. He said something over his shoulder and strode forward.

When he was halfway to Massoud, the boy ran to him, waving his arms and pointing back to Denver.

The man put his hand on Massoud's shoulder and walked him slowly back to Denver. He dipped his head in Denver's direction and spoke in slow, careful English. "I am Massoud's father, Rafi."

"Major Rex Denver, United States Army."

The man nodded. "I know who you are. The American traitor...and I know why you're here."

Chapter One

The chill bit into Hailey's cheeks as she slid from the taxi. She hunched into her coat, crushing her ticket to Alcatraz in her pocket. Even on a chilly January evening, you needed to get a ticket in advance for the ferry to Alcatraz.

If Marten wanted to hit the tourist spots of the city, she would've been happy to oblige and they could've had this meeting over lunch instead of trying to talk on a crowded, windblown ferry. But Marten never made anything easy.

He'd even insisted that she board the ferry without him and wait for him on the boat—as if he didn't want to be seen with her. She could never tell if Marten's penchant for secrecy stemmed from reality or a yearning to play spy.

As Hailey lined up for the day's last ferry to Alcatraz, she pressed a hand against her midsection—and it had nothing to do with seasickness.

Marten *had* been secretive. Had asked her not to mention their meeting to anyone. Had refused to come to her place in Pacific Heights, and now he didn't even want to be seen boarding the ferry with her.

His fear couldn't have anything to do with what happened in Syria, could it? The CIA and the Department of Defense had already debriefed them about the incident and released them—told them to go home. *Ordered* them to go home.

She checked her phone cupped in her palm. Marten hadn't responded to her previous text letting him know she was on her way. She zipped off another one giving him her current status.

The line of people started shuffling forward, and Hailey moved with them. She handed over her ticket and walked onto the ferry, cranking her head back to see if she could catch a glimpse of Marten's black porkpie hat—his signature fashion accessory. He'd even worn it in Syria at the refugee camp, to the delight of all the children there.

Hailey gulped back the lump of tears lodged in her throat.

The faces of the people in the crowd merged behind her and she stumbled, grabbing on to a handrail. Once on the ferry, she walked up two flights of steps to the third level to get a better view of the rest of the tourists pouring onto the boat.

When she reached the top level, she rested her back against the railing and scanned the San Francisco skyline, which stood in stark relief against the dark blue sky. Winter in the city could be crisp and clear and achingly beautiful—too bad she had to waste this moment on Marten and one of his silly games.

The ferry captain made a few announcements as the boat chugged away from the dock. Had Marten even boarded? She glanced at her phone again. Was he going to give her a meeting place or make her wander around the boat looking for him?

The ferry plowed forward, carving its way through

the choppy water of the bay. Hailey spotted a man in a black hat like Marten's on the second level.

Leaning over, she waved to get his attention, but he seemed to be focused on something in front of him. Wasn't Marten even looking for her? Why didn't he just respond to her texts? Typical Marten.

"Excuse me." She squeezed past a bunch of people near the stairs and headed down to the deck below, the heels of her boots clanging on the metal steps. Not the most practical boating shoes, but she didn't plan to hoist a sail or anything.

She followed the path she had seen Marten taking to the front of the ferry as it nosed its way to Alcatraz. Standing on her tiptoes, she gazed at the people milling around the deck, phones out, taking pictures of the shore, Coit Tower gleaming in the distance, and then swinging around and taking pictures of Angel Island and the fast-approaching prison on Alcatraz.

She huffed out a breath of annoyance through her nose. No sight of Marten. What kind of game was he playing with her? There had always been whispers about Marten posing as a relief worker to spy—rumors he'd done nothing to squelch. She'd always brushed them off before, but his actions today sure hinted at covert activity.

Up ahead, a commotion broke out along the railing of the boat. A few people screamed, and a man yelled.

As Hailey drew closer, her heart picking up speed, she heard a man shout, "Man overboard. Man overboard."

A sickening dread punched her in the gut. She pushed her way toward the crowd of people hanging over the side of the ferry, staring at the rough water churning beneath the boat.

As Hailey drew closer to the mayhem, she spotted a black hat on the deck. Her heart stuttered and she lunged forward to retrieve the hat, only to be blocked by a crew member.

With his arm barring her progress, the crew member shouted, "Back up. Everyone back away from this area of the ferry."

The boat cut its speed and started making a wide turn. The people on the upper deck and those inside who didn't know what had happened mumbled in unison, creating a howl that rolled across the bay.

More crew members fanned out on the deck and began herding people to the other side of the boat.

An announcement boomed on the loudspeaker. "Anyone who witnessed the man going over or who has any information about him or the incident, gather inside at the bar."

So, someone *had* gone into the water. Hailey secured the scarf tighter around her neck. Did she have any information? Was that Marten's hat?

She pulled out her phone and texted him again.

A coast guard boat joined them within minutes, and the ferry began to head back to the pier, but they weren't going to let anyone off the boat just yet. A deadly calm and order fell over the ferry as people began to form knots, discussing the incident and complaining about their interrupted trip.

Hailey decided to join the group by the bar. Marten hadn't texted her back yet. Listening to snatches of conversations, it seemed as if nobody had actually witnessed the man falling overboard. A few claimed to have seen a man in the water, but no groups were missing anyone from their party—nobody but her.

She shuffled up to a crew member behind the bar, who raised his eyebrows. "Did you see something?"

"No, but…" Hailey bit her lip. How stupid did her story sound?

The crew member tapped his pen on the pad of paper beneath his arm. "Yes?"

"I—I was supposed to meet someone on board, and I thought I saw him wearing that black hat. He did wear a hat like that."

"What hat?"

"There was a black hat on the deck where the man went over."

He drew his brows together. "I don't know anything about a hat. Go on. You were meeting him on the ferry?"

Hailey flipped one end of her scarf over her shoulder. "He indicated that he was going to be running late and might miss the ferry, so he told me to go ahead and board without him."

"The man's name?"

"Marten de Becker."

He scribbled Marten's name beneath several other notes he'd already taken. "I'm going to radio his name back to the office on the pier so we can check out his ticket and if he boarded the ferry."

Hailey nodded and stepped to the side, folding her hands around the cup of coffee that the crew members had handed out earlier. It couldn't be Marten. Why would Marten jump off a ferry when they had a meeting planned?

Several minutes later, the man turned back toward her. "There was no Marten de Becker who bought a ticket or boarded the ferry. Sounds like you and your friend got your dates or times mixed up."

Hailey's shoulders slumped, warm relief flooding her body. "Nobody is missing yet?"

"The office is narrowing down the names, but we won't release anything until the next of kin is notified."

"It's horrible. Do you have cameras on that area of the ferry?"

"No cameras on the boat, but we do have them back at the loading area."

After several more minutes, people began disembarking, and the captain announced that another ferry would be there to meet them if any passengers wanted to return to Alcatraz and continue their trip.

Hailey didn't have any reason to return to Alcatraz. She'd been there a hundred times. How could people carry on with their plans with the lights from the coast guard boats still illuminating the bay searching for someone?

As her boots clattered over the gangplank, Hailey checked her phone for a text response from Marten, but he hadn't replied. He'd be sorry he missed all the excitement. Marten loved excitement. Her gaze tracked back to the bay and the coast guard boats now in the distance. A chill touched her spine, as if she were out there struggling in the cold water.

Hailey wandered away from the ferry terminal, her head bent over her phone, pulling up a car app. As her finger hovered over the display to accept a ride, a text came through.

She caught her breath when she saw Marten's name. She tapped the message and read aloud, "'Changed my mind.'"

"What?" She clenched her teeth from screaming. After all that trouble and…worry, and he changed his mind about the meeting?

She responded, I thought you were here. Where are you now and why playing games? Call me.

Her gaze burned a hole in her phone as she waited for Marten's response. Someone bumped her elbow and she glanced up.

"Sorry." A woman held up her hand. "Were you on that ferry to Alcatraz?"

"I was."

"What happened? I heard someone went overboard."

"That's what they told us, but nobody seems to be missing anyone. I guess they're checking tickets now and the coast guard is still searching the bay."

The woman hunched her shoulders. "Is that going to be a thing now? Instead of jumping from the bridge, they're going to jump from the ferry?"

"Jump?" Hailey massaged the back of her neck.

"Nobody just falls off the Alcatraz ferry." The woman waved at a man approaching and glanced over her shoulder. "Have a nice night."

Suicide? Who would commit suicide by jumping off the ferry to Alcatraz? Especially Marten.

Hailey shook her head and peered at her phone. She input a row of question marks for the silent Marten.

"Now what?" She crossed her arms and scanned the crowd of tourists streaming along the Embarcadero on their way to and from Fisherman's Wharf and Pier 39 with all its shops and restaurants.

Food. Marten had insisted on the night tour to Alcatraz, and now her stomach was growling. She'd head down to Fisherman's Wharf with the rest of the tourists and pick up some seafood from the sidewalk stands.

Cranking her head over her shoulder, she took a last look at the ferry terminal. Had the man who'd gone overboard been wearing a black hat…like Marten's? Where had the hat gone?

But Marten had never boarded the ferry. He'd never even bought a ticket.

She looked at her phone again. Why wouldn't he answer her? He'd better be prepared for questions when they got together, because she had a ton.

She shoved the phone in her pocket and joined the hordes on the sidewalk. She wove her way through the tourists as they stopped to watch the performers along the street.

When she reached the seafood stands on the sidewalk, she jostled for position, elbowing with the best of them. She leaned forward and ordered some clam chowder in a sourdough bread bowl.

Clutching her plate with the bowl of steaming chowder perched on top of it, she wormed her way back to the sidewalk and walked toward a set of wooden steps that led down to the part of the wharf with the maritime museum and the submarine, both closed at this time of night and affording a little calm from the chaos on the sidewalk above. She'd try giving Marten a call.

When she was about halfway down the steps, someone came up behind her and grabbed her arm. Her heart slammed against her chest, and her dinner began tipping to the side.

The man steadied her plate and whispered in her ear, "Act naturally. Someone's following you—the same person who murdered Marten de Becker."

Chapter Two

Hailey Duvall's slim hand formed a fist, and he clenched his jaw, bracing for a punch to his face.

A shadow passed over them from the top of the stairs, and Joe threw his head back and laughed. Pretending he and Hailey were old friends, he said to her, "I told you to get me some food. I'll take one of these."

A crease formed between Hailey's delicate eyebrows, and her nostrils flared. Her gaze dropped to the bread bowl, steam rising from the chowder. The corner of her eye twitched.

Was she going to toss it at him?

Joe's muscles ached from the smile plastered onto his face. "Can we go back upstairs where it's populated and talk this through?"

"Who are you?" She released the plate they both held with a jerk, and the soup spilled over the edge of the hollowed-out sourdough and ran down the side of the bread bowl.

"My name is Joe McVie. I'm a captain with the US Army, Delta Force."

She blinked her long, dark lashes rapidly, and her chest rose and fell.

That meant something to her. Good.

"I want to talk to you about Marten de Becker and what just happened on the ferry to Alcatraz."

"H-he never made it onto the ferry." She pulled her phone out of her pocket and held it up, her hand trembling. "I got a text from him after the accident. Were you on the ferry?"

"I followed Marten onto the ferry. He was wearing a black hat with a black-and-white-checkered band around it. He never came off that ferry—at least he didn't walk off."

She stepped back from him and twisted her head to the side to take in the mostly empty walkway along where the submarine was docked. Her tongue darted from her mouth and swept across her bottom lip.

Joe took a step up. "Let's go where it's crowded. Where you'll feel safer. I'm not here to scare you."

She tipped her firm chin toward the stairs, not looking afraid in the least. "You first."

Holding the plate with two hands, Joe climbed the stairs and stood to the side to wait for Hailey to pass at the top. "I wasn't kidding about the food. I'm hungry, and this smells great."

She pointed to one of the fish stands on the street. "I got it there. You take mine and find a table. I'll get another and join you…unless I decide to make my escape. And if I do and you try to follow me, I'll call the cops so fast your…red head will spin."

Joe let out a breath on a smile. "You're not my captive, but I think you're gonna want to hear what I have to say. I'll grab a seat on the patio behind us."

Hailey spun away from him and dived into the mob of people clustered around the stand.

If she took off and melted into the crowd, he wouldn't blame her. But something in her sparkling eyes told him the news about de Becker didn't surprise her. Whether or not she believed his claim about someone tailing her just now remained to be seen.

He kept his gaze pinned on her while she ordered another bowl of chowder. Hailey Duvall would stand out in any crowd—tall, dark and beautiful. She wore her wealth with an easy grace. Even a philistine like him could spot the expensive clothes, the designer leather bag slung casually over one shoulder, the perfect hair and makeup that came only from the best products and pampering.

What the hell had she been doing in Syria?

She got her food and ducked between the tourists. Halfway back to the tables on the patio, her step faltered. Then she met his eyes, squared her shoulders and continued her approach.

Maybe she figured if he were going to harm her, he'd have done it downstairs without such a big audience. Maybe she wanted to find out what had happened to de Becker and why.

He could deliver on that for sure.

As she drew within a few feet of the table, Joe jumped up from his metal chair and pulled one out for her, wiping the seat with a napkin. "You never know about these seagulls out here."

"Thanks." She sat down, placing the plate with the bread bowl in front of her. "Where's the man who was following me? Or was that just a ruse to play the good guy and then hit me with your crazy theory about Marten?"

"It's not a theory, and you know it, Hailey."

Her eyes widened. "How do you know my name? Were you part of the military that came to the refugee center…after?"

"No, but I know all about the refugee camp and what happened there."

She covered her eyes with one hand, the big diamond on one finger flashing in the night. "It was horrible, and we were responsible."

"No, you weren't—and neither was Major Denver."

She split her fingers and peeked at him through the space. "That's not what Marten said."

"Was de Becker the only one of your group who identified Denver at that meeting?"

"Meeting?" She picked up her spoon and began stirring her soup as her mouth tightened. "That was no meeting. The other aid workers, our guide and I were all kidnapped. Then they planted a bomb in our car and sent us back to the refugee center—to kill people."

"Sorry, I used the wrong word." He touched the back of her smooth hand with his finger—at least that diamond graced her right hand and not her left, not that her marital status meant anything to him one way or the other. "That must've been terrible for all of you."

"Worse for the people who died in the bomb blast." Hunching her shoulders, she blew on a spoonful of chowder. "So, you know all about me and that…incident. Are you representing the US Army, reaching out to me in some official capacity?"

"Official?" He broke off a piece of bread from the side of the bowl. "Nah."

"What do you know about Marten de Becker?" She puckered her lips and blew on a spoonful of soup before sipping it.

Dragging his gaze away from her pouting lips, he said, "I know he had a change of heart about who exactly kidnapped your group."

"Were you following him?"

"Yes." He dragged the piece of sourdough through the creamy chowder and popped it in his mouth. "I knew he was here to see you. I've been keeping tabs on you, too. All of you."

"You've been following me?" Her eyebrows snapped over her nose.

He didn't have to follow Hailey Duvall to know who she was—heir, along with her brother, to a fortune made in real estate; philanthropist; do-gooder and blessed with a natural beauty that took his breath away. That last part he'd just discovered tonight.

All the magazine pictures and video couldn't do justice to the vitality that radiated from her slender body and shone in her eyes. Hailey wouldn't be one to play tennis and lunch with other socialites. She had an energy about her that made you think she was ready to jump out of her seat and do something important.

"Following you? Not like I was following de Becker. He's the one who fingered Denver."

"You're sure he got on that ferry?" She tucked a lock of dark, glossy hair behind her ear.

"I tracked him from his hotel. I was following the man in the black hat. That man never got off the boat."

She toyed with her spoon. "I gave his name to a crew member and he phoned it in. Marten de Becker never bought a ticket tonight."

"He must've bought it under a different name." Joe shrugged. He had his own suspicions about de Becker.

"I told you before, he texted me after the accident on the ferry. Wrote that he changed his mind."

"Someone has his phone. Probably took it before he pushed Marten overboard."

Hailey dropped her plastic spoon, and it fell on the

ground. "Why would someone kill Marten? Why are you keeping track of us?"

"It all has to do with that kidnapping and what you saw and heard. It has to do with Major Rex Denver." He pointed to her spoon on the ground. "Do you want another?"

"I've lost my appetite."

"Tell me, Hailey. Why did de Becker want to meet you tonight? And why on a ferry to Alcatraz?"

"I have no idea. I haven't seen him since the bombing at the refugee camp. He called me out of the blue yesterday. I invited him to dinner, but he insisted on meeting on the ferry."

"Did he give you any hints about what he wanted?"

"Told me to keep quiet about him and our meeting." She pushed away her plate and folded her hands on the metal table. "He sounded…strange, secretive. All my instincts told me not to meet him—at least not the way he wanted."

"Do you always ignore your instincts?"

She crumpled her napkin in her fist and slammed it on the table. "If you're implying I had any inkling those…terrorists planted a bomb underneath the car for our trip back to the refugee center, you couldn't be more wrong. None of us believed those men waylaid us for that purpose."

"I'm not suggesting that." He held up his hands. "Why would you think they wanted to send a bomb into the refugee camp? But what *did* you think they wanted when they kidnapped you?"

Her dark eyes flashed, and their fire sent a thrill down his spine. The cool, calm and collected princess had a dangerous side.

He spoke in a soothing tone, wary of setting her off.

"I just want to know what you thought, what you all thought. I want to know who first suggested the American with your captors was Major Rex Denver."

She kept hold of the napkin and began shredding pieces from it. "We were coming back to the refugee camp from a supply center in Pakistan. There were five of us—me, Marten, Andrew Reese, the British journalist, Ayala Khan, who's one of the nurses at the center, and our guide and translator, Naraj Siddiqi."

Joe had his doubts about Siddiqi, but he'd keep those to himself right now. "How'd they capture you?"

"Familiar story." She shrugged. "A couple of guys ran our car off the road. They had bigger weapons than our guide and forced us into the back of their truck. They blindfolded us and took us to some bombed-out buildings."

"You couldn't see. How'd you know about the buildings?"

"I could just tell—the dust, the silence, the rubble. While they led us along, they had to keep telling us to step up, step to the side. Even with the warnings, I tripped and stumbled a hundred times. I could tell we were in some bombed-out ghost of a neighborhood."

"Did they mistreat you?" His jaw hardened at the thought of Hailey in the hands of the insurgents in that area.

"No. Offered us tea, but kept us blindfolded."

"And that's when you heard the American? Did he speak to you?"

"We just heard his voice a few times. He spoke French to one of the kidnappers. I could tell he was American from his accent." A flush stained her cheeks. "I—I speak French fluently."

Of course she did. Probably learned it at one of those fancy boarding schools.

Joe ripped off a side of the bread bowl. "The American didn't speak Syrian?"

"No."

Joe crumbled the bread in the remains of his soup.

Hailey hunched forward. "Why? What does that mean?"

"Denver speaks several languages, including Syrian. If he were there, why wouldn't he converse in that language instead of some awful French?"

"I didn't say his French was awful." She tossed her mangled napkin on the table beside her plate. "Maybe that's exactly why he didn't speak Syrian. How many Americans know that language? Maybe he didn't want to give himself away."

Joe snorted. "Major Denver wasn't there. No way. He wouldn't send a bomb into a refugee center targeting helpless people—women and children. No way."

"So that's what this is all about. You, here, following de Becker around. Did the army send you? Delta Force?"

"I'm here on my own, on leave. The US Army has no idea I'm following up on this and it wouldn't be appreciated or condoned…but I don't give a damn about that."

"What makes you so sure Denver didn't go rogue? Didn't he go AWOL?"

"I know him. I'm a good judge of character. He went AWOL because he realized he was being set up. Whoever set him up had already killed an Army Ranger and tried to kill one of our Delta Force team members. The army tried to pin it all on Denver, but that team member, Asher Knight, got his memories back and insisted that he, the Army Ranger and Denver were all set up at that meeting."

"You think our kidnapping is another plot to implicate Major Denver?"

"That's exactly what I think. Who first told you about Denver? Wasn't de Becker the one who initially ID'd Denver as being present at that…gathering before the bomb went off in the refugee camp?"

"It was Marten. I can't even remember how that all came about. I was devastated, in shock after the explosion. They made us all leave the camp—the country—after that." Her voice wavered.

"Did anyone question you?" Joe resisted the urge to take her hand.

"Of course." As if reading his mind, she put her hand in her pocket. "We were questioned there, and people from the Department of Defense came out here to San Francisco to question me and then the FBI sent a couple of agents for good measure. We went through the wringer."

"Did they ask you about Denver and whether or not you could ID him? I know de Becker said that his blindfold had slipped and he saw the American. When they showed him Denver's picture, he picked him out."

"I know that." She straightened out her scarf and smoothed it against the front of her jacket. "My blindfold was secure and I never saw a thing, never saw any of my captors."

Joe slumped in his chair. "So, you never claimed that Denver was there."

"I said I didn't *see* my captors." She held up one finger, her perfectly polished fingernail catching the light from the streetlamp next to their table, making it look like a magic wand. "I did hear them."

"And?" He ran a tongue around his dry mouth.

"And in addition to hearing an American speaking French, I heard someone call someone else Denver."

Joe sank his head in his hands, his fingers digging into his scalp. "No."

"I'm sorry. I did hear that, and I reported it to the military investigators."

"If the major wanted to keep his presence there a secret, why would the others be throwing around his name? That makes no sense."

"I agree, unless someone slipped up." She touched his sleeve. "You still haven't told me why someone would want to kill Marten."

"Because of all this." He swept his arm to the side, encompassing the bay. "De Becker was making noises about taking back his eyewitness statement placing Denver in Syria outside that refugee camp."

"Why is that a problem? Doesn't the army want the truth? Doesn't the CIA?"

"They may want the truth, but there are factions in some high places that want to perpetuate this lie about Major Denver. We just don't know why."

"We?"

"A couple of my Delta Force team members have already uncovered some discrepancies in these stories swirling around Denver. Things are not adding up."

"These highly placed factions are willing to commit murder to further their narrative?" Hailey put a hand to her throat. "To follow around innocent citizens?"

"Your meeting with de Becker never happened. You don't know why he wanted to talk to you." Joe pinched the bridge of his nose between his thumb and forefinger. "If anyone ever follows up with you, tell them you heard the name Denver used for one of your kidnappers and leave it at that."

It was not the speech he'd planned to deliver to Hailey Duvall. He'd wanted her to step forward and question the investigators' insistence that the major was there, that it was ludicrous to believe they'd use his real name under those circumstances. But after meeting and talking with Hailey, all he wanted to do was protect her. Keep her away from this madness.

She'd already been through enough. Her car had delivered a bomb inside a refugee center filled with innocents. Even though it wasn't her fault, she'd have to carry that with her. And he could tell—this would weigh on her.

Why else would an über-rich woman spend her time and money to help people halfway across the world? Put herself in danger to do so? When he'd started this journey, he thought Hailey was a naive do-gooder. Now he felt humbled in the presence of her selflessness.

She tapped her fingers on the table. "If I stick to that story, how are you going to prove Denver wasn't responsible for the bombing of the refugee camp?"

"I'll prove it another way." He swept up his plate with its collapsing bread bowl. "But I'd like to see you home, if that's okay."

Her gaze shifted to the sidewalk, still jammed with tourists. "Do you think I'm in danger?"

He lifted one shoulder. "That guy was probably just following you to see if you'd go to the police with any suspicions about the man who went overboard. If they do have de Becker's phone, maybe you can just play it cool and text him as if he blew off your date."

"I already did text him—and that was no date." She plowed her fingers through her hair. "If Marten was murdered, do you think I can sit back and pretend this night never happened? If it turns out that was Marten, I'm going to go to the police *and* the FBI and tell them about our planned meeting and the texts I received from his phone after his death."

"Not sure that would be wise at this point, Hailey."

"Wise?" Her eyes grew round. "It's what's right. It's justice."

Uneasiness gnawed at his gut. Did he really think Hailey would drop this after all she'd gone through? He should've just made sure she came to no harm tonight. He never should've intervened and approached her. A woman like Hailey spelled danger for him ten different ways.

The truth smacked him in the face, and he swallowed. Once he'd gotten an eyeful of Hailey, he felt compelled to make a move. How else was he gonna meet a woman like this? They didn't travel in the same circles…and that poor boy from South Boston still desperately yearned to be accepted by those women out of his reach—the one that got away. *Pathetic bastard.*

Hailey stood up suddenly. "You can see me home if you like. I was going to call an online car before I got the bright idea that I needed something to eat down here."

"And you never even ate." He pointed to the chowder, cold and soaking into its bowl.

"Like I said, lost my appetite."

As she strolled toward the curb, bent over her phone, Joe grabbed their trash and dumped it in the nearest can.

She held up her cell as he approached her. "I told him to meet us up the street a little to avoid the traffic around here."

"Is Pacific Heights close?"

Sliding a glance to the side, she said, "You really did your research, didn't you? You even know where I live."

"C'mon, Hailey. It's not exactly hard to find out where you live. You're kinda all over San Francisco society news."

"Sometimes this can really seem like a small town." She bumped his elbow with her own. "Let's cross."

He didn't presume to take her arm as they crossed the street, but he wanted to. Everyone she came in contact with must feel that way about her—drawn to her vitality and warmth. He was simply one of many who swarmed around her, wanting to be close.

The phone in her hand rang, and she brought it to her face. "Yeah, right in front of the T-shirt shop. I see you—black Nissan."

As the black car pulled up to the curb, Joe shot forward and opened the door for Hailey.

She slid into the back seat, and he followed.

Hunching forward, she asked, "Do you need directions?"

"I have it on my GPS. Pacific Avenue in Pacific Heights, right?"

"That's it." She settled back and closed her eyes. "When do you think we'll find out about Marten?"

"If he didn't buy the ticket under his own name and they don't—" Joe glanced at the rearview mirror "—find the body, it could take a while. If he washes up somewhere and they can get fingerprints, they'll eventually ID him."

"He's Dutch, you know, a Dutch citizen, and they'll ID him a lot faster when I step forward and report him missing."

Joe put a finger to his lips. He was beginning to understand that once Hailey got her teeth into something, she became a pit bull.

A totally gorgeous pit bull with really nice teeth.

Several minutes later, Hailey tapped the back of the driver's seat. "It's the one on the left. You can pull over here."

The driver whistled as he stopped his car. "That must be a great view during the day. Not bad at night, either."

"It is. Thanks." Hailey turned to Joe. "Do you want to keep the car for wherever you're going next?"

"You're not getting rid of me that easily. I'll see you to the front door."

The driver adjusted the rearview mirror. "I can wait here, but you'll have to call me up again on the app."

"I'll do it when we get up to the house. If you get another fare, take it."

Hailey slid from the car and Joe followed her out and trailed after her as she strode across the street.

His jaw dropped slightly when he got a load of the house looming in front of him. The huge white house, gleaming in the night, had a fountain and a garden in front and what looked like a four-car garage on the lower level. Being in San Francisco, and Pacific Heights in particular, they had to walk up some steps to get to the front door.

"I'm sure it's okay. I even have security cameras." She pointed to the eaves of the house as she charged ahead of him. Then she tripped to a stop and gasped.

His hand shot out to grab her arm, and she spun in his grasp, almost falling into his arms from the step above.

"Are you all right?"

She shook her head and stepped to the side—revealing a black hat with a checkered band resting on her welcome mat.

Some welcome.

Chapter Three

Hailey's knees wobbled and she took an unsteady step down—away from Marten's hat—even though it put her chest to chest with Joe.

His arm curled around her back, and she didn't even jerk away. She needed support right now—and this solid hunk of man fit the bill.

"It's Marten's, isn't it? That's the hat I was following all day until I trailed him to the ferry to Alcatraz. Any doubts now?"

Even Joe's voice, low and rumbling, represented safety.

"How did it end up here? It was on the deck after... he went overboard. Wouldn't the crew have picked it up? Why would they allow some random person to grab the hat of the guy who'd just taken a dive off the boat?"

"There was mass confusion in the moments after the other passengers reported that a man had gone into the water. Anyone could've snatched up the hat."

Someone honked a horn, and Hailey jumped, putting her even closer to Joe and his warm presence.

He squeezed her waist. "It's the driver. I'll tell him not to wait. He'll just think I got lucky."

With her head to one side, Hailey watched Joe jog down the steps to the sidewalk. Got lucky? Was that what he was hoping for? Was that what *she* was hoping for?

As he returned to the porch, Hailey leaned over the hat, giving it a wide berth, and unlocked her front door. She pushed it open and jerked her thumb up to the roof. "I'm going to get a look at exactly who left the hat when I check my security footage, and then I'm going to call the police."

"You're going to call the police on someone for leaving a hat on your doorstep?" Joe crouched down and picked up the hat by its brim. "Maybe the SFPD jumps when someone from Pacific Heights calls, but I doubt this offense would be high on their agenda."

"The hat of someone who was pushed off an Alcatraz ferry?"

"Nobody said he was pushed. There were no witnesses. He could've fallen. Jumped. There's no…body yet."

She turned toward him, still not sure whether or not she was inviting him inside. "Why'd they do it? Why leave Marten's hat here?"

"As a warning? I don't know." He tipped the hat at her. "Let's take a look at that security footage."

He'd made the decision for her, invited himself in… and she didn't mind one bit.

She widened the door and stepped back, holding her breath as Joe crossed the threshold into the foyer. The opulence of the house could make people dizzy—or make them salivate. She'd seen both reactions from men she'd ushered inside—and either way, it had ended badly for her and not too great for them, either.

Joe didn't even blink an eyelash as he placed the hat on a bench in the entryway and touched her arm. "Are you sure you're okay? You look pale. Maybe you should sit down before chasing after that footage."

"I'm fine, thanks." She scooped up a remote control by the door and clicked a few buttons, turning on the lights in the kitchen. "I can bring up the security cam on my laptop."

Her heels tapped on the polished hardwood floor as she walked toward the kitchen, Joe dogging her steps as if he feared she'd keel over in a faint. Despite their cushy surroundings, Joe had to realize she was made of stronger stuff than that, although she didn't know why she cared what Joe McVie thought.

She flipped up the lid on her laptop and tapped the keyboard to wake it up. Her fingers hovered over the keys as Joe leaned over her shoulder.

She flicked her fingers at him. "I'm going to enter my password now."

"Oh, sorry." He circled around until his back was facing her.

Typing in her password, she asked, "Do you want something to drink? I have beer and some white wine in the fridge."

"Just some water, please."

"Bottles are in the refrigerator." She drummed her thumbs on the base of the computer. "I haven't looked at this in a while."

"I can help you, if you need it." Joe held up a water bottle. "Do you want one?"

"No, thanks, but you can pour me a glass of that chardonnay that's open. Glass in the cupboard to your right."

While Joe clinked through the glasses and poured her wine, she navigated to the security program and launched the footage.

"Your wine." Joe clicked the glass on the counter next to the computer and took up his previous position behind her, looking over her shoulder. He jabbed his finger at the screen. "You can get to the date there. Today's date is the default."

"I've got it. Thanks for the wine." She picked up the glass and raised it, tapping it against his plastic water bottle. "Here's to success."

He repeated, "Success."

She sipped her wine as she double clicked today's date and then scrolled through the day. "There's my mail person. I don't think *she* left it."

"You can jump to four o'clock. It had to be after that time."

"I'm getting there." Hailey pursed her lips. She never did meet a man who wasn't bossy. Then she sucked in a breath. "There he is. He left the hat just over an hour ago."

Joe hunched forward, his warm breath tickling her ear. "Damn. Looks like he knew he could be on camera."

Hailey froze the video and traced her finger around the black-clad figure with the ski mask pulled down over his face. "Not very helpful, is it? He's even wearing gloves, so the police wouldn't be able to pick up any fingerprints."

"I can't even tell if it's the same person who was following you on the wharf. He probably would've had enough time to beat us here." Joe blew out a breath and her hair stirred against her cheek. "You're still thinking about calling the cops? Where I come from, the cops would barely move for a dead body on your porch. A hat? They'd laugh in your face."

She twisted her head over her shoulder. "Where do you come from?"

"South side of Boston, although it's been a while since I've been back."

"Rough area?"

"You could say that." He leveled his finger at the display. "Let's see what else he does."

She restarted the video and watched the disguised man—person—drop the hat on the porch, turn, jog down the steps and hit the sidewalk. "Nothing."

"You don't have a camera pointing at the street?"

"Not anymore. It broke and I never got around to fixing it. I doubt this guy would be dumb enough to drive up to the front of the house, anyway."

"You're probably right." Joe slammed his bottle on the counter next to her glass. "They're warning you to keep your mouth shut about Marten and about the abduction in Syria—and you're gonna do it."

She hooked her heels on the bar beneath the stool and snapped the laptop closed on the frozen image of Marten's hat on her porch. "What about Major Denver?"

"We'll figure it out. Don't worry about it. You reported what you heard from your captors, and you told the truth. That's all anyone can ask. That's all I can ask."

"And Marten?"

"He got mixed up in something he should've left alone."

"Wasn't he just telling the truth?"

"Was he?" Joe rubbed a hand across the sexy burnished-gold stubble on his jaw. "I don't believe Marten did tell the truth. Someone got to him, and he lied to promote the Denver narrative. Who knows? Maybe he was paid off. Then he stopped playing the game, and that's when he got into trouble."

Hailey traced a finger around the rim of her wineglass. "That sounds like Marten."

"Does it?"

"Marten was a gambler. Last I heard, he was in debt. I wouldn't put it past him to lie in exchange for money."

"What was a guy like that doing aiding refugees?"

"He liked excitement." She shrugged. "I'm not sure what he was doing in Syria, but I had my suspicions that he'd worked as a mercenary for the Kurds before joining us."

"What about the others? Ayala? The journalist? Your guide, Siddiqi?"

"Ayala's a nurse from Florida. She's already back at the camp. Andrew is back in England writing other stories. Naraj is probably back at work. He's a freelancer for hire. He escorts crazy Westerners around for a price."

Joe pinched his chin and stared over her head. "Convenient."

"Ah, no." She waved her hand in front of his face to break his gaze. "Naraj didn't betray us."

"How'd that group of thugs know you'd be on the road at that particular time?"

"We weren't far from the refugee camp when they took us. They were probably lying in wait for the first opportunity."

"But *your* car, the one eventually heading back to the camp. That explosion derailed the peace negotiations between the Syrian government and the rebels—each blaming each other and getting maximum propaganda points out of the carnage."

"I know." Hailey put a hand over her aching heart.

"You had no way of knowing your kidnappers were going to plant that bomb on your car." He shoved her wineglass toward her, and the golden liquid inside sloshed and sparkled.

Curling two fingers around the stem of the glass, she said, "It's still hard not to feel responsible. We brought that death and destruction into the camp."

"I'm sorry. It's nasty business out there."

Joe placed two fingers on the base of her glass, brushing her hand and causing butterflies to flutter in her stomach.

Must be the emotions of the day that had her so susceptible to this Delta Force soldier on a mission. It couldn't be his dark russet hair and rough-around-the-edges manner. That type hadn't appealed to her since her teen years, when she'd been trying to get her father's attention. It hadn't worked anyway, and the guys ended up being as untrustworthy as the rich boys—just in a different way.

She blinked. "Thanks. I don't think Naraj betrayed us, though."

"Are you safe in this house?" Joe downed the rest of his water and screwed the lid back on the bottle.

He was leaving her.

"Yes, of course. In addition to the security cameras, there's an alarm system."

"I didn't see you set one."

"I didn't. I don't always arm it."

"Why not?" He pushed off the stool and, spreading his arms, did a slow turn around the room. "There's some artwork on that wall over there that could feed a family of five for life."

Heat surged into her cheeks. So he'd only pretended not to notice the luxury of the house. "This is my father's house."

"And you don't care if your father loses his assets?" His brows shot up to his hairline.

"Considering how he amassed his fortune?" She tossed her head, sweeping her hair from her shoulder. "Not really."

"He's a real-estate mogul, not a drug dealer, right?"

"Forget it." She didn't want to go into a petulant first-world rant about her father's wealth in front of Joe. "I will definitely set the alarm system tonight."

"Good, because you're the most valuable thing in this whole house."

And just like that, her heart flip-flopped, but not from fear.

"Do you think I might actually be in danger?" She took a swig of her wine.

"I think you'll be fine if you stick to your original story and don't make waves about Marten."

"That seems—" she swirled the last of the liquid in her glass "—wrong."

"You can't do anything for Marten now, Hailey. Stay on script. Any chance your father is coming home anytime soon?"

"He's in New York with his wife. She prefers it there."

"And your brother?"

Hailey swallowed. Joe really knew her entire family history. "My brother, Win, will be wherever our father is, playing lapdog."

"Speaking of dogs, you don't have a German shepherd hiding out somewhere, do you?" Joe leaned forward as if to peek under the sofa in the next room.

"Mel, my stepmother, can't stand animals. As soon as my cat died, she declared a moratorium on pets in this house."

"Don't you have a house of your own?"

"No. I gave up my apartment near the Haight when I went to Syria. When I came back home, my father asked me to live in and watch his place."

"You could do a lot worse." He crushed the water bottle with one hand. "As long as you're here and as long as there's an alarm system, use it."

"I will now." She held up her phone. "Do you want me to call you a car? Where are you staying, anyway?"

"Hotel back by Fisherman's Wharf." He pulled a wallet out of his pocket. "I'll pay you back for the car."

"Don't worry about it. It'll only be a few bucks." At least Joe didn't assume Miss Moneybags would be picking up the tab for everything.

He waved a twenty in the air before slipping it beneath her wineglass. "Take it for the transportation and the dinner."

"The dinner?"

"I stole your chowder and then ruined your appetite."

"You did do that." She tapped her phone to accept a driver in the vicinity. "Your car's on its way, a white Prius."

"Thanks, Hailey, and I'm sorry I messed up your evening." He held out his hand. "It was nice meeting you."

She took his hand, and it enveloped hers in a warm clasp. "I appreciate what you did tonight—I mean, ensuring my safety. What's next for you?"

"I'll continue looking into the claim that Denver was part of the group that planted the bomb on your car." He flipped up the collar of his jacket. "I might track down the journalist who was with you."

"I told you, Andrew Reese is back in England probably working on other stories."

"Do you have his phone number?"

"I do." She searched through her phone. "What's your number? I'll send it to you."

Joe recited his number, and she saved it in her phone before forwarding Andrew's number to him. "Your car is one minute away."

Hailey suddenly felt a rush of panic, almost as if she had to tell Joe something before he walked out of her life forever.

He started to turn and stopped. "If…if you remember anything else, you have my number now. Feel free to call me—anytime."

Had he felt it, too, then? Something unsaid between them?

She clasped her phone to her chest. "Yes, yes, I will."

When they reached the front door, he tapped the alarm system on the wall. "Set it."

"I will. Goodbye, Joe."

He raised his hand, and she watched him jog down the first few steps before he made the left turn and disappeared behind the bushes.

She clicked the door closed, locked it and punched in the code to set the alarm system.

She picked up Joe's crushed water bottle and pressed it against her warm face. One brief encounter and she'd constructed a mental picture of Joe McVie as superhero to the rescue.

Snorting, she tossed the bottle into the recycling bin. She'd been fooled by that type before. She rinsed her glass in the sink and sighed at the silence of the house.

The wine had taken the edge off a little, but she still couldn't believe Marten was dead…murdered. Maybe Joe had been wrong about everything.

She walked into the den and turned on the TV, flipping over to the local news. The ten o'clock version hadn't started yet, so she ran upstairs and got ready for bed.

Her face washed, her teeth brushed and her hair in a ponytail, she went back downstairs and tripped on the last step when she caught sight of Marten's hat on the coffee table.

What would've happened if Joe hadn't been around to notice the man tailing her? Would that man have delivered the same warning he'd hoped to convey with the hat? *Keep quiet.*

It was not in her nature to keep quiet. Her father had found that out the hard way.

Helping to ID Marten's body was not endorsing any change of heart he might've had about the statements he'd made regarding their abduction. She hadn't even known Marten was going to retract what he'd claimed about Denver's presence with their captors. Surely, giving a name to an unidentified dead man wouldn't get her in trouble.

She sidled into the den, avoiding the hat, and curled up in a recliner with the remote in her hand. She turned up the sound when the local news started. The incident on the ferry was the top story.

Hailey drew her knees up to her chest and wrapped one arm around her legs. The coast guard hadn't found the body yet, and nobody had reported anyone missing from the ferry. The check of tickets on the boat hadn't completely matched up with the tickets sold. People on the boat must've slipped off without showing their tickets to anyone.

How would they ever identify the man who fell overboard? Would they even believe someone *had* fallen overboard? What evidence did they have?

Even the man's black hat was gone.

Hailey sighed again and turned off the TV. She still had some work to do on a fund-raising gala taking place this week, which would be a good way to get her mind off Marten…and Joe McVie.

She swept her laptop from the kitchen counter and tucked it under her arm as she climbed the stairs. She threw back the covers on her bed and settled cross-legged on the sheet, placing her laptop between her knees.

She tapped her keyboard to get things moving and double clicked the folder that contained her guest list and venue layout. Daisy, her event coordinator, had done most of the work these past few months, booking the hotel ballroom, setting up the catering and the decor. All Hailey had to do was look through everything, approve it and write the checks.

She verified the price for the band Daisy had given her and did another count of the guests. Then she opened her email to send Daisy a message.

Before launching a new email, Hailey skimmed through her messages, deleting most of them. An email with an attachment from something called the Syrian Refugee Campaign caught her eye, and she opened it.

The message had no text except for a link. She almost deleted it, but the subject line jumped out at her. It contained a name—Andrew Reese, the British journalist who'd been captured with her.

She squinted at the date. It had been sent tonight. Maybe it was from Andrew. Maybe he'd heard something about Marten.

Her heart thumped as she clicked the link. A video filled her screen, with no sound or introduction.

The video took her down a long, dark hallway, and

Hailey stopped breathing. The blood thrummed in her ears. A door came into focus, and the shaky video continued as someone reached out and opened the door with a gloved hand.

It swung open on a dark room, a single light in the corner, but the camera stayed away from the light, tracking along the shadows instead.

Hailey's fingers curled around the edge of her sheet, bunching the material into her hands. The camera took her farther into the room, suddenly swinging toward an object in the corner under the light.

Hailey gasped at the hooded figure tied to the chair, chin dropped to his or her chest. Was this some kind of sick joke? Some snuff film?

A hand appeared in the frame and whipped the black hood from the person in the chair. The poor soul's head bobbed, but still hung down, long hair obscuring his face.

The hand made its way into the frame again and prodded the man in the chair. Slowly the captive raised his head, looked into the camera from eyes sunken into his swollen face and in a hoarse voice whispered, "Help me, Hailey."

Chapter Four

Joe stretched out on the king-size bed and toed off his shoes. The TV newscast hadn't done much of a story on poor old Marten. Would his body ever wash up?

Joe regretted not getting right to the point with Marten to find out who put Major Denver's name on his lips in the first place. He'd wanted to hold off to see where he went and who he met. He hadn't thought the guy would wind up dead. He'd underestimated the enemy.

A tingle of fear crept across his flesh. Hailey didn't know anything, hadn't retracted her story about hearing one of the terrorists address Denver by name—and now she wouldn't.

His phone, charging next to the bed, rang, and he checked the display. He'd memorized Hailey's number, and he bolted upright to answer her call.

"Hailey, did you remember something?"

"Oh my God, Joe. It's Andrew. They have Andrew now."

"Wait. Slow down. What are you talking about? Who has Andrew?"

"The same people who killed Marten. I'm sure of it. They have Andrew, and they have my email address."

Joe swung his legs off the bed. "Someone sent you an email?"

"It's horrible, Joe. It's Andrew. Th-they've tortured him."

A knot formed in Joe's gut. "This was a video sent to your email address?"

"Yes." Hailey sniffled. "I didn't recognize the email address, but Andrew's name was in the link, so I thought it might be something he was sending. I'm sorry I clicked on it."

"Was anyone else in the video?"

"No, just the cameraman's gloved hand, and I'm pretty sure the video was taken with a phone. It's shaky." She drew in a long breath. "I—I don't know where he is, but we have to help him. We have to call the FBI."

"There are no hints in the video? Background."

"It's horrible, Joe. Andrew's in a room, tied up. They had a hood over his head. When they pulled off the hood, I could tell they'd tortured him, beaten him, but Andrew still mentioned my name."

"He said your name?" Joe launched from the bed and stuffed his feet back into his shoes. He had to see this video for himself.

"He asked me for help." She sobbed. "It was terrible. I'm sick to my stomach."

"I'm coming right over."

"Y-you are? I can forward the video to you."

"I want to see the original email." Did that sound like a good enough excuse? He didn't need an excuse. "You shouldn't be alone right now, Hailey, not after everything that happened tonight."

"If it's not any trouble, I'd appreciate your input."

"Did you set the alarm system on the house?"

"I did."

"Okay. I'm going to download that car app right now

and grab a ride over. Fifteen minutes? Don't open the door to anyone else."

"Do you think I'm crazy? I wouldn't open my door to the police chief himself right now."

"Stay in that frame of mind."

Twenty minutes later, Joe bolted from the car and ran up the steps to Hailey's house. He'd texted her from the car, and she must've been watching from the upstairs window. Seconds after he rang the bell, the door swung open.

Hailey grabbed his arm and practically yanked him across the threshold. "Thank you so much. I'm jumping at every little squeak in the house."

He shut the door behind him. "Arm the system."

She reached past him to punch in the code, and he inhaled the fresh scent that matched her fresh face. Devoid of makeup, her hair pulled back, Hailey looked like a college girl—a scared college girl.

"Show me this email and video."

"My laptop's upstairs. I was just going to do a little work on a fund-raiser that my foundation is sponsoring when I tripped across the email." She hugged herself and hunched her shoulders. "I don't know how I'm going to go to sleep with the image of Andrew's poor face in my mind."

She said all of this while climbing the stairs with her head twisted over her shoulder. In her agitation, she tripped a few times, and he put out his hand to steady her so she wouldn't take him with her as she tumbled down the stairs.

He followed her into her bedroom, his gaze riveted by the sway of her hips beneath a very nonsexy pair of flannel pajamas with pink clouds on them.

She turned at the door and pointed to the laptop on the bed as if gesturing toward a rattlesnake ready to strike.

The computer sat at an angle, probably where it landed after she'd pushed it from her lap.

He sat on the edge of the bed and pulled the laptop toward him. "Is the video up?"

"It should be. I didn't close it out or turn it off." She crept up and hovered over his shoulder, one bare foot on top of the other.

Joe tapped the keyboard, and the still of a dark hallway appeared on the monitor. He clicked the arrow in the lower-left corner and watched the sickening display with a dry mouth.

Hailey had backed up and turned away before the video ended and stood across the room twisting her fingers in front of her. "What do you think?"

"These are some seriously sick people." He didn't tell Hailey he'd seen a lot worse. Of course, she'd been at that refugee center when it had been bombed. She'd seen a lot worse, too.

"Can we report this to someone?"

"The police aren't going to know what to do with it, but you can call the FBI. Do you still have the contact info of the agents who interviewed you when you got back?"

"I have their cards. I'll call them tomorrow. Do you think they can do anything?"

"They can at least touch base with their British counterparts if Andrew is in England and this occurred there. They may be able to do some computer forensics and find out where this came from."

"And why?" She crossed her arms over her midsection. "I have to know why this is happening. Why Marten? Why Andrew? Why me?"

"You all have one thing in common."

"We were all kidnapped by the terrorist group that bombed the refugee camp and destroyed the peace talks."

"And in one way or another, you all called out Major Denver as being one of them." Joe closed the video and shut the lid of the laptop, as if that could keep the horror away from Hailey. "What about the other two? Have you had any contact with Naraj and Ayala since the incident?"

"Not with Naraj. I exchanged a few emails with Ayala just to check on things at the center, send some money and tell her about the fund-raiser."

"When was the last time you heard from her?"

Hailey's dark eyes got huge in her face. "A few weeks ago."

"Did she mention anything out of the ordinary?"

"No. Should I contact her again?"

"You don't have to tell her what's going on over here. Just feel her out."

"I'll do that now." She waved a hand at the laptop. "Is the video off?"

"I closed it and the email." He opened the computer and turned around to face her. "It won't bite."

She approached the bed and dropped to her knees. Using the bed as a table, she launched her email and typed a message to Ayala. "I'm just asking her for a progress report and an accounting of the money I sent. I need that for my tax guy, anyway."

She hit the send button with a flourish. "I'd better not find out anything has happened to Ayala, or I'm going to lose it. Do you think Andrew's okay? Did those injuries look life-threatening to you? They're not going to kill him, are they?"

"Like they killed Marten?"

Covering her mouth, she sat back on her heels. "What do you want, Joe? Do they want to shut us up? We're not saying anything—at least, Andrew and I aren't saying anything."

"You don't know what Andrew has or hasn't said."

"Are you trying to tell me he also retracted his story about Denver? Someone is going to a lot of trouble to keep driving that narrative forward."

"You have no idea." Joe bent his head forward and pinched the tight muscle at the back of his neck.

Hailey braced her hands on her thighs. "It's more than us, isn't it? They have more on Denver than just a few aid workers implicating him in a bombing, don't they?"

"There's a whole framework around him." He shifted to the side and patted the bed. "Come up off the floor and have a seat."

Her gaze darted to the spot he'd indicated, and she licked her lips.

Was she afraid of him? Afraid he'd make a move. She had called him when she got the video, so she must trust him on some level—maybe just not the sitting-with-him-on-her-bed level.

He pushed off the bed and grabbed the laptop. "Where do you want this?"

"You can plug it into the charger on the nightstand." Rising, she wrapped her ponytail around her hand but still didn't sit on the bed. "I'm going to call the FBI tomorrow morning. Do you want to be there when they question me? If they question me?"

"I'm sure they will want to talk to you, but I'm not gonna be there. I don't want any government official to know I'm involved in this. I'm supposedly on leave, and I don't think my superiors would appreciate my interference."

"You're not the only one…interfering, are you? You said they have more evidence against Denver that others debunked?"

"They do, and two of my Delta Force team members were able to poke holes in that evidence, but that hasn't cleared Denver's name or changed the course of this investigation. We need names. We need motives. Right now I have no idea why anyone would want to set up Denver."

"I wish I could help you. How *can* I help you?"

Joe raised his brows at Hailey, arms folded, clutching the material of her pink-cloud pajamas. "Why do you want to help? Why do you go to places like Syria? It's dangerous. You could be playing tennis and lunching like most rich women do."

She tilted her head to the side, and her ponytail swung over her shoulder. "Is that your image of most rich women?"

"That's what they seemed to be doing in Beacon Hill all the time."

"And you know this how?"

He shrugged. "My mom used to clean house for them."

Hailey blinked. "Oh. Well, some of us do more than that. I don't even like tennis."

"You must have something driving you. Guilt?"

A pink tint crept from her neck to her face, matching her pajamas. "What does that mean?"

"I don't know. Some rich people feel guilty about being rich and then try to make up for it by doing philanthropic stuff." He jerked his thumb at her laptop on the bedside table. "Like fund-raisers and running off to dangerous countries to try to make a difference."

Hailey bit her bottom lip, her face still flushed.

"I'm sorry. That was rude." He took a turn around the bedroom. "I don't care what your motives are and they're none of my business anyway. You're obviously generous with your money *and* your time and willing to take risks to make a difference. That's more than most people do. I respect that."

"I didn't take offense." She flicked her ponytail back over her shoulder. "Crazy rich people and their money. But I really was serious about wanting to help. Why wouldn't I? Marten has been murdered. Andrew is in danger. What next?"

Joe clenched his jaw. He didn't want to scare her any more than she already was, but *she* just might be next. "Maybe the FBI can tell you when you talk to them tomorrow. I guess I should be going."

He didn't want to leave her, but he couldn't exactly invite himself to spend the night. She'd be safe here with her tricked-out alarm system and cameras.

"Should I—should I tell you what happens after I talk to them?"

"If you don't mind. I'm going to try to look into Andrew Reese on my own—at least find out what he told the army about Denver and if he had a change of heart lately."

Joe started backing out of the room, waiting for one sign from Hailey that she wanted him to stay.

"I'll call you tomorrow. Thanks so much for show-ing up tonight. That video creeped me out."

"It would creep anyone out. Do you feel okay now? Safe?"

"I do. I'm fine."

They said goodbye for the second time that night, and Joe assured Hailey that he'd call for a car when he got to the bottom of her steps.

Instead, once he hit the sidewalk, he rubbed his hands together and huddled into his jacket. He loped across the street and stationed himself on a bench bor-dering a small park with a view of the bay…and Hai-ley's house.

Hell, morning wasn't far off anyway, and if he couldn't be guarding Hailey from inside the place, he'd guard her from outside. Either way, she *did* need guard-ing. And he'd just appointed himself the man for the job.

THE NEXT MORNING Hailey woke with a start. She sat up, her heart pounding in her chest. Marten. Andrew.

She threw off the bedcovers and padded to the win-dow. As she peeked through a crack in the drapes, she saw a man with reddish hair ducking into the back seat of a car.

She curled her fingers around the material of the drapes as the car sped off. Then she blinked. That was Joe in the car. Had he tried coming over this morning?

She spun around and grabbed her laptop, plopping back down on the messy covers of the bed. She'd bet-ter get used to accessing her security footage, anyway.

She brought up the video of her front porch and scanned back through the previous half hour—noth-ing, nobody. If Joe hadn't been at her front door, what had he been doing on her block?

She fell back on her bed, the computer still resting on her thighs. What did Joe hope to accomplish? If someone embedded in the army or the government, as Joe had implied, wanted to paint Major Rex Denver as a traitor, the words of some lowly aid worker were not going to stop that train.

Huffing out a breath, she draped an arm over her forehead. Joe burned to do the right thing. She could understand that sentiment. She had the same fire.

She showered and dressed and then turned on the TV news when she got downstairs. Marten's body still hadn't been found in the bay, and authorities were beginning to question whether anyone actually went overboard or if a few passengers had overactive imaginations.

But she had Marten's hat. Her gaze darted to his familiar headgear still perched on top of the coffee table. She planned to tell the FBI everything today.

After breakfast, she placed a call to one of the agents who'd interviewed her when she returned from Syria and left a message. Avoiding the email with the video of Andrew, she returned to the work she'd planned to get done on the fund-raiser last night. When her phone rang, she jumped.

She'd programmed Joe's name and number into her phone, and seeing that name now sent a warm ribbon of relief down her spine. "Hi, Joe."

"Everything okay this morning?"

"As right as it can be with Marten presumed dead and Andrew bruised and battered probably somewhere in England."

"No more emails or late-night visits to your porch?"

She swirled her coffee in the mug. "Nobody but you."

Joe sucked in an audible breath.

"That was you this morning getting into a car, wasn't it?"

"Guilty."

"You spent the night outside my house?"

"Technically across the street from your house."

"Are you nuts? If you thought it was a good idea to keep watch over me last night, why didn't you say so? You could've spent the night on the couch or in one of the many bedrooms in this house."

"Hailey, we'd just met. I didn't want to crowd you."

"You also didn't want to worry me. You really believe I need a bodyguard?"

"A lot happened yesterday. We didn't know if they were finished warning you or not. Just playing it safe."

"Well, thanks, but now I feel guilty."

"Do you always automatically feel guilty about everything?"

Hailey clasped her hand around her cup. Joe obviously never had any reason to feel guilty about anything.

"Okay, scratch that. Not guilty, but you should've told me. You must've been freezing out there, and I could've at least offered you breakfast." Maybe she would've offered him much more than that.

"I've stood watch under worse conditions, and I had breakfast at my hotel. Did you call the FBI yet?"

Hailey let out a silent breath. Joe McVie was all business. Even if she had offered more, he probably would've turned her down. "I left a message with one of the agents. He hasn't called back yet."

"I did a little research this morning on Andrew Reese."

"Already? Did you get any sleep?"

"A little." Joe coughed and continued as if to brush

off his lack of shut-eye. "The only thing I could find on Andrew was a story he wrote about Syria for an on-line geography journal. He did report on the bombing of the refugee camp and the effect it had on the peace progress."

"Maybe that was enough to get him noticed. I'm not doing anything to get noticed."

"Are you sure? What's this fund-raiser you men-tioned?"

Hailey swallowed. "I-it's for the children of Syria affected by the civil war."

Joe's silence hung over the line between them.

"Who could object to that?" As soon as she uttered the words, she answered her own question. "The very people who indiscriminately bombed those refugees."

"Can you cancel it?"

"Cancel it? It's scheduled for this week. There's no way I can cancel. Too much work has already gone into the event—invitations sent, money spent."

"Watch your back."

"Thanks for stating the obvious." Hailey cleared her throat. "Would you like to come and watch my back for me?"

"At the fund-raiser?"

"It's just a party for rich people—food, music, danc-ing. I have to give them something for their generous donations. Your donation can be my safety."

"You want me to be your bodyguard?"

"How about my date?" She held her breath.

"A bodyguard posing as your date."

All business. "Sure, if you want to think of it that way—but the date part requires a tux."

Joe snorted. "Damn, forgot to pack one of mine."

"I can send you to my dad's tailor to get suited up. He'll do it quickly and put it on my dad's account."

"I don't—"

She cut him off. "Listen, McVie. I'm not going to pay you for this bodyguarding gig, so you might as well take what you can get—and that's a tux."

"Yes, ma'am. Where is this tailor?"

"Mission District. I'll give you the address and let Tony know as soon as we get off the phone. He'll hook you up."

"You're your father's daughter after all."

"If I were my father's daughter, you'd be paying for the tux and thanking me for it."

As soon as she ended the call with Joe, she placed one to Tony, her father's longtime tailor, and gave him the heads-up on Joe. Then she returned to her laptop, flexing her fingers before launching her email. She didn't need any more surprises this morning.

Sucking in her bottom lip, she scrolled through the new messages. When she reached the end, she slumped against the sofa cushion. No more torture videos.

She picked out the message from last night and wrinkled her nose. The little paper clip indicating an attachment had disappeared from the email icon.

With a sweaty palm, she grasped the mouse and double clicked on the message—nothing in the body and no attachment.

Had she deleted it by accident? Her pulse racing, she searched her deleted items and then all the videos on her laptop. Not that she wanted to see Andrew's battered face again, but she needed some evidence to show the FBI.

She pushed the computer from her lap and jumped

up from the couch. How had they done that? How had they gotten into her computer and removed a file?

She jerked as her phone rang, and then she lunged for it. When she saw the FBI's number on the display, she blew out a breath.

"Ms. Duvall? This is Agent Porter returning your call."

Hailey's gaze shifted to the laptop abandoned on the couch. "I need to meet with you—today."

"Is this regarding the incident at the refugee camp?"

Hailey squeezed her eyes closed for a second. "I think so. Did you hear about the man who fell off the Alcatraz ferry last night?"

Porter paused for two heartbeats. "Let's not discuss this on the phone. We'll meet you this afternoon."

"Now. We need to meet now."

"Name a place close to the Financial District and we'll be there."

"Do you know Caffé Luce on Columbus?"

"We'll be there in thirty minutes."

Hailey placed a call to Joe and put her phone on speaker as she scrambled around the room, stuffing her laptop in its case and her feet into a pair of boots.

Joe answered after several rings. "Are you checking up on me? I'll be heading out to Tony the tailor's in a few hours."

"It's not that. The video from last night showing Andrew is gone. Someone deleted it from my computer remotely—at least I hope it was remotely—and I'm on my way to a meeting with the FBI."

Joe whistled. "At their offices downtown?"

"No, we're meeting at Caffé Luce in Little Italy."

"You won't have anything to show them."

"No, but I'll have plenty to tell them."

"I don't have to ask you not to say anything about me, do I?"

"Don't worry, but I am going to tell them about Marten last night and the video. I mean, they have to be connected, right? Why would anyone care about what happened in Syria? It happened. The terrorists were successful. Why revisit it now?"

"Because there are elements about that incident that someone doesn't want revealed."

"I know. I know. Major Denver's involvement—or rather, noninvolvement."

"Get to your meeting. I'll get fitted for my tux."

"I'm going to tell them everything—except about your presence here."

"You should. Keep me posted."

"Lunch later?"

"Yeah, a debriefing."

Debriefing? Joe was determined to keep their…relationship on neutral territory. "Yeah, whatever. And, Joe?"

"Yes?"

"No velvet on the tux."

She ended the call and strapped a purse across her body. She didn't have enough time to catch public transportation, and she had no intention of driving and trying to find a place to park, so she called up a car on her phone.

Fifteen minutes later, she stepped out of the car and jogged across the street to Caffè Luce. One look around the half-empty coffeehouse, crowded with small tables, told her she was a little early.

She ordered a cappuccino and cupped the big mug in her hands as she carried it to a table outside. She set it down and dragged a wrought-iron chair from another table to hers. Agent Porter had mentioned that *they* were going to meet her. FBI agents usually traveled in pairs, so he must be bringing his sidekick, Agent Winston.

Two suits with matching Ray-Bans hustled up the sidewalk, and Hailey lifted her hand to Agent Porter. She'd discovered the man had played football at Stanford, and he still carried himself like an athlete.

The two agents stopped at her table, and Porter said, "We'll go inside to get some coffee. Do you want a refill?"

She tapped her cup. "All set."

Hailey watched the thin crowd on the sidewalk—too late for morning rush hour and too early for lunch…also known as debriefing, according to Joe McVie.

Her head jerked up at the squeal from a car's tires, and her eyes narrowed behind her sunglasses as she watched some idiot making a U-turn where six streets intersected. The car continued to careen down the street and swerved sharply.

Hailey's heart slammed against her chest as the car leaped the curb, one set of its wheels on the sidewalk.

The out-of-control driver plowed through some foliage and knocked over a wooden sign, and still he kept coming straight toward the tables on the sidewalk…straight for her.

Chapter Five

Joe's legs were pumping before the car even hit the sidewalk. By the time he made it to the other side of the street, several tables had been knocked on their sides, their spindly legs pointing at the sky.

Hailey, wide-eyed and white-faced, had plastered herself against the side of the building, debris from the wreckage at her feet.

The blue sedan that had jumped the curb squealed in Reverse, and Joe threw himself at the hood. The driver punched the accelerator. The car disappeared from beneath him, and Joe landed on the sidewalk in a belly flop, the smell of burning rubber and exhaust scorching his lungs.

"Joe!" A hand grabbed the back of his shirt and practically ripped it off him.

He rolled to his side and squinted up at Hailey looming over him, her sunglasses shoved to the top of her head.

"Are you crazy? He could've run you over."

"Did you get a license number?" He scrambled to his feet, smacking his hands together to dislodge the grit embedded in his palms.

"It's running through my head right now." Hailey held up one incredibly steady finger. "Wait."

As she dashed inside the coffeehouse, sirens wailed down the street, and the two FBI agents Hailey was meeting hovered over the scene.

They wouldn't recognize him, would they? He'd never met them before, but he could bet they'd know his name and his connection with Major Denver. Joe ducked his head.

Hailey rushed back to the sidewalk, waving a white napkin with not a hint of surrender on her face. "I have it. I have the license plate."

The two agents approached her, and the tall African American spoke first. "Are you all right? Did a car come up on the sidewalk? From inside it sounded like an explosion."

Hailey's gaze darted from the agent in front of her to Joe. He shook his head once.

"Yeah, the car jumped the curb, and I know why."

The agent's eyes bugged out from their sockets. "You think it was deliberate?"

In a harsh whisper just loud enough for Joe to hear several feet away, she said, "Someone was trying to stop our meeting, trying to stop me."

The agent lifted his shoulders. "Ms. Duvall, nobody knows about this meeting."

"I wouldn't count on that." She flicked the napkin in his face. "I got the car's license number, and I'm giving it to the police."

The agents hadn't noticed him, so Joe busied himself with brushing off his jeans and then helping the store's employees right the tables and chairs.

A cop car pulled up to the curb, and an officer stepped out. Before the cop could get one word out of his mouth, Hailey rushed up to him with her napkin.

"I got the license plate."

"Slow down." He plucked the napkin from her fingers. "What happened here?"

Hailey launched into her description of the events and jabbed her finger at the napkin in the officer's hand when she reached the end of her narrative. "That's the license number of the car, a blue four-door sedan."

"Nobody was hurt?"

"I was the only one sitting outside, and the car didn't reach the building."

"Did the driver lose control of the car? Did he ever get out of the vehicle?"

"It was a hit-and-run. He rammed the tables, backed up and took off." Hailey licked her lips and flicked a gaze at Joe. "It might have been deliberate. I was here to meet with a couple of FBI agents about…another matter."

The officer raised his brows as the agents crowded Joe and Hailey.

"Ms. Duvall, we'd like to talk to the officer privately for a few moments. We'd still like to hear what you have to say. Can you meet us inside? All this—" the agent swept his arm across the scene "—hasn't scared you off, has it?"

"Absolutely not." She charged past the agents and into the coffeehouse.

Joe followed, hot on her heels, and leaned over her shoulder at the counter as she ordered another cappuccino. "Add a black coffee to go to that order and I'll pay for both."

Hailey cranked her head around. "Are you okay after that stunt you pulled?"

"Stunt? I was trying to stop the car. I figured I could drag the guy out and get some answers from him."

"Looked like he was ready to drag you down the

street under his wheels. We'll leave it up to the police to get answers."

"Do you really think that car is going to come back to the person who tried to interrupt your meeting with the FBI?"

Her cheeks flushed, and she flicked her bangs from her eyes. "So you believe me?"

"Oh, yeah. That was a warning. Would he have done that with the FBI agents sitting next to you? I'm not sure about that, but he saw an opportunity and took it."

"Someone must be following me." Her gaze tracked over his shoulder and scanned the street behind him. "Do they really think that's going to scare me off?"

"I'm sure it would do the trick for anyone else." Hearing the agents' voices, Joe put his finger to his lips as he reached past her and grabbed his coffee. "Remember, keep my name out of this."

She shot a glance at the two Fibbies coming through the door. "Got it."

Raising the cup to his lips, he whispered through the steam, "Meet me at the tailor's shop when you're done."

She nodded and then lifted her chin toward the two agents. "Table by the window?"

Joe slipped out of the coffeehouse and sipped from his cup as he leaned against the pole listing the schedule at the bus stop.

Hailey would have quite a story to tell those agents, but would they believe her with no proof? And could they protect her, or would that be up to him?

AN HOUR LATER Hailey yanked open the door of the tailor her father had used for almost thirty years and tripped to a stop. A dapper man in a black tux tugged on the cuffs of his shirt and did a half turn in front of the mirror.

"Are you sure this slim fit is the thing?"

"It's made for a build like yours, sir."

Hailey dabbed the corner of her mouth to make sure no drool had escaped and then strode across the floor of the small shop.

"Working your magic, Tony?"

"He's got the physique this particular designer had in mind when he created this tux."

Joe shrugged out of the jacket. "Tony doesn't have anything cheap in here, but you probably know that."

"Don't worry about it. I told you this is your payment. After you sit through that boring evening, you're going to understand that I'm coming out ahead in this deal."

"How'd the meeting go?"

"I'll tell you over lunch." She ran a hand across a rack of jackets, the silky material sliding through her fingers. "Are you almost done with him, Tony?"

"I will return him to you as soon as he picks out a vest, and then he's all yours."

Hailey's mouth watered at the prospect of Joe McVie being all hers.

Joe unbuttoned his pants, and her mouth watered even more.

"I'm done. Maybe Hailey will do the honors and pick out something for me while I get dressed. I trust her taste a lot more than mine." He retreated behind the dressing room curtain.

"He's lying, you know." Tony winked as he gathered his tape measure and pins.

"About?" Wouldn't be the first time or the last a man lied to her.

"Joe has impeccable taste."

"Then I'd better do him justice." Hailey selected a

black vest for Joe. He didn't need any colors or gimmicks to show off. The man could shine wearing nothing but his skivvies—and she might even pay to see that.

She signed off on the purchase just as Joe made his way out of the dressing room, the slacks and shirt draped over one arm.

He dropped them on the counter, and Hailey shoved them toward Tony. "Joe told you this was a rush job, didn't he?"

"He did. Good thing he mentioned your name before he said he wanted it in a hurry or I would've told him to hit the bricks."

She squeezed Tony's arm. "Now you're the liar. You'd never tell a customer to get lost, but I appreciate your service, Tony."

As she and Joe stepped through the door, Tony called after her, "Give my best to your father."

"Will do." She waved behind her.

Joe took her arm. "Back to business."

"And lunch. Chinese? We can walk to Chinatown from here."

"I could use some fresh air."

Hailey kept the conversation casual as they strolled to Chinatown, and Joe didn't seem to mind the chitchat after all his talk about business. Why was he so afraid to mix a little pleasure with their work?

They joined the hustle and bustle of Chinatown, the sights, smells and sounds putting an end to any communication between them except for the occasional jab in the ribs or a pointing finger.

When Hailey spotted Superior Best, her favorite Chinese restaurant, she tugged on Joe's sleeve and leaned in close. "We're eating there."

They cut sideways through the crowd and ducked into the dark embrace of the restaurant.

Lottie Chu, matriarch of the Chu family and its businesses, greeted Hailey with a spark in her dark eyes and a curt nod. "Table for two, Hailey?"

"Yes, please, Lottie. This is my…friend Joe."

Lottie clasped the ornate menus to her chest, drumming her fingernails on the embossed covers and narrowing her eyes. "You a good friend to Hailey, Joe?"

"I think I've been a good friend so far, but you'll have to ask Hailey."

Hailey rolled her eyes. "Joe's a good guy, Lottie. Can we please sit down now?"

The old woman hunched her thin shoulders and led them to a table in the back of the room. She smacked the menus on the table. "Sit. Good table for good guy."

When Lottie turned and scurried to the front door to intercept a family of tourists, Joe pulled out Hailey's chair and swiped the back of his hand across his brow. "Whew. I'm glad I sort of passed that test."

"I've known Lottie for years." Hailey turned over her teacup and whipped the napkin into her lap. "My father used to take me here when I was a little girl, and Lottie has gotten somewhat protective over the years."

"Yeah, just a little. She seemed ready to bite my head off, though she doesn't even look five feet tall."

"She's not, but don't let her size fool you." Hailey thanked the waiter for the tea and held the pot over Joe's cup. "Tea?"

"Sure."

She shoved one of the heavy menus toward him. "Any preferences?"

"I'll let you do the honors—just no octopus or anything else I can't identify on my plate."

"I'll stick to chicken, beef and pork."

When the waiter returned, Hailey ordered some safe dishes and then picked up her teacup and inhaled the light scent of the green tea before taking a sip. "The car was stolen."

"Figures." Joe slammed the cup back into the saucer, and his tea sloshed into the saucer.

"That license plate I was so proud of identifying? It came back to a stolen car from San Jose. One of the officers told us that while we were still at the coffeehouse."

"That doesn't surprise me." Joe dragged the napkin from his lap and wiped the tea from his hand. "Were there any cameras? Did the coffeehouse or any of the other businesses have cameras on the street?"

"They did, and the police may or may not look at that footage."

"You're telling me they're not taking this very seriously."

"That's right—a single-car accident, he didn't injure anyone and the damage was minimal, even though it was a hit-and-run." She clinked her cup back into the saucer. "I thought they might at least want to recover the stolen car, but I guess it's not a high priority right now. I also suggested that the guy might be a terrorist just to light a fire under them, but since the sidewalk was mostly empty—except for me—the police didn't buy that theory."

"And the FBI? Did the agents believe it might be someone trying to stop your meeting with them?"

She wrinkled her nose. "They didn't discount that idea, but I guess they would've been more convinced if I'd wound up dead."

"Too bad you had to disappoint them." He drained

the small teacup, which looked like a thimble in his hand. "You told them about Marten and Andrew?"

"I did, but there's still no proof Marten was ever on that ferry, and they're not interested in his black hat. There's not even any proof that someone went overboard."

"And you don't have that video with Andrew to show them."

She smacked the edge of the table with her fingertips. "I should've sent it to them as soon as I received it. I should've sent it to you."

"You had no idea someone would wipe it clean from your computer, but I should've thought of that and had you send it to me."

"I had no idea that was even a thing." She smiled at the waiter as he rolled a cart up to their table with a host of covered dishes.

Joe's eyes widened. "Is there an army you plan to feed when we're done?"

"I thought you might be hungry after all the excitement today." She rubbed her hands together as the Szechuan spices tickled her nose. "I know I am."

"I took you for one of those women who eat a stalk of celery and one cracker and call it a day."

"Ah, the narcissistic socialite type you ran into on Beacon Hill." She dug into the kung pao chicken and ladled it over her steamed rice. "Should I be offended?"

"I know damn well you're not a narcissistic socialite. No socialite I know would put herself in danger to help others halfway around the world."

"Know many socialites other than the ones your mom worked for?"

"Um, not really." He sucked some sauce off the

edge of his thumb. "But now you're the gold standard of all socialites."

Heat rose to her cheeks and she hadn't even sampled the spicy entrées yet. "Anyway, I'm tall and naturally skinny, and I do like running up and down these hills in the city."

Joe cleared his throat and dipped his chin to his chest, as if he'd just become aware that their banter had veered toward the personal and she'd given him too much information.

"So, the agents didn't believe you." Joe scrutinized his forkful of food before putting it in his mouth.

"I wouldn't say that, but without any proof that someone is offing the aid workers who were duped into bombing the refugee camp, there's not much they can do. You know how it goes."

"Nobody brought up my name, did they?"

"You don't trust me?" She pinched a piece of chicken between her chopsticks.

"I trust you. I'm just curious as to whether or not I'm on their radar. I told you that two of my Delta Force team members have already delved into the mystery behind Major Denver's actions. I'm wondering if the FBI or CIA has started connecting the dots yet."

"There are dots to connect? Is this a planned and concerted investigation?"

"Planned and concerted?" Joe shook his head. "Try haphazard and blundering, but we're all committed to doing our part to look into what we know is a setup. Denver would do no less for one of us."

"Nobody mentioned your name or Denver's. I told them I thought someone was trying to keep the four of us quiet, starting with Marten and continuing with

Andrew and even taking a chance on me right before the meeting."

"Speaking of the four of you, have you heard back from the nurse yet?"

"Not yet." Hailey checked her phone just to make sure Ayala hadn't sent her an email in the past hour.

"Did you offer any suggestions for the motive behind these attacks?"

"I did not, and the agents wondered the same. While they didn't dismiss my fears out of hand, they did question why someone would want to muzzle us."

"After what my two teammates discovered about Denver so far, I would've thought they might put two and two together. But that would require them to think outside the box and to entertain the idea that someone on the inside—CIA, DoD, the army or maybe even their own agency—has some kind of vendetta against Denver."

"I can tell you right now, that's not how they're thinking." She aimed a chopstick at his plate. "Do you like the food?"

"It's great—better with this." He held up his fork. "Gets the food to my stomach faster than chopsticks."

"I knew you'd be hungry." She placed her chopsticks across the edge of her plate. "So, the FBI is no use, although the agents did say they'd look into Andrew's whereabouts."

"And Marten's? They could start with his phone. Did you tell them someone texted you from Marten's phone after the ferry incident?"

"They're going to put in an order to ping his phone."

"Have you tried texting the phone since the time right after the incident on the ferry?"

"I've texted him a few times, but there's been no response, and they don't look like they're being delivered."

"More tea, Hailey?" Lottie had returned to the table with the check on a tray with some fortune cookies. She placed the tray firmly in front of Joe.

Hailey covered her smile with her hand. "None for me. Lunch was delicious as usual. You could send the waiter back here with some to-go boxes, though."

Lottie raised her hand over her head and snapped her fingers. "Danny. Boxes over here."

Joe made a show of grabbing the check and taking out his wallet.

Lottie looked down her nose and pursed her lips into a smile. "Good guy. You keep, Hailey."

Laughing, Hailey shook her head at Joe, whose face almost matched the red wallpaper in the restaurant, which was a couple of shades brighter than his hair. "He's not mine to keep, Lottie."

"Maybe you see it in fortune." Lottie tapped the tray, and the fortune cookies jumped.

When Lottie scurried away to another table, Joe held up a twenty-dollar bill. "Do you think this is a big enough tip? Lottie scares me."

"She's just toying with us. She likes to play the role of tiger mom for the tourists, but she's actually an extremely astute and modern businesswoman. Her son and daughter run the family's financial empire now, but Lottie is the one who grew it."

"I can believe that."

Danny, clearly in awe of Lottie himself, not only brought over the to-go containers, but he filled them up with their leftovers. Once he'd bagged them, Joe handed him the check along with several bills.

Hailey wiggled her fingers over the cookies. "I love

fortune cookies. Superior Best gets theirs from the fortune cookie factory around the corner, so they're super fresh."

Joe snatched one of the cookies from beneath her fingers and cracked it open. "Ah, but are they accurate?"

"Well?" She tapped a chopstick against Joe's teacup. "What does yours say?"

His eyes widened, and he twisted his head around to track Lottie's flitting progress across the restaurant. "She planted this."

"Not possible. C'mon, out with it."

Pinching the little slip of paper between his thumb and forefinger, he read aloud. "'You will meet a dark-haired beauty. Take a chance.'"

"No! You're lying." She snatched the fortune from his fingers and held it up to her face. The exact words he'd just read danced before her eyes. "I wouldn't put it past Lottie, but I don't see how she could've managed that. I could've picked that one."

"Could've gone either way." Joe batted his eyelashes at her. "Are you implying I'm no dark-haired beauty?"

"It didn't say dark *red*." She crumpled up the piece of paper and threw it at him.

He caught it and closed his fist around it. "Let's see what yours is, and then we'll know for sure if Lottie tampered with the fortunes."

With a smile playing about her lips, Hailey broke the remaining cookie in two and pulled the slip of paper from one half. As she read the words, her mouth twisted, killing her smile.

"What's wrong?"

"It's just one of those stupid, generic fortunes that could apply to anyone." She dropped the fortune as if it scorched her fingertips.

"No tall red-haired strangers in your future?" Joe swept up the piece of paper, a frown creasing his brow.

He read this one aloud, too, but he didn't have to. Hailey had already memorized it.

"'Be on the lookout for coming events. They cast their shadows beforehand.'" He dropped the fortune, and it floated to the table. "You're right—just silliness. I guess Lottie didn't rig the cookies."

"Coming events casting shadows? That sounds ominous." She flicked the piece of paper away from her—the farther, the better.

"Hailey." He entwined his fingers with hers. "Those are printed words someone baked into a cookie around the corner."

"Yeah, I know that." She bit into the cookie, catching a shower of crumbs with her hand. "I just don't think I've ever gotten a serious fortune like that one before."

"I get those all the time." He smoothed out his own fortune with his thumb. "It's the sexy ones like this I never get."

She cracked a smile, feeling like an idiot. She may have a lot of problems right now, but a warning from a cookie wasn't one of them.

Her phone buzzed, and as she reached for it, she noticed Joe folding his fortune and slipping it into his wallet. He'd probably done that to make her feel better.

Uneasiness fluttered in her belly as she glanced at her phone's display. "I don't know what this number is, but it's local. Hello?"

A man's voice answered, his words carrying a slight accent. "Is this Hailey Duvall?"

"Yes, it is. Who's this?" She shrugged her shoulders at Joe's raised eyebrows.

"My name is Joost Palstra. I'm a friend of Marten's."

Hailey gripped the phone tighter. "Have you seen Marten lately? We were supposed to get together and he never showed."

Joe tapped the leg of her chair with his foot and she held up her finger.

"I saw Marten yesterday afternoon. He was staying with me. That's why I'm calling. He took off, but he left some stuff here."

"D-did he tell you he was going somewhere?"

"You know Marten, sketchy on the details. Anyway, he did ask me to call you if he didn't return, so I'm doing that, but I'm thinking his disappearance might be related to his gambling."

Hailey's heart stuttered. "What makes you think that?"

"He has a lot of people looking for him all of a sudden—and they don't look like the type of guys you want to disappoint."

Chapter Six

Hailey's eyes grew round, and she put one hand over her heart.

Joe shoved a napkin and pen toward her and tapped on the napkin with his fingertip.

As she continued to talk to Marten's friend, she scribbled on the napkin.

Joe squinted at the words she'd written—*people looking for Marten*—and cocked his head. If they'd killed him, why would they be looking for him?

Before he could write a question back, Hailey ended the conversation on the phone.

Snatching the napkin back, she said, "Marten had been staying with Joost and told him to call me if he didn't return, but now people are looking for Marten."

"Wait." Joe held up his hands. "Is this guy at a hotel?"

"A hotel? No." Hailey looked up, pen poised above the napkin. "Why do you think that?"

"Don't forget, I followed Marten from the airport. He went to a hotel in some ritzy area of the city—Nob Hill, I think. That's how I tracked him to the Alcatraz ferry last night. He wasn't staying with anyone." He leveled a finger at her phone. "How do you know this guy is legit and not trying to lure you into a trap?"

"Marten has mentioned this friend before, and why

would he warn me about unsavory characters searching for Marten if he *were* an unsavory character?"

"Maybe to gain your trust. Does this Joost know who these people are?"

She wrote an address on the back of the napkin. "Nope, just that they're pretty shady looking."

"Joost…" He stopped and scratched his chin. "What kinda name is Joost, anyway?"

"He's Dutch, like Marten. Has a very slight accent."

"So… Joost didn't think there was anything strange about Marten not returning to his place?"

"Marten warned him that he might be taking off at any time and told him if he did, he was supposed to call me."

"And tell you what?"

"That he wants me to pick up whatever Marten left behind." Hailey's gaze had locked onto her crumpled fortune on the table. "Joost wants me to come by and get Marten's stuff."

"From your side of the conversation, I gather you're going to pick it up now at Joost's place?"

"Of course. Whatever Marten left for me might contain a clue or something as to what he was doing here and why he wanted to see me."

"You're not going alone." He jerked his thumb over his shoulder at the plate-glass windows overlooking the chaos of Chinatown. "There still might be someone following you, although I kept a close watch on the way over here."

She put a hand over her mouth. "You were watching to see if we had a tail? I didn't even notice. Why didn't you let me in on it?"

"And make it obvious that I was on the lookout? We weren't followed here, and we're not going to be followed to Joost's." He gulped down some water and put the glass on top of the fortune that had spooked Hailey. "Where does he live and how do we get there?"

"He's in the Sunset District. We'll need a car to get there." Hailey picked up the bag containing their left-over food and swung it from her fingers. "I suppose I can't lug this around the city."

"We can have the car make a stop at your place and put it in the fridge. Then we can pick up your car at the same time."

"That's okay. I don't want to drive over, and I know how to make good use of the food without throwing it away." She pointed to the cell phone in his hand. "You want to order a car on that app? Have him pick us up two blocks down so he doesn't have to drive into this mess."

"Sure." While he tapped his phone, Hailey spoke with Lottie and put something in the bag with the food.

On the way out the door, Joe waved to Lottie, who gave him a secret smile. She *had* planted that fortune, and he just might follow its advice.

They meandered down the sidewalk, their pace slowed by the tourists ducking in and out of the shops and restaurants that lined the streets.

When they reached the end of Chinatown, Hailey tapped his arm. "Hang on. I'll be right back."

He watched her walk, her long stride eating up the pavement beneath her feet, the plastic bag banging against her leg. When she reached a small park, she cut in toward a set of benches where a couple of home-less guys were lounging. She held out the bag to the man on the first bench, said a few words and spun around, heading back toward him.

Joe mumbled under his breath, "Do-gooder."

Hailey reached him seconds before their car pulled

up to the curb. He got the door for her, and as she slid onto the back seat, he asked, "Do you do that often?"

"Give my leftovers to the homeless? When it's convenient for me to do so, like today."

"Yeah, right. Don't downplay your charitable heart." He squeezed her knee. "I told you, I'm impressed as hell."

The driver twisted his head over his shoulder. "How are you folks doing today? Sunset?"

"Yes." Hailey pulled the napkin from her pocket and rattled off Joost's address. Then she turned to Joe. "I hope he's there before we are. He was on his way home."

"We'll wait for him outside. At least it's not raining."

The driver sped up and down the hilly streets until they reached wider roads with more suburban-type housing.

Joe pressed his hand against the window. "This is different."

"This area's a little more residential. Joost lives in the garage apartment of a house. He told me to go around the side of the house for his front door. There are a lot of rentals like that here—cheaper."

The driver pulled up to a light blue clapboard house with a motorcycle parked on one side of the driveway.

They exited the car and circled around to the side of the house.

"That's it." Hailey gestured toward a sliding glass door. "That's his front door."

"What do we do? Knock on the glass?" Joe stepped up to the slider, and something crunched under his feet.

He lifted his right foot and stirred the broken glass with the toe of his shoe. "What's this?"

"Joe." Hailey was bending over, her face close to the glass door. "Look."

He zeroed in on her fingertip and saw a square of glass cut out from the door near the handle. He whistled. "Looks like Joost's place has been burglarized."

He stuck his finger through the hole and was able to flick down the lock on the door. "How thoughtful. The thief locked up after himself."

"Maybe he was hoping Joost wouldn't notice, or maybe Joost is the one who locked it after he got home." Hailey rapped on the glass and called out. "Joost? It's Hailey Duvall. Are you home?"

Joe cocked his head, listening for a response. Then he kicked the glass out of the way and said, "Nope, the burglars locked up after they did their business."

Joe had already unlocked the door from the inside, so he grabbed the handle to yank open the slider.

Hailey put her hand on his arm. "What are you doing?"

"I'm going to see what happened to Joost's place. If we're lucky, the thieves will still be here and I can get some answers out of them."

"Is that always your first response?" Hailey wedged one hand on her slim hip. "That's what motivated you to jump on that car this morning, too."

"Damn straight. You can't let the bastards get away when they're under your noses." He slipped his gun out of its holster and pulled open the door. When he stepped inside, he thought he'd made a wrong turn into a computer lab. Rows of monitors blinked at him, and others displayed scrolling data.

Hailey took a slow turn around the room. "I guess the burglars weren't after computer equipment."

Joe put a finger to his lips and crept toward the bathroom, the only other room in the apartment. When he saw it was empty, he returned to the other room, where

Hailey was standing next to the door. He shook his head at her. "Nobody here."

"What were they after?" Hailey picked up an up-ended sofa cushion and dropped it. "Loose change?"

Joost's place was that of a bachelor—his living room doubled as his bedroom, and the large bed in the corner had been searched, its mattress askew, the covers ripped off and tossed aside.

Hailey traced her fingers down the spines of the books that had been pulled off the shelves and restacked, helter-skelter. Folding her arms over her chest, she turned toward him. "Are you thinking what I'm thinking?"

"That someone knew Marten was staying here and decided to look for his stuff?"

She nodded. "That about covers it."

"Then, yeah, we're on exactly the same page."

"Stop right where you are."

Joe spun around, stepping in front of Hailey and aiming his gun at the door. He stopped when he caught sight of the curly-haired blond wielding a baseball bat like Babe Ruth on steroids.

"Joost?" Hailey waved her arms. "I'm Hailey. This is my friend Joe. We just got here and saw that someone had broken into your place."

The Dutchman tightened his grip on the bat and then dropped it and rushed to the bank of computers, jabbering in what had to be Dutch.

Joe cleared his throat. "Doesn't look like those have been touched."

"I hope not. I have about a year's worth of work for this one customer cranking away on these computers."

"Your books, your bed, every other piece of furniture, however, suffered a good going-over." Hailey flung out one arm to encompass the disheveled room.

Joost pushed the curls from his eyes. "Good luck finding anything of value other than the computers."

Joe asked, "Is there anything missing? Can you even tell?"

Joost surveyed the mess. "The only thing I can think of is in the bathroom. Did they ransack the bathroom, too?"

"Couldn't tell at first glance. I just poked my head in there to make sure the thieves were gone."

The bat dragging on the floor behind him, Joost loped into the bathroom and threw open the mirrored door of the medicine cabinet. He spit out an expletive, which sounded a lot more expressive in Dutch.

"They took my meds."

"Your meds?" Hailey glanced at Joe and tapped her head.

"My medication. I suffer from what you'd call social anxiety. The drugs I take for that are in high demand on the black market."

"Oh, sorry." Hailey grimaced. "Can you get them replaced?"

"I'll call my doctor."

"What about the police? Are you going to call the police?" Joe folded his arms and wedged his shoulder against the bathroom's doorjamb.

"I have to if I want my doctor to give me refills. I think I have to submit a police report or something."

Hailey nudged Joe's back. "Is there anything else missing, Joost?"

"Not that I notice." Joost hunched his rounded shoulders. "I'm just glad they didn't touch the computers."

"Don't you think that's weird?" Joe stepped back as

Joost made a move to leave the bathroom. "Thousands of dollars of computer equipment and the thief takes a couple bottles of pills?"

"He was probably a junkie. Didn't care about the computers, probably didn't have the means to move them out of here."

Joe pointed to the sliding glass door. "A junkie with burglary tools? That was a glass cutter."

"I don't know." Joost ran his hand over the top of one of his monitors in a caress. "I'll let the cops figure that out. It's not like they're going to catch him. The SFPD doesn't put much effort into catching petty criminals."

"If that's what he was." Hailey perched on the arm of a sofa covered in comic books, dumped there from the basket lying on its side next to a cushion from the same sofa.

"Why wouldn't he be?" Joost drew a pair of shaggy blond eyebrows over his nose.

Hailey tapped the toe of her boot. "Joost, we came here because you called me about Marten, told me he'd left something with you and had asked you to call me if he didn't return. Then Marten mysteriously disappears, nefarious types start looking for him and someone breaks into your place. You still think this was some junkie looking for a high?"

Joost's round face crinkled. "Marten disappeared mysteriously? He just left. He was here one day and the next day…gone. Those guys searching for him? Probably bookies. I grew up with Marten in The Hague. Marten was born mysterious, so nothing he does surprises me. Are you worried about him?"

Hailey placed her hands on her knees and hunched forward. "We were supposed to meet on the last ferry to

Alcatraz yesterday. You heard the news about someone falling or jumping from an Alcatraz ferry?"

Joost nodded, his pale blue eyes wide.

"*That* ferry." Hailey compressed her lips into a thin line.

"You think that was Marten who went overboard? Last I heard it was a hoax and nobody went over."

"I thought I saw him on the ferry that night, and he—" she jerked her thumb at Joe "—followed Marten right onto the ferry, but he never came off and I haven't heard from him since."

Joost transferred his gaze from Hailey to Joe. "Why were you following Marten?"

Joe threw up his hands. "That doesn't matter. We think he was pushed off that boat…murdered."

"That wasn't Marten. He could've survived in the bay." Joost shook a finger at Hailey. "He was half a second away from making the Olympic swim team for the Netherlands. The coast guard hasn't found a body yet."

Joe preferred the angry, bat-wielding Joost to this mellow dude who had an explanation for everything.

Hailey pressed the heel of her hand to her forehead. "I don't know if Marten is dead or alive. I don't know what happened on that ferry, but there are too many strange coincidences going on, and now your place has been burglarized minutes before I get here, ready to collect Marten's things."

"Hours."

"Excuse me?"

"I've been gone since this morning. The break-in could've happened hours ago."

"Okay, whatever." Hailey rolled her eyes at Joe.

Joe took a deep breath. "We don't know what happened to Marten, but what we do know is that someone broke into your place and you don't even know if Marten's things were stolen. Have you looked? Was his stuff in this room?"

"Things?" Joost blinked his eyes. "Did I say 'things'? It's just one thing Marten left for you in case he didn't return, and that couldn't have been stolen."

"And why is that?" Joe gritted his teeth, feeling the last bit of his patience slip away.

Joost patted his chest. "Because I have it right here with me."

HAILEY SLID OFF the arm of the sofa and collapsed against the cushion, the comic books crinkling beneath her. "Why didn't you say that to begin with?"

"I didn't realize you were concerned about what Marten left for you."

"That's why we're here." Spreading her arms wide, Hailey kicked up her feet on the messy coffee table.

Joe held out his hand. "So, what did he leave her? A note?"

"No." Joost reached into his front pocket and withdrew something pinched between his fingers. He held it up, and it caught the light from the window and winked. "A key."

"A key?" Hailey swung her legs from the table and jumped up. "A key to what?"

"I don't know." Joost bounced the key in his palm before dumping it into Joe's outstretched hand.

As Joe studied the key, Hailey sidled next to him, her hair brushing his forearm.

"Why would he leave me a key without an explanation?"

"Maybe he was afraid it would fall into the wrong

hands." Joe plucked up the key chain, a cardboard circle ringed with metal. "There's some writing on this."

Hailey squinted at the white circle as Joe held it up. "The letters are rubbed out. Looks like an *M, I, S…* Trust Marten to leave me a clue that needs another clue to figure it out."

"Born mysterious." Joost tapped the side of his nose. "That label had something written on it in pencil. I may have rubbed it off with a sweaty thumb, or maybe Marten did."

Joe ground his back teeth. "Did mysterious Marten tell you anything about this key, like maybe what it unlocked?"

"Marten told me nothing. He called last-minute, asked if he could crash at my place for a few days, didn't bring any luggage with him, and I barely saw him. Yesterday morning, he gave me that key and told me to give it to Hailey if he didn't return. He didn't return, and I called Hailey at the number he gave me." Joost held up his hands. "That's all I know. I'm sure Marten is fine. He has nine lives, like a cat."

"Cats don't swim." Hailey hitched her bag over her shoulder. "You have my number. Let me know if you happen to hear from Marten."

"At least you have the key." Joost had turned to face his precious computers, his duty to Marten done.

Joe dangled the key from its key chain. "Yeah, a key to nowhere for Miss Nobody."

"If I remember anything, I'll call you."

Joe snapped his fingers. "Did he tell you he also had a hotel room? Maybe that's why he didn't have any luggage with him."

"Didn't say anything about a hotel. Maybe he's holed up there to escape his gambling debts."

"Thanks, Joost." Hailey made a face at Joe and pointed to the sliding door with the square hole in the glass that Joost didn't seem very concerned about.

They stepped outside, and Hailey swung around to face him, her eyes throwing sparks. "Why would Marten leave me a key and not tell me what it's supposed to unlock?"

"Maybe the name on the key chain would've told you if Joost hadn't rubbed it off with his sweaty thumb."

"I'm not sure about that. Really, when was the last time you ever referred to anyone as Miss? Most people, including Marten, use Ms."

Joe used Miss a lot, but he probably shouldn't let Hailey in on that. "Maybe it's like one of those schools, like Miss Watson's School for Wayward Boys."

Hailey punched him in the arm, and he tightened his bicep.

"Is that the one you went to?" She rubbed her knuckles.

"Close to it." He twisted his lips into a smile. "Are you ready to go home?"

"I'm ready to locate the owner of this key. What do you think Marten left for me?"

"Maybe the retraction of his statement to the CIA regarding Denver's involvement in the Syria bombing, or whatever it was he was going to tell you at your meeting. Sounds like he had a feeling he'd never make it to the meeting."

Hailey bit her bottom lip as she put a hand on his arm. "Would you mind coming back to my place with me? Maybe we can figure out this key thing together."

"I was going to suggest the same thing." He didn't mean to scare her to get the invitation, but that seemed to be the effect of his words.

"I'll order a car." She dug into her purse and pulled out her phone. "Looks like I missed a call from Agent Porter."

"Do you want to call him back while we wait for the car?"

"He left a voice mail." She tapped her phone and listened with the tip of her tongue lodged in the corner of her mouth. She shook her head at him and mouthed, "Nothing."

When she finished listening to the voice mail, she said, "The police found the stolen car abandoned in San Jose, no prints. Agent Porter put in a request for MI6 to look into the whereabouts of Andrew. That's all they have. No news on Marten."

"Are you going to tell Porter about the key Marten left you?"

"No. I have a feeling if I gave the key to him, it would disappear into the black hole of this noninvestigation." Her eyebrows formed a V over her nose. "Unless you think I should."

"They don't know what we know, and they don't believe what I believe. They're not going to take it as seriously as I do, but I'm not going to tell you *not* to contact them with what you have and suspect."

"Suspect." She skimmed a hand through her dark hair, somehow making messy look chic. "That's the key word, isn't it? I don't even have the video of Andrew tied to that chair." She covered her eyes with one hand. "Andrew asked me for help in that video, and I haven't been able to do a damn thing."

He put a tentative hand on her back. "That's not true. Porter just said MI6 is going to track down Andrew. You're doing everything you can, Hailey."

"I did try calling him, but there's no answer and no

opportunity to leave a voice mail. I just wish I could do more."

"You can't save the world, even with all your father's money."

"I can give it a try." She pointed her phone up the street. "Our car is coming."

Twenty minutes later the car dropped them off on Pacific Avenue in front of Hailey's father's house.

Hailey trod up the stairs ahead of him, her steps heavy. Joe wanted to solve this mystery to clear Major Denver, but now he had another motive—to protect Hailey.

As they turned toward the last few steps to the porch, a woman rose from behind the bushes and raised a hand clutching a gun toward Hailey.

Joe's reflexes kicked into high gear. He threw himself between Hailey and the dark-haired woman, grabbing the woman's proffered hand and twisting it behind her back.

As the woman screamed, Hailey yelled behind him, "Joe, stop. That's Ayala."

Chapter Seven

Hailey grabbed a handful of Joe's jacket, trying to pull him off Ayala. Had he gone insane?

He stepped back, releasing his hold on her friend. "God, I'm so sorry. I thought you had a gun in your hand."

Ayala, her dark eyes wide and glassy, pointed to the rolled-up umbrella she'd dropped to the ground. "I-it's an umbrella."

"Are you all right? Did I hurt your arm?" Joe swept up the umbrella from the porch and handed it to Ayala.

Ayala smoothed one hand over her skirt, shooting a gaze at Hailey over Joe's broad shoulder. "I'm fine."

Hailey scooted around Joe and hugged the nurse. "I'm so sorry, Ayala. What are you doing here?"

"Heard you were having a fund-raiser. How could I miss it?" Her eyes shifted toward Joe as she folded her arms, clamping her umbrella to her chest.

"I thought you couldn't make it, but I'm glad you did. I sent you an email yesterday. Did you get it?"

"I'm sorry. I just have my cell phone with me, and I hate reading emails on my phone. Wh-who's your friend?"

"Ayala, this is Joe McVie. Joe, this is Ayala Khan, the nurse who worked with me at the refugee camp."

Joe stuck out his hand. "Nice to meet you. I feel like an idiot."

Ayala's lips turned up in a quick smile as she clasped Joe's hand briefly with her own and then shoved hers in the pocket of her coat. "I'm fine, really, even though it's not the greeting I expected."

"Of course not." Hailey chuckled. "We're a little on edge here."

Joe poked Hailey in the back, and she straightened her shoulders. Did he think she was going to keep all of this from someone who could be in the direct line of fire? "Come on in, Ayala. How long have you been waiting out here and why didn't you call me?"

"It was all last-minute. I went home to Florida first, and I wanted to surprise you. I didn't realize what a stupid idea that was until I landed on your porch and you didn't answer the door."

"But you knew I'd be in town because of the gala." Hailey pushed open the front door and ushered Ayala inside while scowling at Joe.

He made his fingers into a gun and placed his index finger against his temple before scooping up Ayala's bags and following them into the house.

"Can I get you something to drink? Water? Juice? Tea?"

Ayala tilted her head back and spun around the room. "Wow, this is some place you have here."

"Full disclosure." Hailey held up two fingers. "Not mine."

"I know it's your father's. Still, it's a fancy place to crash." Ayala waved her hands. "Not that I'm crashing here. I was just getting ready to call a few hotels when you came home."

"Don't be ridiculous. The house is huge. I think I can find a spare bedroom or two for you to occupy."

"I don't want to—" Ayala nodded at Joe, who was stacking her bags in the corner of the room "—intrude."

"Joe's just a friend. He's staying at a hotel." She didn't even sound convincing to her own ears.

Joe finally finished his task, which he'd obviously drawn out to give her and Ayala a chance to talk, and brushed his hands together. "Did I hear my name? Not calling the cops on me, are you?"

"Oh, please. It's already forgotten." Ayala tipped her head to one side. "It's clear you were trying to protect Hailey. Does she need it?"

Hailey cleared her throat. "How about that tea?"

"Thanks. I'd like some." Ayala patted her purse. "I can also get on the phone to a hotel and book myself a room."

"Don't say another word about that. We'll work out a fair trade." Hailey flicked her fingers in Joe's direction. "Just ask Joe about that."

"Uh-oh. What am I getting myself into?" Ayala's gaze darted between her and Joe.

"You always speak so passionately on behalf of the refugees." Hailey made a move toward the kitchen and crooked her finger at Ayala. "I'm hoping you can give a speech at the fund-raiser. Nothing long, just a little recap of the work you do there."

Ayala trailed after her into the kitchen. "You mean the work *you* do. It's money from people like you and your guests that keep things moving there. Don't expect me to stand up and toot my own horn."

"Anything you want to say, just talk about the work that needs to be done to get them to open their wallets and checkbooks." Hailey reached into the cupboard for two cups and called into the other room, "Joe, would you like some tea?"

"I'm all tea-ed out, thanks."

Ayala sidled up next to Hailey at the counter and nudged her with a sharp elbow. "If he's not taken, do you mind if I try my luck? He's hot."

"Oh." Speaking of hot, Hailey's cheeks flamed. "Y-you— Sure, if you want."

Ayala raised one dark brow. "So that's how it is. You're not fooling me, Hailey Duvall. You might be calling him a friend today, but you want more tomorrow. Am I right?"

"Well, you said it." Hailey winked. "He *is* hot."

"Where and how did you meet him? Is he military?"

"How'd you guess that?" Hailey shoved the teakettle beneath the faucet and filled it half-full.

"The way he carries himself, his clipped manner of speaking. Don't forget, I've been around plenty of American servicemen."

"He's Delta Force."

Ayala's eyes flickered.

Did she remember that Major Denver was Delta Force?

"Is he someone you met in Syria?"

"No." Hailey cranked on the burner and then turned to face Ayala, taking her arm. "We'll explain everything to you—together. It's been a crazy few days, and I can't tell you how happy I am to see you here."

Joe straddled a stool at the center island in the kitchen. "Maybe Ayala wants to freshen up a little."

"Great idea." Ayala drummed her fingers on the counter as she swept out of the kitchen.

Hailey hissed. "That was rude. What was that about?"

"Do you really think we should tell her everything that's been going on?"

"Why not? She's involved in it as much as I am—more, as she's still working at the refugee camp."

"Giving her knowledge could put her in danger."

Hailey jumped as the kettle whistled. She grabbed the handle and poured the boiling water over the tea bags in the two cups. "The way I see it, she's already in danger, Joe. Telling her everything just might give her a chance to stay safe. If anything happened to her and I had neglected to give her the 411 about Marten and Andrew, I'd never forgive myself."

Ayala suddenly appeared at the entrance to the kitchen. "Oh, no. Hailey has a hard time forgiving herself for a lot of imagined infractions. I wouldn't want to pile on." She perched on the stool next to Joe's, crossing one leg over the other and swinging it back and forth. "You'd better tell me everything."

Hailey placed a cup in front of Ayala. "It all started with a call from Marten de Becker."

Hailey told Ayala about everything that had gone on the past few days—except that she'd become dependent on Joe McVie as her savior and bodyguard. Ayala had already figured that out anyway.

As Hailey came to the end of her story, she fished Marten's key from the front pocket of her jeans and slid it across the counter. "Here's the key Marten's friend gave me, but I have no idea what it unlocks. Any ideas?"

Ayala picked up the key and turned it over, running her thumb over the cardboard key chain. "Mis? Could it be someone's name?"

Joe spoke up. "That's what I thought."

"It looks old." Ayala bounced the key in the palm of her hand. "What could Marten have been into? This could all just be about his shady lifestyle, his gambling, his women."

"Maybe, but what about the video of Andrew?"

Ayala shivered and tipped her hand over, dropping the key on the counter. "That's horrible. The only thing I have going for me is that I never ID'd Major Rex Denver as one of the men who held us, and I'm not writing an article about the incident."

"Is that what Andrew is doing?" Hailey wrapped her hands around the cup, warming them. "That's probably why these guys got to him. They probably don't want any further attention focused on the bombing in case Andrew brings more information to light about Denver."

"Then why you?" Ayala touched Hailey's hand. "All you did was bring up the fact that one of our kidnappers spoke French with an American accent and someone called him Denver, which I completely missed. You aren't changing that story…are you?"

"I have no reason to change it."

Joe folded his hands together and hunched forward on the counter, resting on his forearms. "We're beginning to think the people involved are tracking Hailey because Marten reached out to her—or tried to reach out to her."

"Then maybe you should just forget about Marten, Hailey. I know that sounds callous, but you can't help him now." Ayala traced the edge of the key on the counter. "Toss this out and forget about everything. If someone is framing Major Denver, let the US Army figure it out." She shot a quick glance at Joe. "Sorry."

"No need to apologize to me." Joe rubbed his knuckles across the stubble on his chin. "I agree with you. The US Army needs to be doing everything in its power to investigate the matter as a setup, and there's more and more evidence leaking out that it was a setup."

"Where *is* Denver?" Ayala raised her cup to her lips, her dark eyes watching Joe over the rim.

"Nobody knows. He went AWOL after a meeting he'd arranged with an informant went south."

"In Afghanistan?"

"Yes."

Ayala carefully wiped her lipstick from the cup with the edge of her thumb. "Maybe he's already dead."

"I don't believe that." Joe's hands curled into fists against the granite.

"Again, I'm sorry. I know you're concerned about your Delta Force commander, but I'm concerned about my friend."

"I'm concerned about Hailey, too. I don't want her mixed up with this, and I'm not expecting her to go to bat for Denver."

Hailey waved. "Hello. I'm standing right here. Neither one of you needs to be worried about me. And I'm not going to forget about Marten, Andrew, Denver or any of them."

Joe's and Ayala's eyes met, and they said in unison, "Do-gooder."

"Now you're ganging up on me, but I'm serious." She put her cup in the sink and turned toward Ayala. "Do you want more tea, or would you like to get settled in a room upstairs?"

"If you're sure I'm not putting you out."

"Are you prepared to say a few words at the fundraiser?" Hailey held her breath. Ayala could be such an asset at this event, but she was shy.

"I'd be happy to talk *briefly*."

Hailey clapped her hands. "Then make yourself at home."

"I'm going to get back to my hotel." Joe straightened up and stretched, and Hailey tried not to stare at the way his shirt molded to his chest, although Ayala didn't seem to have the same reservations.

"It was nice to meet you, Joe, and thanks for looking out for my friend." Ayala draped an arm around Hailey's shoulders.

"I'm glad she has company here." Joe grabbed his jacket. "Can I take you ladies out to dinner tonight?"

"Of course." Hailey wrapped one arm around Ayala's waist to make sure her friend knew she wouldn't be intruding. "We'd love dinner."

"I don't—" Ayala jumped when Hailey pinched her side. "Sounds good to me."

Ayala extricated herself from Hailey and headed for her bags in the corner. "I'm going to pick out a room now."

"Stick to the first two on the right. They share a connected bathroom. Clean towels in the cupboard."

"Just like a hotel but better." Ayala hitched her carry-on bag over her shoulder. "See you later, Joe."

"See you." Joe peeked around the corner of the kitchen to watch Ayala go up the stairs and then joined Hailey at the sink. "Speaking of hotels, I think it's worth it to check out Marten's."

"Do you think he still has a room there?" Hailey reached around Joe's solid form to pick up Ayala's cup.

"Why wouldn't he? I told you, I picked up Marten's trail from the Pacific Rim Hotel, not from some house in the Sunset District. He went straight to the ferry from the hotel. If he never returned, he never checked out."

The cup slipped from Hailey's fingers and clattered

in the sink as it broke in two pieces. "You didn't tell me it was the Pacific Rim."

Joe sucked in a breath. "Did you cut yourself?"

"No." Hailey held up her hand. "The Pacific Rim, are you sure?"

"Yeah, fancy digs. If Marten was gambling, he must've had a good run."

"That's where my fund-raiser is going to be." She picked up the broken teacup by the handle and dropped it into the trash. "I wonder if Marten knew that."

"If he did, why wouldn't he just set up a meeting at the hotel?" Joe pinched the other piece of the cup between his thumb and forefinger and threw it away. "If you're having the fund-raiser there, do you think you can get access to Marten's room?"

"Don't worry. I can get access to Marten's room, no problem."

"Do you know a manager at the hotel?"

"Better than that. I know the owner—it's my father."

JOE ADJUSTED THE scarf around his neck and turned his back to the wind as it whipped around the corner of his hotel. He'd rather be having dinner with Hailey alone tonight, but with Ayala in town he now had a package deal.

Hadn't his fortune at lunch today encouraged him to take a chance on a dark-haired beauty? Ayala had dark hair and beauty to spare, but he had eyes for just one brunette. He'd already taken a chance on a blonde and failed. Would hair color make a difference?

A sleek white Jag pulled up to the hotel's loading zone, and the passenger window buzzed down. Hailey leaned over the seat and called out the window. "Hey, stranger, need a ride?"

Joe slid into the car and onto the warm leather seat. "Never thought I'd appreciate a seat warmer, but that wind off the bay cuts right to your bones."

Ayala leaned forward from the back seat. "Can you imagine how I feel coming from Florida?"

"Yeah, don't knock the seat warmers." Hailey skimmed her hands over the steering wheel. "Where are we having dinner?"

"I made reservations at a steak house in the Financial District—Jackson's on Jackson. Is that okay?"

"Good choice. You must've read the reviews." Hailey pulled out of the hotel and into traffic.

Joe twisted his head around. "Is that okay with you, Ayala? If you don't eat steak, they have fish and even some vegetarian entrées."

"Steak is fine by me."

It didn't take long for Hailey to navigate the traffic, and twenty minutes later she was handing her keys to a valet attendant.

They took an elevator up to the top floor of the office building, where the restaurant commanded a view over the glittering lights of the city and the Transamerica Building formed a triangle in the sky.

Would've been a romantic spot if not for the third wheel. Joe pulled out Hailey's chair and then made a grab for Ayala's chair. He'd already twisted the woman's arm behind her back; he didn't want her to know his real thoughts.

She smiled her thanks and took her seat as a waiter scurried over to deliver water and a basket of bread.

Hailey sighed. "This is nice."

Ayala raised her water glass to her lips and gazed over the rim at the view. "A long way from Syria, isn't it?"

Joe asked, "Are you going back soon or staying in Florida for a while?"

"Just two weeks in Florida before returning to the refugee camp."

"It must get—" Joe waved a piece of bread in the air "—depressing. How long have you been doing the work?"

"For a few years now. It's not depressing to me. Those are my people, you know. My parents immigrated to the US from Syria. I have an older brother who was born there. I'd been working as a nurse, and as soon as I learned about the need for medical care during the civil war, I knew I had to help."

Joe bowed his head. "I am humbled to be in the presence of two such selfless, generous people."

"As Delta Force, you do your part, too—just in a different way." Hailey opened the wine menu. "Should we share a bottle?"

"I'm not much of a wine drinker, but you two go ahead. I'm a beer guy—you can take the boy out of Southie, but you can't take the Southie out of the boy."

Ayala shook her head. "All I can handle is one glass, Hailey, so unless you're prepared to polish off that bottle yourself, we should probably stick to single drinks."

"You've been in Syria too long. You used to be able to drink us under the table." Hailey wrinkled her nose. "But if you're opting out, I'm not going to order a whole bottle for myself."

The waiter approached their table. "Can I get you something to drink?"

Hailey ordered a glass of cabernet, Ayala ordered a martini and Joe stuck with a beer.

When the waiter left, Joe offered the basket of bread

to Ayala. "Tell me about your experiences in Syria. Think of it as prep for the speech you owe Hailey."

Ayala waved off the bread. "I've been working out there for about three years. While I was at a symposium in Florida on emergency room treatments, I—I ran into a few nurses who had been working at some of the refugee centers. The work sounded incredible and I was stuck in a rut, so it was perfect timing for me."

"And for them." Hailey ran a fingertip up the outside of her water glass. "The need couldn't be greater right now."

"It's so dangerous, though, as you both found out. Do you feel safe there, Ayala?"

"Most of the time. What happened to us—" she glanced at Hailey from beneath her eyelashes "—that was an aberration. A onetime thing."

"I know it put a damper on the peace negotiations. Have both sides recovered from the damage that bombing caused?"

The waiter appeared with their drinks, and Ayala sank back in her seat and took a long pull from her martini glass before he and Hailey even had their drinks in front of them. He'd have to steer the conversation in another direction. Either the violence bothered Ayala more than she let on, or she didn't want to talk business tonight.

Once they ordered their food and all had their drinks in hand, Hailey raised her glass. "To my bodyguard and keynote speaker and a successful fund-raiser."

They clinked glasses and Ayala took another big sip of her drink. "Keynote? I'm saying a few words, right?"

"As many or as few as you like." Hailey swirled the ruby wine in her glass. "I think I mentioned already that our keynote speaker is Dr. Nabil Karam-Thomas. You remember. He visited us at the refugee center."

Ayala raised her napkin to her face, covering the lower half. "I—I do remember. He's much more eloquent than I am."

"You don't have to speak at all if you don't want to, Ayala. I was joking about earning your keep at the house."

"I know you were, and I really don't mind talking. I just don't like going into the graphic details or the political landscape."

Was that directed at him? He'd definitely be changing the topic, but if he were involved in such a selfless endeavor, he'd want to tell everyone about it. Maybe Ayala thought he was trying to glean information from her about Denver. At the house, Ayala had suggested Hailey stay as far away from the inquiries into Denver's involvement in the bombing as possible, and it seemed as if she were taking her own advice.

Joe took a sip of beer through the thick head of foam. "Where do you live in Florida, Ayala?"

Ayala preferred talking about Florida to Syria and seemed to finally open up and lose her reserve—or maybe that apple martini she'd been guzzling had something to do with it.

When the food arrived, both women ordered a second round of drinks while Joe nursed his beer. Someone would have to drive home.

Hailey tapped Ayala's empty martini glass. "Looks like we could've finished that bottle of wine together."

"Oh, this?" Ayala pinged her glass. "It's sour apple. It doesn't taste like alcohol at all."

Hailey rolled her eyes. "Like I said before, you've

been in Syria too long. Those are the most dangerous kinds of drinks. Right, Joe?"

"I wouldn't know." He curled his fingers around the handle of his mug. "I'm a beer guy."

By the end of dinner, Joe knew a lot about Florida and San Francisco but very little about the two women who lived in those cities. Ayala kept her conversation surface level, and while Joe wanted to know more about Hailey, he didn't want to make those discoveries with an audience.

Ayala excused herself to use the ladies' room, and she hadn't been joking about being a lightweight. As she rose from her chair, she staggered and grabbed the edge of the table to steady herself.

"Are you all right?" Hailey put a hand on Ayala's arm.

"I'm fine. Just got up too fast."

Hailey watched her friend as she wended her way through the tables in the dining room. Then she rested her elbow on the table and buried her chin in her hand. "Thank you."

"For what? Dinner?" He fingered the check the waiter had placed discreetly at his elbow. "I haven't paid for it yet."

She cracked a smile. "Oh, that, too, but I'm thanking you for engaging Ayala in conversation. I've never heard her so animated and open."

"That was open?"

"For her it was. She's very reserved and has gotten even more so the longer she spends at the refugee center."

"Sounds like she might need a break."

"I know I did after..." Hailey drained her glass,

and her lips in the candlelight appeared stained red with wine.

"Are you going to be okay to drive home?"

"Probably not." She twisted her head to the side. "Where's Ayala?"

"She's *definitely* not okay to drive. I'm glad one of us stayed sober." Joe slipped his wallet from his pocket and slid a credit card onto the tray.

The waiter picked up the check and the empty glasses and asked them if they wanted anything else—twice—before Hailey pushed back from the table. "I'd better check on Ayala. She's been in there long enough to wash her hair in the sink."

As she walked away from the table, Joe called after her, "Be careful."

Or maybe she just imagined his warning. Why should she be careful on her way to the ladies' room in a restaurant? Regardless, a little chill caused a rash of goose bumps to race across her arms. She rubbed them and headed toward the bar.

She hesitated at the entrance to the dim hallway that led to the restrooms and an emergency exit. A man brushed past her, and she jumped. Hailey straightened her spine and marched to the ladies' room.

She pushed open the door and poked her head inside. "Ayala?"

A woman washing her hands at the sink met Hailey's eyes in the mirror and then looked away.

Hailey took two steps into the bathroom, which contained three stalls. The doors to two of the stalls yawned open. Hailey rapped her knuckles against the closed third door. "Ayala?"

The woman at the sink plucked a paper towel from

a stack on the sink. "That stall was occupied when I walked in, but I haven't heard anyone in there."

The doors to the stalls reached the floor, so Hailey couldn't peek beneath. With her head pounding, she knocked on the door again. "Ayala?"

This time, a soft moan answered her and Hailey gasped. "Did you hear that?"

"I did." The woman was literally clutching her pearls. "Should we call the manager?"

"Go, go." Hailey shoved into the stall next to the locked one and climbed onto the toilet seat. She peered over the top and yelped. "Oh my God. My friend's passed out."

Hailey managed to clamber over the top of the separator between the two stalls and opened the door before crouching next to Ayala.

Another woman stood in front of the stall, gaping. "What happened?"

"My friend's ill. I think someone went to get the manager. Can you call 911?"

"Of course."

Hailey curled her arm beneath Ayala's head. "Ayala. Ayala, what's wrong? What happened?"

Her friend groaned as white foam bubbled from her lips. "Help me. I've been poisoned."

Chapter Eight

The woman who'd left to get the manager stumbled back into the bathroom. "Is she okay? I called 911."

Hailey peeled her tongue from the roof of her dry mouth. "She lost consciousness. Can you sit with her for a minute while I get my friend? What's your name?"

"Marcia." The woman knelt beside Hailey and put her hand on Ayala's forehead. "She's clammy."

"I'll be right back." Hailey charged out of the bathroom and emerged from the hallway into the dining area.

Joe must've been watching for her. He immediately jumped up from the table and strode to her side. "What's wrong?"

"It's Ayala. She's been poisoned."

Cursing, Joe charged past her to the restroom. "Is she in the ladies' room?"

"She's in the last stall."

"Conscious?"

"Barely. Someone already called 911."

"Good." Joe pushed into the ladies' room and crouched next to Marcia.

"Thank you." Hailey put a hand on Marcia's back. "How's she doing?"

"Still unconscious, but her pulse is strong…and the foaming has stopped."

Joe looked up from his assessment of Ayala. "She was foaming at the mouth?"

"A little when I first found her." Hailey helped Marcia to her feet. "Could I ask you for one more favor? Could you please tell the manager that there's an impaired woman in the restroom and that 911 is on the way? I don't think that other woman ever alerted the manager."

"Absolutely. I hope she's going to be all right. I've seen a lot of people passed out from booze, but not with foam coming out of their mouths." Marcia backed out of the bathroom.

Hailey dropped to the floor next to Joe, who'd rolled up his jacket and shoved it beneath Ayala's head.

"What the hell happened?" His harsh whisper echoed in the empty bathroom.

"When I came in here to look for Ayala, there was a woman at the sink and a locked stall. I called Ayala's name at the door of the stall, but she didn't answer. The woman at the sink told me the stall had been locked when she came into the bathroom. I banged on the door and heard a groan."

"Was it Marcia at the sink?"

"No, that woman took off. Marcia came in later." Hailey broke off as someone barreled through the bathroom door.

The manager poked his head in the stall. "Is she all right?"

Joe pressed two fingers against Ayala's neck. "She's still alive but unconscious. Are the paramedics here yet?"

"Not yet, although I saw them arrive street level."

"Could you do me a favor and keep everyone out of here, and when the paramedics arrive, guide them in here? Let them know the woman mentioned poisoning before she lost consciousness."

The manager jerked back. "Poisoning? Not in my restaurant. More like alcohol poisoning."

"Just let them know that's what she mentioned. It might be helpful when they treat her." Joe tipped his chin toward Hailey when the manager swept out of the bathroom.

"That's what she told you, right?"

"Yes. When she wouldn't respond or open the door, I climbed onto the toilet seat in the stall next to hers, saw her slumped on the floor and hoisted myself over the top. She was mumbling and foam or spittle was forming at the corners of her mouth. When I got down next to her, she said she'd been poisoned, and then she passed out. I asked Marcia to get the manager and call 911, and then I ran out to get you."

"How could her food or drink have been poisoned here? Maybe it happened before she got to your place?"

"I don't know. If it was here, someone followed us. Were you watching out again?"

"Always. I'm always watching out." Joe put his finger to his lips as the paramedics burst through the bathroom door.

Hailey told them as much as she knew about Ayala's condition, and they took over.

An hour later, Hailey collected her keys from the valet and Joe held out his hand.

"I think I've completely sobered up by now, Joe."

"If you're sure. It might be better if you drive, anyway."

"Why is that?"

"Because you know how to get to the Pacific Rim Hotel."

She curled her hand around her keys until they

bit into her flesh. "You want to look for Marten's room now?"

"I think it's past time. These people are getting bold...or desperate, and we need to put a stop to them." He opened the driver's-side door for her and she slid onto the seat.

She didn't even need the seat warmers. Joe's presence made her feel warm and secure, but she wanted to match his decisiveness. She couldn't depend on him forever.

"I'm going to call Agent Porter tomorrow and tell him what happened to Ayala."

"We don't know what happened to her yet."

"Just another attack on one of the kidnap victims in Syria. They have to pay attention now. They have to take it seriously—Marten, Andrew, me and now Ayala. How much more proof do they need?"

"They need actual proof, not suspicions and supposition—Marten's body never turned up and nobody has reported him missing, we haven't heard anything back about Andrew, and we don't have the video. The attack on you could've been a wayward driver, and if Ayala *was* poisoned... I guess we'll see."

"Yeah, details, details." She swung out of the hotel's parking lot. "Let's see if Marten's room can offer us any proof."

The Pacific Rim was a hop and skip from the restaurant, but a car couldn't hop and skip through the San Francisco traffic. On the way over, Hailey tossed her phone into Joe's lap. "Can you please call the hospital where they took Ayala? It's San Francisco General."

Joe got the number from information, which then connected him to the hospital. He kept the phone and asked about Ayala.

"We're the ones who were with her. She's visiting

from Florida. She doesn't have family here." He rolled his eyes at Hailey. "I'm on hold."

"Mention my father's name."

"What?"

"He raises a ton of money for that hospital."

Joe pressed his lips into a thin line, and Hailey's eyelid twitched. She sounded as bad as her father on one of his worst days—throwing around his weight and money. But this was for a good cause.

"I understand. Just a minute, please." He held out the phone to Hailey. "You're the expert. I wouldn't even know how to begin using that leverage."

Hailey swallowed and took the phone from him. "Yes, hello. This is Hailey Duvall. My father, Ray Duvall, helped fund the burn unit there at the hospital. Ayala Khan is my friend. She was visiting me and we were out to dinner when she became ill. I'd appreciate any information you could give me about her condition."

In her haste to give Hailey whatever she wanted, the nurse sputtered and stammered but was able to communicate that Ayala was doing well, had regained consciousness and would be ready to receive visitors tomorrow morning.

"Thank you so much. What's your name?"

"Shailene Franklin."

"Thanks, Shailene. I'll make sure to tell my father what great employees work at San Fran Gen the next time he meets with Mr. Sharpe, the director of operations."

Hailey ended the call and dropped her phone in the cup holder, ignoring Joe's gaze burning into the side of her face like a laser.

After several seconds, Joe cleared his throat. "Wow, so that's how it's done."

Hailey was thankful for the darkness of the car's interior, which hid the warm blush on her cheeks. "I learned from the best."

"You keep saying that, and yet you seem to scorn *the best*, as you call your father."

Her hands tightened on the steering wheel. "What are you saying, Joe?"

He flashed his palm at her. "Look, I'm not criticizing you for using your father's name and influence to get what you want."

"Need."

"What?"

"To get what I need, not what I want."

"Okay, okay. I'd do the same. Anyone would, but you seem to heap scorn on your father for supplying you with the means to use his influence and money. It's kinda…"

"Hypocritical?"

His hand inched over to her thigh, and he skimmed his knuckles across the denim of her jeans. "You know what? You can just ignore me and my stupid judgments. I'm probably just jealous that the only string my pop could pull for me was for a free brewski at the corner tavern."

His apology felt as warm as his hand on her knee—heartfelt, sincere. Apologies flowed from his lips freely, as if he were accustomed to making them. What would Joe McVie have to apologize for in his life? Seemed as if he'd soldiered through a rough childhood and then made his way onto an elite military unit. He had loyalty and protectiveness—and muscles—to spare. He had no reason to be apologetic about anything, especially criticizing a spoiled rich girl.

She shrugged her shoulders with a quick lift and

drop. "You don't have to apologize for expressing your honest opinion, but you can bask in the knowledge that you're running with someone with some different connections from your father—although you should never knock a free brewski."

He squeezed her knee before releasing it. "How'd you get to be such a guy's girl?"

"I'll give credit to my father for that, too. He raised me to take over his business."

"Not your brother?"

"I'm older." She pressed a hand to her chest. "And more responsible. Dad groomed me to handle the family business, until…"

"Until what?"

"There's the hotel. I'm going to swing around for the valet."

Joe whistled through his teeth. "Nice. How the hell did Marten afford this, and why would he want to stay in that hovel with Joost when he had a room waiting for him here?"

"I don't know. Maybe just to leave him that rusty old key to give me." She pulled up to the curb and stepped out when the attendant opened her door.

"Good evening, Ms. Duvall."

She peered at the valet's name tag. "Hello, Henry. How are you doing tonight?"

"Just fine, ma'am. I'll take good care of your car."

"You'd better." She winked at him. "It's my father's."

Joe placed a hand on her back and steered her through the front door. Leaning his head toward hers, he said, "How is this going to go down? Are you just going to tell them you want to get into Marten's room?"

"Pretty much." Hailey squared her shoulders and marched up to reception. She may have learned at her father's knee, but she could never master his full command over any and all situations. Hailey parked herself at the corner of the front desk while two clerks handled guests.

One of them looked up from her keyboard and smiled at Hailey. "I'll be right with you, miss. If you need the concierge, the desk is behind you, to your left."

Hailey opened her mouth to respond that she'd wait, but before she uttered one syllable, Timothy Tang, one of the night managers, came bustling from the back.

"Carmen, this is Ms. Duvall."

Two red spots exploded on Carmen's cheeks. "Oh, I'm sorry, Ms. Duvall."

Hailey waved her off. "Please. I wanted to speak to Mr. Tang, anyway."

The manager walked to the front desk, straightening the collar of his impeccable jacket. "What can I help you with, Ms. Duvall?"

"A friend of mine, Marten de Becker, has a room here but got called away to a business meeting in Sacramento for a day or two. He asked me to get something from his room, and I was wondering if you could let me in."

Mr. Tang's eye twitched for just a second, and then he said, "Of course. Let me check Mr. de Becker's room number."

"Thank you so much."

As Mr. Tang tapped on the keyboard, he asked, "Is everything going as planned for the gala? Gretchen has been working mostly with Josie, the event planner, but I've had an opportunity to make a few small contributions."

"Gretchen is really happy with how everything is

working out." Hailey shot a glance at Joe, who was tapping his toe, arms crossed.

He said he wasn't going to judge.

"How do you like being night manager, Mr. Tang? Are you interested in event planning?"

"Oh." Mr. Tang met her gaze over the top of the monitor. "Josie is quite good at what she does, although I do like to chime in here and there—and I think she appreciates it."

"I'm sure she does."

"Seventh floor, room 728. That's Mr. de Becker's room." Mr. Tang slid a key card across the counter, his hand covering it until the last minute when Hailey snatched it up. "You can just drop the key off in any key receptacle on your way out, Ms. Duvall."

"I will do that. Thanks again, and I look forward to seeing you in a few nights."

Mr. Tang nodded quickly and then turned on his heel and disappeared into the back.

Turning toward Joe, Hailey plunged her hands in the pockets of her jacket, her fingers tracing the edges of the key card. "That wasn't bad."

Joe clapped his hands slowly three times as they veered toward the bank of elevators. "I'm in awe. I can't imagine your father, or anyone else, doing it better."

She snorted. "My father would have Mr. Tang thinking it was his idea and thanking him for the pleasure of serving him."

"You weren't too far off the mark." Joe thumbed the call button for the elevator. He ushered her in first when the doors opened. "Do all the employees have pictures of your family taped to their computer screens or something? They're all supposed to recognize you?"

"I wouldn't put it past my father to require that, but

I don't care." She tugged on his sleeve. "You believe that, right? I don't care about that stuff."

"If you did, you wouldn't be running off to war-torn countries like Syria."

Hailey let out a little puff of breath. "My brother, on the other hand."

"Likes the perks, does he?"

"Revels in them. At first he just reveled in the money—drugs, booze, parties, women. Then when he realized that I had fallen out of favor with Dad, he began to clean up his act to suck up to him. Now he's his lapdog."

"How did you fall out of favor with your father?"

"Oh, this and that." She flicked her fingers.

Joe quirked one eyebrow. "So, your brother's in line to take over the family's holdings now?"

"Some, not all. Our father still doesn't trust him."

"Like he still trusts you."

"Sort of."

The elevator pinged and settled on the seventh floor. The thick carpet swallowed their footsteps as they made their way along the hallway to Marten's room.

When they reached his door, Hailey stuck the card in the slot and slid it out again. The green lights signaled entry, and Joe pushed open the door.

Entering the dark room on tiptoes, Hailey crossed her arms over her chest. She whispered, "Marten?"

Joe stabbed at the light switch on the wall by the door, and two lamps lit up the recesses of the big room.

Hailey scanned the area, nodding toward a suitcase in the corner. "His stuff. No wonder he didn't bring anything to Joost's place. He had it all here."

"Except for the key."

A chill skittered down her spine and Hailey made a half turn toward the door. "Lock it."

Joe flipped the latch at the top of the door to block entry from the outside.

Hailey pulled Marten's key from her purse. "Could it be a luggage lock?"

"I think it's too big, but give it a try." Joe made a move before she could and crossed the room to hoist Marten's single suitcase onto the king-size bed. He grabbed the zipper and pulled it across. "His bag isn't locked and doesn't even have a lock on it."

Hailey squeezed past him and flicked on the lights over the bed. "Maybe whatever this key unlocks is inside the suitcase."

"Maybe." Joe plunged his hands inside the suitcase, burying them in Marten's clothes.

Hailey reached past him and grabbed a fistful of shirts. "I don't think we have to worry about disturbing his things."

They pawed through the contents of Marten's suitcase, spreading shirts and pants across the bed.

Joe patted the outside pockets of the bag. "We're probably not going to find anything in his clothes."

Hailey let Joe search the zippered side pockets while she surveyed the room, hands on her hips. "Where's his laptop? I'm pretty sure Marten never went anywhere without it."

"Is there a safe?"

Hailey crossed to the cabinet beneath the TV. "It's in here."

Crouching in front of the cabinet, she threw open the doors. The safe gaped open, completely empty. "That's weird. Nothing in the safe—no passport, no money, no laptop."

Joe knelt beside her with socks clutched in his hands. "Nothing in those side pockets, either, except these."

"Bathroom?" She bumped Joe's solid shoulder with her own.

He rose to his feet, extending a hand for her. She took it and he helped her to her feet. He didn't let go as he led her to the bathroom—and she didn't want him to.

The housekeeping staff had cleaned up since Marten's last day in the room. Clean towels towered on a rack, and fresh bottles of hotel toiletries lined the vanity.

"You'd think housekeeping would be curious as to the guest's whereabouts."

"As long as his departure date hasn't come and gone, I don't think they care or pay attention." She grabbed the handle of the bathroom door and pulled the door forward.

Marten's toiletry bag banged against the door.

Joe snatched it off the hook and dumped the contents on the counter of the sink.

The usual suspects rolled and spilled from the bag— shaving cream, razor, comb, condoms.

Hailey pinched a foil pack between her fingers. "Typical Marten. Wouldn't leave home without a stash of condoms."

"At least he played it safe in *some* areas of his life."

Hailey sank to the edge of the tub. "There's nothing here. Nothing. Why did he want me to have that key? How am I supposed to figure out what it matches?"

"Come on. Let's get his clothes back in the suitcase." Joe shoveled Marten's toiletries into the bag and hung it back on the hook on the door.

Placing her palms against the cool porcelain of the

tub, Hailey pushed up. "I'm disappointed. I was so proud of myself that I got us in here, and it all came to nothing."

"We didn't check all the drawers in the room. Maybe he stayed at this hotel because he knew you could get in here, and he left a note for you." Joe backed out of the bathroom.

"Why didn't he just leave a note with the key? Better yet, just leave me a note telling me what he was going to reveal to me on the ferry?"

"All of that would be too easy for someone else to find. He's obviously protecting this information." Joe crossed the room to the desk by the window and yanked open the top drawer.

Hailey placed one knee on the bed and plucked up one of Marten's shirts. As she folded it, a thump outside the door caused her to clutch the shirt to her chest.

"What was that?"

Joe squinted at her over the top of a piece of hotel stationery. "Maybe just housekeeping."

Hailey dropped the shirt and tiptoed to the door. Placing one hand against the solid wood, she leaned forward and put her eye to the peephole.

She jerked back, her eyebrows colliding over her nose.

"Someone out there?" Joe crept up behind her.

"I can't see out the peephole. It's blocked or something."

Joe drew up beside her and nudged her over. "Let me have a look."

He peered through the peephole and immediately reared back, jamming his thumb against the peephole.

Hailey swallowed. "What's wrong?"

"Someone replaced the peephole with a camera. We're being watched."

Chapter Nine

Hailey staggered back from the door. "Are you serious?"

"Deadly." Keeping his finger against the door, Joe reached for the front pocket of his jeans. He pulled out a knife. "Open this for me."

With shaky fingers, Hailey pulled out the blade and handed the knife back to Joe. "What are you going to do?"

"Get rid of it." He slid his thumb from the peephole and held his hand cupped over it instead while he worked the point of the blade around the edge. After several minutes, he dug the device out of the door and closed his fist around it.

Tipping the back of her head against the wall, Hailey asked, "Someone was watching us this whole time?"

"Someone has had their eye on this room for who knows how long. That camera could've been there when Marten was still here."

"And after he…left—" Hailey licked her lips "—they wanted to see who came in here. They must've already searched this room. Maybe they took his laptop. Where else would it be? He didn't leave it at Joost's place."

"Hailey, I'd love to stay here in this comfortable room talking to you all night, but we've gotta get out of here. The person or persons on the other side of this camera could be on their way right now."

A stream of adrenaline rushed through her body so fast it made her head hurt, and she pressed two fingers against her temple. "Oh my God. I didn't even think about that."

"Are you okay?" He encircled her wrist with his fingers. "Do you need to sit down for a minute?"

"I'd rather get out of here." She jerked her thumb at the mess on the bed. "We can leave that."

"Wait." He strode across the room, shoveled Marten's things back into the suitcase, zipped it up and placed it in the corner. "Let's go." When they got to the elevator, Joe looked over his shoulder. "Too bad we didn't notice that camera before you literally looked into its lens. We could've pretended we didn't see it and I could've waited for the person who planted it."

Hailey punched the elevator button three times. "Too late for that now?"

"They know we saw the camera. They lost their element of surprise—and so did we." When the elevator opened onto the lobby, Joe dropped the device into a trash can. "Hope they like looking at garbage."

TWENTY MINUTES LATER, Hailey let the Jag idle at a stoplight. She flexed her fingers on the steering wheel. "Joe, would you mind spending the night at my place tonight? I— This isn't a come-on or anything. It's just after what happened to Ayala and finding that camera... I don't want to be in that big house by myself—security system or not."

"Do you have an extra toothbrush?"

"Tons."

"Then I'm your man."

Oh, she was beginning to believe that.

"Great." She punched the accelerator and the car leaped forward—pretty accurately mimicking her heart.

On the way to Pacific Heights, Joe theorized about the hidden camera and what Marten's key unlocked, but all Hailey could hear was *I'm your man*.

If only Joe meant it the way she felt it. She could be confusing Joe's natural protectiveness for genuine tenderness, but the way he touched her went above and beyond. Then he'd catch himself and draw back—except for tonight.

For all she knew, they could get to her place and he'd take up his post across the street again…after brushing his teeth with one of her many toothbrushes.

She drove into the driveway and opened the garage door. She pulled into the three-car garage that housed her father's '66 Thunderbird and her stepmother's Range Rover.

Joe whistled. "Now, *that's* a car."

"You can take it for a spin if you like." Hailey cut the engine and pressed her lips together. Did that sound like she was trying to bribe him?

"That would be the type of car I'd like to take on Highway 1 down to Big Sur."

"You've taken that drive before?"

"Not in a classic T-Bird."

Hailey stepped from the car and waved toward the open garage door. "We have to go back outside and through the front door. There's no connection from the garage to the house."

"I'm disappointed. I would've expected a car elevator."

She snapped and pointed her finger at him. "I'll have my dad get right on that."

She entered the code on the side of the garage door frame and turned away.

Joe caught her arm. "Don't you stay to make sure nobody sneaks into the garage while the door is closing?"

"If someone did that, it would trigger the garage door to go up again."

"You—" he touched a finger to her nose "—need to be more careful and aware of your surroundings. You think you're safe just because you're in San Francisco instead of Syria?"

"I know I'm not safe here anymore." She waited until the garage door settled and spun around again. "And maybe if I'd been more alert in Syria, I would've suspected that the people who kidnapped us wouldn't have been willing to just let us go. We should've known they weren't done with us."

"If anyone should've been suspicious, it was Siddiqi. He's a guide in the area, for God's sake. He should've known the drill."

Hailey stopped on the bottom step and twirled around to face Joe, almost meeting him eye to eye. "Get off that idea. Naraj didn't set us up. In fact, maybe he's in danger, too. I should ask Agent Porter to request a check on him."

"That might not be a bad idea. Did you ask Ayala about him? If she'd seen him?" He joined her on the next step, and his clean, masculine scent invaded her senses.

She bobbed her head up and down. "As a matter of fact, I did. She hasn't seen him around."

"Put it on your list for Porter." He nudged her up the stairs.

She opened the door, stepped aside to let Joe through and then immediately armed the alarm system.

The peephole in the center of the door caught her eye, and she peered through it. "It's just a peephole."

"That's good news." Pinching his shoulder, he rolled it back. "I could use a beer, if you're offering."

"You and me both." She pointed to the kitchen. "You know the way. I'm going to call the hospital again to check on Ayala."

While Joe strolled into the kitchen, looking more at home than she felt here, Hailey placed a call to the hospital. She got a different nurse this time, but the word must've gotten around, because this one reported Ayala's progress without hesitation.

Hailey unzipped her boots and padded into the kitchen, where Joe had parked himself at the center island, sipping his beer.

"Ayala's doing fine, resting and will be able to check out tomorrow. I tried calling her cell, but it's dead or she turned it off."

Joe slid a beer toward her on the granite counter. "Did they confirm the poisoning?"

"The nurse was willing to tell me how Ayala was doing, but she didn't give me any details like that. We'll have to ask her tomorrow when we pick her up."

"You're bringing her back here?"

Was that disappointment in Joe's voice?

"Of course. I'm not sending her to a hotel after what she just went through."

"Yeah, yeah, of course not." Joe took a gulp of beer. "What *did* she just go through? What was all that about? Someone followed us to the restaurant? Knew we were going to be there? Slipped something into that martini?"

"I don't know." She tilted her head and wrapped her hair around one hand. "What are you saying?"

"Why was Ayala so quick to yell poison? Didn't she

just get through telling us she couldn't hold her booze? I imagine a martini in San Francisco is a powerful thing."

"You saw her." Hailey ran a fingernail down the damp label on her bottle. "She was passed out on the bathroom floor. Did that look like a woman who'd imbibed two appletinis to you?"

Joe lifted his shoulders. "I don't understand how someone could've poisoned her at that restaurant."

"The same way someone replaced a peephole in a hotel door with a mini camera."

"But they knew Marten was staying at that hotel. Who knew we were going to that restaurant, and why hit Ayala only? Why not spike your wine or even my beer?"

"For someone who's spent the better part of two days telling me my life was in danger because of that kidnapping, you're doing an about-face."

"Not at all. Your life *is* in danger…and so is Ayala's. I'm just not sure how this all went down."

"Maybe we'll have a better idea after talking to Ayala tomorrow."

Hailey took a sip of her beer and rolled her shoulders back, loosening up a few muscles…and a few inhibitions. "So, do you still live in Boston when you're not deployed?"

He put his beer on the counter and caught a bead of moisture with his thumb on the outside of the bottle.

The pause lasted so long, Hailey had a chance to gulp down another mouthful of beer.

"I don't live in Boston anymore. I have a place in Colorado—fresh air and a view ringed by mountains."

Warming to the subject, Hailey asked, "Is your family still there? Your mother?"

"My mom will never leave South Boston, but at least we got her settled in a nicer place."

Hailey's heart skipped a beat. "We?"

"My siblings and I—my two brothers and one of my sisters."

"*One* of your sisters? How many do you have? How many in your family?"

"Five of us—I have two younger brothers and two younger sisters. My youngest sister is still living with Mom, and she…has issues."

"I'm sorry." She let the words hang in the air between them. She didn't want to overstep the boundaries here and have Joe clam up.

He lifted and dropped his shoulders. "Nothing to be sorry about—she chose drugs and alcohol, following in our father's unsteady footsteps."

"I know what that's like. My brother was the same— never met an altered state he didn't want to try."

"He cleaned himself up?"

"Who knows? He must've cut back being around my father, because my father wouldn't tolerate that behavior, but I find it hard to believe Win doesn't indulge when he parties with the beautiful people in Manhattan."

"Win?"

"Winslow Chandler Duvall."

Joe snorted. "I'm sure Win and Jenny are going to very different parties to get their drink on."

"Different parties, same outcome."

He clinked the neck of his bottle with hers. "You seem to feel guilty about everything and everyone else—why not Win?"

"Why would I feel guilty about him? My brother has had every opportunity in the world and chose to squander those privileges." She put her elbows on the counter and cupped her chin in one hand. "Do you feel guilty about Jenny?"

"Oh, yeah, and not just her."

"Not the rest of your family? If they're all helping out your mom, it sounds like they're doing okay."

"They're doing great. One of my brothers is a software engineer, the other's in law school, and my sister is a buyer for a big department store."

As he listed the accomplishments of his siblings, Joe's face almost glowed.

"You did that for them, didn't you?"

"Me? Hell, no. They're successful because they worked hard and stayed out of trouble."

"And because they had a big brother setting an example for them. Keeping three out of four on the right path is something to be proud of. What happened to Jenny?"

Joe's jaw tightened, and his eyes took on a dangerous glitter. "Fell in with the wrong crowd. People determined to see her fail."

"Boyfriend?" Hailey swirled the liquid in her bottle and took another swig.

"My ex-wife."

Hailey choked and the beer fizzed up her nose. She covered her mouth with her hand. "What?"

"My ex, Deirdre."

"I—I didn't know—didn't realize you'd been married."

"It was a long time ago. We dated in high school, and then before my first deployment, she got pregnant, so we got married."

As Hailey's world tilted sideways, she blinked. "You have a child?"

"Deirdre miscarried—and I wasn't even there."

"I'm sorry." She stroked the back of his hand with her fingers.

"When I got home, she blamed me for not being there, but I heard from other people, including my sister, that she'd been drinking and partying."

"Oh." Hailey pressed a hand to her heart. "Is that what led to the divorce?"

"It didn't help. It also didn't help that she'd tricked me into the marriage by getting pregnant on purpose. Told me she was on the pill, but that was a lie."

Hailey rubbed the back of her hand across her nose. Despite Deirdre's misdeeds, Hailey couldn't help but have a little pity for her. Once you had Joe McVie, how could you ever let him go?

"Wait—so is that why she targeted your sister? To get back at you?"

"I think so, not that Jenny needed much encouragement." Joe finished off his beer and clicked the bottle onto the counter decisively. "I failed both of them."

"You can't seriously blame yourself for Jenny's behavior."

"I ended the marriage, and it led to a downward spiral for Deirdre."

"Who wouldn't end it? Her reckless actions probably caused the miscarriage, and it sounds like that spiral started before the marriage ended."

"You take vows, you should make it work. I could've given it a try. She would've changed."

"Ha!" Hailey tipped her head back and laughed at the ceiling. "That never happens. Ever."

"I had other reasons for ending that marriage."

"You mean besides being tricked into it, losing your baby and being stuck with a hard-partying wife?"

"I'd met someone else."

Hailey's world tilted again, and she narrowed her eyes. "You cheated?"

"No, I'd just met this woman. There was nothing between us—then—but she and Deirdre couldn't have been more different. Deirdre represented everything I wanted to escape…and Lisette represented everything I wanted to run toward."

"Sounds like you wanted to escape from Deirdre before you ever met Lisette, and you would've ended the marriage even if Lisette hadn't made an appearance." She traced her fingertip around the lip of the bottle. "What happened to Lisette?"

"We dated briefly and then she dumped me."

"Uh-huh." As if any woman would dump this man.

"What does that mean?" He cocked his head.

"My guess—" she held up her finger "—is that you felt guilty about Deirdre and made a relationship with Lisette impossible."

"Wow." He shook his head and ran a hand through his hair. "Not only did you get me to spill my guts, you psychoanalyzed me in the process."

She grabbed both of their bottles with one hand, dumped her beer out in the sink and placed the bottles in the recycling bin. "I figured it was about time. You came in knowing so much about me and my family."

"Because it's common knowledge, or at least there for the mildly curious."

"Is that what you are? Mildly curious?"

He encircled her wrist with his fingers. "There's nothing mild about how I'm feeling right now."

Hailey swallowed, wishing she had the rest of that beer she'd just dumped down the drain.

He dropped her wrist and stepped back. "I'm sorry."

"Don't apologize." She pushed some hair from her

overheated face. "I'm guessing all the personal questions I threw at you gave our conversation an intimate quality even though we're…strangers."

"Is that what you think we are? Strangers?"

"I—I mean we barely know each other. We've been chasing after phantoms and keys to nowhere, and when we finally have a minute to catch our breaths and the conversation turns personal, we slipped into an easy familiarity."

"That's a lot of words." Joe raised his eyes to the ceiling and then focused on her like a laser, his blue gaze smoldering. "I like you, Hailey, a lot."

"I like you, too." She ran her tongue around the inside of her mouth. "And I appreciate…"

He sliced a hand through the air. "I don't want you to appreciate me or be grateful or want me to be your bodyguard or your driver or your security guy."

"Is that how you think I see you?" She plopped back down on the stool, because her knees were in danger of giving out.

"Not sure." He brushed his knuckles against the stubble on his chin. "When you're not thanking me, you're outfitting me so I can be presentable for your fund-raiser."

Hailey's jaw dropped. "You're kidding. I guess I've been successful at keeping you at arm's length, then, because I've been trying like hell to keep my hands and my dirty thoughts to myself."

A slow smile spread across Joe's face, the kind of smile that made her heart do jumping jacks.

"Dirty thoughts, huh? Like what?"

She reached across the counter and grabbed a handful of his shirt, pulling him toward her. When they were nose to nose and she could see the faint freckles on his forehead, she said, "These thoughts are better expressed across a pillow."

Joe's nostrils flared right before he plowed his fingers through her hair, drew her close and planted his lips against hers.

The edge of the counter dug into her ribs and her toes cramped as she curled them against the tile floor, but she never wanted this kiss to end.

He broke it off way too soon and coughed. "You're strangling me."

She blinked. "Sorry." She loosened her hold on his shirt and flexed her fingers.

"Are you going to lead the way to that pillow?" He folded his arms, tucking his hands under his arms. "Or have you changed your mind?"

"Because that kiss you laid on me was supposed to deter me?"

"It wasn't meant to deter or persuade. It just…was. If you haven't noticed, I've been trying to keep you at arm's length, too. I'm not sure I'm capable of that anymore, unless you want me to. Then I'll try like hell just to keep you close."

"That's a lot of words." She moved around the corner of the counter and cupped his jaw with one hand. "Why are we pretending? Why are we fighting against what's been clear from the minute we met on Fisherman's Wharf?"

"Because you have baggage and I have baggage. Because we don't know if this is real or we're feeling it because we have a shared threat hanging over us."

"Right now—" her hand slipped from his face to his neck, where she wedged her fingers beneath his shirt and caressed his warm skin "—I don't care about any of that."

He clasped her hand and raised it to his lips. He kissed each one of her knuckles. "Right now, there's just this single moment."

Lacing her fingers with his, she took a step back and pulled him along with her. "You've never been upstairs, have you?"

"I've never been invited."

"I'm inviting you now. I even have toothbrushes up there."

"Then it's a done deal."

Still holding Joe's hand, she walked upstairs with him trailing behind her. She didn't say another word, afraid of breaking this spell between them.

Her bedroom door stood open. She dropped his hand and crossed the room to the window. "You have to see the view."

He stood still at the entrance to the room, his solid frame outlined by the doorjamb. He whispered across the darkness, "I'm looking at the only view I wanna see right now."

His words sent a thrill through her body, which tingled in all the right places. She never would've guessed Joe McVie would have all the right moves *and* all the right words.

She stretched out her hands. "Come to me, Red."

His long stride ate up the distance between them, and he took her hands, squeezing them lightly.

She made room for him at the window, and their shoulders nestled together. Dropping her head to the side into the crook of his neck, she said, "Isn't it beautiful?"

He draped his arm over her shoulder and twisted his head to the side to look at her. "The most beautiful view I've ever— Oh my God, get down!"

And the tender moment ended with Joe hooking his arm around her neck and yanking her to the ground as glass shattered around them.

Chapter Ten

As his heart practically jumped out of his chest, Joe caught a bead of blood on Hailey's cheek with the pad of his thumb.

"Are you hit? Are you all right?"

"Hit?" Her glassy dark eyes widened. "Hit by what? Why did you throw me down? Where'd the glass come from?"

Joe ran his hands over her body in a poor imitation of what he'd had planned for her in that giant bed. "Hailey, the glass is from the window. Look."

She raised her eyes to the window that looked out on the spectacular view of the bay, which now sported a jagged hole. "What happened?"

"Someone took a shot at you through the window."

Her body, still safe beneath his, jerked. "What do you mean?"

"Someone had you pinned down with a laser on your forehead. Thank God I saw it before he got off the shot."

She began to shake. "No. That can't be. That's not possible. It was a light from the street."

"A red dot of light on your forehead?" He wrapped his arms around her trembling frame. "I'm Delta Force, remember? I know what a night-scope laser looks like."

She buried her face in his chest. "What if you hadn't come over to look at the view?"

"Not possible. You called and I came." He kissed the top of her head and then brushed some slivers of glass from her hair. "Can you move? I want you to crawl to the bed and then get on the other side of it, on the floor."

"Where's my phone? I'm calling 911."

"Your phone's downstairs. Use mine and do it behind that bed." He handed the phone to her, closing her fingers around it. Rolling from her body, he said, "Move."

"Where are you going?"

"Going to pop my head up and have a look."

She stopped midcrawl and grabbed his shirt. "No, you're not."

"Just a peek. Get on that phone."

She huffed out a breath but continued a damn good army crawl across the carpet.

Joe got on his knees in front of the window and yanked the drapes closed. He parted them at the middle and put his eye to the glass at the bottom of the window. "What is that building across the street from you?"

"That's a house."

"It's huge. Who lives there?"

"Some stockbroker and his wife and kids. I don't think he'd be renting out any rooms to snipers."

"Are they home?"

"I don't know. Hang on."

As he listened to Hailey make the 911 call, he continued to scan the scene across the street. "There's that small park. There are several trees tall enough to give someone a view of this room."

"The police are on their way." She sucked in a noisy breath. "Joe?"

His heart stuttered again. "Are you okay?"

"I'm fine, but I think there's a bullet in my wall."

"Good. Let's leave it for the police to dig out."

"Someone shot at me through my window from a tree? Do you see anyone in the park?"

"Nope. Maybe he made his escape after he took the shot, while we were on the floor."

"Maybe he thinks he hit me."

Joe did another scan of the park and then crawled toward Hailey. He found her stretched out on the floor, on her back, clutching his phone to her chest.

She flung her arm out to the side and pointed to the wall. "Bullet."

"You're right. At least the police will be able to identify the type of weapon used."

"And the FBI. I'm reporting this to Porter, along with the attempt on Ayala's life. Someone is desperate to shut us up, whether we have anything to say or not."

"That's a bold move, all right."

Sirens screamed from the street below, and Hailey rolled her eyes. "That'll get the neighbors talking."

"Are you ready?" He touched the small cut on her cheek. "The glass hit you. Scared the hell out of me when I saw the blood."

"Better the glass than the bullet." She grabbed his hand and kissed the inside of his wrist. "Thank you for saving my life."

"Anytime." He nudged her to start crawling out of the bedroom. "You first."

She rolled onto her stomach. "I suppose we should stay down just in case he's waiting out there to take another shot through the window."

"At least until we get out of the bedroom." He scooted to the side to let her pass. "I'm actually glad the shooter took aim at you first."

"Thanks." She kicked her foot out at him as he crawled behind her.

"Think about it, Hailey. Would you have noticed a red dot on my forehead? If he'd taken me out first, you would've been in shock, confused and an easy mark for his next shot."

"You're right. I literally would not have known what hit you…and then me." She shifted to her side when they reached the hallway. "Okay to stand up now?"

"The police are at the door."

One of the officers pounded on the heavy door and shouted, "Police! Did someone call the police?"

Hailey scrambled to her feet. "I guess that's me."

ABOUT AN HOUR LATER, the police left and Hailey collapsed in a chair in the living room. "So, somebody climbed a tree in the little park across the street and took aim at my bedroom window."

"That's what the officers seem to think after finding that broken branch, but your neighbors didn't see or hear anything except your window shattering." He sat on the arm of her chair and brushed her hair back from her forehead. "You still have a few grains of glass in your hair."

"Don't cut yourself." She shook her head back and forth. "I hope Agent Porter follows up with the SFPD. He said he would when I talked to him tonight."

"Call the police department tomorrow to make sure they're going to send the report to Porter, like they said they would."

"I will." Hailey yawned and curled her legs beneath her. "Do you think they came after us once they saw us nosing around Marten's hotel room?"

"Maybe. It's clear they haven't found anything in his

hotel room, either, but they must think whatever he had or was going to say is important enough to risk raising a red flag for you and Ayala, because you two weren't going to refute the story about Denver being among your kidnappers."

"We need to find out what the key opens." Hailey yawned again and her eyes drifted closed.

Joe swallowed his disappointment. This night hadn't ended the way he'd anticipated, but he couldn't expect Hailey to be in the mood after a sniper had put her in his crosshairs.

He smoothed a fingertip over the small cut on her face. He'd thought at first his attraction to Hailey had come from his memories of Lisette, the woman who had been out of his league and out of his reach years ago, but Hailey and Lisette occupied two different planes.

Lisette frittered away her parents' wealth on selfish pursuits and status items meant to dazzle the poor boy from the wrong side of the tracks. Hailey put her father's money to good use, helping others. Hailey used wealth as a tool, a means to a very good end.

And in the process, her goodness had done more to dazzle this poor boy than all the gold in Fort Knox could.

"Hailey." He slipped an arm beneath her back. "Do you want me to carry you up to bed?"

She murmured and burrowed deeper into the chair.

He pushed up from the arm of the chair and grabbed a knitted blanket from the back of the couch. He shook it out and tucked it around her body. Then he kissed her cheek and whispered, "Good night, Hailey."

Holding his hands out, he backed away from her sleeping form. He dashed upstairs, found the promised toothbrush and brushed his teeth. Then he grabbed a blanket from the bed that had been reserved for Ayala. As he reached for the pillows, he stubbed his toe on a hard edge beneath the bed. He flipped up the bedspread and nudged Ayala's laptop farther under the bed. He swung by Hailey's room and snatched a pillow from her bed for good measure.

When he got back downstairs, he wedged her pillow on the right side of Hailey's body and threw the other two at the couch.

He eyed the length of the couch and shrugged. He'd spent the night in worse conditions than a too-short couch in a Pacific Heights mansion with a beautiful woman sleeping in a chair across from him.

He toed off his shoes and pulled down his jeans and socks all at the same time. He unbuttoned his shirt, yanked his T-shirt over his head and folded everything into a neat pile on the coffee table.

He settled one half of the blanket on the couch, anchored it with his body and pulled the other half on top of him for a cover. It took him several minutes to get comfortable. He made the best of it by rolling to his side and hanging one leg off the edge of the couch.

On his side, he had a clear view of Hailey snuggled into the chair. He had no intention of leaving her downstairs on her own.

What worried him was the growing feeling that he could never leave her side again.

HAILEY TURNED HER head and caught her breath. Was the crick in her neck from sleeping in a chair all night or from Joe's life-saving technique of tackling her to the ground?

She rubbed her eyes, and a vision appeared before

her. She rubbed her eyes again to make sure she wasn't dreaming, and the vision only got clearer.

Joe's bare leg hung from the couch, his toes touching the floor, the blanket slipping off his muscled thigh. The other edge of the blanket draped across his torso like a toga, and he certainly did resemble a Greek god.

The muscles she'd imagined and felt beneath layers of clothing appeared before her in an awesome display of maleness.

If that shooter had to take aim at her last night, why couldn't he have waited until after she and Joe had made love? How inconsiderate of him to ruin the moment.

"Is the chair that comfortable?"

Hailey jerked upright. Joe's words wrenched her gaze from his perfect pecs to his slightly amused blue eyes. She pulled the afghan close around her body as if she were the one half-naked and exposed.

"This chair is extremely comfortable. I've crashed here on more than one occasion, usually with a book or tablet abandoned on my chest."

"I felt bad about leaving you in the chair. I thought about carrying you upstairs to bed when you fell asleep, but I didn't want to wake you and I didn't want you sleeping in that drafty room with the shattered window."

"That's fine, but you didn't have to take the couch. I told you there were plenty of rooms upstairs." She punched the pillow under her head. "Hell, you could've taken my room if you don't mind a nice, brisk temperature."

"I didn't want to leave you…here by yourself."

His low voice rolled over her like a warm breeze.

She tucked her hands beneath her cheek. "I'm sorry we were interrupted last night."

"I'm sorry someone took a shot at you."

"And were you also sorry we were interrupted?"

"What do you think?"

"I—I think you don't want to appear callous by being more upset our carnal desires weren't satisfied than the fact that someone tried to kill me."

He grinned and her heart melted around the edges.

"That's a fine line to walk. Can we agree that we're pissed off at that sniper for trying to kill you *and* for splashing cold water on our…carnal desires?"

She pulled the afghan up to her nose and peered at him over the edge. "I can agree to that. Can we also agree that the danger is gone and maybe it's time to return to our original plan?"

He threw off his blanket and placed both feet on the wood floor. "Danger? What danger?"

Hailey squirmed beneath her cover. The only danger she could see now was the fire in Joe's blue eyes.

Before she had a chance to answer his rhetorical question, Joe tossed the blanket behind him and crossed the space between them on his knees. He pulled the lever to recline her chair and she shot forward, her feet swinging to the floor.

He crouched before her and said, "I didn't undress you last night when you fell asleep because I didn't want to…take liberties."

Gripping the arms of the chair with both hands, Hailey lifted her hips. "By all means, take as many liberties with me as you like."

Joe unbuttoned her jeans and tucked his thumbs beneath the waistband on either side. He yanked down her underwear along with her pants and pulled them from her legs. He threw them over his shoulder, never breaking eye contact with her.

A thrill skipped through her body, anticipation making her mouth dry. She didn't have to wait long.

Joe hooked his arms beneath her knees and pulled her forward. He positioned her legs over his shoulders and tucked his hands beneath her bottom.

When his lips touched her throbbing flesh, the world stopped spinning for a split second. When it started again, it seemed to career out of control. She dug her fingernails into his scalp as if that could ground her.

His tongue toyed with her, teased her, and she panted out his name. He stopped his exquisite torture, but she craved more.

She gasped. "You can't stop now."

"I thought that's why you were saying my name… You'd had enough."

"You're a tease." She yanked on his earlobe. "Why are you even talking?"

"Yes, ma'am."

He buried his face between her legs and resumed his exploration of her body and all its sensitivities—and he was a fast study.

Her hands slipped from his russet hair to his shoulders, which she squeezed and molded as he kept taking her to unimaginable heights of pleasure.

She reached the precipice of her climax a few times only to have Joe shift his attention to her inner thigh or to a freckle just above her mound. Her frustration quickly morphed into a searing need that built up in her core and heated her blood beyond the boiling point.

After yet another detour, Joe swept his tongue across the pulse beating between her thighs. The ache in her belly exploded into a million pieces, and she arched her back, driving herself against Joe's mouth.

He didn't pull away, which made her orgasm tumble into infinity, wave after wave of pleasure engulf-ing her body.

Drained and sated, she slumped back against the chair, her legs still dangling over Joe's shoulders.

He eased back, cupped her heel and kissed the arch of her foot. "How was that?"

She opened one eye. "You have to ask? That was incredible."

"Hard to deliver something to the woman who has everything."

"I do now." She wiggled her toes at him. "Well, al-most everything."

"What else can I give you?"

"For starters, you can slip off those boxers and let me do what I do best."

"What you do best?" He raised one eyebrow.

She placed one foot against his chest. "You said it yourself. I'm the giving type, generous to a fault."

"I don't remember saying it was a fault of yours." He hooked his thumbs under the waistband of his boxers and pulled them down his powerful thighs.

Her heart rate, which had been returning to normal, spiked again. She slid from the chair and knelt in front of him, wrapping her arms around his waist.

"You know what?" He scooped his hand into her hair. "I didn't even properly kiss you."

"Whatever you just did couldn't be called 'proper,' so I'm not holding my breath for a proper kiss, either."

He hunched forward, pulling her head toward him and slanting his mouth over hers. His tongue, which had just teased her to crazy heights of pleasure, continued its assault as his lips pressed against hers.

When he finally released her, breathless and wanting more, she gasped. "If that's a proper kiss, sign me up for propriety."

Joe rose to his feet and started to take his place in the chair, but she wrapped her hands around his calves.

"I want to taste you, too." She took his erection into her mouth and skimmed her tongue along the length of him.

He moved against her and sucked in a breath. "I can't last long like this." He gasped. "Especially when you do *that*."

He pulled away from her and sat in the chair, yanking her down on his lap. "Is this a very expensive chair?"

She straddled him. "Very."

"Oh, well."

He plunged into her and she rode him. At one point the chair flipped back into a reclining position, but it barely put a hitch in their rhythm—and they did have a rhythm.

Having Joe inside her felt more right than anything she'd ever experienced. He seemed attuned to every nuance of her body to bring her maximum pleasure, which made her feel safe in his arms.

When her climax took her this time, it flooded her body, rocking her gently up and down. That blissful ease didn't last long as Joe reached his own pinnacle. He thrust against her madly, hungrily, clawing at her backside in a futile effort to purchase some stability.

It didn't work. He yelled and howled like a crazy man and took them both over the side of the chair.

They lay on their sides, their limbs entwined, laughing and gasping, clinging to each other as if they'd never let go.

Hailey didn't want to ever let go.

When the pounding on the front door started, reality came crashing down on their pretty dream.

Chapter Eleven

"Ms. Duvall? It's Agent Porter."

Joe groaned and flung his forearm across his eyes. "I can't believe the FBI is interrupting my postcoital haze."

"Is that what this is?" Hailey scrambled to her feet and lunged for her jeans and panties.

She still had her top on, and Joe couldn't believe he hadn't explored those beautiful breasts along with the rest of her body.

As she stepped into her jeans, she nudged his bare backside with her toe. "Move. I'm not inviting Porter in with you sprawled out on my floor naked."

"I would hope not." Joe gathered up his clothing, the pillows and both blankets and headed up the stairs, two at a time.

He slipped into Hailey's bedroom, chilly from the cold air seeping through the hole in the window. Porter's banging on the door and this cold slap to the face both served as reminders of his true mission here in San Francisco—and that wasn't to finally land the rich girl.

The murmur of voices carried upstairs. He tossed Hailey's pillow back on her bed, messed up the covers and dropped the knitted blanket on the foot of the bed. Then he dragged the other blanket to the guest room

Ayala was supposed to occupy before she was poisoned at dinner and put it and the pillows back on the bed.

He clicked the door closed, made up the bed and got dressed just as Hailey led Porter upstairs.

He pressed his ear to the guest room door and heard Hailey's voice. "I had a friend with me and he noticed a red dot on my forehead and pushed me down."

"Where's your…friend now?"

"He went home. You don't need to talk to him, do you? He doesn't know anything, and the cops already interviewed him last night."

"The police took the bullet?"

"Dug it right out of the wall over here."

The voices faded out to the point where Joe could just hear a word or two.

He paced the room while he waited, feeling ridiculous hiding out. Would Porter even know who he was? Recognize his name? He didn't want to take any chances. Major Denver needed him active and engaged, not sidelined and reprimanded. So, for now he'd hide out like a thief in the night.

He walked past the bed for the hundredth time and kicked the cord connecting Ayala's laptop to an outlet under the bed.

Finally, he heard the front door slam and Hailey's footsteps on the stairs.

She tapped on the door. "Are you decent?"

He called back, "Does it matter?"

The door swung open, and Hailey stood on the threshold, one hand on her hip. "I was hoping you weren't."

He swooped toward her and kissed her mouth, just because he could. "How'd it go? Did you finally get Porter's attention?"

"Oh, yeah." She wrapped her hands around his waist and tucked her hands in his back pockets—probably because she could. "He figures it was a high-powered rifle, and this time, unlike the car on the sidewalk, whoever took aim at me had deadly intent."

"No kidding. You told him about Ayala?"

"I did, and he's taking that seriously, too. I also asked him to check on Naraj and if he'd heard anything from the UK about Andrew yet."

"And?"

"The FBI was actually one step ahead of me. They've tried contacting Naraj, but nobody can find him." She bit her lip and shook her head at him. "Don't even say it."

"What about Andrew Reese?"

"MI6 hasn't contacted him yet, or at least the CIA hasn't let Porter know anything about Andrew. I think Porter turned over the request to the CIA, so they're looking into Andrew's whereabouts."

"Gotta love that cooperation between agencies. Do you see now why my teammates and I are taking the investigation of Denver into our own hands? We can't get anyone to believe us about the conspiracy, even after what Cam and Asher uncovered."

"I think I'm making some progress with Agent Porter, though. That sniper attack on me rattled him…and he's not easily rattled."

"The Fibbies tend to be a stoic bunch." Joe ran a hand through his hair. "I need a shower if we're going to head over to the hospital and pick up Ayala."

"She won't be discharged until later today, but let's get breakfast and I have a few last-minute errands to run for the event." Placing her hands against his chest, she whispered, "I'd offer to shower with you, but then we'd never get out of here."

"God, I'm glad you're safe." He enfolded her in his arms.

"Thanks to you. I'm glad you accosted me on Fisherman's Wharf. I don't know where I'd be if you hadn't."

"Maybe you would've been safer." He rested his chin on the top of her head. "Maybe they're targeting you because of me. If you'd kept your head down, accepted that Marten had changed his mind about the meeting and had gone about your business as usual, you might not have ended up with a red laser beam on your forehead."

She stepped back from him, and strands of her hair stuck to his chin, keeping them connected. "Don't be dumb. Marten involved me the minute he contacted me when he got here, the minute he decided to leave me a key."

"You might be right."

"I am right." She placed her hands on his shoulders and squeezed. "And if you hadn't been around to protect me, I'd be in big trouble right now…or dead."

A knot twisted in his gut, and he pulled her close again, inhaling the musky scent of morning sex that clung to her body. His own body responded, and he took a step back so she couldn't feel his erection. He cleared his throat. "When are you getting that window fixed?"

Her gaze dropped to his crotch as a smile tugged at one corner of her mouth. "I'll call someone today to fix that… The window, I mean."

"You have a dirty mind, Ms. Duvall." He pinched her chin between his thumb and the side of his forefinger.

"You have no idea, Captain McVie." She patted his backside before spinning around. "But unless you plan to use what you're packing there, we need to get ready to go to the hospital."

"Towels?"

As she reached the bedroom door, she looked over her shoulder. "That was a fast recovery. Should I be insulted?"

"Even the thought of a cold shower will do that to a guy, so no."

"Clean towels and everything else you'll need are in the bathroom."

She swept out of the room, and he said to the closed door, "Not everything I need."

LATER AS HE sat beside Hailey in the Jag, he turned toward her. "Do you think Ayala will be able to make it to the fund-raiser?"

"If she doesn't have any lasting effects from the poison, she should be okay, but I don't know if she'll want to attend now. Why would she want to broaden that target on her back, especially once she hears what happened last night?"

"She didn't seem that enthusiastic in the first place."

"Yeah, she's shy and definitely doesn't like to brag about her efforts."

"I got that. Didn't seem interested in talking about the refugee center at all. Most of the time, people who do work that's close to their hearts like that can't stop talking about it."

"Ayala's reserved." She swung into the passenger loading area on the side of the large hospital's emergency entrance. "I think we can leave the car here as long as we're picking up a patient."

"And if we can't, you can always drop your father's name."

She threw the car into Park and pointed a finger at him. "I'm gonna take that as a joke, McVie."

"I'm only half joking. I'm getting accustomed to the perks afforded by Ray Duvall."

She snorted and exited the car.

The parking attendant tucked a ticket beneath the windshield wiper of the Jag, and Joe took Hailey's arm as they walked into the cavernous hospital.

They passed the emergency waiting room, and a man called out to Hailey.

Joe's protective instincts flared, but before he could embarrass himself again by taking down one of Hailey's friends, Hailey waved to the man.

"Patrick, how's it going?"

"Great." Patrick walked toward them, a slight limp hindering his gait. He gave Hailey a hug, and a different kind of instinct flared in Joe's gut.

Hailey pulled away first and gestured toward Joe. "Patrick, this is my friend Joe. Joe, Patrick."

As he shook Patrick's hand, Joe childishly applied more pressure than necessary. What made it worse was that Patrick's eyes twinkled, reading him like a cheap paperback novel.

Hailey touched Patrick's arm. "I hope you're not here for yourself."

"Naw—" he jerked a thumb over his shoulder "— one of the guys took a fall this morning."

Joe gazed over Patrick's shoulder at a transient, holding his head in his hands.

Hailey followed Joe's line of sight. "Patrick runs a homeless shelter in the Mission District."

"Mission Hope." Patrick jingled a large key chain in

his hand. "Hailey's foundation has contributed a lot of money to our cause."

As usual, Hailey brushed off the praise. "Tax deduction."

Patrick's keys fell out of his hands, and Joe stooped to retrieve them. "Let me."

He scooped up the keys. As he shook them out, his pulse jumped. "What is this key?"

"Which one?" Patrick's eyebrows created a V over his nose.

Joe plucked out a key with a round cardboard tag attached to it. He studied the tag, but the writing on it in pencil had been smeared off—just like another key.

"That's a key to one of the lockers at the shelter."

"The shelter called Mission Hope. *M-I-S-S...*"

Hailey's eyes widened as she snatched the key from Joe's hand. "It looks the same. Marten knew about my work with Mission Hope, knew I'd been there before."

Patrick's head turned from side to side as if he were watching a tennis match. "What are you two talking about and can I please have my keys back?"

"Sorry." Hailey dropped the key chain into Patrick's outstretched palm. "Someone left me a key, and we've been trying to figure out what it unlocked."

"Do you have it on you?"

Hailey patted her pockets. "I left it at home, but it looks the same, doesn't it?"

"It sure does. Patrick, what did the writing on this circle say before it was wiped off?"

"'Mission Hope.'"

Joe asked, "Who gets keys to those lockers?"

"They're first come, first served. If a homeless person comes to the shelter and has valuables, or at least what he considers valuables, he can leave them in a locker while he's sleeping at the shelter or when he goes out to panhandle." Patrick extended his hand to Joe. "You're welcome to come by and check out the lockers at any time…as long as you bring a check or some food or toiletries. Nice to meet you. I have to get back to Michael."

Joe shook the man's hand—without the extra pressure this time. "Thanks. We'll do that."

"Great to see you again, Patrick." Hailey gave him a hug.

Patrick returned to Michael and sat next to him in the plastic chair.

Seemed he was surrounded by do-gooders. Joe touched Hailey's back. "Looks like we found the match to our key."

"I think so. Marten was at the shelter for some reason and thought it was a good idea to get a locker."

"Maybe because he figured nobody would think to look in a locker at a homeless shelter—except for his philanthropic friend who just might recognize a key from Mission Hope."

"As soon as we get Ayala settled at my place, we'll grab that key and pay a visit to Mission Hope with food and toiletries in hand."

Hailey checked in at the desk and joined Joe at the wide double doors leading to the treatment rooms of the emergency wing.

"The nurses told me she's doing fine and is ready to leave."

They found Ayala's bed, which occupied one of four curtained-off areas in a large room.

Hailey whipped back the curtain and rushed to Ayala's bedside. "Oh my God. How are you doing? I was so worried when I found you on that bathroom floor."

Ayala, her dark head propped up against a snowy-white pillow, gave Hailey a weak smile. "I can imagine."

Hailey whispered, "Was it poison? Did the police come by and talk to you?"

Ayala gave a shake of her head. "It wasn't poison, Hailey."

"What?"

Joe pushed a chair against the backs of Hailey's legs before she collapsed, and she sank into it.

He put a hand on Hailey's shoulder. "What did the doctors say, Ayala?"

She shrugged, and the hospital gown slipped from one shoulder. "A stomach upset and too much alcohol."

Hailey hunched forward. "You don't believe that, do you?"

"I don't know what to believe. I've been drunk before. This didn't feel like too much alcohol. Maybe it was all our talk before, but I immediately thought someone had poisoned me."

"But the doctors didn't find any poison in your system." Joe sucked in one side of his cheek. "I suppose there are certain poisons that can be masked."

"Are there?" Ayala folded her arms. "I wouldn't know, but I do want to get out of here."

Hailey squeezed her hand. "We're here to pick you up and take you back to my place, but I should warn you, someone took a shot at me through my bedroom window last night."

Ayala gasped and clutched the sheet. "This is crazy. You should get out of this city, Hailey. We both should."

"I'm planning on it, but not before the fund-raiser. You'll be safe at my place for now. How are you feeling?"

"A little weak, but fine. They did pump my stomach, so if it was some kind of stealth poison, it's out now." Ayala closed her eyes. "Hailey."

"Yes?" Hailey shot a sidelong glance at Joe.

"I can't do that gala now. I'm sorry. I just want to get back to Florida."

"Of course. Don't even think about it."

A nurse bustled into the area, clutching paperwork to her chest. "Ms. Khan, you just need to sign a few forms and you're on your way." Ayala scribbled her signature a couple of times, and the nurse left some papers with her. "Hope you're feeling better."

Ayala swung her legs off the bed. "I'll feel better when I get out of this hospital gown and away from the guy hacking up his guts next to me."

Hailey stood up and retrieved Ayala's neatly folded clothes from a shelf. "Will you be okay if we leave you at my place on your own for a while?"

"Sure. Why?" Ayala took the bundle of clothing from Hailey.

Joe gritted his back teeth. Why did Hailey feel the need to spill the beans to everyone? That key was need to know, and Ayala Khan didn't need to know.

"We think we might've found out what Marten's key unlocks."

"Oh?"

"By chance, I ran into a friend of mine who runs Mission Hope in the Mission District, and he had a key on him that looks just like Marten's."

"Be careful, Hailey. I still think you should let this go. I'm not sure the doc knows what he's talking about. That was poison coursing through my veins." She held out one hand to Joe. "Tell her, Joe."

"You know Hailey better than I do."

Ayala sighed. "You're right. Just take care of her. Now, if you two don't mind, I'm going to get out of this ugly gown."

"We'll be in the waiting room." Hailey patted Ayala's hand. "Take it easy."

Joe kept quiet down the corridor, which buzzed with new arrivals, a crying baby and nurses weaving in and out of the rooms. When they got back to the waiting room, he plopped down in a plastic chair that wobbled beneath him.

"That was strange."

"Ayala? I know. Why was she so sure it was poison?"

"Maybe she lied to get out of the speech at the fund-raiser."

Hailey punched his thigh as she sat down. "Be serious. It could've been poison that the doctor didn't or couldn't detect."

"That's a possibility." Joe nibbled on a rough cuticle on the side of his thumb.

"Are you biting your nails over this?" Hailey grabbed his wrist and folded both of her hands around his.

"Don't tell me you're going to send me in for a manicure before the big event." He splayed his free hand in front of him. "Delta Force don't do manicures."

"I prefer your rugged hands to a pair of soft, polished ones."

"Good."

"Whatever got Ayala, it spooked her."

"Shh." Joe tipped his head toward the double doors as the subject of their conversation walked into the waiting room.

Hailey tilted her head at him. "I don't know why you want to keep her in the dark about everything."

"I don't know why, either. Habit." But the words

fell on deaf ears as Hailey launched herself toward her friend.

Joe stayed put, rising from his chair when the women approached. He pasted on a concerned expression. "All ready?"

"So ready to get out of here." Ayala hooked her hand through Hailey's arm. "It totally slipped my mind, but an Agent Porter from the FBI visited me right before you showed up."

Hailey whipped her head around. "He did? I met with him this morning about the shooting and told him about you. That was fast. What did he say? He didn't tell you about the shooting?"

"He didn't mention it, and he didn't have much to say about anything else once he saw my toxicology report. There was nothing in my system except alcohol."

Joe allowed the women to exit before him, and Hailey pulled out her car keys and punched the remote. The Jag beeped once.

Joe opened the door for Ayala, and as she slid into the back seat, he asked, "If you saw Porter before, didn't he tell you about the sniper shooting at Hailey?"

"Oddly enough, he did not." She dipped her head to reach for her seat belt, and her long hair hung like a curtain over the side of her face.

"Did he tell you why he was visiting you and how he knew you were at the hospital?"

Ayala snapped the seat belt in place. "He said Hailey told him about my incident last night."

Joe shut the back passenger door and climbed into the front. "Agent Porter never mentioned the shooting to Ayala. Isn't that odd?"

"You said it yourself." Hailey cranked on the engine. "Fibbies play it close to the vest."

"Did I say that?"

"Or maybe you were talking about Delta Force." Hailey peeled out of the parking lot. "Are you hungry, Ayala?"

"Ugh, the thought of food literally turns my stomach right now. I'll take some tea when we get back to your place, though…and I'll get it myself. You two should head over to Mission Hope. Maybe you can put a stop to all this once you check out that locker."

"We can only hope."

When they arrived at the house, Hailey pulled the car into the driveway. She turned to Joe. "You can wait here. I'll see Ayala in, show her around the kitchen and head right back down."

Joe clicked open his door. "I need the exercise."

Hailey caught her breath, realizing he still wanted to keep tabs on her. "Sure you do."

Joe kept Hailey and Ayala in front of him as they climbed the stairs. As always, he'd kept watch to make sure they hadn't been followed, even though the bad guys knew exactly where Hailey lived, and now he had to look out for snipers in the treetops.

Safely inside, Hailey patted the couch that had served as Joe's bed last night. "Have a seat. I'll make you some tea."

"Don't be silly. I can walk into the kitchen and make a cup of tea."

"Let me at least get it ready for you." Hailey charged into the kitchen as if she were ready to turn out a full-course meal instead of boiling some water.

Joe took up a station near the front window. "Should we check that security footage, Hailey?"

"We can do it when we get back. Do you want some water or anything before we head out again?"

"Just a glass of water, please."

Hailey held a glass to the ice maker on the outside of the fridge and filled it with water. She took a few steps out of the kitchen when the teakettle blew.

Ayala pushed up from the couch and sauntered into the kitchen, taking the glass from Hailey. She brought it to Joe and joined him at the window. "See anything interesting out there?"

"Thanks." He took the glass from her. "Not much. Not high enough to see the bay, either."

Hailey called from the kitchen, "Milk?"

"Yes, please." Ayala rolled her eyes at Joe. "Really, I can make my own tea."

Hailey ignored her and continued banging around the kitchen. "What are you going to do the rest of the afternoon? You should take a nap. Bed's all ready for you."

"Maybe."

Joe took a gulp of water. "And your laptop is still under the bed."

Ayala jerked her head around so fast, Joe thought she saw something out the window.

"Did you see something?"

"I—I thought maybe something by the bench in that little park." As she pointed out the window, the red stone on her ring caught the light, flashing a beam on her face not unlike the one centered on Hailey's forehead last night.

Joe cupped his hand over his eyes as he peered through the window. "I don't see anything. Hailey's house has an alarm system. Just stay away from the windows and you should be safe enough here."

"Tea time." Hailey carried a steaming mug into the living room. "I left a few more tea bags on the counter for you, the kettle's on the stove and milk is in the fridge if you want more."

"Thank you so much. I'll be fine here—go."

Hailey swept Marten's key from the counter and grabbed her purse. As she hoisted her bag over her shoulder, she turned at the door. "Set the alarm when you get the chance—5806."

Ayala waved.

When they stepped onto the porch and Hailey had shut and locked the dead bolt, Joe poked her in the side. "Now you have to change that code as soon as you get home."

"I had to give it to her. How else was she going to arm it?"

"Just sayin'. Reset it."

Hailey saluted. "Aye, aye, Captain."

"I'm not in the navy." He poked her again. "Are we taking your car?"

"There's parking around the back, and I know Patrick's car, so I can block him in if I have to."

"There you go with your friends in high places again."

As they got in the car, Joe glanced up at the window, partially obscured by the bushes in the front garden. The drapes stirred and then dropped into place. "Looks like Ayala didn't waste any time setting the alarm."

Hailey said, "Good. She seemed nervous."

"She thought she saw something in the park." Joe clicked his seat belt.

"Did she?"

"It was her imagination. There was nothing there."

Hailey nodded. "Yeah, nervous."

Hailey navigated like a pro through the busy San

Francisco streets, driving past Union Square, where the Christmas tree still towered above shoppers.

Two blocks later the shoppers had thinned out, replaced by shopping carts pushed by raggedy men and women looking to score a quick buck or two.

"How often do you come down here?"

"Not enough. My assistant, Gretchen, delivers care packages from the foundation occasionally." She hit the steering wheel. "Shoot. We forgot to bring the food and toiletries."

"I'll write a check instead. I'm sure there are a fair number of vets out on the streets here. Let me feel the glow of a good deed for a change."

"I have a feeling you do plenty of good deeds." She wheeled around the back of a gray stucco building sporting a neon sign announcing the Mission Hope, only the *P* and the *E* had burned out at the end.

Joe nudged her and pointed at the sign. "I'm sure that's not what Patrick wants to advertise."

Hailey giggled. "It could be worse if the *I, O* and *N* on the end of *mission* were also burned out."

She parked behind a black Prius with a Coexist bumper sticker.

"Let me guess." Joe leveled a finger at the car. "That's Patrick's."

"That's why I'm parking here."

Joe kept a tight hold on Hailey's arm with one hand and a tight hold on the barrel of his gun with the other as they walked through an alley leading to the back door of the shelter.

A few homeless guys loitering with cigarettes dangling from their lips held out their hands. Joe brushed past them.

When they stepped inside, a cook hovering over a

boiling pot called a welcome without looking up. "Dinner doesn't start for another few hours and you can't start lining up for another hour—around the front."

"Actually, we're here to see Patrick."

The cook glanced up from his work. "Oh, sorry. Yeah, Patrick's out in the van rounding up some poor souls for dinner."

"That's okay. Are the lockers still in the front room, on the other side of the dining hall?"

"They are." He put his spoon down and swiped a towel across his forehead. "You lookin' for something in particular?"

Hailey held up the key and dangled it in the light. "Just checking on my friend's locker."

"Okay, go ahead, then. What was your name again?"

"It's Hailey. Hailey Duvall."

"Ah, why didn't you say so? I know the name, and now I know the beautiful face behind all that generous giving."

"This place couldn't run without people like you." She closed her hand around the key and backed out of the kitchen.

She led the way past a dining area with rows of empty picnic tables lined up. "The locker room is on the other side of this."

A couple of transients looked up from their card game as Hailey and Joe walked by a common room.

Hailey entered another room where banks of metal lockers hugged the walls. Some of the lockers had keys hanging from them.

Joe flicked one of the familiar keys with his finger. "How much to rent one?"

"I think it's still a quarter." She placed her hands on her hips and surveyed the room. "There's no number on this key chain, so I have no idea which one it belongs to."

"I'm wondering how these guys remember which lockers are theirs, especially if they come in here drunk or drugged out."

"They're not allowed in here when they're high."

"Let's face it. Some of them are just high on life, if you know what I mean—they're in a permanently altered state without any substances to help them along."

"I'm sure Patrick and the rest of the staff help them out."

"We don't have that luxury right now." He banged his fist on the first locker to the right. "You ready to try your luck?"

"At least we can rule out the ones that already have keys." She stepped forward and tried to insert Marten's key in the first locked locker. "Nope."

Hailey tried the lockers on the top row, with no results, and crouched down to start on the bottom row.

A transient with a hat pulled halfway over his face shuffled into the room, and Joe nodded at him.

The transient tipped his head and then stuffed his hands into the pockets of his bulky overcoat, mumbling to himself.

"None of these." Hailey popped up, bumping Joe's arm with the top of her head, noticing the homeless guy in the corner for the first time. She zeroed in on him and said, "Do you need help finding something?"

Joe tapped the side of her boot with his toe.

She scowled at him, reserving her smile for the transient. "Can we help you?"

"No!"

Hailey jumped back at the shout and put a hand to her throat. "All righty then."

"Keep moving, Hailey." Joe tapped the next locked locker.

She inserted the key, and it clicked. "This is it."

Out of the corner of his eye, Joe detected a flash of movement. He reached for his gun, but the fake homeless guy beat him to the punch.

By the time Joe spun around with his weapon in hand, the transient had his arm around Hailey's neck and a gun to her head.

Chapter Twelve

Hailey twisted her head to the side and tried to sink her teeth into the arm that held her, but the man tightened his grip and she choked.

Joe stood in front of them, blocking Marten's locker, his gun pointed at the man who held her.

The man, who didn't smell homeless at all, shoved the cold metal of his gun against her temple. "Don't even think about it, or I drop her right here. Place your gun on the floor and kick it toward me."

"Don't do it, Joe. He's going to kill me anyway. You know what happened at the house."

Joe waved his gun at the man. "Who are you, and what do you want?"

The man chuckled, his hot breath blasting her ear. "I'm holding all the cards here. Why would I tell you anything? Now step aside so I can get whatever it is de Becker left there for Hailey."

Hailey blinked rapidly at Joe and mouthed the word *move*.

Without releasing his gun, Joe took a few shuffling steps to his right.

The man spit out, "More."

Hailey gave Joe a wink, and he moved farther from the locker but still kept his gun trained on Hailey's captor.

The man descended on the open locker, dragging Hailey with him and keeping one eye on Joe.

He probably didn't want to shoot her here because of the men in the other room playing cards. A gunshot in a homeless shelter would be a very big deal. Of course, once he took her out of here, all bets were off...if he did take her out of here.

Still facing Joe, the man made a half turn toward the locker and plunged his hand inside the small space, the sound of his fingernails scrabbling across the metal echoing in the room. "What the hell?"

He made another sweep of the empty locker and ended it with a thump of his fist. "What did you do with it?"

"There was nothing in there."

"Liar." He pushed Hailey back, and her head banged against the bank of lockers.

Joe growled and took a step forward.

"Don't move. I swear I'll kill her."

"You're not going to shoot anyone in here. This place probably has a hotline to the SFPD."

Joe's cold voice had her swallowing hard. How could he be so sure?

"Look, I don't have anything. I didn't take anything out of that locker because it was empty." She spread her arms out to the sides. "Search me."

Someone laughed from the other room, and the man's eye twitched.

What would he do if they were interrupted? Would he start shooting? She couldn't allow that to happen.

"Take me out of here, and I'll show you. I have nothing on me."

"Hailey, no." Joe moved closer. "I'm not going to let him take you anywhere."

"What the hell is going on in here?" Two of the men from the card game stumbled into the locker room and hovered at the doorway, their eyes wide as they looked from Joe's gun to her captor's.

"None of your business. Get the hell out of here… losers."

The two men turned, and then one of them grunted and charged at Hailey and the man holding her.

The attack surprised her captor. He swung his gun from Hailey's head toward his oncoming attacker and took a shot.

Hailey screamed.

Joe lunged forward and pushed her behind him.

The homeless hero fell on top of the shooter and they grappled on the cement floor, the gun between them.

Joe raised his own weapon, taking aim at the two men rolling on the floor.

"Be careful, Joe. Don't hit the homeless guy."

Cheers and shouts filled the room and Hailey's mouth dropped open as she saw the men crowding the doorway and rooting on their guy as if this were an MMA fight instead of a life-or-death struggle.

Joe got closer to the melee on the floor and shouted, "Stop. Stop."

A shot sounded, and Hailey covered her ears as the sound bounded off the walls. She plastered herself against the lockers, her mouth dry as she watched the two men on the floor slowly separate.

The transient rolled off the other man, breathing hard and clutching his bloody leg. He coughed and then laughed like a crazy person.

Hailey's gaze shifted to the man who'd had her at gunpoint.

Joe crouched beside the form sprawled out on the

cement, blood pumping and spurting from a wound on his chest. Joe had his fingers at the man's pulse and was furiously whispering something in his ear.

Patrick stormed into the room. "What the hell happened here? Someone call 911. Trace, are you okay?"

The transient on the floor groaned and rolled to his side. "The guy shot me in the leg. They saw it. Self-defense, man. He had a gun on that woman."

Patrick stepped away from the carnage on the floor and grabbed Hailey's arm. "Is this true?"

"It's all true. That guy—" she pointed at the man expiring on the floor, Joe still beside him "—had a gun on me, and Trace came in here and charged him."

Joe straightened up, rubbing his hands on the thighs of his jeans. "He could've gotten Hailey killed, and himself, but Trace definitely saved the day."

Trace grabbed his bloody leg. "The guy called us 'losers.' I'm no loser. I'm a US marine."

An hour later, Hailey slumped behind the wheel of the Jag with Joe beside her. "Since you're all over that police report, is it going to get back to your superiors?"

"Oh, yeah. I'm just glad Trace kept his mouth shut about *my* gun. That would've been a whole lot harder to explain without a concealed-carry license here in California."

"I'm just glad the guy didn't decide to shoot me first before Trace got to him."

"Trace had the element of surprise going for him. Never been happier to see a marine." He traced a finger down her throat. "It's still red. The only thing I regret is not killing the bastard myself."

"You were too busy worrying about me." She smoothed a thumb against the crease between his eyebrows. "Did you get anything out of the dead guy?"

"What do you mean?"

"I saw you talking to him, or at least trying to talk to him as he lay dying. Did he give you any answers to your questions?"

"He was too busy trying to catch his last breaths." He patted his jacket pocket. "I did get his prints, though—just in case the SFPD doesn't care to share his identity."

"I stuck as closely to the truth as possible—my friend left me a key to his locker at Mission Hope and that man attacked us and held me at gunpoint to get whatever was in the locker."

Joe massaged his temples. "Which was empty, anyway."

"Not. Quite." Hailey slid a slip of paper from inside her bra and proffered it to Joe between thumb and forefinger.

He jerked forward. "You got this out of the locker?"

"My hand was already inside the locker when the fake transient made his move. I snatched the piece of paper and shoved it down my top, pretending to hold my hand against my heart."

"I'll be damned." He punched on the dome light with his knuckle and read aloud. "'I'm still alive. MDB.'"

"Marten. Marten's still alive."

"And this—" Joe waved the slip of paper in the air "—is how he decided to tell you? That son of a..."

Hailey snatched the paper from his hands, crumpled it up and swallowed it.

His eyebrows jumped to his hairline. "Why'd you do that?"

"I don't want anyone to see it. Nobody needs to know that Marten survived that push or fall or jump from the ferry." She patted her stomach. "Nobody knows."

"I think you're taking this subterfuge a little overboard." He smacked the dashboard. "He put you in all kinds of danger by leaving you that key just to tell you he was among the living."

"I don't think that was his original intent, Joe. I believe he left me something in that locker, and when he survived, he returned to the shelter to collect it and replaced it with that note."

"You're probably right. That makes the most sense." He drummed his fingers on his knee. "Why hasn't he come forward with his info yet? It would be stupid to change his mind now because the people after him don't care and wouldn't trust him, anyway."

"He must be in hiding, waiting for the right moment."

"The right moment is now, to protect you and get these people off your back. Doesn't he realize he's put your life in danger with his silly spy games?"

"Maybe he's not aware of the attempts on my life."

Joe clenched his jaw. "He should've been able to figure that out. He knew people were following him. He knew enough to arrange a secret meeting with you and to leave you the evidence in case something happened to him."

"I'm just amazed Marten was able to survive in the bay that night."

"You heard Joost. Marten was some kind of Olympic swimmer."

"That survival is a story I hope to hear someday—straight from Marten's lips." Hailey started the engine and cranked up the heater. "I hope Trace is going to be okay. What do you think the police are going to find out about the dead guy?"

"Probably whatever his bosses want them to know. That's why I took his fingerprints myself." Joe sawed his lower lip with his teeth as he stared at the alley behind the shelter.

"What's wrong?"

"The twenty-five-million-dollar question."

"Which is?"

"How the hell did anyone know about that key? How did that man know we would be at the shelter at precisely that minute?"

"He followed us from the house."

"Dressed as a transient?"

"He…he— Wait." She braced her hands against the steering wheel. "You can't be implying that Patrick had anything to do with this."

"Patrick? He's not the only other person besides us who knew about the key and the shelter."

Hailey knitted her brows. "Not Ayala."

"She's the only person outside of Patrick and us and maybe Joost who knew about the key."

"That's not possible." A flash of heat claimed her body, and Hailey turned down the car heater. "Ayala was attacked last night. Poisoned."

"Was she? That's not what the toxicology report indicated."

"But we all agreed that the poison could've been something undetectable. She passed out in the bathroom. I saw her, felt her clammy skin."

"That could've been the result of anything—even playacting."

Hailey clutched her hair at the nape of her neck as her head swam. "Are you saying you think she set up the whole poisoning scene? For what possible purpose?"

"For this purpose." Joe drew a circle in the air with his finger. "To throw us off her trail. If Ayala is a victim just like you, how could she be responsible for the attacks on you?"

"Joe, this is crazy. I worked with Ayala for over a year in the refugee center."

"What did you learn about her in that time? You said she was reserved. Where's her brother? Her husband?"

"Husband? She doesn't have a husband."

"Fiancé? She wears a ring with a single red stone on the ring finger of her left hand."

"She does?"

"She was the only one of you, Marten and Andrew who didn't ID Denver. Just like the poisoning, she's trying to keep a low profile. Here I was thinking Siddiqi was the mole when it could very well be Ayala. She knows the area, the language, the people."

"That's just it. She cares for those people. You haven't seen her in action."

"She might care for them on one level, but they'll never trump her ideology. I've run across several extremists. They don't think like the rest of us do."

Hailey pinned her unsteady hands between her knees. "You think she came out here to monitor the situation? Gain my trust and then strike?"

"I do. Maybe her associates had already put the plan with Marten in motion, and when they realized Marten had communicated with you, they sent for her to cozy up to you, find out what you knew or suspected."

"You were suspicious of her from the beginning, weren't you? Maybe it was your instinct kicking in when you first saw her that told you she posed a threat to me."

"I took her down because I thought her umbrella was a gun."

"Makes perfect sense to me, because an umbrella

looks just like a gun." Tipping her head back, she closed her eyes. "I still can't believe it. You might be wrong."

"I'm not wrong, Hailey. Nobody else could've tipped off the gunman that we were at Mission Hope looking for Marten's locker."

"So she got on her phone as soon as we left the house and alerted someone."

"She did it before that—when we left her to get dressed in the hospital. She knew about the key then. Who knows? She could've even left something in this car, like a GPS to track us. She could be on her computer right now cooking up the next plot."

"She didn't bring her laptop."

"Yes, she did…" Joe snapped his fingers. "Now I know it's her. She told us she didn't have her computer, didn't she?"

"That's why she didn't see my email. She doesn't like reading emails on her phone and said she didn't have her laptop."

"She does have it. She left it charging under the bed, and I stubbed my toe on it while I was waiting for you to finish up with Porter this morning."

"Oh my God. So she lied about the computer. What else?"

"A lot." He turned toward her and grabbed her arm. "Hailey."

"What?" His tone sent a river of chills down her spine.

"She knows I'm on to her."

"How do you know that?"

"I mentioned that she could pass the time this afternoon on her laptop, totally forgetting she wasn't supposed to have it here. It gave her a start when I said it."

Hailey shook her head, trying to clear the fuzz in her

brain. "When we show up alive, she's going to be even surer that we're on to her."

"If she hasn't heard from her contact by now, she's going to assume the plan didn't work. She already knows we're on to her."

"And she's alone in my house."

"I doubt she's going to be hanging around, but step on it anyway."

Hailey squealed out of the lot behind the shelter and made good time, despite the traffic. She hoped Ayala wasn't there. She wouldn't know what to say to her. How did you confront someone you thought was your friend but who was capable of such evil?

As she pulled into the driveway, Joe put a hand on her arm. "Let's take it easy."

"You said she wouldn't be here." She clenched the steering wheel, her white knuckles practically glowing in the dark. "I don't want to see her...ever again."

"I do. I want to finish what I started when I first laid eyes on her, but she's not gonna be sitting in that chair with a cup of tea waiting for us."

"Then what are we waiting for?" Hailey yanked on the door handle.

"Hailey, we don't know what kind of surprise she might've left us. Her henchman at the shelter wasn't successful, and these people don't give up."

Hailey ducked her head. "Don't tell me there's going to be another sniper waiting for me in the tree across the street."

"I don't know what might be waiting for us. That's why we're going to be careful and take it slow and easy." He swung open his door. "Wait for me."

In the rearview mirror, Hailey watched Joe shrug out

of his jacket. When he reached the driver's-side door, she cracked it open for him.

"Okay, come on out, slowly."

She grabbed her purse from the center console and hugged it to her chest as she slid out of the car.

Joe stepped around her immediately, placed his body between her and the sidewalk, and draped his jacket over her head. With one arm firmly around her shoulders, he walked her up the steps.

She stumbled once or twice, but Joe steadied her.

"No red laser beams on the back of my head?"

"Nope. We're almost at the door. Keys."

As she handed him her key chain, she tossed off the jacket and looked over her shoulder. "Safe here?"

"Yeah." He stretched up and felt along the top of the doorjamb, his fingers trailing over the wood. Then he knelt down and inspected the base of the door and curled up one corner of the mat.

Hailey held her breath through the search when a thought hit her square in the chest. "The food. She could've even poisoned my food."

"Good point." Joe slid the key into the lock and turned it slowly. He released a breath when it clicked. "Get behind me when I open the door, Hailey."

She licked her lips. "Do you think she set up an automatic firing squad when the door opens?"

"I wouldn't put anything past her. Would you?"

"Now that I know she's responsible for the carnage at the refugee camp? No." She took a sideways step to huddle behind Joe's solid frame, putting one hand on his back.

He eased open the door, every muscle in his back tensed and ready for…something.

"No firing squad." Still feeling exposed on the

porch, Hailey started forward, her purse swinging from her hand.

Joe shouted, "Hailey, stop!"

A funny smell assaulted her nostrils, but before she had time to analyze it, Joe grabbed her around the waist and pushed her over the back of the porch into the garden below.

And then the world exploded around her.

Chapter Thirteen

The ringing in his ears drowned out Hailey's screaming, or maybe no sound was actually coming from her mouth, wide-open and showing off all her pearly whites.

Joe rolled onto his back, the branches of some bush gouging his bare skin. Black smoke billowed from the porch, the acrid wisps swirling around him, causing his eyes to water.

Voices came from somewhere. He shook his head and spit what looked like dissolved charcoal out of his mouth.

Hailey. His head fell to the side and some leaves scratched his face, but he got a good look at Hailey next to him—in one piece. Maybe.

"Are you hurt?"

She choked in response, and black spittle formed at the corners of her mouth.

The voices he'd heard before seemed to be closer now, and with great effort, he turned his head away from Hailey.

A clutch of people had gathered on the steps up to the house and were leaning over the railing into the garden where he and Hailey had landed like a dazed Adam and Eve.

Joe moved an arm and then a leg. They still seemed

attached to his body. The fall into the various bushes and plants had done more damage to him than the bomb had.

Because that was a bomb—not a very good bomb, but it probably could've torn them to pieces if they, instead of Hailey's purse, had crossed that threshold.

Joe struggled to extricate himself from the thorns and sticks that clung to his clothing and skin, trying to make him part of the mulch.

He didn't want to be mulch. He snatched his arm away from a particularly vicious bush and scooped it beneath Hailey's back, lifting her up. "Are you all right? Say something to me."

Her dark eyes clicked into focus, and then they widened and she let loose with a scream right in his face.

It was the sweetest sound he'd heard in a long time. "Are you hurt? Let me help you up."

One of the neighbors on the steps yelled out, "We called 911. The fire department is on the way, but it looks like the sprinkler system shut down the fire. Is Hailey okay?"

Joe finally maneuvered into a crouched position just as one of the onlookers decided to clamber across the front garden. Since the garden sloped down to the street, the man lost his footing and started to slide down.

Joe held up his hand. "It's okay. I've got my bearings now. I'll help Hailey. She doesn't seem to be hurt, but she's still in shock."

The sirens racing toward the scene were the second sweetest sound he'd heard today.

Joe gently pulled Hailey toward him with one hand while detaching her from her thorny bed with the other, as she whimpered.

He whispered as he worked. "You're fine. You're gonna be okay, my love."

The sirens stopped, and a commotion erupted on the street as the firefighters unraveled their hoses.

Just as Joe had Hailey up in a seated position, a firefighter clomped into the garden with his boots and protective gear.

Joe called out, "Careful. There's an incline. We're being held in place by a few strategically placed bushes."

"Were you thrown by the explosion?"

"We jumped."

"Probably a smart move."

Another firefighter joined him with a stretcher on his back. "Let's roll her onto this. Does she have any other injuries?"

"Not that I can tell, but she's still in shock. She gets clarity every now and then and screams bloody murder, but her most serious injuries are from the fall and this damn foliage poking us."

They secured the stretcher next to Hailey and eased her onto it.

"You need a stretcher?"

"No, but I'm coming with her in the ambulance and don't even try to stop me." Joe stood up and hoisted one end of the stretcher.

When they got free of the garden, Joe tipped back his head and surveyed the damage to the door. The explosives had blown the door off its hinges, and it now lay on the sidewalk at the curb. It must've sailed over him and Hailey, and he said a silent thanks to God that it hadn't landed on them.

They loaded Hailey into the back of the ambulance, and Joe climbed in after. On the ride to the hospital, the EMT checked her vitals, cleaned her superficial wounds and put an oxygen mask on her face. Through it all, Hailey maintained consciousness but couldn't seem to speak or make sense of what was going on around her.

Joe kept hold of her hand, stroking the back of it with his thumb and murmuring ridiculous sentiments like how he'd never leave her side and he'd take care of her forever.

He cranked his head around to the EMT. "Where are you taking her?"

"San Francisco General, emergency."

"You're not taking her to the emergency room. She's going to a private room and seeing a doctor who isn't too busy to spend more than thirty seconds with her."

The EMT opened his mouth, and Joe sliced his hand through the air to silence him. "Do you know who this is? This is Hailey Duvall. Her father, Ray Duvall, practically owns San Fran Gen. So just do it."

The EMT hunched forward and stuck his head into the cab of the ambulance.

Joe glanced down at Hailey. Was that a smile playing about her mouth underneath that oxygen mask?

He leaned down and touched his lips to her ear. "I learned from the best, baby."

An hour later, with Hailey tucked into a hospital bed in a private room with an IV in her arm, Joe pulled up a chair and laced his fingers through hers.

"Feeling better?"

She croaked in her new raspy voice, "I'm fine. What about you? Has anyone checked you out yet?"

Lifting up his shirt, he twisted around to show off the bandage on his back. "That's the worst of it. Some sharp branch speared me. Why didn't your father's gardeners plant some ice plant in that area?"

"Let's be thankful there weren't more rosebushes in there."

"There were enough." Joe held out his arm where a hodgepodge of gauze patches created a pattern on his skin.

She kissed her fingertips and pressed them against the biggest gauze square. "Did the police talk to you yet?"

"They did, and Agent Porter is on his way." He scooted his chair closer to the bed. "Turns out Ayala must've gotten a C in bomb-making class."

"I don't know." Hailey folded over the edge of the sheet and creased it with her fingers. "That sounded like an A-plus effort to me."

"She didn't use enough chemicals to take down the house, but we definitely would've been severely injured if we'd stepped across that threshold."

"My purse set it off, didn't it?"

"I saw the wire inside the house at about the same time you moved forward and swung your purse in the doorway."

"You saved us again. If you hadn't seen the wire, hadn't suspected Ayala of setting us up, the EMTs would've been picking up our body parts from that front garden." She covered her eyes with one hand. "It felt like…felt like…"

"What you experienced at the refugee camp." Joe smoothed his hand over her leg beneath the sheet.

"Only that was much worse. There was shrapnel with that one, horrible, horrible injuries. How could a nurse perpetuate that kind of violence?"

"Something else is more important to her now. If a few children have to die for the greater good, she's down with that."

"Exactly." Agent Porter tapped on the open door. "We're looking into Ayala Khan's brother and her boyfriend."

"Agent Porter, this is Joe McVie."

Porter stepped into the room, his large frame making it appear even smaller, and extended his hand to Joe. "I know all about Captain McVie, Delta Force. You've been busy on your leave, Captain."

"Call me Joe. I feel like we're old friends."

Porter drew up a chair on the other side of Hailey's bed. "Are you okay, Hailey? You've been through the wringer since… Joe showed up, haven't you?"

"You think I'm a target because of Joe?" She struggled to sit up, punching a pillow behind her. "If you're going to blame anyone, outside of the real culprits, blame Marten de Becker…and help him. He's still alive."

"So is Andrew Reese."

"Thank God. Is he talking?"

"I got nothing from the CIA except Reese took a beating and refused to finger his assailants."

"Unlike me."

Crossing his arms, Joe extended his legs beneath Hailey's bed. "What are you doing about Ayala Khan?"

"We have her on the terrorist watch list, the no-fly, and we've contacted Interpol. Everything we can do."

"Is the CIA ready to admit Major Denver didn't have anything to do with the bomb in Syria?"

"Hold on." Porter held out a hand. "All we know is some group is targeting the relief workers who were kidnapped. We don't know why. Maybe they think they can ID their captors."

Joe snorted. "I don't think some random terrorists in Syria would be too worried about that. The connection is the ID of Major Denver and the fact that Marten de

Becker, who had positively identified Denver as one of the kidnappers, decided to change his mind."

"You're making a lot of assumptions, McVie."

"Are you forgetting what my Delta Force teammates discovered? The original emails implicating Denver were fake, and the claim that Denver shot an Army Ranger when he went AWOL was force-fed to Asher Knight through mind control." Joe bunched his hands into fists and shoved them into his pockets.

"I heard some of that."

"Those claims that Major Denver kidnapped the aid workers and planted the bomb for their car to take back to the refugee center are also false. This is one big setup."

"I'm not here to get into that with you, McVie. I'm here to make sure Hailey is okay—" Porter flashed his teeth at Hailey "—and to glean any more information she might have about Ayala Khan."

"It sounds like you already know more about her than I do." Hailey took a sip from her water cup beside the bed. "I didn't know about any boyfriend, and I had no idea her brother had links to any terrorist organizations."

Joe hunched forward, elbows on knees, and asked, "Do you know anything about a boyfriend or fiancé?"

"Nothing yet. How do you know she has one?" Porter's eyebrows collided over his nose.

"How *do* you know that?" Hailey grabbed a napkin to dab at the water she'd spilled on the front of her hospital gown.

"I'm just guessing, because she wears a ring on her left ring finger." Joe shrugged. "A lot of times women get lured into these causes with some misplaced sense of romanticism."

"We'll be looking into any and all of her contacts."

Joe felt Hailey's gaze boring into him and glanced up to meet her narrowed eyes. "I—I'm just generalizing. Most women have minds of their own."

Porter rescued him by asking Hailey another question and then stayed on another twenty minutes, taking notes about what Hailey remembered of Ayala's day-to-day activities at the camp. Then he tucked his notebook into his breast pocket and pushed up from the chair. "I'm glad neither one of you was seriously injured. You were lucky to have Delta Force on your side when you went back to your house, Hailey."

"I've been lucky to have Joe around on several occasions." She flicked at the IV running into her arm. "Agent Porter, can Marten come to you with his information?"

"Any of you can come to me at any time. I thought I made that clear in the first set of interviews stateside." He squinted at her. "Why? Have you had contact with de Becker?"

"Not yet, but I'm sure it's coming. He's alive and he wants to stay that way. The only insurance he has is the truth. Once that's out, there's not going to be any more reason to silence him."

Porter lifted his linebacker shoulders. "There's always payback."

Hailey's face drained of color, and Joe jumped from his chair. Pumping Porter's hand, he said, "Thanks for coming by."

As Porter reached the door, Hailey called out, "I expect to see you at the fund-raiser tomorrow night, Agent Porter."

The Fibbie spun around at the door and smacked the wall. "You're still going through with that?"

"Of course. I wasn't injured in that blast, and it's great advertising for what we're battling out there."

"If you plan to be there, the SFPD is going to have to ramp up security."

"I'm counting on it." She winked at him.

When he left, Hailey sank against her pillows again and closed her eyes.

Joe perched on the edge of her bed and traced a line from her temple to her jaw. "Are you sure you're up for the gala?"

"Oh, yeah." Her dark lashes fluttered on her cheekbones. "I have a feeling about tomorrow night."

"I have feelings about tomorrow night, too, and none of them good."

"That's why we have to carry on with our plans. Dark forces are surging in this city, and they're going to converge at the Pacific Rim tomorrow night. My fortune cookie said so."

"Whoa, that's deep." He pinched her soft earlobe. "Hailey?"

Her breathing had the deep, rhythmic quality of someone in REM, which didn't surprise him, as some of that juice in her IV was a strong sedative to help her cope with the shock of the explosion.

Joe straightened out her covers, tucking them beneath her chin. He kissed her parted lips and then returned to his sentry position beside her bed.

As he slumped in the chair, stuffing a pillow behind his back, he said, "My fortune cookie told me to take a chance on a dark-haired beauty—and am I glad I did."

A BRIGHT LIGHT FLASHED. Black smoke curled in the distance. A horrible stench like hellfire permeated the air. And the children screamed. The children screamed.

Hailey shouted and kicked out her limbs.

The side of the bed dipped, and a warm hand clasped hers. A soft touch smoothed the hair back from her forehead.

Her eyelids flew open, and a savior with red hair hovered above her.

"Shh. You're okay. You're in the hospital and I'm right here with you."

And he'd never leave her. Didn't he say that before? He'd never leave her side again.

She threw her arms around Joe's neck. "Oh, God. The dreams. The visions."

"The explosion at your father's house brought it all back, every wretched detail." He stroked her glossy hair. "You should see someone, Hailey, a professional."

"You're probably right." She tried to swallow, but with her parched throat, it ended in a cough.

"Here you go." He handed her the water cup and placed the straw in her mouth. "You seemed to be sleeping soundly before. Do you want the nurse to give you some more sedative?"

"Oh, God, no." She slurped up every last drop of the water. "That stuff makes me thirsty, and I think it's partially responsible for giving me hallucinations. What time is it, anyway?"

"It's five a.m. The gala is tonight, if you're still game."

"Damn straight." She eyed Joe's tousled hair and scruffy chin. "You've spent another night in less-than-ideal conditions, haven't you? Let's see—since we've met, you've spent one night in a park across the street from my house, one night on a too-small couch and now a night cramped in a chair. You need a good night's sleep in a real bed."

"I intend to spend a night in a real bed, real soon, but I can do without the sleep." He quirked his eyebrows up and down at her.

So, he didn't intend to rush off the minute the danger ended?

"That can definitely be arranged. Now, when can I get out of here?"

"Whenever you like. You're a VIP, remember? But let's not take off just yet. There's a small problem. You can't stay at the Pacific Heights house."

"Oh, boy." She smacked the heel of her hand against her forehead. "I need to call my father."

"He already knows."

"What?"

"He's already called the hospital once." Joe slipped his phone out of his pocket and dropped it on Hailey's lap. "Do you want to call him? It's eight o'clock in New York."

"Might as well get this over with." She entered her father's number in Joe's phone. "He's not going to answer an unknown number." To his voice mail, she said, "Dad, it's Hailey. Everything you heard is true. I'm in the hospital after an explosion at the house. Call me back at this number."

She ended the call, keeping the phone cupped in her hand. "In five, four, three, two..." Joe's phone vibrated. "Dad, it's Hailey."

"What the hell is going on out there? Why is someone rigging a bomb at the Pacific Heights house?"

"I'm fine, Dad." She winked at Joe.

"Don't play that pity card with me. I already know you're fine. I talked to Dr. Owens for a good twenty minutes. He told me you were in perfect health except for a few bumps and scratches. What he couldn't tell me is why someone is bombing my house."

"It has to do with—"

"Don't tell me. It's that Syria mess, isn't it? Give it up, Hailey. You've put your life in danger too many times to count. Come back to the fold and get back into the business. Your brother's a pretty face, but he's useless on the day to day. I need you."

"I don't like the way you do business, remember? And if you haven't changed your ways, I wouldn't think you'd want me around to blow the whistle on your unethical practices again." This time she avoided Joe's gaze, which she felt burning the side of her face.

Her father harrumphed over the phone. "You think I give a damn about that now? You ratted us out, I paid my fine and it's over. I'd still rather have a snitch like you around than Win."

"A snitch?"

"Face it, that's what you are, Hailey. A snitch and a do-gooder."

"Someone else I know calls me a do-gooder."

"Smart man."

"How do you know it's a man?" Hailey met Joe's questioning blue eyes with a smile.

"You think I'm a fool? You think I don't know you? Dr. Owens also informed me that you have some military guy keeping watch over you there like some kind of damn bodyguard. If you're letting some man that close to you, it means something."

"It does, Dad."

"Good. Then get that door repaired once the cops let you back in and keep this military guy close."

"Oh, I will." She ended the call and pressed the phone against her heart.

Joe propped on the frame of her bed. "You blew the whistle on your dad's company?"

"One of them. He was engaging in unfair business practices, bordering on the criminal."

"Sounds like he still wants you back."

"I guess things aren't working out with Win, but what he wants first is for me to repair his house." She handed the phone back to Joe. "I didn't even see it. How bad was the damage? I know there was a fire."

"Your father's extensive sprinkler system put that out quickly. Like I said, Ayala flunked bomb making. The door landed on the sidewalk, the foyer is scorched, and you and I pretty much destroyed that front garden."

Hailey snapped her fingers. "All fixable."

"But not livable. You won't be able to stay there until the police and the FBI finish their investigation. You're welcome to stay with me at my hotel in Fisherman's Wharf. I'll even buy you another chowder bread bowl."

"Better yet, you're welcome to stay with me at *my* hotel."

"Your hotel?"

"The Pacific Rim."

"You mean that place where the forces of evil are converging?"

"That's the one."

"I'd be honored."

AFTER SHE WAS discharged from the hospital, Hailey used Joe's cell phone to place a few calls while a car took them to Joe's hotel to pick up his things.

When they finished at Joe's hotel, Hailey braced herself to face her father's house and the damage there. What she faced was yellow police tape ringing the property and a patrol car stationed out front.

The officer got out of his car when she and Joe stepped onto the sidewalk. "Can I help you?"

"I'm Hailey Duvall." She waved her hand at the house behind her. "This is my father's house, and I'm just here to pack a bag and take a look at the damage."

"Just be careful on the porch. The investigators are almost done."

"Will do." She kicked Joe's suitcase on the sidewalk. "Put these in the garage by the Jag. We'll take the car over to the Pacific Rim."

Joe wheeled his bag into the garage and parked it at the rear of the Jag. "Ready?"

On shaky legs, Hailey climbed the steps. Joe must've sensed her trepidation, as he kept a firm hand at her back.

He pointed into the foliage to the right. "That's where we landed."

"Looks painful."

"It was." He picked up a chunk of cement on the top step. "Part of the porch."

"Nice of them to return the door." Hailey nodded at the scorched and splintered door leaning to the right of the gaping entrance to the house.

Black burn marks smudged the doorjamb and the porch. Evidence of water damage from the sprinkler system and the fire hoses stained the wood floor in the foyer, and a scorched tapestry decorated the wall.

"I hope that wasn't expensive."

"It's all expensive, but my father has insurance." Hailey sniffed the air and swallowed. Smell more than anything triggered her memories. She covered her nose and mouth.

"You doing okay?" Joe rubbed a circle on her back.

"Yeah. Let's get this over with. Can you take some

pictures of the damage? I'm going to send them to my dad, and he can forward everything to his insurance company."

While Joe took out his phone, Hailey glanced around the living room to make sure Ayala hadn't helped herself to some valuables on her way out.

She caught her breath when she saw the mug with Ayala's lipstick on the rim. She hadn't even processed Ayala's betrayal yet—her betrayal of the people who'd counted on her in the refugee camp, yes. That was stunning. But the personal betrayal from a woman she'd admired and worked beside hadn't hit home yet. Hailey curled her hands around the sink and leaned forward. Just one in a long line of betrayals from people she trusted.

But not Joe. This whole journey with him hadn't just been about his dedication to justice for Major Denver, had it? Her involvement had definitely drawn the perpetrators out of the woodwork. If they hadn't come after her, Joe never would've been able to get close to Marten—at least not in the same way—and in her bed, in her heart.

She jumped as he touched her shoulder.

"Do you want to wait in the car? Just give me a list and I can pack up for you."

Swinging around, she threw herself into his arms. "You would do that, wouldn't you? For me. Just for me."

His arms, strong, secure, wrapped around her body. "Don't ever doubt me, Hailey. I would do anything for you. I'd go to hell and back to protect you, and even though you're completely out of my league..."

She put two fingers over his lips. "Don't ever say that again. Money is just money, Joe. It doesn't buy integrity, loyalty, courage. Hell, it doesn't even buy class."

"You have all of that *and* money." He kissed the corner of her mouth.

"If you think I have all those qualities, then I must be in your league and you're in mine." She returned his kiss, and as his hand cupped the back of her head, she never felt safer.

In an instant, those feelings of security evaporated as Joe's body jerked and he whipped out his weapon.

"Hold it right there. Don't come any closer."

Hailey twisted her head over her shoulder, her mouth dropping open at the sight of a raggedly dressed man waving a crutch in front of him.

"You don't wanna shoot me, man. I just came here to get that hat." He pointed to Marten's black hat on the coffee table. "And return it to its owner."

Chapter Fourteen

"Hey, you!" The patrol officer from the front of the house charged through the front door, his gun drawn. "Drop that crutch."

"If I drop the crutch, man, I won't be able to stand." The transient tapped his leg. "I got shot yesterday, saving this young lady's life...and that tough-as-nails D-Boy's, too, come to think of it."

Hailey blew out a breath and dabbled her fingers down Joe's corded forearm. "It's Trace from Mission Hope."

"You shouldn't sneak up on people like that unless you have a death wish...man." Joe pocketed his gun. "It's all right, Officer. We know this guy."

The young cop wiped a bead of sweat from his brow. "Ms. Duvall?"

"It's okay. Everything he said is true. I was...attacked yesterday and Trace saved the day. You can leave us."

The officer holstered his gun and squared his shoulders. "Don't do that again. When an officer tells you to stop, you stop."

"Yes, sir, Officer, sir." Trace saluted and pushed back his hood.

Hailey waited until the police officer walked through the gaping hole that used to be the front door and then took a few steps toward Trace with Joe hovering behind her. "Is your leg okay?"

"Just a flesh wound." Trace grinned. "I've had worse."

Joe cleared his throat. "You're straight with the police over the shooting? They're not filing any charges against you, are they? If so, we'll be happy to speak on your behalf."

Hailey nudged Joe with her elbow. "You're catching on. You could be Deputy Do-Gooder."

"Yeah, yeah. I'm good with the cops." Trace held up his middle and index fingers together. "Like this now. I didn't even shoot the guy. His finger was on the trigger, so he shot himself. I just directed the gun away from me."

"What brings you here?" Joe folded his arms over his chest, widening his stance. "How do you even know where Hailey lives?"

Trace leveled a stubby finger at the hat. "Told ya. I'm here to pick up something for a friend. He told me about the house."

"Where is Marten? He's alive?" Hailey dived for the black hat and skimmed her fingers across the rim.

"Isn't that what the note said?" Trace leaned on his crutch and fetched a cigarette from his other pocket.

Joe lunged for Trace and snatched the cigarette from his hand. "No lighting up in here. Are you crazy?"

"Some say I am." Trace tapped his head. "But you know about that kinda crazy, don't you, soldier?"

"Are you getting any help for that?" Joe handed the cigarette back to Trace. "Not in the house."

"Here and there. Couple of shrinks volunteer at Mission Hope." He pocketed the cigarette.

"How do you know about that note? About Marten?" Hailey twirled Marten's hat around her hand.

"Crazy dude, that Marten. Talks kinda funny, too."

Joe asked, "Where'd you meet him?"

"Met him on the rocks down by Fisherman's Wharf. He was comin' out of the bay like one of those escaped prisoners from Alcatraz."

Hailey shook her head. "No prisoners ever escaped from Alcatraz—and lived to tell about it."

"They never found that bunch, just their makeshift rafts." Trace winked. "You never know."

"Back to Marten." Joe tapped the toe of his boot.

"Yeah, came out of the water, told me he was hiding from some people and just faked his own death. I told him the best way to be invisible in this city was to be homeless. Got him suited up and took him to the shelter with me for a meal."

"Did he say he was pushed from the ferry?" Hailey perched on the arm of a chair. "Do you want to sit down?"

"Not staying that long." Trace scratched his scruffy beard. "Dude said he jumped."

"I thought he was dead."

"I guess that's what he wanted."

Joe glanced at her, his eyebrows peaked over his nose. "Nice of him to worry his friend. Is that when he got the locker, when he went to the shelter with you?"

"Yep. Saw the locker and figured it suited him just fine."

"Wait a minute." Joe held up his hands. "If he got that locker after he nose-dived off the ferry, how did he get that key to Joost?"

"Joost must've been lying."

"Joost is the big blond guy—" Trace held his hand a few inches about his head "—talks funny like Marten?"

"That's him." Hailey clenched her teeth.

"Then Joost lied, 'cause Marten dropped off the

locker key with him after making a copy for himself. Then I guess Marten lived longer than he expected, because he went back to the locker and replaced the letter he had in there with the note telling you he was alive."

"How in the world did Marten expect me to know what that key unlocked?"

"Has 'Mission Hope' written right on it." Trace cocked his head.

"It was worn off." Joe rubbed the back of his neck. "Did Marten tell you to keep an eye on the lockers?"

"Yeah, and I did. I saw you two going in there and I would've been there sooner if I'd noticed that guy following you, but I kinda got caught up in the card game. I still saved you, didn't I?"

"You did." Hailey flipped up the hat and put it on her own head. "Where is Marten now and what does he have planned next?"

"I don't know where he is. What he has planned next?" He tipped his head toward Hailey. "He wants his hat back."

Joe pushed off the sofa where he'd been leaning and jumped at Trace, causing him to drop his crutch. "You tell that selfish SOB to come forward now and admit the truth so Hailey doesn't have to keep looking over her shoulder. You see all this? It's all because of that crazy…dude, Marten."

Trace hopped backward, away from Joe. "I'll tell him, I'll tell him. Just don't follow me, man. Don't expect me to take you to him. He'll disappear again. He warned me about you."

"Joe." Hailey rose from the arm of the couch and rubbed his back. "Let Marten do it his way."

"While he plays games and puts your life in danger? Why should I?"

"Because he might just disappear, like Trace said, and then we'll have nothing."

Joe wagged his finger in Trace's face. "Tell him to hurry up or he's going to have another enemy after him."

"On it. I'm on it." Trace's gaze dropped to his crutch on the floor.

Hailey dipped down and retrieved it, tucking it beneath his arm. Then she swept the hat from her head and handed it to Trace. "Anything else? Would you like to take some food with you?"

"I could use a beer."

"Out." Joe pointed at the doorway.

Trace grinned and swung around, using his crutch as a pivot.

"And, Trace?" Hailey called after him.

"Yeah?"

"Tell Marten I'm glad he's alive."

When he hobbled out of the house, Hailey brushed her bangs back from her face. "I am glad he's alive, but I can't believe he staged that whole ferry accident. He knew what I'd think."

"Maybe that was his way of protecting you. If he were dead, then there's no way he could've told you what he knew about the setup of Denver." Joe stroked his chin. "What do you think he has planned?"

"I don't know, but he'd better speak up soon or this danger will continue to hang over us both."

Hailey packed a bag, including her toiletries and her evening gown for the fund-raiser.

WHEN JOE SAW the long dress draped over her bag, he swore. "In all the excitement, I forgot to pick up my tux."

"All taken care of. I called Tony when you were at

your hotel, and he's having it delivered to the Pacific Rim. If you need him for a fitting, he'll be happy to come over to the hotel."

"The fit of my tux is the last thing on my mind." He pounded a fist against his chest. "As long as there's room for my shoulder holster."

"That request must've driven Tony nuts. It will definitely ruin the drape of the suit."

"Do you want your bodyguard to keep you safe or look good in his tux?"

She ran her hands across his chest. "Lucky me, I don't have to make that choice."

They loaded their bags in the trunk of the Jag and drove to the hotel.

As soon as Hailey checked in, her assistant, Gretchen Reynolds, appeared at her side. "I can't believe you're going through with this after what happened at the Pacific Heights house."

"Great to see you, too, Gretchen. This is Joe McVie. Joe, my assistant, Gretchen."

As they shook hands, Gretchen gave Joe the once-over. "He'd better be here to protect you."

"I am." Joe leaned close to Gretchen. "And I'm not the only one here in that capacity."

Gretchen's eyes bugged out. "Is the SFPD ramping up security because of what happened at the house?"

"Yes." Hailey patted Gretchen's hand. "Don't worry. Everything is under control, and you did a beautiful job. We're going to raise lots of money."

When they got up to the suite, Hailey slid open the closet door. "Tux is here. Do you want to try it on?"

"I'm sure it's fine, Hailey." Joe collapsed on the bed. "You wanna give me the lowdown on the festivities tonight?"

"I'll take you to the ballroom where it's being held so you can look around." She hung up her dress in the closet. "At seven o'clock cocktails and hors d'oeuvres. A few speeches—none by Nurse Ayala Khan—buffet dinner, and then dancing and more cocktails."

"That's all *you* have planned, anyway, but what's planned for you?"

"Whatever it is, I'm sure you and the SFPD and maybe even Agent Porter will take care of it. Ayala has been outed."

"She's just the face we know. What about all the other faces we don't know? I'm sure there are others like her—outwardly dedicated to one cause and secretly supporting another."

"Whatever's gonna happen is gonna happen."

"Those forces of evil?"

She shrugged. A sense of calm had descended on her after she'd left the hospital. Maybe it was knowing Joe McVie was on her side. "I forwarded the guest list to the FBI."

"Recently?"

"Today."

"Hate to break it to you, but they don't work that fast. Don't tell Agent Porter I said that."

"My lips are sealed." She drew a finger over the seam of her lips. "Do you want me to give you a tour of the ballroom now?"

"Dinner at eight?" Joe rubbed his stomach. "I'm starving. Let's eat first and then I'll check it out."

"There are a couple of great restaurants in this hotel." Hailey reached for her purse.

"Room service." Joe bounded up from the bed and slid the embossed leather folder on the desk toward him. "We're eating in. The less exposure you have, the better. The danger is not over, Hailey, just because Ayala's on the run."

"I know that. It's coming. I feel it coming—but now I'm ready."

THE REST OF the afternoon passed with both of them working on their laptops. As day shifted into night, Joe stretched and rubbed his eyes.

Hailey looked up from her screen. "Are you in trouble?"

"What?" Folding his hands behind his head, Joe kicked his feet onto the desk next to his laptop.

"You've been awfully busy over there, typing away. Are you writing out your defense?" Hailey stretched out her legs on the bed and wiggled her bare toes.

"Answering some emails and, yeah, explaining myself."

"I repeat. Are you in trouble?"

"No." He spun his cell phone around to face him. "But we will be if we don't start getting ready for this damn gala."

"We have over an hour. I don't know about you, pretty boy, but I don't need that long to get ready."

Joe swung his legs off the desk and stalked toward the bed. "I do, when I plan to shower with my protectee and ravish her in the process."

Hailey shoved her computer off her lap. "Then what are we waiting for?"

Just about an hour later, completely sated and clean in the bargain, Joe faced the mirror in his monkey suit.

Hailey came up behind him, her shimmery silver dress floating around her legs. She reached around him and straightened his bow tie. "You look very handsome."

"You look—" he flicked the skirt of her dress "—stunning."

She kissed the side of his neck and then twirled away to snag his jacket from the back of a chair. "I'll help you into your jacket."

"First things first." He slid open the closet door and retrieved his shoulder holster. "You can help me into this before the jacket."

She sighed. "Poor Tony."

"It'll be fine."

After he strapped on his holster and secured his weapon, Hailey held out his jacket for him. He slipped into the jacket, and Hailey patted his chest.

"More than fine, Red. You're going to have to stick by me when we walk in, because I don't have a ticket for you. Gretchen sent one over and I thought I printed it out at the house, but with the sniper fire and bomb blast, who knows what happened to it?"

"I plan to stick very close to you."

As soon as they left the safety of the room, all of Joe's senses went on high alert. If someone wanted to take out Hailey or make some kind of statement about the war, this gala provided the perfect venue.

Damn that de Becker. What was he waiting for? The longer he kept quiet, the longer Hailey faced danger.

The guards at the door of the ballroom patted him down after Hailey told them he was with her and was providing personal security, so they skimmed over his weapon.

Joe blinked at the dazzling decor of the ballroom. This place couldn't be farther from that Syrian refugee camp. Maybe after the keynote address, all the wealth and comfort were supposed to make the guests feel guilty.

Hailey understood that.

Joe declined the champagne floating around on waiters' trays, but Hailey grabbed a glass of the bubbly and downed half of it before coming up for air.

"Is that a good idea?" Joe raised one eyebrow.

"You're the only one who has to stay sober, Red."

The guests began to filter in through the doors after being checked out by security, and the level of noise in the ballroom increased minute by minute.

Joe nodded toward Agent Porter, his football-player frame dressed to the nines. He was here as a guest, too, but he had his eyes wide-open.

Putting him firmly in the guest column, Hailey introduced Joe to her foundation's board members and acquaintances as a…friend. If the *friend* designation allowed him to continue doing all those things to her body that he'd just done in the hotel suite, he'd take it.

The dais at one end of the room sported a podium, long tables on either side and a screen behind it. Would images of the devastation in Syria be projected on that screen, or would that be going too far for this crowd?

A small commotion stirred around the side door to the right of the dais as two security guards ushered in a tall, lean man and two women.

Hailey followed his gaze and said, "That's Dr. Nabil Karam-Thomas and Dr. Lynne Roberson. The other woman is Dr. Roberson's date, I believe."

"Dr. Karam-Thomas, the keynote speaker."

"That's right. He's done a lot to recruit volunteers in the medical field."

"Thomas?"

"English father, Syrian mother, I believe." Hailey deposited her champagne flute on a passing tray. "They're coming this way."

As the small group approached, Hailey sailed forward, extending her hands. "I'm so happy you could make it tonight, and everyone is looking forward to your speech, Dr. Karam-Thomas."

"So good to see you again, Hailey, and please, call me Nabil."

"Dr. Roberson, welcome." Hailey took the woman's hand. "This is Joe McVie. Joe, Dr. Roberson and…"

Dr. Roberson gave Joe's hand a firm shake. "This is Valerie Guida."

After shaking hands with both of the women, Joe made a half turn toward Dr. Karam-Thomas.

"Nice to meet you, Valerie." Hailey turned toward Dr. Karam-Thomas. "Dr.—Nabil, this is Joe McVie. Joe, Dr. Nabil Karam-Thomas."

As Joe shook hands with the doctor, Karam-Thomas tightened his grip, his ring squeezing against Joe's knuckle. When they released, Joe glanced at the large gold band on the doctor's right hand. It looked like a wedding band that belonged on his left hand.

Joe glanced at Karam-Thomas's left hand and cocked his head. The ring on the doctor's third finger boasted a red stone, unusual for its dark color. Where had he seen a stone like that recently?

He slid a gaze at Hailey's hands, expressively gesturing as she spoke to the doctors, her long fingers adorned with three diamond rings. The lady obviously preferred diamonds to rubies, or whatever that stone was.

Joe tuned back into the conversation just in time to hear Dr. Roberson ask about Ayala Khan.

"I've heard great things about the work Ayala does at the refugee center near the Turkish border. Will she be here tonight, Hailey?"

Hailey pinched the sleeve of Joe's jacket. "Sh-she wasn't able to make it."

Not done singing Ayala's praises, Dr. Roberson turned to Dr. Karam-Thomas. "Have you met Ayala Khan, Nabil? She's Syrian, too."

Karam-Thomas flashed his easy smile and held up his hands. "I can claim only half Syrian ancestry. I have not met Ms. Khan, but I've heard wonderful things about her. Maybe next time our paths will cross."

"Hailey—" Joe held up a finger "—I thought you said Dr. Karam-Thomas had visited the refugee center when you were working there. Wouldn't he have met Ayala then?"

Hailey's body stiffened next to his.

She obviously didn't want to put a damper on the evening by announcing that one of the Syrian Florence Nightingales was fomenting terror and destruction, and he had no intention of outing her now. He just thought it strange that Karam-Thomas wouldn't have remembered meeting Ayala. The guy was probably too much the superstar to remember all the underlings.

"That's right." The doctor snapped the fingers of his left hand, and the red stone caught the light and glinted. "I *did* meet Ms. Khan on that visit—amazing nurse. Now, if you ladies and gentleman will excuse me, I'm going to press some flesh."

"That would be advisable." Hailey swept her hand to the side as if to make a path for him.

Joe watched Karam-Thomas's ramrod-straight back as he melted into the glittering crowd, glad-handing and probably flashing that smile. "That's weird."

"What?"

"That he didn't remember meeting Ayala."

"Why?" Hailey smiled and wiggled her fingers at

Dr. Roberson and her companion as they moved away to mingle. "Why are you even bringing her up?"

"I didn't. Dr. Roberson did."

"But why call out Dr. Karam-Thomas like that? I don't want her involvement in the bombing of the center to come out here, of all places."

"I'm sorry, Hailey. I just remembered that conversation we had with Ayala when you mentioned he was going to be the keynote speaker and thought it was odd he didn't remember her."

"Not really." She tipped her head toward the doctor, who was in the center of a group of adoring fans. "He's a very popular and busy guy. Speaking of which, I need to make some opening remarks before the food and Nabil's address."

Hailey's speech seemed to go smoothly. Joe didn't comprehend one word of it as he watched the crowd, his senses alert to every cough and scrape of a chair leg.

The audience met Dr. Karam-Thomas's speech with resounding applause, and Joe's muscles relaxed—just a tad. The evening seemed to be progressing without a hitch...and without any attempts on Hailey's life.

The knots in Joe's gut prevented him from enjoying or even eating much dinner. Hailey had wanted him up on that dais with her and the doctors and several Syrian dignitaries, but Joe felt more comfortable roaming the crowd.

As dinner began to wind down and the coffee was served, a ruckus erupted at the entrance to the ballroom. Joe went on high alert, pushed off the wall where he'd been leaning and strode toward the noise.

Two security guards held a struggling man between them—a man wearing a black porkpie hat with a checkered band.

"Let me in. Tell Hailey Duvall who I am. She'll know."

Agent Porter sidled up next to Joe. "I'll be damned. It's Marten de Becker."

Joe whistled. "And this is the venue he's chosen for his reveal—public and safe."

Porter made a move. He badged the security guards. "Let him through. Ms. Duvall is going to want to see him, and even more, she's going to want to hear what he has to say. We all do."

Security released de Becker, and he brushed off his clothes and tipped his hat at Joe when he sauntered by under Porter's protective watch.

Joe followed them up to the dais.

When Hailey saw de Becker, she jumped up from her chair and lifted the skirt of her dress to jog down the steps to the ballroom floor. She threw her arms around him and whispered something in his ear.

Joe clenched his jaw. She'd better be telling him to get up there and spill his guts once and for all.

While the other notables on the dais continued eating their desserts and drinking their coffee, Dr. Karam-Thomas had eased out of his chair and headed toward the opposite side of the dais from where Hailey was still talking to de Becker…even though the doctor's seat was steps away from them on the same side.

Joe watched his descent from the stage through narrowed eyes. Karam-Thomas seemed to be in a hurry without trying to appear he was in a hurry—and that megawatt smile had disappeared.

The doctor slipped one hand in his pocket—the right hand—and once again, Joe caught a glimpse of that unusual ring. The same ring Ayala wore on her left hand.

Adrenaline surged through Joe's body, and he lurched forward to follow Karam-Thomas as he wove his way through the tables, barely acknowledging his admirers as they reached out to him.

Why did he have his hand bunched in his pocket? That small space couldn't accommodate a gun—even a small one.

Joe slipped his hand beneath his jacket to grip the handle of his own weapon as he continued to follow the doctor, who was completely unaware he had a tail.

Joe planned to keep it that way. He circled around to the right, keeping Karam-Thomas in his sights.

When Hailey's voice boomed over the speaker system, the doctor tripped to a stop and cranked his head over his shoulder.

"We have a surprise guest tonight, someone who worked in Syria with me, and he'd like to say a few words."

Karam-Thomas's feet seemed rooted to the floor, his face a white oval as he listened to Hailey's introduction of Marten de Becker. Then he lurched forward, not even trying to mask his hurried pace.

Joe continued circling to the doctor's right.

Karam-Thomas pulled his hand from his pocket, and Joe focused on the way the doctor's fingers curled around the device in his hand, his thumb positioned on the top of the item.

Joe drew closer, and his heart slammed against his rib cage as he recognized a remote clutched in the doctor's hand, his thumb pressing against the release.

Joe knew those triggers. Once the doctor released his thumb, it would set off an explosive device. But where was the device? Was this a suicide mission for the doc? Did he have something strapped to his body?

Hailey's voice carried across the ballroom. "So, I'd

like to turn over the microphone to my fellow aid worker in Syria, Marten de Becker."

Applause rippled through the ballroom as de Becker approached the podium.

Licking his lips, Dr. Karam-Thomas glanced over his right shoulder. As Marten began his speech, the doctor lurched toward the exit, his hand wrapped around the remote.

A deadly calm descended on Joe as he made his decision. In four long steps he reached the doctor's side before he got to the exit door.

With his left hand, Joe grabbed the doctor's hand clutching the device and covered his thumb with his own, pressing down on the release with all his strength.

Karam-Thomas bucked under the assault. He dipped his left hand in his pocket, and a knife flashed before a searing pain ran up Joe's thigh.

Gritting his teeth, Joe squeezed the doctor's hand in a death grip, raised the gun to his temple and growled, "You're not ruining this party."

Then he pulled the trigger.

Chapter Fifteen

The gunfire echoed in the ballroom…and in Joe's ears. People screamed and ducked.

De Becker shouted into the mic, "Get down, get down."

Karam-Thomas jerked once and then his body slumped, heavy against Joe's, his head falling to the side, blood running down his face and soaking Joe's jacket. The doctor's hand holding the remote began to slip from his, and Joe crushed the dead man's fingers, repositioning his thumb over Karam-Thomas's.

As a security guard rushed him, Joe dropped his gun and wrapped his arm around the doctor's chest. He could either prop him up in a macabre dance or hit the ground with him. Then he had no choice. As Karam-Thomas slipped to the floor, Joe had to go with him, every ounce of his energy focused on covering the doctor's thumb with his own.

He fell on top of the body. A gun clicked in his ear, and a boot kicked him in the back. "Get off him. Roll over."

"Can't do that." A bead of sweat rolled down Joe's face and hung off his chin. He raised his arm, his hand still engulfing Karam-Thomas's and the remote, his thumb going numb with the pressure. "Once this trigger is released, something's gonna blow—I don't know where it is or what it is, but this death switch is the key. Get everyone out of here. Find FBI agent Porter and evacuate. Now."

Another security agent joined the first one. "I know who Agent Porter is. I'll get him, but keep your weapon trained on him. We don't know what's going on."

People began streaming past Joe and the dead man beneath him, giving them a wide berth. Blood covered the front of his shirt, and the leg of his trouser sported a rip from the knife Karam-Thomas had swung at him. Tony would never forgive him.

He shouted to the security guard, "Direct these people to the other exits, for God's sake. They don't need to see this."

Seconds later, Hailey crouched beside him, the hem of her sparkly dress brushing the pool of blood on the floor. "Oh my God, Joe. What happened? You're not telling me Nabil planted a bomb in the ballroom. How did you know what he was planning?"

"His ring. Look at his ring, Hailey. It's the same one Ayala had. They're a couple. He probably recruited her. Hell, they might even be married, for all we know."

Hailey choked and then scrambled to her feet. Was she overwhelmed by guilt and remorse for trusting those two? For inviting Dr. Karam-Thomas into this world? She had to stop doing that to herself. People took advantage of her because she had a kind and giving heart— he hoped she'd never change.

Less than a minute later, Hailey returned with several white napkins from the tables. She pressed them against the wound on his thigh. "Your leg is bleeding. How long are you going to have to hold down that button?"

"As long as it takes." Porter loomed above them.

"Good work, McVie. How long *can* you hold on? The bomb squad is on its way."

"Like you said, Porter. As long as it takes."

De Becker joined the crowd encircling Joe and Karam-Thomas's inert form. "Damn, I didn't even get to talk."

Joe growled low in his throat. "This is your fault, de Becker. Why did you lie about Major Denver in the first place?"

"Money and intrigue." De Becker straightened his hat. "Money first, I'll admit, but I was able to draw out the terrorist group behind the bombing and behind the setup of Denver. Isn't that worth something to you?"

"Not as much as Hailey's life."

She leaned forward and kissed him—dead guy and all.

Ten minutes later the ballroom had been cleared and the bomb squad arrived with explosive-sniffing dogs.

A member of the team leaned over Joe and slid a device between the doctor's thumb and the remote to keep the trigger in place. "You can release now, buddy. Amazing job."

Joe rolled onto his back, shook out his hand and flexed his fingers. "Why didn't I have one of those?"

Hailey crouched beside him and waved her arm in the air. "Hey, did someone bother to call an ambulance? Joe's been stabbed in the leg."

"It's nothing. He barely got me."

Porter said, "Police and EMTs are out front. A few people got hurt in the scramble to get out of here, and they're being treated at a triage center away from the hotel. The entire hotel is being evacuated."

One of the German shepherds started barking furiously at the front of the ballroom.

"We got a hit. Let's move these people out of here."

Agent Porter and Hailey helped Joe to his feet, and he limped out of the ballroom between them. They moved toward the curved staircase that led from the lobby to the ballroom.

When Joe spotted de Becker on the top step, his blood boiled all over again. He had put everyone's life in danger playing his stupid spy games.

A woman stepped up beside de Becker, and Joe stumbled to a halt as Hailey gasped.

"Ayala!"

"What have you done? What have you done with Nabil?" The gun she held to Marten's head trembled in her hand.

"It's over, Ayala." Joe struggled forward as both Hailey and Porter held him back. "Nabil's dead. The bomb squad has located the explosive device. Your plan failed."

Her dark eyes flashed. "It's not over. We have more people than you can even dream of for our cause. People you trust."

"But not Major Denver. You lied about him. You lied about his presence at the kidnapping. Why? Why him?"

Ayala laughed. "You're wrong. We do have Major Denver."

De Becker took a step away from Ayala. "That's not true. I was paid to lie about hearing Denver there and then threatened when I decided to tell the truth."

"You don't know anything, Marten."

Ayala's weapon had slipped an inch or two, and Joe nudged Porter.

"Our cause will continue with the help of people like Denver…and others."

"What is your cause, Ayala?" Hailey reached out a

hand. "I thought we shared the same cause—to help innocents affected by war."

"Short-term casualties for a long-term goal, Hailey. You will never understand our goal."

"Try me." Hailey edged away from Joe toward Ayala as he made a grab for her hand.

Now was not the time for philanthropy.

"And you will never understand our commitment to it." She cried out, "Nabil!"

Then she turned the gun on herself.

Epilogue

Hailey joined Joe at the window, curled her arms around his waist and drank in the view of the San Francisco Bay. "It's a beautiful day for January."

"It might be sunny, but it's still cold." He twisted his head over his shoulder and kissed her mouth. "Let's go back to bed."

"Oh, no, you don't, Red. We've been in bed for the past two days while it's been cloudy and raining." She patted his bandaged thigh. "Time to stretch out that leg."

"You're a stern taskmaster. I just took down a terrorist, shooting him in the head and hanging on to that detonator for dear life as he fell to the floor." He wove his fingers through hers. "Don't I deserve a break?"

"You're lucky that was a detonator in Nabil's hand and not a remote control for the projector."

"I had it and him all figured out by the time I took him down. When I recognized that ring, I knew he was the one who recruited Ayala at that symposium in Florida. They were lovers, shared the same ring, shared the same passion—a passion for destruction."

"Agent Porter showed me video footage from the hotel of a woman, who I ID'd for him as Ayala, using a ticket to the gala to get into the ballroom. That's when she set up the explosives beneath the dais, but did she and the doctor know Marten was going to show up?"

"I think that was just icing on the cake for them. They planned to disrupt that fund-raiser one way or another, with or without de Becker there. Maybe Karam-Thomas's hand was forced when de Becker showed up, and he sped up the timeline."

"I'm just glad you were suspicious of the doctor and kept an eye on him. I never would've guessed he'd be involved in trying to block a peace process in Syria."

"Why would you? The guy was smooth."

"And Marten got to make his announcement in public, just like he wanted."

"Clearing Major Denver of any involvement in that bombing, despite what Ayala claimed."

Hailey smoothed a thumb over the crease between his eyebrows. "Doesn't that make you happy?"

"It does, but Denver's still out there. He has no way of knowing we've been slowly chipping away at the evidence against him. I just wish there were some way we could reach him. If he came in now, he might have a chance of completely clearing his name."

"The CIA and the army still believe he's in league with a terrorist group, and Ayala's statements before her death didn't help matters."

"They do believe that, but now we'll have a better idea of which group it is as the CIA and the FBI start to sort through Nabil's connections. I did believe one part of Ayala's admission before she ended her life."

"That we'd never understand their cause?"

"No. That they have people in high places on their side."

"Those people will be exposed eventually." Hailey

slipped between Joe and the window and rested her hands on his broad shoulders. "Now it's back to work for you, isn't it?"

"Once my leg heals." He cupped her face with his hands. "Are you going to wait for me? Because I'm telling you right now, Hailey Duvall, I can't live without you."

"Of course I'll wait. I love you." Turning her head to the side, she kissed his palm. "But if you think I'm going to be cooling my heels on a tennis court or sipping mimosas at brunch during your next deployment, you've got the wrong socialite, Red."

He rolled his eyes. "Where this time?"

"I thought I'd play it safe and volunteer to build some homes in Guatemala."

"Just as long as there are no bombs involved."

"I would hope not." She broke away from his embrace. "Right now, though, I'm not averse to sipping a couple of mimosas."

"In bed?"

His hopeful tone brought a smile to her lips.

"One-track mind." She tapped her temple. "I was thinking of this little place in Big Sur, but I need a driver."

"I'm your man." He saluted.

"Good, because there's a '66 T-Bird in the garage, and it's been cooped up a little too long—just like a redheaded D-Boy I know."

Joe's eyes, as blue as the bay behind him, lit up. "That offer just might be better than sex."

"Watch yourself." She shook her finger at him. "Of course, if we see any needy people on our way out of the city, we might have to stop and help them or maybe even take them along with us. Would that be a problem?"

He reached out and pulled her into his arms again. As he nuzzled her neck, he murmured, "Do-gooder."

* * * * *